Heart Fire

Robin D. Owens

BERKLEY SENSATION, NEW YORK

THE BERKLEY PUBLISHING GROUP
Published by the Penguin Group
Penguin Group (USA) LLC
375 Hudson Street, New York, New York 10014

USA • Canada • UK • Ireland • Australia • New Zealand • India • South Africa • China

penguin.com

A Penguin Random House Company

HEART FIRE

This book is an original publication of The Berkley Publishing Group.

Berkley Sensation Books are published by The Berkley Publishing Group.
BERKLEY SENSATION® is a registered trademark of Penguin Group (USA) LLC.
The "B" design is a trademark of Penguin Group (USA) LLC.

Berkley Sensation trade paperback ISBN: 978-0-425-26395-2

An application to register this book for cataloging has been submitted to the Library of Congress.

PUBLISHING HISTORY
Berkley Sensation trade paperback edition / November 2014

PRINTED IN THE UNITED STATES OF AMERICA

10 9 8 7 6 5 4 3 2 1

Cover art by Cliff Nielsen.
Cover design by George Long.
Interior text design by Kristin del Rosario.

To all those who love Celta,
thank you, you amaze me.

Acknowledgments

I want to thank here those who helped me compile a complete cast of characters of the series, and most particularly the speaking (or yowling) parts for the audio books on Audible, in random order: Erica Brown, Antonia Witt, Kelly Self, Frances May, Kathleen Mancini, Nykki Williams, Cathy O'Connor, Sandi Dreer, Megan Bamford, Faith Bodley, Kathleen Courtade Collins, Darla Maxwell, and Christy Aaron.

And to my beta readers, including Crystal Jordan, friend and author, Michelle Kaye, and Sandra Kaye . . . the rest didn't say they wanted named, so I am respecting their privacy. All wonderful and helpful!

Characters

Antenn Blackthorn-Moss: Hero, architect, Fam Pinky (a cat who became a Fam).

Tiana Mugwort: Heroine, FamCat Felonerb.

The Turquoise House (TQ): Intelligent House.

Antenn Blackthorn-Moss's Family:

Mitchella Clover D'Blackthorn: Adopted mother, interior designer, FirstFamily GrandLady (heroine of *Heart Choice*).

Straif T'Blackthorn: Adopted father, FirstFamily GrandLord, tracker (hero of *Heart Choice*).

Ilex Winterberry: Cousin by marriage of Trif Clover Winterberry, Chief of all the Druida City guards (police), (hero of *Heart Quest*).

Draeg Betony Blackthorn: Adopted cuz, warrior (upcoming hero of *Heart Legacy*).

Tiana Mugwort's Best Friends:

Camellia Darjeeling D'Hawthorn: GreatLady D'Hawthorn, businesswoman/cook, owner of teashops (heroine of *Heart Search*), FamCat Mica.

Glyssa Licorice Bayrum: FirstLevel Librarian (heroine of *Heart Fortune*).

Tiana Mugwort's Family:

Artemisia Mugwort Primross: Sister, Healer (heroine of *Heart Secret*), FamRaccoon Randa.

Quina Mugwort: Mother, devotee of the Intersection of Hope religion, Healer.

Sinjin Mugwort: Father, former judge, writer of legal articles.

Garrett Primross: Brother-in-law, private investigator (hero of *Heart Secret*), FamCat Rusby.

The Temple People:

High Priestess GrandLady Ulmaria Meadowsweet D'Sandalwood: Of GreatCircle Temple.

High Priest GrandLord Alb T'Sandalwood: Of GreatCircle Temple.

Lucida Gerania of GreatCircle Temple: FirstLevel priestess and rival of Tiana Mugwort.

The Intersection of Hope Ministers:

Chief Minister Younger: Reflecting the childlike self.

Chief Minister Foreman: Reflecting the vital adult.

Chief Minister Elderstone: Reflecting the older, wise guide.

Chief Minister Custos: Reflecting the inner guardian spirit.

Others, in order of appearance:

GreatLord Muin (Vinni) T'Vine: Friend of Antenn, *the* prophet of Celta.

GraceLord Hymale Equisetum: Enemy of the Mugworts, founder of the Traditionalist Stance movement.

Mica: FamCat to GreatLady Camellia D'Hawthorn.

Brazos: FamCat to GreatLord Laev T'Hawthorn.

Rusby: FamCat to Garrett Primross.

GreatLord Rand T'Ash: Jeweler/smith (hero of *HeartMate*), Fam-Cat Zanth.

GreatLady Danith Mallow D'Ash: Animal Healer (heroine of *HeartMate*).

Arvense Equisetum: Farmer, cuz to GraceLord Equisetum.

GraceLord Majus T'Daisy: Newssheet owner and editor.

GrandLord Walker T'Clover: Statesman (hero of the novella *Noble Heart* in the collection *Hearts and Swords*).

GentleLady Avellana Hazel: Daughter of a FirstFamily House, artist, fiancé to Vinni T'Vine.

GreatSir Tinne Holly: Owner of The Green Knight Fencing and Fighting Salon (hero of *Heart Fate*).

GreatSir Nuin Ash: Eldest son of T'Ash and D'Ash, fire mage.

One

*B*OOM! *BOOM! BOOM! Three explosions shook the narrow
two-story house, followed by an ominous whoosh and crackling.*

*Pinky, Antenn Moss's cat, yowled in terror. Antenn used all his
twelve-year-old speed to snag the cat and run from the kitchen.*

*Trif Clover met him in the hallway, her face pale with fear.
"Fire. We can't get out. Fire blocks both doors, windows, stairs."
Wrapping her arms around herself, she said, "I don't know how to
teleport."*

*"Me, either," Antenn said. His voice was high but didn't shake
or crack. Good. "You have Flair, psi power. Yell mentally to
EVERYONE. I will, too. Neighbors will call." The space between
his house and others was narrow.*

*"I know the best place, this way." He grabbed her hand and ran
with her to a far corner of the mainspace, then put Pinky down.
"There's a little foundation crack here. Maybe we will be under the
smoke." He yanked Trif and tried to put her next to Pinky, but she
was twenty and bigger and stronger. She pushed him down and
curled around him like he did around Pinky.*

*Using a little Flair, Antenn widened the crack, hoping to pull
more air in just for them, and he prayed, and yelled with his mind.*

And listened to the fire eat its way to them.

This was no natural fire. Must have been firebombs. Though he was only twelve, enemies wanted him dead for what his brother had done. Was this revenge?

His home was gone. If he survived, he knew gut deep, bone deep, everything would change.

A rough tongue rasped over his face, prickling his beard, and Antenn's eyelids whipped open to see too-close Pinky whiskers and teeth. He grabbed his plump Fam and sat, panting from the nightmare that had been the past.

Bad dream, Pinky sent telepathically. He could do that now. The cat had transformed to a Fam.

"Yeah." Not surprising. That had been one of the most memorable experiences of Antenn's life, and today, hopefully, would be another. He kicked off the covers and put Pinky down, not wanting any kneading paws on his lap. "Heading into the waterfall now."

The small Fam's nose wrinkled. *Time for breakfast!*

"Not quite," Antenn said, but saw his Fam trot to the door in the wall and out.

Padding to the waterfall room in his Family home, T'Blackthorn Residence, which he'd moved into the day after the fire, Antenn passed the tunic and trous he'd laid out for the day. Very professional cut, but sturdy enough and bespelled enough to handle tramping all over the site of the cathedral on the Varga Plateau.

The cathedral. He dragged in a deep breath, caught the smell of panic-sweat the dream had coated him with, and grumbled. Not a good way to start the day.

Very big day. If his clients signed the contract for the cathedral, Antenn would prove to all he was a valued member of Celtan society. His name would go down in history, Antenn Blackthorn-Moss, a FirstLevel Architect. He'd finally settled on Blackthorn-Moss instead of Moss-Blackthorn. Knew himself better.

Knew bone deep that today, everything could change.

Heart Fire   *3*

* * *

I know you desire my position, dear," the High Priestess of GreatCircle
Temple, *the* main priestess on the planet, said to Tiana Mugwort.

Tiana stumbled over a small rock in the meditation path. Her
mentor's comment caught her off guard. She'd been concentrating
on keeping her new, expensive, and *white* formal robe from catching on some of the twiggy bushes along the trail instead of watching
where she was going.

"Most FirstLevel Priestesses would be honored to have your
position," she said. No help for it, she'd have to use psi power, Flair,
to coat her gown. She'd anticipated this career review would take
place in an office instead of one of the winding paths near GreatCircle Temple.

With a huge, hopefully discreet breath, she used nearly the last
of her Flair to protect her robe for a half septhour. Surely that would
be enough. She'd spent her psi energy recklessly this morning with
several teleportations before the meeting.

She'd thought there'd be tea and flatsweets. Instead she needed
to catch up, both on the path and with the conversation.

Of course she shouldn't have expected her own ambition to
become the High Priestess—no matter how masked behind a quiet
manner—to have been overlooked by the savvy woman.

"And despite the rumors, I am not ready to retire within the next
few years." The older woman, GrandLady Ulmaria D'Sandalwood,
paused in their trek and smiled with good humor plumping her
round cheeks, kindness showing in her sparkling dark-brown eyes.
"I may never be ready to retire. Nonetheless, it is time to evaluate
you for your next step up this career ladder you wish to pursue,
yes?"

Warning! Tiana began to sweat even in the shade of the thick
trunks of blossoming trees blocking the morning sun.

Ambition and spirituality didn't often mix well, and everyone
who'd chosen to become a priestess or priest knew it.

With great care, Tiana smoothed her gown away from the wild

underbrush, hoping her spell would work to keep her gown from tangling. The robe had cost a full month's salary and was appropriate for her work in formal rituals more than anything else.

Seeing the lady's gaze on her, she straightened one of her long rectangular sleeves embroidered in gold with her rank as FirstLevel Priestess and her Family designation, mugwort leaves.

The High Priestess's robe showed embroidery of her birth Family and her HeartMate's Family. Both of those Families had much more clout than Tiana's disgraced one.

That disgrace was a thorn in Tiana, spurring her *need* to reach the greatest pinnacle in their religion, one of the highest positions in their culture. She had to prove that she—and her Family—were honorable people. Her eyes stung as she glanced around the area that she wanted for her own—a permanent place in GreatCircle Temple. She'd wanted this ever since the Lady had come to her as a child, had walked with her in dreams, had called her to serve.

Now she and the High Priestess walked along one of the looping trails in the Temple environs, this one outside the manicured lawns and gardens, just beginning to show color. She knew the seasons of GreatCircle Temple and cherished them.

Soon the tall trees overhead and the hearty bushes would give way to a broader path through tall, dense hedges that would accommodate three, though Tiana didn't think the High Priestess's Heart-Mate, the High Priest, would be joining them. Tiana hoped not; she felt more unprepared than she'd anticipated.

Looking to her right she could see the Temple itself, her sanctuary, her heart's home. "I don't want to leave GreatCircle Temple and be transferred to another temple." The statement spurted from her lips without passing her brain first, appalling her.

GrandLady D'Sandalwood's plump hand swept over a bush full of tiny spring flowers, releasing a gentle scent that soothed, as it was meant to, even as Tiana's mind raced to amend her words and mitigate her mistake.

But the High Priestess continued, "There have always been two paths to the top ranks of the priests and priestesses of Celta. One way is to stay here in GreatCircle Temple; the other is to prove your worth by rising as the priest or priestess of small to medium temples, then graduating to more influential ones. Then when the time comes to choose the next High Priestess your name is known."

"I understand," Tiana said, pushing her impatience with this conversation down, down, down. This was the next step on her life plan.

"Something you should also consider is that due to our rituals, the High Priest and High Priestess are sometimes mates. Either husband and wife or HeartMates. We find ourselves drawn to those in our profession." The High Priestess paused delicately. "I believe you have a HeartMate."

Tiana dredged up the expression she put on and the words she said every time that particular issue was raised. "Yes, but he hasn't come looking for me." She fought hard to keep the bitterness from her voice. She'd tried several times to connect with him emotionally and hadn't been able to do so. "Because of the disgrace of my Family, perhaps."

"Perhaps." The other woman flicked her hand as if that event, the most influential and disastrous event in Tiana's life, were of absolutely no matter. Tiana bowed her head to keep her irritation from showing, watching the trail they walked. Oh, yes, this extremely intelligent lady tested her.

"You don't anticipate looking for your HeartMate?" the High Priestess asked, smiling and waving at some picnickers, then back to Tiana.

Tiana's gaze shot to her mentor's. "No . . . I didn't . . . no!" Too forceful, dammit!

"A HeartMate is one of the greatest blessings of life, yet you turn your back on it? This concerns the High Priest and me."

"I don't know who he is. He doesn't want me!" Tiana burst out. "He'd have come if he'd wanted me!"

The priestess's curved and groomed brows lifted. "You know his mind and heart so well, then? You have such a strong bond you know this?"

"No."

"So it is your mind and hurt that prevent you from searching for him."

"I . . . I had not thought so." Eyes prickling, fingers twitching with the need to fist them, sweat slithering down her spine, Tiana said in a low voice, "But you must be right. I will have to meditate on this." She'd just given up on him, concentrated on her career. There weren't really many couples, even HeartMates, that became priests and priestesses.

"Indeed."

"And," Tiana swallowed, adding in a tiny voice, "I will need more mentoring on this matter." She faced an awful truth she hadn't known inside her. "I will need a . . . steadier mind and emotions with regard to my HeartMate before I proceed with any search for him." She'd need the support of not only her mentor, but her two best friends.

"I see." The High Priestess gestured to the right-hand fork in the path that avoided the hedges and led back toward the Temple. Tiana wasn't sure what that indicated. Her pulse bumped hard through her body. Had she just ruined her career?

The path had widened, and she moved to walk next to the High Priestess between garden beds showing shoots of green, tiny spears of hope that Tiana could no longer match.

A long moment of silence passed before Tiana raised her eyes, needing to see more of D'Sandalwood's reaction. And found quiet contemplation . . . not at all what Tiana had expected.

"Lady?" she croaked.

"I am not She, not the goddess," the priestess said. "Not today at this time. Her aspect is not within me. But I think we can leave this HeartMate matter to Her and Her Lord."

That wasn't a notion that sat well with Tiana, that the main deities of Celta might mix in her personal life. They had so many others to care for.

"They care for us all," the priestess said. "And we Celtans believe in destiny in some things, do we not?"

"Yes, High Priestess."

D'Sandalwood inclined her head. "Very well, we shall set aside the concern regarding interacting with your HeartMate for the moment, but you do know it is a point of growth that must be addressed in the future, don't you?'

"Yes, GrandLady D'Sandalwood." Tiana began to feel like the veriest novice instead of a priestess who'd been accepted into the highest rank, FirstLevel. She'd been an apprentice at the Temple: a journeywoman, third-level, then second-level priestess. Still she had more personal problems than she'd anticipated before she could progress in her career.

"So let us touch on the matter of your wish to become the highest priestess in our land . . . eventually."

Tiana swallowed. The floral scent of spring blooms dried on her tongue like the sharpness of dying flowers.

"I don't think you are ambitious in the right way, or for the right reasons." The High Priestess sounded more severe.

Though all Tiana's muscles clenched and her mind scrambled, she projected a relaxed manner as they strolled.

"You are very good at seeming serene," said the priestess, a hint of admiration in her tone.

"Thank you." Tiana managed not to croak out the response.

Then D'Sandalwood's face folded into sternness. "You have ambition, but I believe the fire that burns in you to become High Priestess is because you want to prove to everyone that you are a fine woman who is deeply spiritual in our Celtan culture." She paused, eyes intense. "Though your mother is a member of the Intersection of Hope Church, popularly known as Cross Folk."

"There's nothing wrong with being a member of the Intersection of Hope religion. We welcome all religions here on Celta."

"That's true." GrandLady D'Sandalwood nodded but continued inexorably. "But you want to prove to all that it was wrong for a Noble enemy of your father's to accuse your Family of being a part of the Black Magic Cult, to have your title ripped from you, to exhort a mob to set fire to your home, and to force your family into hiding."

Tiana repressed a shudder at the litany of the destruction of her

life, at the desperation and despair that had followed. The High
Priestess had slammed her with that list for shock value, of course.

Then the High Priestess stopped and turned and took Tiana's
hands, and Tiana realized she'd allowed her eyes to blur with scenes
of the past; she blinked and met the older woman's steady gaze.
"But, Tiana, we all know that all those events that happened were
wrong."

"He's still in power, GraceLord T'Equisetum," Tiana ground
out. He was the lowest level of a Noble, "Grace," as her father, her
Family, had been.

"But his power has been checked. He was a rising star in the
NobleCouncil until he let his hatred of your father, of your mother's
religion, make him act impulsively and wrongly by requesting that
the NobleCouncil strip your Family of their title and wealth in perpetuity."

He'd done it from calculated greed, not from wrongheadedness
as most people thought, used the quick fear the NobleCouncil had
had about the Black Magic Cult murders to spearhead that effort.
Furthermore, Tiana deeply believed that he'd been behind inciting
the mob that firebombed their home and drove them away.

But the High Priestess continued. "He had hopes of being Captain of All Councils, you know."

Tiana wasn't surprised; her nostrils pinched at the thought. But
unlike the High Priestess, Tiana still believed, *felt*, the man was
dangerous. He remained an enemy.

"You are still angry at GraceLord T'Equisetum, and don't open
your heart to forgiveness."

Lifting her brows, Tiana said, "One can forgive after the wrong-
doer acknowledges his or her harm and regrets the harm they
caused. Despite what you said, GraceLord T'Equisetum has never
stated he was wrong, never acknowledged in a public manner that
he did my Family wrong. Just goes on spewing hate for anyone and
anything *he* doesn't consider good." She stopped herself from adding that the man was a canker.

"He has a right to hold his own beliefs."

"The main tenet of our religion, of our culture, is to harm none! He hurt my Family," Tiana said quietly, when she wanted to shout it. They had never recovered the lost title, the Family estate, the home. Justice had not been done. Her parents had retreated to the secret sanctuary of Druida and were only now taking first steps out of it, years later, since her sister, Artemisia, had married.

"Yes, he hurt you and your Family." Lady D'Sandalwood squeezed Tiana's hands, and she felt the boundless caring from the woman. "And that is the root of your ambition, dear Tiana, not that you want to serve the Lady and Lord, give yourself over to the Lady in selfless service, let her speak to you and through you."

"I am a good priestess!"

"Yes, you are, but you will be a better one if you understand what you truly want, and I don't think it is becoming the High Priestess of Celta. You serve best when you perform rituals with small groups and intimate circles. And your crafting of new rituals is better than that of anyone else in the Temple with your years. *Those* are the skills that High Priest Lord T'Sandalwood and I believe embody your calling."

Not rising to the top of the pyramid of success, but creating rituals for those at the top to use. Working with small circles. Hurt speared through Tiana.

But she wouldn't quit, wouldn't modify her plan right now. She could still become High Priestess. She had years to try.

"You love your mother." A final squeeze of the hands by D'Sandalwood before she loosed Tiana's fingers.

"Of course I do!" Tiana replied instinctively.

The GrandLady began strolling again toward GreatCircle Temple. "And your mother believes truly in the tenets of the Intersection of Hope, that there are four parts to one divine being."

"Yes, it is a religion based on good to others, also. A religion that is a derivation of a major religion of old Earth but developed in the starships during the long voyage here."

Lady D'Sandalwood finally smiled with great approval, the smile everyone near her wanted to see. Tiana relaxed.

"We teach of the other religions in our programs, and most people, including our priests and priestesses, understand, intellectually, what they are. But you, Tiana, have an open heart in this matter, and truly understand and accept those who worship in other ways than our own."

This was no idle conversation; the woman was leading somewhere.

"Let us proceed to my office," D'Sandalwood said.

Office for official business. Tiana's back, her whole gait, stiffened, but the High Priestess didn't seem to notice as she picked up her pace and Tiana matched her. And hoped that the birdcalls overrode the gurgle of her stomach. She'd been too nervous for breakfast.

They entered GreatCircle Temple through the huge eastern doors of rock quartz carved with designs of wind and air. These doors were the closest to the city and the ones most people used.

There was a short hallway the depth of the priests' and priestesses' offices with walls covered in a mosaic of crystals that caught the light from the armorglass ceiling and reflected prisms in the small space. Tall, pale pine doors led to the corridor that curved through the round building.

The High Priestess turned left, toward the southern curve of the circle. Just beyond the due-south door, they entered the High Priestess's suite and passed through the sitting room and into the office, an inner room with no windows.

Tiana sat with the High Priestess in the gloom for only an instant before the woman waved a hand and the roof glass thinned to nothing, letting in the scents of turned earth ready for flowers. A slight breeze ruffled the stray papyrus on D'Sandalwood's desk, nearly lifted the covers of the thick deep turquoise of Tiana's personnel file and a new, thinner folder of heavy cream-colored papyrus edged with gold. Did that cream and gold indicate her next position? Tiana's eyes sharpened. What did those colors mean?

The moving air swept around her head, lifting her hair and cooling the perspiration on her neck. It felt good. The sun slanted in, touched a wall lined with plaques of their faith—a pentacle within a leafy circle, the green man, the antlered Herne, the face of the Lady. Those soothed Tiana. She was still in the Temple, the place she loved, a building imbued with positive energy.

She sat in the deeply cushioned seat with just the right amount of springs to keep a person comfortable and watched GrandLady D'Sandalwood sink into her comfortchair, one that conformed to her body.

"FirstLevel Priestess Tiana Mugwort." The woman's voice plucked chords of obedience and deference in Tiana, no mistake, that. "You have stated that you will abide by my and High Priest Lord T'Sandalwood's decision with regard to your next assignment."

Tiana bowed her head. "I will."

She had no choice if she wanted to continue in her career, and she knew now that what they asked of her would be tough.

Two

*T*he duty we assign to you must be fulfilled in an acceptable manner
for you to continue to rise in the ranks of the priestesses of Celta.
Of course you can choose to stay at your current level and you will
be assigned a permanent temple of your own." The intensity of the
High Priestess's gaze had Tiana looking up and matching it.

D'Sandalwood smiled. "We would be pleased to grant you the
CircleTemple and Sacred Grove in Landing Park."

One of the premier small temples in Druida City, the temple
nearest to the great starship *Nuada's Sword*, a gem of a temple, a
plum of a job. Tiana's until she retired. But it wasn't GreatCircle
Temple. It wasn't here.

She swallowed with a dry throat.

"If you do not take the offer of Landing Park CircleTemple, it
will be offered to another and you will miss your chance to have it."

"I understand."

"Your other choice will have you remaining here, but with a
suite of two rooms instead of one. Your counseling will diminish
and your leading ritual circles will remain the same, and you will
take on a new assignment." The High Priestess watched with sharp
eyes and Tiana thought the woman had seen her concern, then her

pleasure that her circle work would continue as is. Tiana loved leading circles.

She didn't speak, but waited, and the silence between them filled
with the chirp of birds—always continual and melodic around the
Temple. A hint of floral fragrance swirled around them from the
High Priestess's personal meditation incense.

Calm trickled through Tiana and her mind began to subside into
a meditative trance. The priestess nodded and smiled. "Well done. I
thought you might never relax during our time together, and a
priestess must always be able to reach for serenity . . . and joy."

Tiana smiled back.

Lady D'Sandalwood opened the cream and gold folder. "We
have been approached by one of the Chief Ministers of the Intersection of Hope to give our approval for them to build a cathedral on
the Varga Plateau outside the Druida City walls.

"We stated that they did not need our approval or blessing for
such an action, of course.

"Chief Minister Custos informed us that they have the land and
the permits and the architect already, and wanted our support. We
told them that they have it, and that we would assign a liaison to
work with them and their architect, Antenn Blackthorn-Moss."

The words jolted Tiana from her peaceful state, reverberated in
a near scream in her head. She'd distanced herself from her mother's
religion since the scandal, the firebombing of her home. Now she
was being pulled back into it. Rumor and gossip would buzz around
her again; her old wounds would reopen.

"Tiana, if we, the High Priest and High Priestess, find your
efforts at completing this assignment worthy, you will be accepted
as one of our main assistants here in GreatCircle Temple and regularly write and perform ritual circles for the benefit of all Celta."

"I . . . I . . ." She shouldn't have started to speak, because she
floundered, showing herself near panic. Being an assistant to the
High Priest and Priestess was a prize. But to do that, she'd have to
work through all her pain from her Family's losses. Of course, that
was the reason she was being given the experience.

"This will be a high-profile project, which will cause a great deal of . . . discussion," D'Sandalwood said.

She really meant outcry.

The High Priestess continued, "There is no room in our world for religious prejudice. That tore apart old Earth on more than one occasion. We will not tolerate it here, and we will make that clear to the All Councils, the twenty-five FirstFamilies who rule, those who are devout in our faith in the Lady and Lord. We will stand firmly behind the Intersection of Hope, this undertaking to raise their own beautiful and substantial place of worship. We will completely support you as our liaison, Tiana. You have our blessing."

Which came close to a dismissal.

"You have an appointment at MidAfternoon Bell with my HeartMate, High Priest Lord T'Sandalwood, to discuss this matter, also. After that, we will give you two days to decide."

Tiana's mind whirled; she couldn't even manage a nod.

GrandLady D'Sandalwood raised a finger. "Though we allow you two days for your decision, we have no control over the timing of other events. The project will be announced, and the Chief Ministers of the Intersection of Hope will be giving interviews to the newssheets and viz press tomorrow morning."

"Before the time I make my decision," Tiana said, grasping the point most pertinent to her.

The High Priestess inclined her head. "We would, of course, like to confirm you as liaison at that time, during our own interviews."

Tiana steadied her breath and began breathing deeply to calm herself.

With a glance at the wall timer, the High Priestess said, "Though we had not anticipated such a task for you, the High Priest and I are pleased that one arose. And though, of course, you *do* have two days to contemplate the matter, events march on and we have had to make definite arrangements to handle the situation. We have set up an appointment with Antenn Blackthorn-Moss for you in half a septhour at his office in CityCenter."

"Oh."

"Will you abide with *our* decision and deal with the arrangements we have already made?"

Sternness lived under the soft aspect of the High Priestess's face. Her plump hands had gestured with sharp movements.

Despite what her mentor had said, Tiana knew she had to decide. Now.

Stay at this level, or go forward. She bowed her head to hide the resentment filling her. Though she believed the High Priestess and High Priest hadn't manipulated her, the situation had done that; she *hated* that she had to make a life-changing decision on a few moments' notice.

Pretty much anything but "Yes, High Priestess," would poorly influence the career she loved, had worked at for years. One she wanted to rise in.

She took another long, long breath and raised her head. "I . . ." Dammit, she couldn't get the words out in one sentence! Had to clear her throat. "I don't need to take two days. I agree to your task."

A fast, beautiful smile came from D'Sandalwood, one that lit her eyes, and an open expression of great approval . . . with a touch of surprise. "Excellent." She paused. "A Temple glider is waiting to take you to your meeting with the architect." Several heartbeats' pause. Definite dismissal.

"Thank you for this opportunity," Tiana mumbled as she stood and fluttered the folds of her elegant, richly formal robe slightly. She'd worn the garment to honor the High Priestess.

Tiana suppressed tears as Lady D'Sandalwood came and embraced her in a soft and caring hug.

"You need to work through your anger, dear girl. Think how you might take steps to release that, more than you have done."

"Yes, High Priestess."

Holding her at arm's length, GrandLady D'Sandalwood smiled in sympathy. "You can do this, Tiana. This is an extremely important situation to us, and we know you will represent us well."

Pride had Tiana's shoulders straightening, and the tears coating her throat drying.

"We know this will be a personal trial to you." The priestess searched Tiana's face. "But we think it will serve your soul's growth well."

Tiana was just fine with her soul as it was. "Yes, Lady Sandalwood."

"Good. You will do fine." She dropped her arms and stepped back, tucking her hands in the long sleeves of her equally formal gown. At least hers was shifting shades of blue; Tiana's was white.

"Go to your appointment with GentleSir Blackthorn-Moss, and don't forget your meeting with my HeartMate this afternoon."

As if Tiana could. Again she bowed her head, and words came from deep inside. "I appreciate your confidence in me."

"Honor your mother and her religion, and us and ours, and yourself, Tiana. Blessed be."

"Blessed be." She concentrated on steady steps to the door and down the hallway, turned to one of the four main entrances, the southern one, and saw her rival, Lucida Gerania, smiling as she left High Priest GrandLord T'Sandalwood's chambers, obviously happy with *her* assignment.

Tiana had to squelch envy hard.

Lucida beamed at Tiana, and then her smile took on a hint of glee. "You don't seem pleased with your new assignment."

A *good* thing that irritated words stuck in Tiana's throat. She rearranged her expression, lifted her chin a little. "It's a challenge," she said, and, to her discredit, liked the beginning of the frown she saw. "And I've been named an assistant and graduated to a two-room suite."

The other's nose lifted. "So have I."

Of course she had.

Lucida said, "I'm just going to check my new offices out. See what furnishings they might need . . . or whether I should tint the walls first . . ." She lifted blond brows.

"A Temple glider is waiting to take me to a pressing appointment," Tiana said. The amount of gilt she could spend on any refurbishment of her new offices was nil.

Envy flashed in Lucida's eyes. For now. Tiana knew the woman would be crowing when she heard of Tiana's duty.

"Blessed be," Tiana said.

"Blessed be." Lucida nodded, then hurried down the wide and curving corridor.

$\mathcal{A}$ *long, sleek, dark-blue glider with the sigil of the GreatCircle Temple* sat under the portico. As Tiana advanced, the door opened upward and she slid into the luxury of soft furrabeast leather. The door whispered shut and the glider accelerated. No driver sat on the front bench, so the vehicle had already been programmed to take her to the offices of the architect, Antenn Blackthorn-Moss. Just from his name, Tiana knew he was adopted by one of the twenty-five First-Families, the Blackthorns, a GrandHouse.

Everyone knew the Blackthorns had problems with sterility and a vulnerability to some common sicknesses, so the couple had adopted several—many?—children. She thought Antenn was the first, but T'Blackthorn hadn't chosen an Heir, from either his children or a cuz and a secondary line. She'd do some research later.

Now she concentrated on resting since she hadn't slept well the night before, nervous about her meeting with High Priestess Grand-Lady D'Sandalwood. And she'd teleported to a couple of stops from the hidden sanctuary where she lived to GreatCircle Temple. Then she'd had to add spells to her dress. Weariness pressed on her.

Still, it wasn't often she'd ride in such classy comfort. One of her best friends, Camellia D'Hawthorn, had married into the FirstFamilies, but Camellia's HeartMate and husband preferred small and jazzy sports vehicles. Tiana's Family had no vehicle at all.

Stooopppp! Let me IN! screeched a mental voice.

Reacting instinctively, Tiana snapped, "Stop the vehicle immediately."

The glider whooped a warning to others, jerked still, deployed the landing brackets, and rocked back and forth on them.

Windooww! yelled something. Tiana turned toward the sound

and jolted as something dark and furry showed beyond the tinted window.

"What are yo—" she began, but saw a whippy cat tail. All right. She commanded, "Thin the back windows to air."

The spell took hold, and the furry animal bolted through, landing close to her. She put out a hand to keep the cat from tumbling onto her and thought she saw drool or spittle flying toward her, too.

Yay! Look at Me! I am with My FamWoman! I have CATCHED her!

Tiana stared at the brindled cat of drab shades of brown and gray. One of his ears was half gone. Obviously not a pampered Fam, but a feral.

He smiled ingratiatingly, showing a broken fang, too, and then his loud and rumbling purr filled the glider.

"FamWoman?" Tiana asked faintly.

His head bobbed. A white scar showed the length of his head and disappeared into the fur near his neck. *I am your Fam.*

"Do you even know who I am?"

The Fam snorted. *Acourse I do. You are the priestess who lives in the secret place that welcomes the really scared or sad.*

Her heart thudded and her mouth dried. That was true.

You are not the Healer who lives there and who has a raccoon Fam. The tom lifted a paw and flicked it as if dismissing such a creature. But Tiana's sister's Fam was young and pretty, especially compared to this one.

So was everyone else's Fam.

Light-green eyes fixed on hers. *I am a good fighter. Like you.*

"I see."

He preened and turned his head and licked a mat by his shoulder. *We will be good together. I have been smelling you for the last two weeks, and knew I had to find you.*

That simply appalled Tiana. "Smelling me?"

He sniffed. *Yes. You are my FamWoman.*

Well, he had no doubt about that.

"I take it you haven't come from GreatLady Danith D'Ash's Fam Adoption Rooms."

The tom made a disgusted noise. *Bunch of soft pussies.*

"We are now ten minutes late to the appointment," the mechanical voice of the glider said.

"Oh! Resume driving!" Tiana ordered.

This is a nice glider, the tom said, looking around, flexing his claws. *I have always wanted to ride in a glider!*

"Don't you dare put your claws in the leather seat—"

But in went the claws and Tiana bit her lip as she watched the cat knead, but when he pulled out his claws, his whiskers turned down at no holes in the leather. A very good trick.

"Ah," she said. "What's your name?"

The cat sat proudly. *I am RatKiller. All the Fams in the world know RatKiller!*

Tiana just stared.

But you may give me a human-gift name, too. A Mugwort name. That will be good. Then I will be Something RatKiller Mugwort.

"Wonderful."

"The destination is in one block on the right," the vehicle said. "Prepare to disembark."

I will ride around in this for a while and see you at your home when you are done.

I am going to T'Hawthorn Residence after the meeting, she replied. To celebrate . . . or at least tell her two best friends how the morning had gone. Everything was already arranged.

The cat stopped licking his foreleg and grinned at her. Yes, one fang definitely had a jagged top. *Even better,* he said. *Tell this glider to go there.*

"I don't think so."

Then I will! GLIDER, AFTER YOU LEAVE CITY CENTER GO TO NOBLE COUNTRY!!

"What!" Tiana sputtered.

"Orders acknowledged," the glider said. Apparently it had spells set to receive Fam telepathy.

Every portion of this day had spiraled out of Tiana's control.

*　*　*

*T*he *Turquoise House hummed to himself, happy with his existence as* much as he'd ever been since his HeartStones had wisped into awareness twenty-two years ago. The tune wafting through his walls was one of the latest that Trif Winterberry had composed for him. He was beloved of the FirstFamilies and had had many wonderful guests.

But he was impatient and it was time to gather in his Family.

He was no longer an adolescent, but a mature adult. He was wealthy from his leases and the belongings his previous Family had gathered over two and a half centuries, but most of all, he was beautiful, with a gorgeous, shiny light turquoise exterior.

No one, not even the person he'd been luring and who had not come back, could resist him now.

And TQ was brilliant. He'd set his plans. Soon he would have his Family, and everything would be perfect.

*T*he *priestess was late. Annoyingly unprofessional.*

Antenn Blackthorn-Moss wanted to pace the flagstoned sidewalk in front of his business, a nicely elegant building with tall rectangular windows set in rough-cut red sandstone that he'd recently redesigned and rehabbed. But he couldn't show his impatience or tension because his client, a Chief Minister of the Intersection of Hope, a stocky man but with an innate elegance, remained serene.

Antenn couldn't even look at his wrist timer, though his preliminary engineering crew awaited them at the building site, a dusty piece of land at the edge of the Varga Plateau, the geographic area Druida City was built on. His forewoman knew what to do, so hopefully they had started without them.

Finally a glider stopped near them and the door rose. A woman gathered a formal robe and stepped out before Antenn could take the couple of paces to offer his arm. When she turned to them, her face seemed flushed with irritation, which immediately annoyed him. *They* were the ones waiting on her . . . but his frustration simply dropped away as he got a good look at her. She'd made an attempt to tame curly brown-black hair by putting it in a bun that might have once been smoothly elegant, but tendrils wisped in fine strands around her oval face.

As she'd exited the vehicle, the fabric of her gown had tightened here and there and he'd seen she was slender but with nice, and nicely proportioned, breasts and hips. Her fine-boned features eased into a standard priestess pleasant expression.

Elegant, dainty. Out of his league. And exasperatingly late.

Chief Minister Custos moved toward her, stopped, and bowed four times. "We of the Intersection of Hope had requested you be our liaison but had not hoped you'd agree. The High Priest and High Priestess stated it was your decision."

The priestess's emerald eyes flickered and Antenn guessed that the Powers-That-Were in the Temple hierarchy had put pressure on her. Yet her manner held the strength and serenity of most priests and priestesses he'd met, along with steely determination.

She inclined her torso. "My deepest apologies, Chief Minister and FirstLevel Architect Blackthorn-Moss, for keeping you waiting." Her lips twitched up. "I was only offered this experience this morning." She pivoted toward Antenn, and he searched for her name, dredging up the knowledge that she traveled in a pack of three: Camellia D'Hawthorn, Glyssa Licorice Bayrum . . . , got it! He gave her his best bow. "No problem, Priestess Mugwort."

Her eyes narrowed as if she heard the hint of his lie. With an automatic smile, he continued, "My team is already at the land at the edge of the Varga Plateau that belongs to the Cross Fo— Intersection of Hope. Perhaps we should teleport?"

She whirled to look at the glider that had taken off a few seconds before, and flushed again. The pink tinting her cheeks added lovely color to a pale complexion that showed she worked inside.

The Chief Minister offered his beringed hands to both of them with a smile. "I have visited the land often and can visualize it in any light, so I can handle the teleportation of the three of us."

Antenn shrugged and took the minister's right hand, leaving the man's left for Mugwort. For some reason he didn't want to touch her—if her touch was as stunning as her looks, she'd be a major distraction for him. He said, "I've got a pretty good image of it, too. The center point with the brass inset, right? I'm contacting my crew mentally to make sure the area is clear."

Chief Minister Custos smiled placidly. "I can send a mental claxon noise also to warn everyone."

Nodding, Antenn said, "Please do."

FirstLevel Priestess Mugwort—what *was* her first name, something pretty—said, red deepening her cheeks, "I'm sorry but I won't be able to contribute much Flair to our teleportation." Her breasts rose. "I've used a lot of psi power this morning."

"Both I and the boy"—Custos gestured to Antenn—"have sufficient Flair for this."

"Thank you," she said, but Antenn knew she gritted her teeth.

"Let's go."

Three

A few seconds later the three of them landed on the edge of the plateau where Druida City was built . . . but outside the city walls. A wind had picked up and flung gravel and dirt around, tugging at Tiana's hair despite the spells. She bit her lip to stop a cry of protest at tromping around in the empty field full of dead brush and rocks.

She'd better focus on serenity, on clearing her mind and the irritation from her manner. Chief Minister Custos was as knowledgeable as the High Priest and Priestess with regard to people. Tiana was a FirstLevel Priestess and able to order her emotions, so she should act like one. Custos was probably already aware of her feelings. She had to shape up.

The three of them walked around much of the jut of land, significantly higher on this southwestern edge than Druida City. The architect and minister discussed the area and the views.

The Chief Minister and she were introduced to Blackthorn-Moss's small crew. Tiana knew her new shoes, at least not nearly as expensive as her gown, would be ruined.

Blackthorn-Moss stated, "The site and the underlying rock is such that I don't think we can give you the cathedral in the exact spot you and your Elders wished within the budget you wanted. Heavy-duty

Flaired building-mages would have to be used, or we would have to rent the old Earthan machinery from the starship *Nuada's Sword* and its Captain."

Chief Minister Custos frowned, lines snaking across his wide forehead. "Is that so?"

"Yes. If we progress with the original plans, due to the composition of the land, the cathedral would have to be angled several degrees from the northeast-southwest axis you prefer."

"That is not acceptable." Chief Minister Custos tilted his head toward Tiana and said, "Absolutely one of the reasons I wanted First-Level Priestess Mugwort to work with us. I'm sure you have reviewed your notes on our religion, FirstLevel Architect Blackthorn-Moss, but you would not have a *feeling* for us as Priestess Mugwort does. Can you briefly explain our religion to the FirstLevel Architect, Tiana? And may I call you Tiana?"

Another test! Tiana dipped a tiny curtsey. "I'm honored, Chief Minister." More stiltedly than she wanted, she said, "Pursuant to the Intersection of Hope beliefs, there are four parts to one divine being." She cleared her throat, calmly crossing her arms so her hands disappeared into the opposite sleeves, a more formal pose. "It's a religion concerned with the individual, and compassion to all. A belief system set in terms of a journey that rose during the long voyage here." She smiled at the Chief Minister and saw approval in his kind eyes, and the architect seemed to be actually listening to her. "The four aspects of the divine are the childlike self always open to possibility; the mature individual full of vitality and purpose; the older and wise guide; and the inner guardian spirit. All four points of a cross that meet in the middle to form the perfect human being, the ideal spiritual person whom each member of the religion strives to be."

"Very good!" Chief Minister Custos said. Glancing at Blackthorn-Moss, the cleric spread his hands. "The northwest-southeast axis must be precise, because it is the absolute symbol of our hope, first the stars in the sky in relation to the original voyage, then the direction the starships lifted off." He shook his head. "It is impossible to change the axis."

The architect smiled, and Tiana finally realized he was an attractive man when he wasn't scowling. She thought his resting face wasn't flattering since his expression seemed to shade toward melancholy and older than his years. She couldn't quite gauge what his age was.

His features were even and pleasant. He had pretty brown-green hazel eyes, defined brows, and a stylish professional cut to his thick brown hair the color of rich earth in the summer. He held his lean body with the toughness that came of a very physical man.

But his facial structure showed no hint of any FirstFamily Noble line like his adopted father's would. The highest Nobles tended to breed among themselves unless HeartMates were involved.

She shifted from foot to foot. Some pointy rock had been close to piercing the thin sole of her shoe.

Blackthorn-Moss said, "If we can't change the axis, I have a workaround for you." He opened his hand and a meter-long roll of papyrus appeared in it. He turned to look at his crew at the edge of the plateau, no doubt to gesture to one of his workers to hold the other end. Tiana sighed, then offered, "I can help you with that."

"Thank you. It's a Flaired plan, so we can see the building in both two dimensions and three."

"Naturally, you would have a workaround," Chief Minister said.

Tiana took the end of the plan and walked backward a pace or two . . . and right into a prickly bush that snagged the embroidery on the gown she'd saved for a year to purchase, a work robe to wear during formal rituals at GreatCircle Temple. She stiffened, but the men didn't seem to notice, both of their gazes fixed on the plans.

"It looks to me as if you have also shrunk our cathedral," the Cross Folk priest said.

"I have, to match the dimensions of the best ground on the plateau," the architect said, "but what you might lose in the extreme grandeur of your building, you can use for more elaborate craftsmanship, more details, in the stonework outside and inside. The actual building would be four-fifths the size that you wanted. Unless you wish to consider one of your two alternative sites."

The Chief Minister hummed in acknowledgment, then pleasure

as two holographic models of the same equal-armed-cross building rose: one larger and plainer, the second smaller and prettier.

Tiana stopped trying to carefully pluck her embroidery off the bush to study the images as they rotated; then the first disappeared, leaving the smaller second, and the outer walls thinned to show the exquisite sculpting of carved stone inside.

They all studied the holo for a moment, and Blackthorn-Moss's body relaxed from the tension Tiana now realized he'd carried. The Chief Minister lifted his stare from the papyrus plan to scan the ground. "Yes," he said slowly, "I can visualize this revised building." Equally slowly, he shook his head. "I'm not sure I want to move to another site. This one resonates with the proper energies for me."

Antenn Blackthorn-Moss tapped the plan and it snapped shut with Flair, taking Tiana by surprise, jerking her forward with a ripping sound.

Her formal robe!

"Oh, my dear!" The minister stepped forward, stared, like her, at the jagged thirteen-centimeter tear in her gown.

Tiana forced back tears. "It's not much."

The canny old man's brows winged up at that, but he nodded.

Blackthorn-Moss strode over, shook his head. "Dam—" He cleared his throat. "My apologies."

"An accident," Tiana managed.

He nodded, then turned back to his client.

Her gown wasn't totally ruined, but it would take a substantial amount of gilt to repair it so she could wear it in rituals at GreatCircle Temple.

Not to mention how she'd have to scramble to look presentable before her meeting with the High Priest this afternoon. She didn't have the Flair to teleport home and back.

Chief Minister Custos gave a little cough.

"Yes, Chief Minister?" Blackthorn-Moss asked attentively.

The cleric gestured to the people working on the far edge of the plateau. "Could I ask you to dismiss your crew so that I might, once again, get a feeling for this area now that the dimensions and the layout for our cathedral have changed?"

"Of course," the architect said. He stared across at the forewoman, who turned her head, nodded, and relayed Blackthorn-Moss's orders. The workers all teleported from the site with nearly embarrassing quickness. Those who didn't have the Flair or skill for the transportation linked with others who did. Tiana was impressed.

"Thank you," Chief Minister Custos said, strolling away to the mark that showed the center of his cathedral.

Tiana stood where she was, chanting a few couplets that might calm her. This day, which she'd anticipated, which she'd thought would have her climbing a few more rungs on the ladder of her career, which she'd thought would be triumphant, had turned disastrous.

She was quite sure that her mind wouldn't settle down until she was in bed tonight. All the pleasure she'd felt in her vocation seemed smirched by the events of this one day. Perhaps the Lady and Lord themselves had sent this day to test her. Maybe her life had seemed too smooth to fate. But the inner peace she'd built over the last few years now felt like a shell encompassing a seething mass of emotions that she'd suppressed, or that she'd hidden from herself . . . or something. Definitely not time to think about that now.

She stood in the chill wind of spring and watched the Chief Minister stroll around. Antenn Blackthorn-Moss had drifted over to where his team had been, apparently scrutinizing their work or what might need to be done. Still, his body showed a tautness in his muscles and movement that cued her in that this client was extremely important to him. Important enough—or the challenge of the building was important enough—that he didn't care about any controversy that might hit him. She only wished she could be as casual.

The moment her name was linked with this project, GraceLord T'Equisetum would rev up his hate machine. She knew that if no one else did, and hoped the others were taking security seriously.

Closing her eyes, she breathed with the wind, letting it tease more hair from her pins . . . she'd stopped the Flair holding it nicely the minute she'd entered the glider.

Sage and dust and the hint of spring flowers budding teased her nostrils, and underneath the flow of the wind she could feel the slow beat of the land, and its sense of the movement of the ephemeral creatures—humans—atop it.

Chief Minister Custos was right about this place. It held a . . . pristineness that she hadn't often experienced. Neither the early colonists, the Earthans, nor the Celtan people had put their mark on this land. The touch of humans lay very lightly on this edge of the plateau.

It was harder to live in the moment, this moment of this day, than she'd anticipated. The interview with the High Priestess had been so wildly different than Tiana had anticipated.

An atavistic cold whispered down her spine. Something in the wind, now. Not natural. Perhaps a smell; sniffing delicately, she turned in place as if examining the view, glad the men had left her alone. The tinge-taste of rot came from the city along with a whiff of malice. Not something, *someone*. And she'd been wrong; greed and anger and fear and other negative emotions were all too natural. Yes, this project made her uneasy.

Because it brought back wrenching memories. Because she knew that others of her rank in the Temple would see it as low status, a setback in her career.

Because her memories and emotions would not be the only ones stirred up, and there were people who had mobbed her house, driven out her Family because her mother had been a member of the Intersection of Hope, who had never paid.

Her spiritual beliefs told her that they'd paid thrice for that cruel act, for breaking their own religion's rule of "harm none." They should have suffered physically, emotionally, spiritually.

But what would happen to the cathedral if people like Grace-Lord T'Equisetum remained bitterly convinced that the Intersection of Hope folk were bad?

No, despite what the High Priestess thought, Tiana didn't think this project would be good for her.

The wind shifted and she smelled the men, heard their footsteps coming toward her. Chief Minister Custos smelled of the incense that sometimes wafted around Tiana's mother, and of an older man.

Antenn Blackthorn-Moss smelled . . . virile. Sexy. Tiana frowned as she tried to break down the scent into components. And then they were there and that particular moment was lost.

She opened her eyes to see the architect walking side by side with the cleric.

Chief Minister Custos said, "I am quite pleased at all the thought, work, and creativity you have already done for our building, GentleSir Blackthorn-Moss. I have been given permission to tell you that we accept your bid and will sign a contract today or tomorrow. I will speak to our Elders and we will schedule a date to begin the construction."

"Thank you." The architect offered his arm. The Chief Minister grasped the man's arm at his elbow, and Blackthorn-Moss returned the grasp. Then they both bowed.

"Merry meet and merry part and merry meet again," said the younger man.

"Truly, I hope so." The Chief Minister beamed at the architect. Then he turned to her. "Go in peace; may you journey to the center and find your joyful self."

"Go in peace; may you journey in the light," she responded automatically to Chief Minister Custos.

He smiled benignly and teleported away.

"Sorry about your formal gown," Blackthorn-Moss said, in the offhand tone of a man who could buy ten robes like hers that flicked her on the raw.

"You . . . you . . . man. You think I wore this for *you*? I wore this gown for my career-level review with the High Priestess of GreatCircle Temple. I saved for a full year to afford this robe!" With the energy surging from her anger, she teleported away to somewhere she knew she'd be cherished, to her good friends who awaited to hear how her interview had gone. They would be as disappointed as she.

And she went to another of the FirstFamilies Residences, T'Hawthorn's.

*A*ntenn *was in deep trouble. When—not if—his mother, GrandLady* Mitchella Clover D'Blackthorn, the interior designer and a very feminine female, heard this story of him ruining a broke woman's expensive dress, even accidentally, his goose was cooked.

So he damn well needed to tell her himself.

He'd let his hormones get the better of him, and he was old enough to know how to control them. The minute the gorgeous woman had stepped from the Temple glider, his body had reacted, and only the old-fashioned loose and blousy trous that he wore had enabled him to disguise the semiarousal that had plagued him throughout his time with her and the Chief Minister.

He'd had to drag his gaze away from the motion of her hips as she'd walked, the graceful gestures of her hands, the curve of her cheek, to pay attention to his client and this massive job that would bring him fame and respectability.

He'd gotten the impression that the Chief Minister, as a man, had noted his condition and had been amused, thank the Lady and Lord. But Antenn must keep ironclad control of himself if he'd be working with the delectable FirstLevel Priestess Tiana Mugwort. This project was too important to him and every person in his small architectural firm for him to be distracted by a lovely woman.

Checking his wrist timer, he saw it was NoonBell and lunchtime. The consultation had gone a full septhour, seventy minutes, longer than he'd anticipated, but he'd kept the whole day free.

He reached into his pocket for his scry pebble, flicked it with his thumb, and saw the cheerful freckled face of his assistant, Bona Vervain.

She grinned at him, her newly tinted purple hair almost glowing. "How'd it go? The crew said you dismissed them with full pay for the day."

Yeah, that had given him a qualm but the client had wanted a privacy of three—too bad Custos hadn't asked the woman to leave, too—and Antenn had complied.

Antenn let his shoulders ease from a tight, straight line. "I think he went for the revised plan."

Bona and the other two of his office staff whooped. An increase in pay for all of them if they could pull this off.

"I translocated the plans back to my desk," he said.

"We noticed. It has some gold thread on it. Really, Boss?"

Antenn winced. "Accident with the FirstLevel Priestess who'll be the liaison from GreatCircle Temple on the job."

Bona's face showed sympathy. "Oh, that's not good."

"I'm taking lunch now. I'll be back in the office in a septhour or by MidAfternoon Bell at the latest."

"All right, we'll save the champagne until then."

"We'll save the champagne until the client signs the contract."

Bona saluted. "Right, Boss."

"Later." He cut the scry, stuck the pebble in his pocket, stretched, and examined the site one last time. A good place, outside the ancient city walls erected by the original colonists, but the parcel never developed.

The Earthans had constructed buildings in the innermost city and near the starship *Nuada's Sword*, and spread out mostly north and east, since to the west was the Great Platte Ocean. The highly psi-powered, Flaired, FirstFamilies had built castles in the Noble-Country part of the city.

Antenn shook his head. Though the earliest settlers had anticipated their descendants would spread out over the whole of the Varga Plateau, it hadn't happened. The planet Celta was tougher on humans than they'd thought.

He turned in place. This was a good area, the Chief Minister was right about that. Felt nice, and like the older man, Antenn could *see* the beautiful cathedral here.

A movement at the edge of his vision had him tensing, touching the hilt of the blazer sidearm he carried as part of the Noble class, though he rarely used it.

"Greetyou, Antenn," said the tall, lean man walking toward him in dark green tailored silkeen trous and shirt.

"Vinni." Antenn's held breath whooshed from him, and then he noted his friend's face. He wasn't just Vinni. Now the man looked like GreatLord T'Vine, the premier prophet of Celta, who he also was. His eyes had changed color, a bad sign.

Four

*A*ntenn raised a hand to stave off any prophetic words. *"Don't say anything. I don't want to know."*

Vinni joined him, the lines in his face due to his psi making him appear older than Antenn, though Antenn had nearly two years on his friend. Vinni was also taller due to good nutrition all of his life, while Antenn had lived on scraps in the old Downwind with his brother's gang before he'd been adopted. And naturally Vinni had handsome, noble features. Antenn's features tended to the rough.

"This project will stir up a lot of contention," Vinni said, studying the area as Antenn had done. His friend's mouth curved in a half smile; his gaze went distant, the color continuing to change hue. Not good. "But the cathedral will be wonderful, a special place for centuries. If it gets built."

"If it gets built!" Antenn heard a squeak in his voice, stamped his feet to ground himself and send the surge of fearful anger away. "Dammit, Vinni!"

T'Vine blinked and came back to the present, his smile fading. He slanted Antenn a look. "You put enough guards on all shifts." He paused. "And check it yourself. Watch for fire."

Antenn ground his teeth; there went much of his profit margin. "I'll do that. Are you done with the future-forecasting now?"

Vinni inclined his head. "For now." He hesitated, then repeated. "For now."

Antenn sighed. "If you have any urgent feelings about this, let me know."

"The whole situation is in flux." Now Vinni smiled. "Along with your life."

"Thanks a lot."

"You're welcome." Vinni leaned and bumped Antenn's shoulder with his upper arm. "You have some pretty good opportunities in the next little while. Don't let them slip away. What's up next?"

"Lunch with Mitchella. I gotta consult with her on a gown."

Now Vinni's eyes sparkled as if he'd known nothing of that situation, excellent. "A gown."

Antenn gestured widely. "FirstLevel Priestess liaison from the Temple showed up in a formal gown to tour the area." His hand swept to the prickly bush. "Bad results. Guess I'd better damn well replace it."

"A priestess's gown will have additional spells and spiritual workings in it, I'm sure," Vinni added, mock-helpfully.

"Even more expensive," Antenn translated.

"Yep."

"Damn."

Vinni said, "This I've got to see. I'll go to lunch with you at T'Blackthorn Residence." He linked arms with Antenn and 'ported them to Mitchella's home office teleportation pad in a blink. Hardly anybody had the strength of Flair Vinni T'Vine did.

Mitchella, GrandLady D'Blackthorn, glanced up at them, still as beautiful as she'd been when she'd adopted Antenn from the Saille House for Orphans. "Hmm. To what do I owe this pleasure, son?"

He tried to be casual but was sure those sharp eyes already saw through him. Walking over, he kissed her cheek. "Can't I have lunch with my favorite lady?"

She nodded. "Oh, yes, but usually not on a weekday and on the day you informed me at breakfast would be critical for your career."

"Busted," Vinni said.

"I don't know why I even try," Antenn said.

A grunt came from near the window. Pinky, the small peach-colored cat Antenn had found and named in his childhood, rolled to his paws. His fur was sleek, but not his body. His stockiness had turned into plumpness. Setting his front paws on the window cushion, rump up, he stretched long and luxuriously, then twitched his whiskers. *Greetyou, FamMan.*

"Greetyou, Pinky."

"Greetyou, Pinky," Vinni said.

It's lunchtime. A small pink tongue came out and swept over his white whiskers.

Taking advantage of the distraction, Antenn crossed over and picked up his Fam, letting him stay, round tummy up, in his arms. Pinky turned his head and sniffed Antenn's tunic, his pale-green eyes cracked open. *Nice smell. I like.*

Antenn poked a gentle finger in his Fam's belly. "That's good, because I think you should go with me on site with this project."

Mitchella's face softened. Holding a cat and looking as innocent as he could, reminding her of his small and pitiful orphan-self, sometimes worked to get him out of hot water. She dropped her writestick and stood, smiled at him. "Lunch sounds great. You can tell me what trouble you got into that you need me to help you out of. Just the three of us for lunch; your brothers, sisters, and cuzes are elsewhere. Of course you're welcome, too, Vinni."

"Thanks, Mitchella."

The lunch was very green and healthy. Vinni seemed all right with it, but he tended to let his staff—all relatives like in most Noble Residences, but mostly female—boss him around.

Antenn had his doubts regarding the huge multicolored green leaves and a few nuts. He looked across the table in the breakfast room at his adopted mother. "You do realize I spent much of the morning tramping around a nice-sized area of the Varga Plateau?"

Raising her nicely shaped brows, Mitchella said, "And you'll be doing the same this afternoon? Or sitting at a desk?"

With a grimace, Antenn stabbed more leaves. They seemed to have multiplied. "Desk."

Mitchella said, "I'll order you a clucker sandwich."

"Thanks, Mitchella," Antenn said.

While they were drinking their after-lunch caff, Antenn said, "I need to consult with you about a dress."

Mitchella's hand, holding her pretty white china cup to her lips, paused. She set the drink back down and studied him. "I think that's the first time you've said anything of that sort to me since I adopted you at nine."

He grinned.

She cocked a finger at him. "But I know that expression." Her brows lifted. "Whose dress did you ruin?"

"It was an accident," Antenn said. "Mostly. Well, the rip in her gown was, the dirt . . . we were walking a site, for Lord and Lady's sake! It's dirty, it's dusty, and her wretched dress was white."

With his peripheral vision, Antenn saw Vinni wince.

Antenn raised his palms out as he noted his mother drumming her fingers on the linen tablecloth. "Peace. I'll make it good. I'll buy her a new dam—a new gown." He tried a smile. "That's why I came, to ask you how much it'll cost."

"Good job," Vinni muttered from the side of his mouth.

"What kind of gown was this?"

"A priestess's formal ritual gown, I think."

Mitchella winced, lifted her cup, and drank down the strong caff. "Whose?"

"FirstLevel Priestess Tiana Mugwort. She'll be the liaison between GreatCircle Temple, me, and Cross Fo—Intersection of Hope Chief Ministers."

"Ah." Mitchella pursed her lips together, no doubt tracing Family lines in her head or something. "Mugwort, I don't know her Family. What was the dress like?"

Antenn made a futile gesture. "White, heavy material to her ankles. Long rectangular sleeves. You know the sort."

"Traditional."

"Yeah." He frowned. "I think it had some pattern woven into the cloth."

"Embroidery?" Mitchella asked.

"Only around her sleeves and at her shoulders, denoting a First-Level Priestess and her Family."

Mitchella nodded. "All right. I can contact our cuz Amplecta Clover, who's started a tailoring business. I think she can get it done immediately." She scanned Antenn's tunic. "You should switch your custom to her. She'll give you a good rate."

Antenn grunted. He didn't care too much about clothes. "Sure."

Naming a figure for the gown that made him wince, but wasn't as expensive as the highest cost he'd earmarked in his mind, Mitchella held out her hand for the gilt.

He got it out of his wallet and handed it over.

"Measurements?" she asked.

His eyes nearly popped. "How should I know?"

Vinni laughed.

"I'll contact GreatCircle Temple, why don't I? They'll know her measurements because they regulate their priestesses' and priests' garments." Mitchella smiled as she tucked the gilt into her own gown pocket.

"Yeah, yeah. I gotta go." He stood, walked around the table, and kissed her on the cheek. "I'll be home for dinner with the rest of the gang." Then he walked back, buffeted Vinni on the shoulder, and said, "Later, man." Leaning down, he picked up Pinky. "You're coming with me to the office."

Nice, Pinky purred.

With a last wave, Antenn hopped onto the teleportation pad and 'ported to his office, where he was boss and he made damn sure things ran as smoothly as humanly possible.

*T*iana had no sooner arrived on the teleportation pad in Camellia Darjeeling D'Hawthorn's sitting room when her nose twitched at the smell of grilled clucker, her favorite food and made by the hands of her best friend, Camellia, herself.

"How'd it go?" chorused Camellia and the other of their trio of friends, Glyssa Licorice Bayrum.

Camellia gasped. "Your poor robe! What happened?"

Like the cork popping from the champagne bottle that she couldn't drink from because she had *another* interview this afternoon with the High Priest, words flew from Tiana's mouth.

She was hugged, her gown whisked from her body and handed to a commiserating housekeeper to see what damage could be repaired, and she was draped in one of Camellia's thin silkeen houserobes.

Her friends murmured all the words of support that Tiana wanted to hear, but she didn't miss the sharpening of their gazes or a couple of quick, shared glances between them . . . and her spirits dampened.

When they were all done with brunch, she sighed herself and held up a palm before either of them could work their way around to gentle comments. "I know, I know, some of what the High Priestess said is true."

"So are you going to work with Antenn?"

Tiana blinked. "You know him."

Camellia rolled her eyes. "He's been reconstructing the Mistrys-Suite for me here, I *told* you."

Glyssa said, "And, though I don't recall meeting him lately, he was the one who drew up the plans for the town at the excavation of *Lugh's Spear* where I'll be living. I've already helped construct one of his buildings, the community center, there."

"He's part of that whole younger Noble group," Camellia said. "You know, along with Laev and Vinni T'Vine."

They all gave a tiny shudder at Vinni's name. No one ever wanted to see the prophet.

Glyssa chuckled, tucking a strand of red hair behind her ear. "Camellia and you will be my rich, Noble friends."

"Camellia, maybe," Tiana said.

"No, Tiana," Glyssa softened her voice. "You *know* that if you're aiming for High Priestess you will be mixing in with the FirstFamilies."

"And be held to the highest standard of behavior in all of Celta." Camellia wrinkled her nose.

Two sets of eyes, brown and gray, stared at her. Tiana blinked her own.

"We've never talked about that," Camellia said. "Do you really want to watch everything you say and do more than you do already?"

"Uh—"

Glyssa brushed the question away with an impatient gesture. "I don't think they'll accept someone who isn't in the HeartMate bond."

Tiana flinched, staring at both her friends, who'd settled into their HeartMate status with their husbands.

Leaning forward, Glyssa said, "Being part of a HeartMate couple influences everything in your life."

Camellia waved her hands and sounded equally passionate about the issue. "It's wonderful."

Tiana dampened her lips, and her own voice was high. "The High Priestess accepts that I don't need to search for my HeartMate right now. Why are you pushing?"

Another shared look between her two friends, one that excluded her, as their new experiences excluded her. Lady and Lord, she hadn't realized she felt that way. Not acceptable. She would have to meditate on it.

Camellia translocated a tier of plates from her kitchen, each holding a different dessert. She plucked a small white cake iced with pink frosting and handed it to Tiana. "We want you to be as happy as we are."

"Now is not the time to think of HeartMates," Tiana said severely. "I have enough to juggle with these new duties and a Fam." Her smile was lopsided. "And it isn't as if GrandLady D'Sandalwood will be retiring soon, as she very well told me." All right, a hint of bitterness had entered her tone. More meditation on *that*, too.

"Speaking of your Fam," Camellia said. "We'd love to meet him."

"He'll show up," Tiana said. Recalling her interaction with the disreputable tom amused her. Good, that showed she could poke a little fun at herself. She tilted her head. "In fact, I bet if I thought *FOOD* to him, he'd be right here." She did, sending a picture of the furrabeast bites she'd seen Camellia feed her own FamCat.

Pop! The cat lit on the table, tipping over the dessert holder with a crash, knocking Glyssa's plate onto the floor, yowling and whirling, tail smacking cups of tea into the air. He lunged for a clucker leg, snagged it.

Crash! More plates and cutlery hit the floor. Good thing it wasn't Camellia's prized tea set.

Tiana reached for her Fam, caught him close. Camellia and Glyssa stood, staring at the destruction.

I'M HUNGRY! RatKiller yelled mentally as he ate.

"What is going on?" The Hawthorn housekeeper popped in, holding Tiana's gown. She stared, and then with one sweep of her arm, all the plates and utensils levitated to a large silver tray sitting on a side table.

"Manners, Fam!" the housekeeper ordered.

"He doesn't have any," Glyssa choked.

"That is one interesting Fam," Camellia said, grinning.

Tiana eyed the cat, chomping at the clucker leg, and didn't think she dared take it away from him. It smeared grease along the front of Camellia's robe.

"What. An. Interesting. Fam," the housekeeper said between gritted teeth.

Mortification flooded Tiana. "I am *so* sorry. I will be pleased to clean up—"

"Thank. You. No." The housekeeper gestured and Tiana's dress hung in the air. Then the woman gave one sharp clap and the room seemed to depressurize.

The remaining platters of food shifted to a sideboard. Camellia grabbed the teapot as it floated by, and then the tablecloth folded itself over and vanished somewhere it could be tended to.

Doors opened on a cabinet and a clean, pale-pink tablecloth draped over the polished wood of the table; more silverware laid itself at places, followed by china also in pale pink with red roses outlining the rim. Tiana shared a glance with Camellia, who rolled her eyes at the fussy spell but said nothing.

Unlike the two cats who shot through the open doors, the Fams of Camellia and her husband, Laev T'Hawthorn.

We smelled a new FamCat. A new FamCat has come to visit us and play? Mica, the young female calico asked. She scanned the room and Tiana holding her Fam. The cat screeched and leapt onto Camellia's shoulder. *It's RATKILLER!* she yowled.

Five

*T*he calico cat, *Mica, screeched, He hurt me when I was a feral kitten!*

Tiana's Fam stopped gnawing on the clucker leg and looked at the new arrivals, Mica first. *I just gave you a tap.* He smiled, and because of his half fang it seemed more like a leer. *A looove tap.*

Brazos leapt in front of Camellia's feet, bristled and bottle-tailed. *She is mine. Mine, mine, mine, mine, mine, MINE. MY mate.*

RatKiller snorted.

"RatKiller." Glyssa's lips twitched.

"He'll need a new name, of course," Tiana said.

"Do you want more tea, GreatLady D'Hawthorn?" the house-keeper asked, using Camellia's title. Not the first time the three friends had been viewed with disapproval by Laev's Family staff. It didn't bother them.

Camellia lifted the pot she held. "Thank you, GentleLady. I can heat this up." She looked at the remnants of their meal. "The food can be cleared, but could you translocate another dessert plate with little cakes and flatsweets?"

"Yes, GreatLady." Back stiff with offense, the housekeeper ges-tured and the two massive trays, one of no-doubt antique Haw-thorn china and the other of food, floated with her from the room.

RatKiller went back to chewing the clucker leg.

You are a Fam now? the long-haired, nicely groomed black Brazos sneered. *Took You long enough. I didn't think You'd ever find a person to like You.* He lifted a paw, licked it, and smoothed the fur over his ear. *You see this Residence? I live here, I am the TomCat here. I have a rich FamMan.*

Sniffing, RatKiller nuzzled his head, and the bone in his mouth, against Tiana's upper chest. She now had small shreds of meat on the robe. The second garment she'd ruined today. *MY FamWoman lives in the hidden garden, where Your FamMan can't go. Where only Special People can go.*

Brazos growled. *My FamMan was there once.*

"Enough!" Tiana said, then cleared her throat as her cat widened his eyes in a pitiful manner. "Are you still hungry?"

He burped around the bone. *I could eat more.*

Camellia stroked her FamCat. "Mica, will you show our guest, um, RatKiller, the Fam no-time storage unit outside against the patio wall?"

Yes, the calico sniffed, too, and, adding Flair to her jump, sailed across the room to land in front of the open door. She crooked her tail. *Come on, Brazos. Come on, RatKiller.* She flicked her tail and sauntered out.

I would like hot, hot furrabeast bites! RatKiller said. *And cold, cold milk! Does your no-time have that?*

Mica said, *Of course. My FamWoman makes all our food and drink.* And a no-time would produce the food and drink at the same temperature it went into storage.

RatKiller licked under Tiana's chin before he jumped from her arms, leaving the picked-clean bone behind. *I will see you later, FamWoman.* He didn't walk, he swaggered. Brazos, the black cat, followed, prowling, ready to pounce. Well, better any fighting take place outside the house.

Tiana glanced down at herself and caught both her friends looking at the smeared and dirty robe. At least it didn't look like it had any cat-claw holes.

Her friends' lips were twitching when she glanced up again.

"RatKiller!" Camellia gasped.

Glyssa just shook her head. "You have interesting times ahead of you."

"I guess so. I'm sorry about the robe, Camellia."

"A cleansing spell will take care of it. Here, let's examine your gown."

"I should have known better than to wear white," Tiana grumbled.

"Why? You thought you'd stay inside the Temple," Glyssa said absently. She stroked the sleeve of the heavy cloth. "Whoever worked on this did an incredible job. It appears to be new."

"It *is* new," Tiana said, and walked over to check out where the ragged tear had been. She couldn't see it.

"They rewove the threads." She hummed in approval. "Heavy-duty Flair."

"Your general protection spell on it as well as the fact that it is quality material and workmanship helped," Camellia said. She was a little flushed, still new to all the wealth and skill she could command as a GreatLady.

Tiana nodded. Her perscry, a personal communication pebble that she'd placed on an end table, glowed and pinged. "Twenty minutes until your meeting with High Priest T'Sandalwood," the calendar sphere part of the perscry announced.

"I need to go," Tiana said.

"We'll help you with your gown," Glyssa said, murmuring the spell to release the dress as Camellia came around and took her robe back with not-very-suppressed chuckles. She shook her head and said, "Fams."

Tiana stood for a moment in her undergown while her two friends slipped the formal robe over her head, murmuring more spells as they did so. The dress now fairly hummed with Flair.

With a last twitch at the skirt, Glyssa stood back. "There, you look great."

"Take some flatsweets," Camellia urged. She smiled at Tiana's narrowed eyes. "They can't hurt. And I think GrandLord High

Priest T'Sandalwood particularly likes the ones with white cocoa bits." She offered a little papyrus bag that smelled great. But no time for dessert for Tiana.

"And I'll, ah, take care of this." Glyssa's mouth twitched as she picked up the clean leg bone from the carpet that Tiana hadn't noticed. She closed her eyes and flushed, even though these were her best friends.

Glyssa kissed her on the cheek, took the bag from Camellia, and thrust it into Tiana's hands. "A goodwill offering. Especially since you think he's going to be as hard on you as his lady, High Priestess D'Sandalwood."

"Glyssa," Camellia protested.

"Well, it's the truth."

Tiana grimaced. "I've had a lot of the truth today." She rubbed her hand over the robe, and it soothed her. Narrowing her eyes, she looked at her friends. They both tried to appear guileless; Glyssa did it better. Tiana shook her head. "Thank you for whatever serenity spells you added." She frowned. "I don't think we're allowed—"

"They are spells fueled by the love of friends, and primarily to protect an expensive gown." Camellia nudged Tiana. "Go."

"You can nail this interview!" Glyssa said. Of course, *she'd* already gone through her tests and been promoted in her career. As for Camellia, she was a businesswoman and worked for herself, so she didn't have to deal with performance reviews.

Hauling in a deep breath, Tiana shifted her stance as she also tried to shift her state of mind into tranquility. Mostly it worked, though some niggling, worrying bit chittered in the back of her brain, which she ignored.

"I love you both!" She concentrated on her friends, on the warmth she had for them, the love, drew it through her, along her nerves.

"We love you!" they chorused. "Blessed be!" They boosted her Flair for the teleportation.

"Blessed be." She smiled with real sincerity and 'ported to the GreatCircle Temple's priest and priestess lounge.

"There you are." GrandLord T'Sandalwood, the High Priest, smiled at her, but his eyes were sharp.

She might need the flatsweets.

*S*ince *Antenn had been in the office too long and the afternoon had* warmed, presaging summer, he took the box with the replacement gown for FirstLevel Priestess Tiana Mugwort and went to the teleportation pad in the lobby of his offices. "I'm heading out for the day. I'll be in tomorrow at the regular time, or I'll come back if Chief Minister Custos needs me here to sign papers. Scry me, then."

His assistant, who worked the reception desk, finally smiled at him. She'd made a point of announcing loudly to the whole place when the robe had arrived a half septhour before. "Later, Boss."

"Yes." With his Flair, he checked the public teleportation pad near GreatCircle Temple's east door and found it clear, flicked the switch to show he'd be using it, and 'ported.

The huge, beautiful cream-colored stone building dominated the beginning-to-green landscape. He stopped to admire it—some long-ago Earthan whose name had never been recorded had designed the temple for their new religion, and the colonists' machines had built it. Without those machines, with just the more powerful Flair that Celtans had, they might, just might, this generation, have been able to raise a building like this.

Or make a cathedral like he aspired to do. That building wouldn't quite be like the old ones on Earth that Antenn had researched. The Intersection of Hope religion was not an Earthan religion. The Cross Folk had different symbols, but the cathedral would have four equal arms, towering arches, and flying buttresses.

The Temple grounds seemed busy. If Priestess Mugwort was having a review, others might be also. He asked a passing, cheerful journeyman where he might find FirstLevel Priestess Mugwort's chambers.

The young man eyed him. "She's closeted with the High Priest." The journeyman glanced at his wrist timer. "But they should be finished shortly. Use the north door."

"Thank you."

"Blessed be."

"Blessed be," Antenn replied.

"I *am* blessed! I made ThirdLevel Priest today!" He grinned.

"Congratulations," Antenn said rotely, his mind on the information he'd garnered. He'd thought she'd already had her interview when she'd accompanied him this morning. She was with the High Priest now? What of her ripped gown? Dammit! He could only hope that she'd been able to do spells before the interview to fix it . . . maybe an illusion spell . . . no, a High Priest would see through a simple illusion spell, wouldn't he? And religious people of all sorts emphasized honesty.

The box in his hands felt heavier as he recalled his offhand attitude about the dress.

He didn't really like to recall his own past reviews as apprentice, journeyman, the last one for master. His many yearly reviews. He was an excellent architect. He was not so good at being an employee.

Shrugging the past off and trusting that the Lady and Lord would be helping their priestess, Antenn strolled along the stone path that circled the temple. Flowers and bushes were planted close to the building, then the path, cobbled in reddish stone, then a sweeping lawn. Just the beginning green sprouts of early spring flowers poked a few centimeters from the ground.

The north door wasn't as busy with priests and priestesses and whoever else wanted to use the Temple.

Sitting in the middle of the walk, focused on the great double doors of oak outlined in brass and inlaid with a stone mosaic of a mountain scene, sat a very ugly tomcat.

He turned his head as Antenn approached. Staring, the cat said, *Greetyou.* He made no effort to move from the center of the walk. Good thing it would accommodate three abreast.

"Greetyou," Antenn said, turning to go up to the doors. The cat rose to his feet and trotted along. *You are going in? Good. You can hold the door for Me.* His smile neared a smirk.

"Are you allowed in?" Antenn asked. He'd taken his own Fam,

Pinky, to several rituals, but it had been understood that Fams were welcome at those times. He didn't know whether they were on a day-to-day basis.

The cat lifted his nose. *I am sure.*

Antenn wasn't. "Who are you waiting for?" he asked casually, pausing before the doors, and taking time to admire the fine craftsmanship.

Every muscle of the cat's body swelled with pride, his head lifted, and his tail waved. *I am waiting for My FamWoman, Tiana Mugwort.*

Antenn let his hand fall from the handle of the door. "You? You're FirstLevel Priestess Tiana Mugwort's FamCat?"

The cat's half ear twitched. *Just today, We became Fams. A Very Important Day.* Again his tail thrashed.

Antenn's lips twitched. "No doubt."

We will go in. The Fam stopped, expecting Antenn to open the heavy doors for him. Glancing down, Antenn considered. He'd never seen a less impressive cat. One who thought the world revolved around him. Even Zanth, T'Ash's Downwind Feral Fam, was somehow more civilized than this one.

"I don't think *we*—" Antenn started, then broke off as he received a telepathic communication.

Greetyou, GentleSir Blackthorn-Moss. This is High Priest Alb T'Sandalwood; please come in, and, ah, escort the cat.

As you wish, Antenn said. Before he could open one of the doors, they swung in.

*D*espite the High Priest's efforts to make her relax, his own innate peace, and the flatsweets, Tiana remained tense throughout their interview. Now and then she'd grab futilely at a thread of grounding calmness, only to have it unravel. She felt that the great man was very aware of her miserable efforts to be composed.

They'd touched on her ambition again, the fact that the other forerunner for High Priestess was Lucida Gerania, that Tiana wasn't Heart-Bonded with her HeartMate and didn't, in fact, know who he was.

Worst of all, she had to admit, once more and aloud, that she hadn't managed to forgive GraceLord T'Equisetum. She nearly squirmed in her seat.

The High Priest contemplated her under his bushy black and white eyebrows, then waved the topic aside and pushed the plate of flatsweets toward her. "If we didn't care for you, see great possibilities in your career should you open yourself more, we wouldn't both have spoken with you today." His lips curved up. "Neither of us wanted to yield the career interview to the other."

She supposed she should feel well supported by them, but instead felt battered and couldn't regain her normal confidence. "No one else had an interview with both of you today?" Like Lucida Gerania.

His smile deepened. "No, only you."

Tiana was so lucky.

"Ah . . ." Lines had dug into T'Sandalwood's face and his smile had vanished. The caff pot on the sideboard drifted over to Tiana's cup on a tiny table next to her and refilled it. She'd have to use a little Flair to steady her hands before picking up the delicate china cup in the form of an open flower blossom.

Arching her brows, she said, "You have something else very important you want to say." Which was why he was adding a dollop of white mousse to the top of her caff, to break it a little more gently. She did love her white mousse.

He nodded, serious, the instant's hesitation gone. "The Lady High Priestess and I think that the destiny stone is pointing in your direction."

"Fateful events are moving around me," Tiana said by rote. She didn't know what divination the High Priest and Priestess did privately, but she knew of omens.

GrandLord T'Sandalwood watched her with an intense gaze until Tiana gave voice to the correct conclusion. "Fate will be moving me."

"That's right." He dipped his head, his expression went slightly remote. "And the High Priestess and I will be finessing it along." He paused. "You should drink your caff."

She remained stiff with shock when his long, mobile face turned curvy with another smile, dimples on the sides of his mouth, eyebrows high and rounded. Tilting his head, he obviously sent a telepathic thought to someone. Then he leaned back in his comfortchair that conformed to his body and intertwined his fingers over his flat middle.

"We'll wait a moment, why don't we?"

Six

Tiana had no clue what he was talking about, but he was the High Priest and not to be questioned unnecessarily. Again she deliberately loosened her muscles. She'd had no idea the day would be so trying. When she'd awakened this morning, she'd had such high hopes!

There came a scratch on the door; it opened and a smell wafted in. Her body tightened. Already she knew that smell.

FamWoman! RatKiller grinned his broken-fanged grin and hopped right onto her gown.

"Ah, Fam," she said aloud. She was *not* going to call him Rat-Killer . . . though from the smell it seemed he had, indeed, done some kind of dispatching, and perhaps eating, since the last time she'd seen him at T'Hawthorn's.

"Greetyou, Fam," said the High Priest, laughing quietly under his breath as his chair straightened.

GREETYOU HOLY MAN. I AM RATKILLER!

"So I noticed. Greetyou, GentleSir Blackthorn-Moss."

"Greetyou, High Priest T'Sandalwood," said the man behind her. She hadn't noticed before that his voice had a timbre that resonated well, was deeper than she'd expected, and slid right along her skin.

She was absurdly grateful she wasn't alone with T'Sandalwood anymore.

"What is that you carry?" the High Priest asked.

Antenn Blackthorn-Moss inclined his torso toward Tiana, guilt on his face. She gave him a smile.

"While we were touring the Varga Plateau for the cathedral this morning, FirstLevel Priestess Mugwort's dress tore on a bush."

"Humph." The High Priest stared at her. "Good mending job."

Tiana picked up the caff. The back-and-forth discussion—and maybe her Fam's presence—relieved her enough that her fingers didn't tremble. After a lick under her chin, RatKiller jumped down and began checking out the large suite. T'Sandalwood didn't seem concerned, so she hoped it was Fam-proofed.

"The mending wasn't my work," Tiana said, "but that of the T'Hawthorn Household." She nodded toward the box. "And my great, great thanks for your generosity."

"The least I could do," Blackthorn-Moss muttered. He placed the gown box on the arms of the chair she was sitting in, and it was large enough to trap her in the seat, if it had been a heavy object.

"Let's see it," T'Sandalwood said. His long nose twitched. She'd forgotten how curious he could be. The box was fastened all around the bottom with Flair.

Before she could say a Word to open it, Blackthorn-Moss tapped on the top with a finger. The box top lifted and settled on the floor, and the gown itself unfolded to hang in midair. Simply beautiful. The dress was unmistakably a formal robe for Temple rituals but had a slight difference of cut of the sleeves, the shoulders, the waist that made it unique. The creamier color would complement her better than the white she currently wore, and she had no doubt that it would fit. The gold-thread embroidery denoting her rank was not just on the shoulders but twined up the sleeves in a harmony of Celtic knotwork.

"Ohhh." Her throat tightened. She couldn't recall the last time she'd been given a new dress. Hadn't even understood that she'd wanted such a gift. "It's wonderful."

"It's a little different style, but perfectly acceptable," T'Sandalwood said, then nodded. "I like it."

"And you provided it so quickly!" Tiana blinked hard.

"Mostly my fault your gown was torn." Blackthorn-Moss shrugged. "I have a cuz who makes dresses and asked her to hurry one up for you." He frowned. "I didn't know you had an additional review this afternoon. My apologies."

"It's nothing." Maybe, maybe, the day was turning around for her . . . despite all the spiritual work she needed to do.

Beau-ti-FUL! RatKiller leapt onto the corner of the High Priest's desk, scattering papyrus, then launched himself at the gown.

"No—" Tiana yelped.

But the cat hit a Flaired shield about five centimeters from the dress and gently slid down it, all his claws bared but giving no purchase.

T'Sandalwood began coughing.

Blackthorn-Moss looked to the heavens and said a couplet. The dress whisked to the box and folded itself inside and the top flew back on. "Best if you translocate the dress as soon as possible, I think."

Bending over and touching the top of the box—which was warm with Flair—Tiana scraped up the very last of the Flair she had and made the box vanish to a cache she and her Family used outside the walls of their home. Teleporting and translocating people and objects into the secret sanctuary was always problematic . . . as was getting out.

RatKiller righted himself to sit and yowl protest.

"Quiet!" Tiana said, then waved him to jump to her lap. Better that she had her hands on him to keep him in order.

The yowl transformed to a large and rumbling purr as he settled his odoriferous self on her lap.

High Priest T'Sandalwood gestured, and a chair angled for Blackthorn-Moss. That man's face went blank, then masked before he sat and said, "You have something to discuss."

"Indeed," T'Sandalwood said, talking over RatKiller's purr.

"We, the High Priestess and I, had planned on speaking with you later, but here you are." He raised his brows. "I want to verify that Chief Minister Custos of the Intersection of Hope has commissioned you to build a cathedral."

The architect crossed his legs at the ankles. "I'm not sure that is any of your business."

With a short laugh, T'Sandalwood shook his head. "I assure you, we of GreatCircle Temple are enthusiastic about the cathedral."

Antenn Blackthorn-Moss jiggled his foot, then said, "Chief Minister Custos has seen the plans I've drawn up but has not actually signed a contract, yet."

"You're sure the Intersection of Hope will build a cathedral?" T'Sandalwood asked.

"Yes."

Now the High Priest leaned over his desk, expression as serious as she'd ever seen. "We, the High Priestess and I, are dedicated to this project. It is extremely important to us. So, both of you, feel free to call on us to help you at any time."

"Uh—" the sexy architect said. Yes, now Tiana could admit the man was extremely appealing.

"Can I see the plans? I promise you I will keep the information completely confidential," the High Priest said.

There was silence as the men studied one another. Tiana said nothing, but she recalled the plans, and the holo model, fairly easily. T'Sandalwood hadn't asked her about that, though.

"All right." A casual flick of his hand brought an architectural drawing to T'Sandalwood's desk, smaller than what she'd helped hold that morning.

Tiana frowned. It reminded her of something.

"The first thing I believe you, FirstLevel Architect Antenn Blackthorn-Moss and FirstLevel Priestess Tiana Mugwort, should do is to consult with the Chief Ministers of the Intersection of Hope to formalize a ritual to raise security spellshields." T'Sandalwood tapped his forefinger on the map.

His gaze went to Tiana. "One of the reasons we want you on

this project is you *can* craft such a ritual, blending our beliefs with that of the Intersection of Hope." He stood. "Please consider working on the ritual as your highest priority, and include all the Priests and Priestesses in GreatCircle Temple. The High Priestess and I will request that all our people here attend." He paused and appeared a little thoughtful. "I'll put out a notice to the rest of the Druida City temples, too, and we'll see who confirms they will be there."

Tiana foresaw a huge circle, larger than she'd ever written a ritual for . . . and the most challenging ritual she'd crafted in her life. She gulped.

T'Sandalwood said, "GentleSir Blackthorn-Moss, I would appreciate if you spoke about this security spellshield ritual to your father and mother, your whole Family. Please ask your father to spread the word that a ritual will be forthcoming that the First-Families might wish to participate in, since they regularly like to affect our world."

Dizziness made Tiana want to lower her head, and she was glad she yet sat.

"I can do that," Blackthorn-Moss said.

"And my HeartMate and I will contact the other, smaller, religious groups in Druida and ask for their participation," T'Sandalwood said, then directed his next words to Tiana. "Plan for a multicultural, multidenominational ritual that will incorporate several faiths and cause no offense to any."

"Of course," Tiana said faintly. She kept her chin and her head high as she stood, curling her toes in her fancy—and still ruined—shoes.

Antenn Blackthorn-Moss stood, too.

RatKiller purred louder, and despite herself she tightened her grip on him solely for his animal comfort.

The architect said, "GrandLord T'Sandalwood, I'd like to translocate that plan back to my office. Would you release it, please?"

With a sigh, the High Priest lifted his hand. The papyrus whisked away, the Flair used looking effortless. Tiana quashed the pinch of resentment that she'd tapped out her Flair.

"It's been a pleasure speaking with you both," T'Sandalwood said.

Antenn knew dismissal when he heard it. Priestess Mugwort placed her disreputable Fam on the floor and curtseyed deeply to the High Priest. Taking his cue from her, Antenn bowed as if to a FirstFamilies Lord or Lady.

He strode to the door and opened it. RatKiller sauntered out, scruffy tail waving.

The priestess lagged behind. In fact, she appeared pale. The day had obviously been hard on her. *He'd* made it harder on her than it needed to be, and he regretted that.

So he stood aside and waited politely until she exited and closed the door behind them. Since she still appeared a little shaky, he took her arm and pulled it through his own and nearly staggered himself at the touch of her. For a moment his mind felt as if he'd plunged into a cool, pellucid green lake, all niggling anxieties vanishing. Complete serenity.

That was his mind.

His body, particularly around his groin area, heated with a surge of lust he hadn't felt for a woman upon simple touch for a long, long time.

"Did you have lunch?" he found himself saying. His body leaned close to her . . . protectively, without his knowledge. Then more words escaped. "Would you like a snack?"

She smiled wanly up at him. "I look that bad, do I?"

He grimaced. "I *hated* career reviews."

"Thus the reason you are a master, a FirstLevel Architect, and work for yourself," she said, a little zip in her answer. Her shoulders and posture had straightened, too.

"Thus," he agreed.

They left the corridor to traverse the huge round inner space of the main temple. Several paces into the temple, RatKiller shrieked telepathically, *MOUSE! I SEE A MOUSE! DON'T WORRY, RATKILLER WILL GET HIM!* and took off in the opposite direction, the southeast, bounding along with an odd gait.

"Ah-hmm," the priestess said.

Antenn kept his mouth straight, his eyes kind. "Fams." He shook his head.

"You have one?" she asked, with a little more enthusiasm than she'd shown for him so far.

"Yes, a cat, since I was a boy." He shook his head. "Pinky."

Her lips twitched. "Pinky."

"That's right."

"I'm not sure that it's any better a name than RatKiller."

"Got me there."

A young woman also wearing FirstLevel robes, these the standard pale blue, of an equally fine quality as those of Tiana Mugwort, crossed their path. Her steps hesitated and her eyes narrowed as she scanned him. He got the impression that she discreetly studied his not-so-noble features and his excellent and costly clothes.

She stopped, nodded a greeting at FirstLevel Priestess Mugwort. Something in her air toward Tiana seemed condescending and irritated Antenn. *He* lived with being ignored, patronized, and looked at with disdain by Nobles . . . or downright loathing by the survivors of those his renegade brother had killed. But he didn't like it and certainly wouldn't put up with anything like that to Priestess Mugwort.

"Greetyou," he said, coolly.

The woman was a pretty blonde, well aware of her appeal. She dimpled a smile at him. "Greetyou—"

"FirstLevel Priestess Gerania, let me introduce GentleSir Antenn Blackthorn-Moss," Tiana said with a lack of enthusiasm.

As usual with strangers interested in status, Antenn saw her lips turn down at his non-Noble title, then purse as she caught the First-Family Noble surname. She probably recalled that his adoptive father hadn't chosen an Heir yet, so Antenn *might* someday become one of the premier lords of Celta. After only an instant's calculation in her eyes, she curtseyed to him as if he were already a FirstFamily Lord. He hated that.

"Blessed be," she purred.

"Blessed be," he replied.

His FirstLevel Priestess—that is, Priestess Mugwort—smiled in a way that looked all right but he sensed was strained. "Lucida was also promoted today."

Antenn tightened his arm against Tiana's in support. He liked being connected to her. Dipping his head, he said, "Congratulations," then looked at Tiana. "What does that include?" Her body relaxed beside his. Nice. He got to be slotted into friend status vis-à-vis the other priestess instead of the one left out as the priestesses bonded.

"We both have been given larger offices here in GreatCircle Temple and our duties have been expanded and been more defined," Tiana said.

"Oh, like that big ritual GrandLord T'Sandalwood said you'd be leading," Antenn contributed, not at all guilelessly.

"Yes." Tiana's lips curved.

FirstLevel Priestess Gerania arched elegant brows. No doubt she came from a long-standing Noble Family. Antenn Moss had never known his natural father, let alone any blood relative other than his mother and brother.

"A big ritual?" the other priestess asked.

Tiana nodded. "That's right. The time hasn't been set."

"Must be in the next couple of weeks," Antenn said, thinking about the building schedule.

"No doubt," Tiana agreed. "You'll be notified, of course. The High Priest and Priestess want everyone associated with GreatCircle Temple to take part."

"That was my understanding," Antenn said, but still shuffled plans in his mind. He nodded to Gerania, then looked at Priestess Mugwort. "We should get some food in you," he said, and Tiana withdrew a little. Dammit!

Addressing the other priestess, he started the Noble good-bye bit. "Merry meet."

"And merry part," she replied.

"And merry meet again," he finished. With a tug, he encouraged Tiana Mugwort to move. A few strides from the other woman, he

said, "Lead me to the nearest teleportation pad. Would you mind
going for a snack—tea, whatever—at Darjeeling's HouseHeart? It's
close to my office."

She stopped walking. He glanced at her again and recalled her
friends; this time he acknowledged it aloud. "You're the third of the
trio of friends with Camellia Darjeeling D'Hawthorn and Glyssa
Licorice Bayrum."

"That's right."

"Oh. Ah. Will going to Darjeeling's HouseHeart be all right?"
he asked.

"You mean, will Camellia be there?"

"Yes."

"No, she will not be there. She has business at D'Hawthorn Residence today."

"Good, that's good." He didn't want to make nice to the Great-
Lady. He liked her fine, he just . . . wanted to spend more time in
the company of Tiana Mugwort without anyone interrupting.

The Priestess wetted her lips, and any spirituality he'd attached
to her vanished again.

"Darjeeling's HouseHeart sounds lovely, thank you. I'd like one
of their clucker salad sandwiches and a bowl of cream of veg soup."
A little hesitation. "I have no more Flair to use today."

Antenn shrugged. "I'll handle it." He let the press of her hand
around his arm guide him back into the corridor that circled the
temple and they headed southwest.

"We'll teleport from my new office," she said.

"Fine." He'd like to see it. As an architect he was nosy about
everyone's homes and offices . . . with only one exception.

When they reached a modest oak door in the southwest quadrant
of the circle, he dropped her arm so she could unlock the door with her
palm and a murmured Word. Then they stepped into a slice of curving
office. Right now, it was bare enough that he could see the two rooms.
This one was larger and contained a multipaned window that dominated the wall, showing formal hedge gardens yet twiggy and bare.
The chamber to the right appeared smaller and he got the impression it

was more of a private space—he saw the shabby and chipped corner of a wooden desk with a peeling veneer. Where they stood seemed more public . . . probably for counseling or conferences. He quashed a shudder. He'd been through plenty of those, but not here at this Temple and not by FirstLevel Priestess Mugwort, thank the Lord and Lady.

The creamy stone walls and floors looked scrubbed clean from the last occupant, though a scent of incense remained that included a whiff of heavy musk that he didn't think fit Tiana well.

To the left of the window stood a chaise longue in blue-green, nearly turquoise, which was his least favorite color. But with her dark brown hair and her pale complexion, she'd look good on it. Exotic. Sexy . . . He yanked his mind from those thoughts that pleased his body.

In the inside corner, where the wall to the hallway met that of her inner office, were neat piles of her belongings. The largest was a meter-tall holo painting that had been turned off so he couldn't see the subject.

"Do you want me to help you out here?" Yes, he remained curious. Snoopy, even.

Color flooded her pale cheeks and he cursed inwardly that he'd been distracted. "I'm sorry. You definitely need food." He glanced around. "Is there a preferred area for teleportation, one that will accommodate the Flair more easily?" Not her Flair, but he still had plenty for the day. He wondered in passing what she might have been doing that depleted all of hers. Surely she was as powerfully Flaired as he. She must be at FirstLevel.

She glided over to the far left corner beyond the window. "FirstLevel Priestess Alchemilla had a teleportation pad here." Tiana Mugwort's cheeks reddened even more. "I'll be taping off an area." She set the indicator that the teleportation space was in use and waited for him.

Antenn couldn't stand it anymore. He needed to get his hands on her.

Seven

Walking up to Tiana, he put his hand on her shoulder and slid his fingers down to link with hers. Of course she looked up, and he kept his expression serious. "I overestimated my Flair. Do you mind?" he asked as he pulled her into his arms, her back to his front, leaving just a little gap. Oh, yeah, she felt good and womanly, with that addition of serenity that seemed to seep into his very bones.

"Of course not," she said, though her voice sounded a little strained.

He hoped it was because she felt the same attraction he did.

I'M HERE! RatKiller teleported into the room and leapt for Antenn's shoulder. He jerked his head aside, sucked in too much air with smell-of-death-and-cat, and nearly choked. RatKiller spread his claws all too closely to Antenn's eye, then began to lick blood and fur from them.

Antenn just stood a moment, suppressing annoyance, then said, "All right. On three."

"Do you really want to go to Darjeeling's HouseHeart, Rat-Killer?" Tiana said dulcetly. "They are quite strict there about Fams. I think they'll put a spellshield on your fur."

Antenn figured they damn well better.

SOMETHING AGAINST MY FUR?! NO, NO, NO, NO,

NO, NO! The Fam hopped down, lit lightly, and stood staring at the Priestess's belongings, tail thrashing.

"Maybe you could wait for me at home?" She cleared her throat and glanced up at Antenn. "RatKiller and I only connected today. RatKiller, can you get to my home?"

The tom turned his head. Even in the dimness he looked bad—half ear gone, half fang gone, matted and scruffy fur. He lifted his nose and projected in a more acceptable tone, *I know where you live. I will go there.*

"Dinner is usually in four septhours."

Flick, flick, flick of the gray and dun striped tail. *So late! I know where to go to get more food.* Once again he vanished without any good-bye.

Tiana's body lost some rigidity in Antenn's arms. "He needs caring for," she said, "I can't imagine he has a good diet. That could help his teeth and fur, don't you think?" She looked up at him and Antenn just saw large pupils surrounded by emerald, plush pink lips.

"FirstLevel Architect Blackthorn-Moss?"

He blinked, pulled himself out of spiraling desire that had more than a hint of tenderness. This woman appealed to him on so many levels. What were they talking about? "Yes. Ah, you might take him to the Ashes, the animal Healers, GreatLady D'Ash or her son Gwydion."

Tiana stiffened. "My sister and mother are Healers. I'll see what they can do first. After all, RatKiller will be living with them, too."

"Uh-huh." Antenn didn't have to cast his mind far to understand why the priestess would prefer that solution. The Ashes weren't exactly inexpensive, and he'd already realized Tiana Mugwort lacked funds. He could offer a few solutions—bargaining with the Ashes, having RatKiller go to Gwydion on his own as a feral, which the tom certainly had been before today, Antenn paying the bill. . . . Yes, the cat needed to be cared for. So did the woman in his arms. He felt that more and more just standing with her in the quiet of this not-quite-an-office.

And what was wrong with the High Priest and Priestess that they couldn't see she needed help?

Antenn sure wouldn't say a word about helping her *to* her; he was smart enough to know that would rile her. But he'd keep it in the back of his mind, for sure.

"Teleport on three?" she asked.

"Of course," he said, mentally checking Darjeeling HouseHeart's main teleportation pad and finding it clear. He began the countdown. "One, Tiana; two, Antenn Moss; and *three*!"

They landed easily, though she'd been right, she'd had no Flair to contribute to the transportation.

She moved and he reluctantly dropped his arms. She walked from the teleportation pad to a table near the water fountain that had a "Reserved" sign on it. As the atmosphere wrapped around him and the smells of solid, simple food teased his nose, he realized that this place quieted him. Like Priestess Tiana Mugwort. Both were absolutely true to themselves, delivered exactly what you expected.

In Antenn's experience, people, including priests and priestesses, played a lot of games—mental, emotional, status or greed driven. Lucida Gerania was like that.

Tiana Mugwort was not.

He usually got good service at Darjeeling's HouseHeart. Accompanying Tiana Mugwort, he got exceptional attention. In fact, he thought there might have been gossip had she not greeted the waitress by name and with a sober face and said, "Business meeting."

For that he was grateful.

As he spread his softleaf on his lap, he glanced around to see if anything had changed—Camellia D'Hawthorn *did* do that now and again. He said the words aloud that he often thought when he ate here. "Doesn't look like any HouseHeart I've been in."

Tiana's eyes rounded. "You've been in more than one?"

"I shouldn't have said that." His smile was quick but sincere, self-deprecating. "And I can't say."

She nodded and a distance came to her eyes as if she gazed on secrets of her own. "I understand."

"But, in general, HouseHearts have some, ah, features in common." He paused. "I would imagine." Gesturing around him, he said, "An altar, which here is shown by separate niches to the Lady and the Lord."

"That's one thing I don't care for here," Tiana murmured. "The niches on separate walls. They should be together. They should always be together."

He blinked at the forcefulness of her tone, and a vision of entwined lovers came to his mind. He told himself that it *wasn't* himself and Priestess Tiana Mugwort. He didn't have time for a serious relationship, and everything about the priestess—her demeanor, her honesty, her obvious strong sense of self—indicated she was not one to participate in light, brief affairs. The type of sexual "relationships" he preferred.

Mostly because he didn't dare be so vulnerable to having his spirits crushed when a woman found out about his common origin or his murderous brother and rejected him. That had happened with his first love.

"Don't you think the God and Goddess should share space?" Tiana asked, pretty brows raised.

He managed a half smile. "I would venture to say that most true HouseHearts show them together."

She nodded, then tucked into the platter of small but hearty sandwiches placed before her. After a few bites, her head tilted and she said, "What else would you include in a HouseHeart, FirstLevel Architect Blackthorn-Moss, should you design one?"

He finished swallowing a mouthful of clucker soup. "Any new HouseHearts I design wouldn't become intelligent Residences for a couple of centuries." He thought of the five that he'd been in, one of which was just becoming aware. "Though the time period it is taking the HouseStones to develop sentience seems to be shortening."

Her attention focused completely on him, and his ego expanded even as his heart thumped a little harder.

"So, like people, Residences are becoming more Flaired . . . have more psi power?" she asked.

"I would say that's a true statement."

"Each generation of people is stronger in Flair, and has more of that energy and stamina." Her mouth turned down as if recalling she'd exhausted hers that day. Antenn wanted to put his free hand over hers but didn't. Yet his fingers tingled and shock zipped through him at how much he wished to touch her again. "And, sticking with the subject, naturally every HouseHeart has the four elements, which are very well displayed here." His gaze went from the fountain, to the rocklike walls and plants climbing on trellises, to the wall with an open fireplace oven, and the wind chimes adding slight notes to the ambience.

After daintily nibbling her way through the last piece of sandwich, Tiana leaned back in her chair. "Yes, the whole tearoom is very well done by Camellia." The priestess's face softened with affection and Antenn swallowed, liking how approachable that expression made her. *Not* businesslike, not professional sympathy or interest, all of which he'd seen from her that day.

"I love this place." Her tongue came out to sweep a few crumbs from her lips, and his shaft thickened. He masked his own expression and was grateful for the substantial tables and chairs that would keep his arousal from showing.

Clearing his throat, he pushed his empty bowl aside and reached blindly for the mug of strong black tea he'd ordered. "Good atmosphere. Great food," he said.

Tiana smiled, and it appeared carefree. Feeding her had been the right damn thing to do, for sure. "Have you been to the Ladies' Tearoom?" she asked.

He chuckled. "You think I wouldn't go into something so ultrafeminine? My mother helped Camellia D'Hawthorn decorate it. I saw the whole place in various models before the restaurant was done."

Tiana's gaze sharpened. "Did you help, too?"

With a shrug, he said, "I walked through it." He'd made sure the building was sound and the space would work with D'Hawthorn's vision.

Thoughtfully, Tiana said, "I heard that you remodeled the MistrysSuite for Camellia in T'Hawthorn Residence."

"That's right."

"And my other friend, Glyssa Licorice, said that you drew up plans for the community that's been founded at the excavation of *Lugh's Spear* across the Bluegrass Plains. She bought into the town and worked with others to build the community center."

"I've seen holos and vizes of that building. They did an excellent job." He smiled at the server who whisked their empty plates away and refreshed their teas.

Tiana set her elbows on the table and propped her chin in her hands. "Well, FirstLevel Master Architect Blackthorn-Moss—"

"Call me Antenn," he said.

She straightened and nodded. "And you must call me Tiana. Antenn, we got off to a rocky start."

Looking into her emerald eyes, he found himself giving her a truth. "I was nervous about the job, about walking the venue with Chief Minister Custos and explaining that his original idea wouldn't work and showing him the new plans. I was irritated you were late." Another half smile. "I'm still nervous about getting the commission."

"You shouldn't be," she stated with calm authority. "You work with T'Hawthorn, who is a power in the younger set of Nobles. He's very wealthy, and his FatherSire's influence as Captain of All Councils is still felt. You must be *the* up-and-coming architect."

The back of his neck heated and blood rushed to his cheeks. He inclined his head. "Good of you to say."

Now *she* reached out and touched the back of his hand—when had his fingers clenched into a fist?—his hand tight with the rough denial to not touch her, his mind budding with hope that what she said was true, his career would be set.

"I say the truth as I see it."

"Of course you do, as a priestess."

"I apologize for my tardiness," she said, withdrawing her hand.

He breathed again, his mouth went dry just meeting her serious, direct gaze, so he took another sip of tea. "I think that your being late wasn't your fault."

She glanced away but said nothing. She wouldn't say anything negative about the High Priest or Priestess, of course.

"I'm sorry about your dress." He felt compelled to apologize again.

This time her smile was nothing short of radiant. He blinked.

"You made up for the accident that tore my gown, so very well. My new robe is wonderful!"

"I'm glad you like it." He was, and the last smidgen of resentment at the cost vanished. He'd pleased her. That was worth anything.

The server appeared with a bill. Antenn swiped his hand across the table in payment, adding a good tip, and the waitress stepped back. The priestess rose and he followed reluctantly. "At least your reviews are over," he said.

She stiffened as if reminded of unpleasantness, which should not be, since he couldn't imagine her being less than great at anything. "Tiana?"

"I have a lot of spiritual growth to work on."

"Is that what those who reviewed you said?" he asked.

"The High Priestess and the High Priest?" Tiana said, and Antenn winced. Talk about people with great expectations of a person; she'd had it rough.

Tiana bit her lip. "No. But that's what became evident through our discussions."

"I think you're too hard on yourself." He gestured toward the teleportation pad. "Can I teleport you anywhere?"

Her lips quirked. "No, thank you. So far we don't have a great many places in common." She put her hands in her opposite sleeves, and the prospect of holding one of them vanished, disappointing Antenn.

"I'm sure we'll become acquainted well enough that I can 'port you several places where you'd like to go." He frowned. "I'm sure I could teleport you to T'Hawthorn's ResidenceDen, or even D'Hawthorn's bedroom."

"No." Her eyes widened. "Teleporting into Camellia's bedroom. What would Laev say?" She scowled. "You don't want to irritate any of those very entitled and odd FirstFamilies Lords and Ladies."

His face froze and he stiffened instinctively. "I am adopted by a FirstFamily."

Eight

$\mathcal{N}$*ow her expression went to horror. She put her fingers over her mouth,* stepped back, and sank into a chair, dropping her head in her hands. "Lady and Lord, the insult I've given you, I am so sorry."

All he could see was her reddening neck beneath her fancy hair bun. "Please accept my apologies, GrandSir FirstLevel Architect Blackthorn-Moss. I have no excuse," she mumbled.

His body eased as he realized that for some reason—because she was as attracted to him as he was her?—she could not face him. She'd struck him as fierce, quite the opposite of cowardly, but she didn't lift her head and look him in the eyes.

He let his fingers curve over her hunched shoulder. "No insult taken," he said softly.

A server bustled up, appearing concerned. "Is anything wrong?"

"Perhaps some soothing tea?" Antenn asked.

"At once—"

"Perhaps some tea that will cure I-am-so-embarrassed-I-could-die?" Tiana Mugwort lifted her head and looked at the waitress. The priestess's face was a very becoming pink. Antenn withdrew his hand slowly, letting some tendrils of her hair brush across his fingers. He liked that too much.

"Everything must be all right if you're poking fun at yourself," the waitress said.

"Yes." Tiana smiled. "I'm fine. As soon as my knees get a little more strength back I'll stand and walk out of here. No need of anything more for me to drink."

With a nod the server left them.

This time the priestess matched Antenn's gaze. "I am truly sor—"

"Not necessary." He cut her off and held up his hand, palm out.

"The only thing I can say in my defense," Tiana said quietly, "is that of all the FirstFamily noblemen I've ever met, you are the least inherently arrogant."

Antenn smiled. "I think that's a compliment."

She nodded solemnly. "It is."

WHERE IS MY FAMMAN! shouted a mental cat voice that Antenn knew all too well. Pinky, small and plump, sauntered in through a cat door Antenn hadn't previously noted.

"Now that one wears his status as a FirstFamily FamCat where everyone can hear and see," Tiana said.

"My Fam, Pinky."

"I guessed," she said, but the rich color had faded from her face and left her more pale than Antenn liked.

It is WorkEnd Bell! Pinky said, strolling up to Antenn and sitting before him, stretching to hook his claws in Antenn's trous. Antenn picked him up instead.

Time to go home and EAT DINNER, Pinky said. He licked his muzzle. *Unless you want to feed me here. I haven't eaten here for a while.*

"It is not WorkEnd Bell," Antenn scolded—just as the bell rang in the old timer hung on the wall.

Pinky grinned, showing his fangs. "Yesss," he articulated. *It is.*

"Yes, and I am expected . . . somewhere else." Tiana rose and gave him a deep curtsey, a curtsey low enough for a FirstFamily Heir. Which he wasn't. She inclined her head. "I'll see you later, GentleSir Blackthorn-Moss." Back straight, she moved gracefully through the aisle of tables and behind the counter to the back area of the restaurant. Where he could not go, if he followed the rules.

With a soft paw on his chin, Pinky attracted Antenn's attention so he looked down at his FamCat. *I am hungry. Let's go home to T'Blackthorn Residence. I teleported all the way from your office. A few blocks.*

Antenn squeezed his Fam, liking the warmth and the roundness of him, even though he knew the cat needed a diet. Antenn would speak to the Chef and the Residence about that tonight.

"Let's go home. It's been a long day." It had been, but as he ambled to the teleportation pad, he thought that it must have been worse for the priestess. Reviews, good Lord and Lady! How glad he was that that part of his life was *over*.

$\mathcal{A}$*s soon as she'd let herself out the back door of* Darjeeling's House-Heart *and into the alley*, Tiana allowed her steps to shuffle and her shoulders to sag. She couldn't recall the last time she'd been so tired, so depleted of Flair.

Wait, she could. The night the mob had firebombed the Mugwort home, incited by GraceLord T'Equisetum into thinking her Family was a part of the murderous Black Magic Cult. She and her parents and her older sister had barely escaped with their lives, had teleported away to her father's, the judge's, chambers, then left and ran, ran, ran through the narrowing streets of Druida. They'd been accepted for one night, and one night only, by her mother's relations. The next days had been chaotic: the Family stripped of their title and their possessions and all their gilt; both parents had lost their jobs; and they'd scrabbled to find a place to live quietly.

A terrible time, and all those memories stirred up once again today. And more than once today.

Tiana trudged from the not-too-dirty alley to the street. She considered the public carrier, but taking transportation home would include at least four transfers. And she'd be a FirstLevel Priestess on the vehicle in a formal ritual robe. No.

She could manage to walk the few long blocks to the PublicLibrary and the house across the grounds from it that belonged to her friends, the Licorices. She'd finally take them up on their offer of one of their old and lumbering Family gliders to drive her home.

The Licorices knew, though they'd never asked and she'd never confirmed, that Tiana and her Family lived in the secret sanctuary of Druida. And though every one of the Licorices was more than curious, and they'd check the route of the glider when she returned it, they would not be able to discover where the sanctuary, the legendary FirstGrove and BalmHeal Residence, was.

She only had to get to the Licorices and Glyssa. The recollection that Glyssa kept several changes of clothes for Tiana had her picking up her feet from her shuffle and walking faster. She could get out of the robe. In fact, Glyssa could translocate it to her office—no, Tiana had a new office that Glyssa didn't know well enough to send items. And *that* had a tired smile curving Tiana's face, her back straightening with pride. Perhaps she had more spiritual work to do on her character than she'd anticipated, but she'd still been promoted.

She'd still been given a great responsibility—maybe she'd have to get accustomed to being so involved with the Intersection of Hope as a liaison, but the appointment, at least in the High Priest's and High Priestess's eyes, *was* career making.

As she drew in a big breath of the crisp spring air, she accepted that of all the priests and priestesses of the Celtic religion, she *was* the one best suited for that particular job. The Sandalwoods had been right about that. Tiana had written rituals that incorporated some Intersection of Hope beliefs for Family celebrations.

She had participated in her mother's rituals and written strictly Intersection of Hope rituals. Tiana had helped her mother dedicate and furnish a small outbuilding on the estate as a temple of her faith. Yes, Tiana could do this job like no other.

To be honest, she *liked* writing rituals, had studied under *the* best crafter of specific circles until he'd passed on to the wheel of stars a few months before. As he'd requested, she'd officiated at his Remembrance Circle, the one he'd written for himself, though since he'd been too humble, she'd added an additional eulogy.

Also on the upside of today, she'd been offered a wonderful Temple of her own, though she hadn't wanted it, and been granted the privilege of staying in GreatCircle Temple to do her work. Yes, she had a new, larger office; a new, vital responsibility; and she'd met a fascinating man . . .

With that thought she stopped walking automatically as she faced the door to the Licorices' Residence. The gate had let her through and now the door opened for her.

Friends and Family and a career she loved. She *was* blessed.

*T*iana's *Family ate dinner early since her sister, Artemisia Primross,* had a swing shift at Primary HealingHall. Tiana spoke of her day. Her parents exchanged significant looks at the mention of Heart-Mates, and Tiana became abruptly aware of an inner ache she'd never quite banished when she thought of her own. And now living with two sets of HeartMates had become exquisitely painful.

Garrett Primross, her brother-in-law, was sent to retrieve her new dress, and both her mother and sister admired it.

Her father gently questioned her decision to stay in GreatCircle Temple instead of taking the position of having her own influential Temple at Landing Park, but she satisfied him that she'd have no regrets for her choice.

Much discussion was had about her new job, her mother quietly weeping at the thought of a cathedral being built for her faith. And Tiana decided that she might be able to lure her parents outside the sanctuary gates now and again to see the construction of it, and, later, her mother to worship there.

After dinner the Family retreated to the mainspace and their favorite chairs. They had all been accepted by the Residence.

"What is that *smell*?" Tiana's mother's nose twitched.

'S ME! RatKiller bounded from the Fam door leading outside to the center of the circle of chairs.

"It's blood," Artemisia said flatly.

"Who are you?" Tiana's mother, Quina Mugwort, wrinkled her nose.

I am the GREATEST RATCATCHER OF ALL TIME! I AM RATKILLER! He leapt onto Tiana's lap. *I am HER FAM!*

Garrett doubled over, wheezing with laughter. Artemisia and Quina snickered. Tiana's father coughed.

"Where did you find him?" asked her father, Sinjin, when he could speak again.

SHE DID NOT FIND ME! I CATCHED HER!

"You don't need to shout, tomcat," Sinjin said. "We all hear you fine."

Garrett studied the cat. "I don't recall you being one of my feral informants who help me with my private investigation business."

The tip of RatKiller's tail was gone, too, Tiana noticed as he swished it. He lifted his nose and stared at the big man who was her sister's HeartMate. *I walk by Myself. I am a bounty hunter! I am RATKILLER! I—*

"You kill rats around businesses and leave your prey on steps and get fed scraps," Garrett said. His mouth twitched.

I supported Myself until I found My Person. He only had to stretch a little to lick the underside of Tiana's chin. She flinched.

"Ah, I think you're, um, leaking blood on Tiana's trous," her father said. Yes, her leg felt wet. At least she'd changed into comfortable clothes the minute she'd gotten home and it wouldn't matter that these were ruined.

Not my blood, RatKiller said smugly. Another lick. She suppressed a shudder.

"You're sure you want him?" Garrett asked. "I could roll him into my troop. Find him another good home."

Tiana gazed down into confident light-green eyes, saw a still-smug scarred muzzle, a cat completely assured she would love him for what he was . . . and the love in his eyes for just who and what she was. The *one* of her Family without a HeartMate. She circled her arm around the cat. "He's with me."

Acourse I is! His purr filled the room again. She wasn't sure where it came from because the body she held was skinny. He *did* smell, and more than of blood. She inhaled. "Have you been—"

KILLING SEWER RATS! YES, YES, YES, YES, YESSSS!

This time Garrett had a fit of coughing. When he could speak again, he said, "What are you going to name him?"

Part of My name is RatKiller! The scruffy tom lifted his chin. Tiana scratched under it and he slitted his eyes; his purr took on a smoother note and diminished in volume, like it was a sound, now, only for her.

Love swept from him to her, appreciation and more, a feeling of a hole of loneliness in his heart being filled. Being with her had done that; the cat had had a Tiana-sized need in him that she'd filled. Again the thought of her HeartMate wisped across her mind, the one she thought didn't want her because of the scandal. Too bad.

But she had a Fam.

"Hmmm," Garrett said, his fingers absently rolling a coin in one of his sleight-of-hand tricks. His eyes met those of Tiana's sister's, skimmed over her mother and father, then away. "You know, ah, one of the folk names of Mugwort is—"

"Artemisia," her father said, beaming at his older daughter.

"St. John's plant," said her mother, sharing a smile with her HeartMate.

"Muggons," Tiana offered, such a fun and friendly word.

Garrett shook his head. "A lot of nicknames—"

"I could come up with a couple more." Her father's eyes twinkled. "Naughty Man . . . but I think I know what you're going to say, Garrett."

Nine

❤

*A*nother common name for *Mugwort is 'Felon Herb,'* Garrett stated.

RatKiller abandoned Tiana's skritches to stare at her brother-in-law. *FE-LON. FE-LINE. I like it!*

Tiana choked but didn't have the heart to tell him the meanings weren't close.

I AM FELON RATKILLER MUGWORT. I AM FELON RATKILLER MUGWORT! Tiana's new Fam accompanied his mental shouting with awful yowls.

A Fam! I hear a new Fam! A CatFam! came the cheerful mental stream of Garrett's young cat, Rusby. He shot into the room from the open door of the hallway, a nine-month-old orange tabby cat, stopping pretty much where RatKiller—Felon RatKiller Mugwort—had, sniffing around the spot.

Felon RatKiller's tail slashed as he stared coolly down on the young cat. *You are rude to sniff before talking to Me. But I will not swat You because We are Family.*

The young cat's mouth seemed to drop open in horror, and he leapt backward. *RatKiller. It is RatKiller.* With one leap, the smaller, healthier-looking tom hopped onto Garrett's shoulder, no doubt aided by Flair. Rusby had a lot of Flair, and Tiana wondered how much her own Fam had. As far as she knew, he'd teleported a couple of times, and that indicated solid Flair for a Fam.

RatKiller showed his fangs with a little hiss.

"That's enough, Felon," Garrett said.

Narrowing her eyes at Garrett, Tiana resumed petting the knobby spine of her Fam. "I don't think I want to call him Felon."

I AM FELON RATKILLER MUGWORT!

She rolled right over her cat's loud mental projection. "I think I'll call you Felon Herb. Felonerb. It's more respectable."

I will allow that, the Fam said. He surveyed the room. *So there are only two Fams here so far? The odd coon and the immature tom?*

"That's right," said Tiana's father. "But we expect you to obey the rules of the House, the Residence—"

"And be a clean cat," Tiana's mother added.

"What say you, Residence?" Sinjin asked.

Felonerb's eyes went wide. *I am living in a real Residence?*

"You are living in the *oldest* Residence," said the House in its grumpy-old-man persona. "And you'd better be clean or you will regret it."

Felonerb sniffed wetly, and the Healers, Artemisia and Quina, focused on him.

"We really need to examine him," said her mother. "Or contact Danith D'Ash to do so."

"I doubt Danith or Gwydion Ash will take on such a one as him for free," Garrett said. The coin in his fingers transformed into a metal tag and Tiana didn't see him do it. "I, however, have an account with the Ashes, and especially Gwydion, to look after my feral band. I can have him check out Felon RatKiller."

Gwydion Ash, Felonerb said reverently. *Big, kind man with Flaired hands. I have heard of him. Yessss, I would like to go.* Felonerb articulated, "Yesss."

Garrett held up the tag, spun it so it flashed in the light. "You gotta pay, cat."

Felonerb rose to his feet and did a couple of hops on Tiana's lap.

What? What to pay? How many rats? Would you like a live one? How about just guts? The guts are good eating.

"You have to treat my Fam, Rusby, with respect. *Great* respect. And Artemisia's raccoon, Randa, too."

Felonerb grumbled in his throat, looked at Garrett stroking his Fam, then Artemisia, then up at Tiana.

She said, "I don't have connections with the Ashes." She didn't think they even knew who she was. "My mother or sister can take care of you fine."

"He needs a bath." Her mother put force behind the word but hid a smile.

Felonerb flinched and looked at Garrett. *I agree, Big Man Leader of the Ferals.* He looked at Rusby. *I will treat you very nice, Rusby. And the raccoon, Randa.*

I will treat you nice, too, Rusby said amiably.

"And now I need to go," Artemisia said. She'd already dressed in her green Healer tunic and trous of expensive material because she worked at Primary HealingHall. The Family lived well enough off the land and bounty of BalmHeal estate, but there was no denying that Garrett's gilt and Artemisia's and Tiana's salaries provided what they couldn't grow or make themselves. And Tiana had forgotten to ask exactly how much of an increase in salary she'd get with this next promotion. There were five grades of FirstLevel Priestess and she'd been at grade four; had she moved one up . . . or, perhaps, perhaps, two?

But Garrett and Artemisia were leaving the House, Garrett saying, as he usually did, "I'll see you to the HealingHall, and collect any information my band has on my current cases."

"Have a good shift!" Tiana called belatedly.

"And you should go straight to bed," said her mother.

Tiana acquiesced and pushed herself from her chair, dislodging Felonerb, who'd been grooming his claws and paws. "Yes," she said, though she knew her mother and father also wanted to discuss all the news she'd brought—her reviews, her promotion, and, most especially, the Intersection of Hope cathedral.

She dragged herself to the second floor to her bedroom, following Felonerb RatKiller—what a name!—as he pranced up the staircase. "Residence?" she addressed the cranky entity who liked her less than her sister.

"Yes, Tiana?"

"Can we make a Fam door in my door? I can promise you the energy and Flair to do it. Well, not tonight, but tomorrow."

That is a GOOD idea. RatKiller approved. He stopped on a stair and gave her a broken-fanged grin. She managed a return smile. Not even Gwydion Ash would be able to do anything about that fang.

And she was grateful for Garrett's intervention and offer to pay the Ashes for Felonerb's physical. She *had* given it a little thought on the long ride, then walk, home. She believed one of the Ash children's Nameday was upcoming, and she'd planned on offering a trade of creating a small, special Family ritual for them in exchange for an appointment for her Fam.

"Did you hear me, Tiana?" questioned the Residence, opening and slamming a door. She winced.

"I'm *so* sorry, Residence," she groveled, knowing that it would not be as gracious in accepting her apology as Antenn Blackthorn-Moss. "I am so tired my mind wandered and I didn't hear your very excellent advice."

"I *said*"—it turned up the volume of its voice—"that you are lucky. One of the walls of your room had a Fam door opening onto the corridor at one time. It was a moment's work to remove the wall and clear away the debris."

"Oh, wonderful!" She put energy into her reply.

OH WONDERFUL! screeched Felonerb, hopping around in the hallway. *CAN YOU HEAR ME, HOUSE? I AM THE NEW FAM! THE* CATFAM!

"I hear you," the Residence said sourly. "You do not need to shout, FamCat. And you may address me as 'Residence.'"

"YES, HOUSE!" Felonerb answered with great enthusiasm.

Tiana's teeth snapped together before she pried them apart and rushed into speech. "He meant no insult." Despite her weariness, she sent a telepathic message strictly to the Residence. *I am sorry, but he is a Street Cat and I will work on his manners!*

A floorboard creaked under her feet, a disapproving noise by the Residence. *It is a Rude being.*

Yes, I'm sorry, she said mentally, then aloud, "Oh, look, Felonerb, there's your door!" It was nicely framed in expensive redd-wood, highly polished.

And there was her own door, and behind that door was her bed, and near the end of her bed was her fireplace. She *yearned* for the sooth-ing, unrhythmic pop and crackle of flames . . . the very best way for her to sink into a meditative trance was listening to a fire. But she didn't think she had the energy or Flair to light the kindling. Some other time.

Without another word, Felonerb zoomed through his door, leav-ing the thin wooden flap swinging. A few steps later, Tiana was through her door, out of the public portion of the House, in her own private sanctuary. She tottered to the bedsponge set on a frame just low enough for her to fall facedown on it, sink into the thick feather comforter, and let out a moan of relief at finally being alone and done with this interminable day.

THIS IS A WONDERFUL PLACE. YOU HAVE MORE THAN ONE ROOM. AND YOU HAVE A LITTLE CLOSET THAT DOESN'T HAVE MUCH IN IT. I NEED THAT CLOSET! ALL THE BEST CATS HAVE THEIR OWN CLOSETS. I HAVE LEARNED THIS FROM THAT BRAZOS HAWTHORN CAT. I NEED A CLOSET LIKE HIS.

Felonerb was still shouting. And hopping. He hopped all over her back with little hard paws.

"Please don't shout, Felonerb, my head aches." All of her ached. Every. Single. Muscle.

I will "whisper." He managed to enunciate the last word.

"Wow," Tiana said. "What incredible skill you have vocalizing."

I know, he said smugly. *I will go explore the whole House and look for some pillows for My closet. The House will learn to love Me.*

"I'm sure."

He left and Tiana was finally alone and in silence enough to hear her own thoughts.

Was the High Priestess right? Had she misinterpreted her Heart-Mate? Decided he hadn't come for her because of the scandal surrounding her Family?

There *were* other reasons for men not to look for their ladies—or women not to look for their lords. Her friend Camellia's HeartMate had been married to another woman; her friend Glyssa's HeartMate hadn't believed in love. Had Tiana been wrong about her own Heart-Mate? Wouldn't he love her despite her past? The essential her?

She *did* know that one night had changed all her philosophies about life, that night her Family had run for their lives.

So many of their friends had abandoned them that she thought *he*, whoever he was, had abandoned her, too.

Status and fortune had been ripped from them because Grace-Lord T'Equisetum had managed that, could do it. And though her Family hadn't been broken by those acts, though they'd become a stronger unit, it had been impressed upon Tiana that status mattered.

And she'd believed her HeartMate hadn't come to her because he knew her and her low status and wished not to be tainted by associating with—marrying—her.

She could have been wrong.

Just before she slid into sleep, using all of her small, replenished Flair, she *reached* for the link with her HeartMate.

And found nothing.

*A*ntenn slept and heat rose inside him and he thrashed and had sex dreams and didn't know who the woman was but did know he didn't deserve her. Not he, a common boy from Downwind, brother to a murderer.

He moaned and Pinky patted his face, and he opened his eyes

groggily to see his Fam lick his paw as if it were damp . . . or had salt on it. Burying his head under his pillow, he subsided back into dark unconsciousness.

A yowling screech jolted Tiana from sleep and had her yelling herself, jackknifing to sit, flinging her comforter—and her new Fam, Felon RatKiller—nearly off the bed. Nearly, because he'd hooked claws into comforter. The bundle of him, wrapped in the quilting, wailed even louder.

Her head pounded and she put her hands over her ears, trying to keep the burgeoning migraine from crippling her.

"What is going on!" her mother bellowed.

Tiana whimpered and curled up in a ball.

"Ohhh, shhh." It was the slightest of whispers and Tiana felt the bedsponge sink as her mother sat next to her . . . then her mother's warm hands moving her own from her head and the touch of her mother's Healing fingers and blessed relief.

Except for the shrieking cat.

"You stop that, now!" ordered Quina. "Can't you see you're hurting your FamWoman?"

Felonerb stopped midhowl.

Drawing in a shuddering breath, all too aware that her body had slicked with sweat during the moment of migraine, Tiana began to uncurl.

"This is not a good sign," said her mother in the darkness, then sighed.

No. Once Tiana got a migraine, no matter that her mother or sister Healed it, the thing tried to return all day long . . . unless she slept for a full seven septhours. Not something she could afford to do.

I AM SORRY, FAMWOMAN! Felonerb projected mentally.

"A little less blasting-loud telepathy, Felonerb," Tiana said weakly. She sat again, leaning on her mother.

In the silence a small ripple of sound could be heard. Tiana's scry pebble, stuck in her pursenal atop her bureau. The tune was the one Tiana had assigned to the High Priestess.

"I, too, have a message for FirstLevel Priestess Mugwort," the Residence said.

Her title. Something official, then. She'd have to leave, and fast. Her mouth dried and her pulse thundered in her ears.

Ten

I'll prepare a special shake for you before you leave," Tiana's mother said, and hurried from Tiana's bedroom.

She was left alone to deal with Felonerb and the Residence.

"I could not get your attention," the Residence continued with complaint in its tones. "I was forced to inform the recently arrived Fam."

Me! Felonerb said.

As Tiana's eyes adjusted to the twinmoonslight beaming through the long window, she saw her Fam's ingratiating grin.

"All right. Thank you, Residence." She slipped from bed, knowing that she probably would be using a lot of Flair in a day that started with an early announcement . . . and the first thing to do was to dress quickly.

That meant doing a Whirlwind Spell to bathe and clothe herself appropriately. Then she'd also need her Flair to teleport to the gates of the secret sanctuary and out, and wherever she was needed. She'd be lucky not to succumb to another migraine today.

"Residence, can you please play the message sent to you for me?" she asked.

"Certainly," it said with more than a hint of pomposity in its tones.

FirstLevel Priestess Tiana Mugwort, came the rushed voice of

High Priestess D'Sandalwood. *The four Chief Ministers of the Intersection of Hope have requested an immediate meeting with us and you and the FirstLevel Architect. The High Priest and I are preparing to lead Dawn Ritual. We wish you to open the off-site Temple offices in CityCenter for Blackthorn-Moss and the ministers. Please arrange for breakfast and drinks.* There was a pause, a note of querulousness mixed in with the High Priestess's usual lilt. *None of us have been informed why the ministers wish to speak with us or what they want to discuss.* Another small break. *Perhaps your mother, as a noted parishioner, might have been told? In any event, the High Priest and I will teleport the moment Dawn Ritual at GreatCircle Temple ends.*

Tiana already knew her mother had no information with regard to the meeting, otherwise Tiana would have been awakened first instead of playing catch-up.

"How long ago was this?" she asked the Residence, not wanting to activate the perscry's light spell or the one in the room.

"Seven minutes forty-nine seconds."

"Thank you."

One sharp window rattle came, punctuation from the Residence that equated to a human sniff.

"Residence, can you ask T'Blackthorn Residence if Antenn Blackthorn-Moss has left yet?"

"Surely." Now the House sounded proud, since it was linked to all the current Residences and respected as the oldest by its peers.

"He is teleporting to his office as we speak."

She'd have to hurry or she'd be late to meet him *again*.

"Can you calculate the end of the Dawn Ritual, please?" she asked, continuing to get vital data and soothe the Residence. It loved to feel needed and helpful.

"Twenty minutes."

"Thank you." She sucked in a breath. "Whirlwind Spell, professional meeting." The last of her breath was snatched as air spun her around, hit her like tiny pellets to scour her clean, flung bespelled clothes on her—soft, plain underwear, pantlettes and breastband, an equally soft robe of pale blue, one of her older ones that flattered her. Her hair was pulled and braided into a coronet.

By the time she inhaled she was ready to leave.

I will go with You to breakfast, Felonerb said.

Of course that would be his main priority.

And to support You, he added virtuously.

Her mother came through the door with a large tube of thick cocoa—a Healing potion to stave off a migraine that didn't always work but was better than nothing at all.

Tiana drank it down, gave it a few seconds to settle in her stomach, and walked to the corner of her sitting room that had a teleportation area delineated by a small, meter-square rug.

"Residence can you drop your shields just for an instant this morning so I can teleport out?"

"I would not usually do so, but the GreatCircle Temple, a personage almost as old as myself, has a fondness for you."

It did? News to Tiana. She nearly gasped since she hadn't thought GreatCircle Temple even knew she walked its halls. She bowed her head. "Thank you for this exception, BalmHeal Residence."

"Don't expect it often," the Residence said.

"I won't."

Felonerb made a fantastic leap and attached himself to her shoulder. She felt the small pricks of claws and heard the material tear, and winced.

"I will add shoulder pads to all your clothes today, Tiana."

"Thank you, Mama." It was depressing only because she had so few clothes, especially outside her priestess robes. At least pale blue looked good on her . . . and just *why* had that thought appeared? Because she was going to meet the architect! By the Lady and Lord, had she developed . . . something . . . for him so soon?

He was kind. He was solid. He was ambitious. Three good qualities.

Beautiful hazel eyes. Attractive. Sexy.

Time to go! Felonerb said, turning his head and breathing on her. His breath . . . even his person . . . didn't smell too bad. She sniffed.

I rolled in the herb garden! 'Cuz my name is also Felonerb!

With another discreet sniff she recognized a variety of Earthan chamomile difficult to keep alive and knew her Fam had probably flattened her mother's most prized herb bed.

She gave her mother a big smile. "Yes, time to go! Thanks so much for the Healing and cocoa, Mama! I *love* you!"

Quina narrowed her eyes, tilted her head. "What's going—"

And as Tiana teleported away to the Temple's CityCenter office, Felonerb said with relish, *And SHE wanted to wash ME!*

A cat who believed in grudges. Just what a priestess who had to do work on her own self wanted.

The Turquoise House felt the light of the dawn on his exterior walls and hummed to himself. Soon, soon, soon the first of his Family would come. It would be the woman, because his plan would entice her first.

Yes. And she would bring the man.

Maybe today!

Thunder cracked. He didn't care. Today would be a fabulous day! And tomorrow would be even better!

As soon as Antenn entered the bright and cheerful conference room with easy chairs set around a fireplace, he heard the clattering of china and silverware. His heart jumped. Tiana Mugwort would be here, too.

Since there were no voices, he cleverly deduced she was alone. Cocking his head, he realized the sounds were coming from another room, and he found the door to that room tucked into a corner. Where he might have put the entrance to a setup room or pantry.

With a smile because he'd see her again, he strode toward the half-open door and pushed it wide.

Perfectly groomed, she nodded to him. "Greetyou, FirstLevel—"

He cut her off with a slice of his hand. "I thought we agreed that you don't have to always call me by my professional title or my Noble title. How can I help?" He studied the small room that had a counter running along all sides with cabinets hanging above and inset below.

Her brows raised and she gestured to a tray on the opposite counter where a teapot, caff carafe, sweet bowl, and mugs stood. "If you can put those togeth—"

Crunch, mumble, sluuurrrp.

Antenn glanced and saw the bottom end of RatKiller sticking out of a no-time, tail high and waving with pleasure. "Ah, I would recommend that you not let your Fam gorge—"

Tiana whirled. "I *closed* that. Get out of there, Felonerb."

No response from the cat, of course. She narrowed her eyes, glanced at her nice, professional garb, and said, "I have porcine strips, Felonerb. I don't think there are any more in there."

She'd gone for bribery. Good call.

With a wave of her hand she heated up the pile of strips on a plate and Antenn's mouth watered.

The scruffy cat withdrew from the large no-time compartment that no doubt held full holiday meals. White mousse decorated the tom's face and whiskers. He grinned. *Porcine strips, my FAVORITE.*

A click came as the door to the no-time slid shut. The cat had been quick inserting himself earlier. A whole lot quicker than Antenn's Pinky would have been . . . but Pinky hadn't had to scavenge for food since before Antenn was nine.

He heard a loud gurgle from the Fam's stomach. No, Antenn didn't want to deal with this.

He moved to the far counter and set the caff, teapot, cups, and everything on a large rectangular silver tray.

Tiana plucked a narrow piece of porcine and bent to a small plate on the floor. The cat snatched it from her hand and crunched. Another intestinal rumble. Tiana's eyes widened. She set her hands around her Fam behind his front legs. "I'll just teleport you to the gate home, why don't I? You haven't explored the . . . grassyards . . . yet." In the next second the cat vanished with a yowl that was cut short by a wet whoosh.

Straightening, the priestess murmured, "Dear Lady and Lord, please have had him land where my mother won't have to clean him up."

Antenn snorted and she went red . . . again. He'd gotten the impression that he'd seen her without her professional calm a lot in the last two days—and liked that.

Her lips compressed. "Thank you for loading the tray." Her own hands sped to finish arranging the foodstuffs in some pattern that would look fine to her.

"One never wants one's mother to have to clean up after one's Fam," he said, leaning against a counter. "I speak from experience."

Her laugh was as much a sigh and lightened her face to a beautiful smile. "I'm sure."

A bong reverberated and he straightened. "That's the teleportation signal, the Cross Fo—the Intersection of Hope ministers are here."

She nodded and took the tray of breakfast foods from the counter, walking ahead of him through the door to the main room.

The four greatest ministers of the Intersection of Hope stood in their formal robes, three in primary colors, one in white. All of their expressions were serious bordering on the stern.

Antenn's gut clenched. Trouble, and he couldn't guess what kind so he could head it off, find a workable option.

The one in red, Foreman, who represented adult vitality, aimed his stare at Tiana Mugwort, and Antenn sucked in a small breath. Maybe they weren't taking their business to a different architect, then. "We take exception to the messages from your High Priest and Priestess," Foreman said.

Eleven

Tiana bent her head. "If we have insulted you, please accept our apologies." She set the tray of dishes on a low table in the center of the chairs and gestured as she murmured a couplet. Steam rose from a few of the offerings and Antenn's nose twitched. Cheese bread. He had a weakness for warm, fresh cheese bread. The lightly spiced scrambled eggs smelled pretty good, too, not to mention the porcine strips.

"Please sit so we can work this out." Tiana indicated the plushly cushioned chairs.

"Come, gentlemen," said Custos. He was wearing his white robe that signified the Guardian Spirit. "We have a representative here from GreatCircle Temple. As I said before, something like this is exactly why we asked for a liaison. Let us take advantage of her to express our concerns."

With slight grumbles, and, Antenn thought, some telepathic messages zinging back and forth, the men sat.

The priestess poured out a cup of caff and raised her brows at Antenn. He took it. She poured tea for herself, something dark and strong, asked the others their preferences, and provided the drinks.

After a minute of sipping, the abrasive Foreman stated, "Your Celtan religion that was crafted on the Ships is inclusive." He took a fork and stabbed an apple turnover to transfer it from the common plate to his own.

"Yes, that's true," Tiana said. "Our ancestors were far too aware of the divisiveness that religious fervor could cause if one religion stated it was the *only* correct belief system."

Foreman slogged on. "Your ancestors"—he pointed his fork at Tiana and Antenn—"and ours on the Ships diluted *your* main religious beliefs to accommodate many of the religions at the time. Since then, most of those beliefs that don't quite fit with the belief in the Duology, the Lady and the Lord—"

"—the Lord and the Lady," Antenn murmured.

Foreman shrugged. "The Lord and the Lady or the Lady and Lord, those beliefs that belonged to older religions have fallen by the wayside naturally."

Tiana nodded as if this wasn't a new idea to her, though it was to Antenn.

"But that is not true with our Intersection of Hope religion." Foreman jutted his chin. "Our beliefs were well thought out when our religion was created and are not to be mitigated or expanded or tweaked for expediency's sake."

"We *do* believe we are the . . . maybe not the *only* religion . . . but that we serve the needs of people best," said the youngest man there, dressed in yellow, symbolizing the childlike self, surely a new adult at no more than eighteen.

"I understand," Tiana said with a sincerity Antenn wouldn't have been able to fake. "What is the problem here?"

"We do not want other religions, such as the Celtic religion, involved in our cathedral. We do not want a ritual to set security spellshields up comprising other religious beliefs than our own. We do not want some sort of all-inclusive ritual with a muddle of intentions, of prayers to various spirits. We want our land, our cathedral, our ritual to resonate to our beliefs only."

"That is understandable," the priestess said.

Was it? Antenn didn't know. He stopped chewing and began to reconsider the best commission of his life.

Custos said, "We want our hymns sung, our incense used, our singular faith to infuse our space."

Tiana turned her head slightly toward Antenn as if she'd noticed the muscles on his face had stiffened and said, "It is like a Family would prefer their Residence to resonate to their Family as opposed to some different Family."

She stared with wide eyes at the four ministers. "And it's not as if you are saying those who believe in the Lady and Lord, the Lord and the Lady, or have any other belief system are wrong or evil."

All four men gasped.

"Absolutely not," said the one in blue called Elderstone.

"Of course not," said the one named Younger.

"No," said Foreman and Custos in unison.

"*That* would be wrong. And it is our belief to respect each and every one who is on their journey. Every individual is meeting perils and fighting battles in their personal journey that we might not know or understand," Custos said.

Antenn flinched inside, straightened in his chair. Everyone had inner wars they were fighting. He'd never thought of it that way. He certainly fought for self-confidence every day . . . and though they had a great life, he was sure his parents fought their old personal wars: his mother's sterility, her deepest wound. And his father would never forget that his entire Family had died of a common Celtan disease and that he was a man with great Flair but a genetic flaw he would pass down to any child of his blood.

Words ripped from Antenn. "That is a simple but profound philosophy."

Lips curving, Custos nodded at Antenn, then shared a look with the others. "I knew you were the right man for the job."

Younger smiled sweetly, innocently, and said, "As simple and profound as your own religion's ultimate law 'for the good of all, according to the free will of all, an it harm none.'"

That was true.

After a swallow of a jam-filled pastry that left a squirt of red-berry across his cheek, Younger continued, "We still want our rituals and *only* our rituals on the land." He dusted his hands, flicking crumbs away with abandon. Antenn was reminded of the pure happy gluttony of Pinky. Pretty much everyone else had paused in their eating.

"I understand," the priestess said, and Antenn could have sworn he felt a wash of bitter disappointment from her. She'd been planning on officiating at that ritual, he figured. It took all kinds.

Then he recalled how impressed that rival priestess had seemed, and Antenn knew that it would feel to him like a commission yanked from him—one that would challenge his creativity. He kept his face impassive since the woman wouldn't want pity, but the cheese bread had dried on his tongue and he scooped up his caff mug to swallow.

"Please, eat." She gestured with a serene smile at the food. Antenn glanced at his tunic. The bread hadn't been too crumbly, hadn't fallen on one of his best tunic-trous-suits, so he could retain a professional appearance.

The other men went back to their plates.

From the side of his eyes, he saw Tiana's lovely breasts rise as she took a long, deep breath.

"Would you be open to accepting the High Priest and High Priestess as celebrants in one of your own rituals?" she asked.

That stopped all talk. The ministers' gazes met, and from the buzzing sensation of Flair in the atmosphere, they were consulting telepathically.

"Would they not disavow themselves from their God and Goddess by worshiping with us?"

Antenn looked on in admiration as Tiana poured more of their various drinks into their cups, treating the matter with casual easiness. He wondered if the Sandalwoods knew what a treasure this woman was.

When she put the carafe down, she met each minister's glance in turn. "The Lady and Lord are not jealous beings with regard to their followers. I would say that whether a priest or priestess would honor your four-godhead would depend on the individual's relationship with their own soul and their relationship with the Lady and Lord. The High Priest and Priestess emphasized to me that this project is important to them."

Now she stood and folded her hands in her opposite sleeves, looking every inch the priestess. "You are holy men, filled with belief, with kindness and abjuring hatred and condescension to others. Your religion is kind and worth respect. Why would we not honor and accept you and celebrate *your* journey as you do so yourselves?"

Though she spoke softly, Antenn thought that she might have shamed a couple of them. From his own experience he knew that the outcast, the downtrodden, could hold great anger. These men were of a portion of their culture that was usually ignored and sometimes disdained. No wonder they held tightly to their own rules.

And, if he had to be fair, it was easier for Tiana Mugwort, as a priestess of the main, accepted religion of most Celtans, to be sympathetic and generous.

Foreman's shoulders lowered into what might have been a slump for a less muscular man. He shook his head. "We do not have an appropriate ritual for those who do not believe wholeheartedly in our fourfold God's journey . . ."

The tension radiating from Tiana was massive. She said, "I am conversant with your rituals. If I . . ." She stopped as all eyes turned her way. "If I help *my mother*, a member of your faith, draft a ritual for security spellshields? Naturally, you would prefer only members of your temple—your church—to be there for the consecration of the ground, but that can happen later, in a separate ritual after the spellshields go up."

Silence.

"An interesting offer but one I don't think we can accept," Elderstone stated quietly.

Antenn put his plate down and lowered his torso in a sitting bow. "I don't know what divination systems Your Excellencies use, but perhaps I should tell you that yesterday, at the site of your cathe-

dral, I was approached by GreatLord Muin T'Vine, the prophet."
And damn if Antenn hadn't picked up the ponderous phrasing.
Anything to get the job done. Now everyone stared at him. This
time the quiet Flair humming through the room held an edge.

The tiny muscles of Foreman's face worked, Younger's expression had gone blank, and Custos's and Elderstone's smiles appeared
strained.

"May we ask what the GreatLord told you?" asked Younger, his
voice a little higher than he probably wanted.

"GreatLord T'Vine told me that the future of this venture is in
flux."

Everyone paled.

"He said that security is paramount and that I should put
around-the-clock guards on the project." Antenn turned to look at
Tiana, still standing, hands tucked into her opposite sleeves, then
back at the men. "I would recommend using any and all resources
you have for the spellshields. And that when you announce the
project today to the newssheets, you include the High Priest and
Priestess of Celta."

"We will be happy to be of any service." The resonant tones of
T'Sandalwood came.

Antenn jerked at the man's voice; he saw Tiana give a little
shiver. Had she known they'd arrived? They must have locked down
the teleportation pad from GreatCircle Temple for only their use.
Interesting. Because of confidentiality? Or security?

The Chief Ministers rose, as did Antenn, and faced the couple.
All the men bowed and the women curtseyed. The ministers,
Antenn, and Tiana sat again.

Then Foreman's lips twisted. "Increased security for our temple,
our cathedral. We can't just build it like every other group, every
other Family, erects a home or a community center, like *you* build a
Temple." He sucked in a breath and shook his head and made a cutting gesture. "I need to work on my acceptance of such restraints."

He continued. "And despite those greedy cranks who whipped
up public sentiment against us Intersection of Hope adherents,

burned some of us out"—he nodded toward Tiana—"I must recall that your Celtic religion doesn't seem to attract many fanatics."

The High Priest and Priestess stayed silent but tilted their heads to Tiana. Testing her. Still. Antenn was so fliggering glad he worked for himself and was *done* with employer tests, with people he could never satisfy because he had commoner blood, or maybe just because he wasn't of the Cang Zhu Family that he'd apprenticed with and didn't think like them.

Tiana said, *"An it harm none* is the main tenet of our faith. We carefully try to educate any intolerance from our members and limit any fanatics." Her manner remained completely serene.

But Antenn's last taste of caff dried sourly in his mouth as he scrambled to remember the events they referenced: the Black Magic Cult killings—one of his adoptive cousins, Trif Clover, had been kidnapped by the Cult, and the Family had rallied around her. One of the members had falsely implicated the Cross Folk, easily done since the Cult had used the paralyzing drug pylor in their evil ceremonies. A trace of pylor was included in incense most often associated with the Intersection of Hope.

One Family had been stripped of everything . . . Antenn thought he'd heard his father and some of the younger FirstFamilies Lords and Ladies discuss the incident as political maneuvering, but he hadn't paid much attention. He'd been concerned about Trif, and, as always, he'd been preoccupied with his own problems, struggling as an apprentice with an architectural Family who'd despised him.

He should have damn well researched that situation more because he was missing nuances here. Yet the hair on the back of his neck rose in warning that this was important.

Foreman had leaned forward, staring at Tiana, face set in harsh lines, but another spoke first. "Do you limit fanatics of your Lord and Lady?" asked Elderstone, the oldest man, the one in rich blue, the spirit of wise maturity. He shared a glance with his compatriots. "We wondered."

"We do," the High Priestess stated. "Those who, time and time again, show a hatred for other religions are restricted from our public rites." Now she had her hands in her opposite sleeves in a more formal posture.

"GraceLord T'Equisetum," Younger stated.

Tiana's face became so smooth a mask that Antenn knew that name affected her on a personal level.

The High Priest said, "Yes, he has been restricted from our rites. And, yes, he remains intolerant. He believes that our religion is the only acceptable religion . . . but his hubris does not only apply to religion. He believes only his opinion counts in all matters—such as class. He is a member of the new political group, the Traditionalist Stance."

"Ah," Custos nodded. "Then T'Equisetum doesn't accept that people with increased Flair should Test for, and receive, Noble titles. As far as the Traditionalists are concerned, only those already with titles should be Nobles."

The High Priest inclined his head toward Younger. "We can only discipline in our area. We have done what we can to ensure the man is not accepted by our spiritual community."

"Greedy crank status seekers will use anything to make their points, including religion," Younger said, *not* looking at Tiana.

Custos angled more toward the Sandalwoods and continued in a bland tone, "If you didn't hear, the prophet GreatLord T'Vine believes the future of our cathedral is not set in stone and there could be security issues."

He paused slightly, gathered the gazes of his colleagues, nodded to them and got returning nods, then met T'Sandalwood's perusal. "We originally called this meeting to inform you that we did not wish to include you in a mixed-faith ritual for blessing and spellshielding. However, we have modified that to accept a new ritual written in accordance with only *our* beliefs by Tiana and Quina Mugwort with regard to spellshields."

The Chief Minister continued, "This ceremony will also be performed as an Intersection of Hope ritual, officiated by us. You, High Priest T'Sandalwood, and High Priestess D'Sandalwood and anyone else, are invited to join us as celebrants." He paused. "Celebrating the Intersection of Hope's spiritual beliefs."

"Understood," High Priest GrandLord T'Sandalwood said. He took his HeartMate's hand and drew himself up into a stern and authoritative aspect. "There may be other ministers, priests, priestesses, and potentates of religions who will not join us, but we will certainly be there. We and our highest assistants."

The four men inclined their heads as one. "We thank you for that."

"We must be vigilant. This could be a turning point for Celta down a dark road," D'Sandalwood said. She walked over to a two-seat, sat, and poured herself some hot black caff, and Antenn knew her silence was punctuation for words to come.

After a sip, her gaze met and lingered with each one of them. "We cannot allow our spiritual beliefs—that which should always call to our higher selves—to become a divisive factor in our culture. All of us are descended from people who risked their lives for a new world." As Foreman began to speak, she lifted her hand. "Even the crew members of the starships had a choice. I'm sure they thought being on a ship, going to a new world, was the best thing they could do, personally for themselves, whether it was because they had psi power or because they were penniless and the ships offered good jobs."

T'Sandalwood sat beside her, linked fingers with her, lifted their hands and kissed hers. "Though we seem like a homogenized society, we are not."

"And we *should not* be. But in our lifetimes we *will not* allow anyone supposedly of our faith to persecute any other faith."

"Setting such rules, making outcasts . . . That's how splintered religions are made," Foreman said cynically.

The High Priest rolled his shoulders, his nostrils widened in disgust. "We are not Earth with billions of people and poobahs who rant to masses but do not go among their followers. A person wishing to establish another religion would have to gather like-minded people in a close group, and if such a person preached hatred, acted on hatred, he and his group would break the laws of Celta and be subject to them."

He slanted a sorrowful look at Tiana, then at the ministers.

"The mob that was whipped up against members of your religion during the Black Magic Cult murders had done its worst by the time we were informed. The houses burned, the Families scattered. *Against* our precept 'For the good of all, according to the free will of all, an it harm *none*,' " T'Sandalwood said.

"We will not allow the idea that it is right to hate others for their spiritual beliefs to prosper," the High Priestess emphasized.

"So you say, and so you might believe," Foreman said. He stood and gathered the others to him with a glance. "We agree that you have done what you can, but also agree that it might not be enough." He bowed to Tiana, who'd risen with Antenn. "Neither did we anticipate that security would be a problem. The budget for the cathedral is set and I, for one, do not wish to change it." He flashed Antenn a smile. "I like the new plan for the cathedral very much." Another bow to the Sandalwoods, who had also gotten to their feet. "So, my recommendation to my brethren is to accept your energies and Flair in raising the spellshields." Foreman raised a finger. "*If* the ritual is an Intersection of Hope rite." He switched his stare to Tiana Mugwort. "Can we see a preliminary outline of the ritual tomorrow at MidMorning Bell?"

Antenn *felt* Tiana's inner pressure though she stood casually and calmly. "Of course."

Twelve

♥

Tiana sank into her balance, stilled her anxious mind. She <u>could</u> do
this. Felonerb's piercing yowl outside the entrance nearly shook her
from her general inner peace. She suppressed a wince and addressed
Chief Minister Custos. "Are Fams allowed to attend the ritual?"

His iron-gray brows winged up. "I am not sure. I will have to
consult with my colleagues." He sent them an inquiring glance.
Younger appeared delighted; Elderstone and Foreman frowned.
Custos himself looked thoughtful. "But Familiar animal companions developed on the long voyage of the colonist ships from Earth
to Celta, just as did our religion." He shrugged. "We will consult
together to answer your question. We have a great deal to consult
about . . . however, we *will* be at the press conference in a septhour
at our church offices down the street. We would welcome your presence, High Priest T'Sandalwood and High Priestess D'Sandalwood.
FirstLevel Architect Blackthorn-Moss, we will definitely need you
for explanation of the building and the process."

Beside her, Antenn bowed with easy finesse and walked away.
Tiana wouldn't have to go; good, because she already felt as if she
were behind on an internal schedule.

Foreman strode to the teleportation pad. "Let us use the time between now and then to make decisions and revise our statements."

"Thank you for meeting with us and telling us your concerns," the High Priestess said.

Custos bowed to them. "Thank you for listening. We'll see you later." The four vanished.

"We need to go now, too," T'Sandalwood said.

"One moment," the High Priestess said, and gestured for Tiana to take the few paces to join them.

"Yes, High Priestess?"

"If you require any reference materials to create the rituals, you are welcome to use whatever I have in my office, or GreatCircle Temple has in its library, including the restricted section."

"You can also use any materials I might have," rumbled the High Priest, "and like my HeartMate, I have documents, recording spheres, et cetera from my predecessors."

"Thank you, but that won't be necessary," Tiana said.

Surprise showed on both faces.

"During training we are allowed in the special section of the GreatCircle Temple library, and I examined the materials then for information on the Intersection of Hope." She gave a little cough and a small smile. "I saw that you didn't have anything that was not in the PublicLibrary or my mother's . . . Also, my trainer at the time had a list of each of your office collections."

Tiana looked away. "After my Family found a home again, we reacquired the items my mother felt were necessary for her spiritual needs."

Tiana inhaled and met the Sandalwoods' gazes. "You know that I am a good friend of FirstLevel Librarian Glyssa Licorice Bayrum. Some years ago the PublicLibrarians requested that I ensure their collection was as complete as they could make it with regard to the Intersection of Hope. I did that and I know that they requested and received many materials from the Chief Ministers of the Intersection of Hope, some of which are under seal and not to be revealed without permission."

T'Sandalwood smiled a slow, approving smile. "Excellent, Priest-ess Mugwort."

She gave a little curtsey. "Thank you. I have access to everything I might need."

"Very well. But if you run into problems, let us know," D'Sandalwood said. He bent a look on his wife. "My Temple chambers, HeartMate?"

She nodded, and they teleported from where they stood.

Tiana blew out an irregular breath and let her knees weaken so she half-collapsed on the twoseat.

"Good job," Antenn said, and she jolted.

"I thought you'd left."

"Not yet. I cleaned up the kitchen."

"Oh."

His smile was easy. "Not that there was much to clean up, though if I were you, I'd check the contents of the no-time. If your Fam is anything like mine, he raided more food than you noticed."

She sighed and pushed to her feet. "I have no doubt about that. I'll go through every menu section and have it restocked." She paused, then rubbed her head. Yes, that migraine lurked, ready to hit at her weakest moment. Glancing around, she said a quick housekeeping spell and watched the wrinkles in the cloth of the chairs, the crumbs on the table, vanish with the sweep of Flair.

The scent of herbs used in GreatCircle Temple released by the spell lingered in the air. The familiar fragrance she smelled every day eased the band of pain in her head, and she moved with more energy and confidence into the small kitchen. The spell had swirled through here, too, and every surface that could sparkle did.

Antenn came up behind her, so close she could feel his heat, his breath on her hair, and his Flair impinging on her. She didn't move away. Instead she closed her eyes and let the sensual atmosphere wrap around her and she became aware of another scent . . . Antenn's scent, musk and deep earth as if his roots, his core, went far into Celta and were as solid as any building.

They stayed like that for a long moment, close but not touching, not speaking. Separate, yet together. Sexual awareness fizzed around them. Then she felt his hands on her upper arms. She couldn't recall how long it had been since a man had stirred her so. When? Never.

He tugged and she turned. They stood facing each other, less than a handspan apart. Heat built and seemed to cycle back and forth between their bodies. She tilted her head so her gaze would meet his. His eyes had darkened to brown. Wide black pupils. A flush accented his cheeks and her face warmed, too.

His hand lifted and his fingers touched, withdrew, settled under her chin. He bent and his face came close to hers and his head angled and his lips feathered over hers and she closed her eyes. His mouth pressed against hers, and a rush of need swept through her, pounding through her blood. She reached out, to link her arms around his shoulders, and found air.

Her lashes opened to see him taking more than one pace back, his expression stunned.

"I—" he began, then made a futile gesture and closed his mouth.

She straightened her spine, lifted her chin, and gave him honesty. "It was good. I—"

The scry screen in the outer room pinged. "FirstLevel Priestess Mugwort, I would like to see you as soon as possible in my office," came the voice of High Priestess D'Sandalwood. Tiana saw the flicker that showed the woman was looking into the room and awaiting a response.

"Later," Antenn Blackthorn-Moss said, and didn't even walk to the teleportation pad before he disappeared.

Tiana dragged in a breath and let it out along with some of the sexual tension, she hoped. She didn't want D'Sandalwood to read her expression. With a casual step, she moved toward the screen and answered. "I'll be right there. The chambers here are cleansed, but the no-time needs to be restocked." She smiled with self-deprecation. "I'm afraid I didn't watch my Fam closely enough when we arrived, and he gorged."

The High Priestess's face lightened. "I've heard from my husband about RatKiller."

"His name is Felonerb now." Tiana coughed a little. "Felonerb RatKiller."

"Even better. I'm sorry I missed him. I will send a journey-woman to review the no-time offerings there and choose the menus, a good task for such a one. Please come. I have a new concern."

Tiana crossed to the teleportation pad, checked the various pads in GreatCircle Temple, found a free one, and flipped the switch to show she'd be arriving on it. "I'm coming at once, High Priestess."

Seconds later she was in a tiny northeast teleportation room set aside for staff. She preferred the larger, public pads, but GreatCircle Temple was busy this morning. And as she crossed the wide inner area she saw a lot of furniture being moved around. For an instant a pang went through her at losing her small office with the view of the starship *Nuada's Sword*, but then she assured herself that her new *two-room* chambers, closer to the High Priestess, with a view of the lushest flowering Temple gardens, would suit her better.

And Tiana realized something else in a blinding flash. She held on to the past too tightly. Another damn—wretched—flaw to work on. Her shoulders sank as if under a heavier burden.

She also wondered why Antenn had retreated from her. Was it something about her or about him?

Seemed she'd have to work on self-confidence, too.

A few minutes later Tiana sat in front of the High Priestess's desk. This time her personnel file, the gold file of the Intersection of Hope project, and another, thinner and newer turquoise file were spread before D'Sandalwood.

It appeared that her superior was going to give her another responsibility that affected her career. She stifled a sigh.

"Ah," D'Sandalwood said. Her gaze flicked to Tiana, then upward to the spring-blue sky revealed by the open ceiling.

Tiana wanted to prompt the woman, but that would show impatience.

"The Chief Ministers, the High Priest, and I spoke together and we continue to agree that you will be an excellent liaison."

"Thank you," Tiana said.

"I was impressed and pleased at how you handled the situation this morning." D'Sandalwood smiled the warm smile that filled Tiana with pleasure that she'd done well for this woman.

"Thank you." Tiana smiled back, relieved.

The High Priestess raised a hand. "However, we"—she gestured, encompassing the Temple—"are concerned about your availability."

"Availability?" Tiana asked blankly.

"Ah." Another peek at the sunshiny sky by D'Sandalwood. "We—the High Priest and I—couldn't help but notice that you were quite tired yesterday." She didn't look Tiana in the eyes. "Perhaps due to a great deal of teleportation. And, I think, you have teleported a couple of times today, also?"

"Yes." Tiana had a vague idea of where this was going. The High Priestess was being circumspect about where Tiana and her Family lived . . . BalmHeal Residence and FirstGrove.

"The Chief Ministers of the Intersection of Hope—all of us—want you immediately available. Under, ah, other circumstances, we might assign a glider to you, but we don't think that would work for you, would it?" She paused. "Since you live out of the city."

Tiana didn't know whether the High Priestess and High Priest had any idea where FirstGrove was. She couldn't imagine either of them being desperate enough to find the secret sanctuary tucked in the northeast corner of the city walls. Only the despairing, the near hopeless could find it and penetrate the walls and spellshields.

FirstGrove wasn't easily discovered since a warehouse district had built up between the estate and the rest of Druida City.

Teleportation from the House depended on the whim and mood of the Residence and could be iffy within the boundaries of the land, too. Usually people didn't remember the exact location once their life got better, or they Healed mentally, emotionally, physically.

The Mugwort Family were bespelled not to mention their home.

"No. I wouldn't be able to have a glider," Tiana said. A nice glider parked outside the walls of FirstGrove in the decrepit warehouse district would stand out flagrantly.

"We—my HeartMate and I—didn't think so. And though you responded quite quickly to our urgent request this morning, and, as I said before, we are quite pleased with how you solved a tricky problem, we think it would be better if you were closer to the city, ah—"

"More available," Tiana ended, using the High Priestess's own word. Better if she weren't living in BalmHeal Residence. Moving away from her home and her Family for the duration of this project, for the good of her career.

Again she was presented with a big decision, and again she felt she'd have to decide on the spot, was being pressured to do that.

"Circumstances around this project are moving quickly and not under our control," D'Sandalwood said apologetically.

Tiana's heart beat fast; her mouth had dried so she could barely swallow, hardly speak, but she must. Lifting her chin, she met the High Priestess's gaze. "I will have to request a stipend to live outside my home."

A flash of pity showed in D'Sandalwood's gaze, and Tiana's stomach clenched. She could feel the heat on the back of her neck at having to reveal this and hoped her cheeks weren't too red.

"A stipend will not be necessary," the High Priestess continued smoothly. She gestured at the new turquoise folder on her desk. "You are very lucky."

Sure didn't feel like that, and Tiana's spine went ramrod. So far, nothing about this assignment—except the physical attractiveness of Antenn Blackthorn-Moss—had felt lucky.

"The Turquoise House is between occupants and it has offered itself to you as a domicile."

Tiana blinked as she processed that sentence. "My sister stayed at the Turquoise House for a week last year."

"And so it knows your Family." D'Sandalwood frowned briefly. "I think there might be other connections with you or yours that—

but I don't know for sure." She shrugged. "Currently the House has been empty at its own request for about a half year, and minimally furnished." D'Sandalwood chuckled. "It says it would be happy to decorate for you."

Tiana's mind spun, ideas flitting around, unable to get any traction for her to think through. A sparkling wonder made her smile at the thought of an intelligent Residence taking her wishes into consideration. At *anyone* taking her wishes into consideration . . . putting her first. Incredible concept.

Too incredible. "I . . . uh . . ." She had no clue how to furnish or decorate a House in a pleasant manner. She'd paid little attention to her old home; they'd lived on the run for a year, then had been offered custodianship of the estate of FirstGrove, the ancient Balm-Heal Residence, which was already furnished. About the only thing she'd added to her room was . . . a drawing of the floor plan of the Turquoise House she'd gotten as a gift.

She *felt* her pupils widen.

"The Turquoise House has a relationship with Mitchella D'Blackthorn, the interior designer, who has worked with it before," D'Sandalwood said.

"Antenn Blackthorn-Moss's mother," Tiana said.

"That's right."

Tiana leaned back, staring at all three folders, and a chain of inner personal questions pinged through her brain, quickly asked, quickly needing answers. Her life had twisted and flipped in the last day. The challenges ahead of her, internal and external, loomed big and nearly insurmountable . . . at least so they loomed in her inner vision.

Much was being asked of her. She could quit. She could live in BalmHeal Residence and work on the estate for the rest of her life, become hermitlike as her parents had. Did she want her career? This career? Yes. The Lady had called her when young and she had answered. This was her vocation.

Move on to the next question.

She'd have to root out her anger and pain and fear with regard to the past. Could she do that? She could try. No, not try. She *could* Heal, would Heal whatever wounds lingered inside her. But if she went on, she'd have to deal with those challenges.

She'd have to live away from the bedrock support of her Family, the deep security of BalmHeal estate. That part sounded a little exciting, but scary. And the idea that the Turquoise House would welcome her, decorate for *her* tastes, was near staggering. A huge benefit of these changes.

And there was more at stake here than just one building project, even a huge cathedral, or her career.

She *was* the best person for this particular job. No one could understand both religions as she could. If she withdrew from being the liaison, wouldn't that be hurting society itself? Letting people from two religions stumble through what should be a smooth partnership, perhaps insult and alienate one another? This *did* have the potential to fracture elements of society, have it solidify into rigid structures of distrusting religious differences that might take years to overcome.

The High Priestess watched her patiently, ready to give her all the time she could, Tiana knew, to work through her decision though the joint press conference was within a septhour. D'Sandalwood was a good woman, a good employer, a good role model.

Tiana had help: the High Priest and Priestess, her excellent friends Camellia and Glyssa as well as her Temple colleagues, her Family, even her Fam.

And Antenn Blackthorn-Moss. He'd help.

No, she wasn't totally alone anymore. "I can't make this decision for two of us without input," she said.

Thirteen

D'Sandalwood frowned. "Two of you?"

Felonerb, to me! Tiana shouted mentally. Unlike most humans who usually needed spatial and light cues, Fams could teleport to their persons. Perhaps it was because of their size . . . or their animal natures.

I am here! Felonerb appeared on her lap. This time she wasn't surprised that he smelled a little less than pleasant, or that he dropped a semiclean, unknown-origin bone in her lap. He gave her a lick near her chin, then picked up the bone and began to crunch . . . and little flakes of *stuff* fell on her lap.

He turned to the High Priestess with a grin around his bone. *Greetyou, Holy Woman!*

D'Sandalwood appeared delighted. "Greetyou . . ."

FELONERB RATKILLER MUGWORT!

The High Priestess coughed. "Greetyou, Felonerb RatKiller Mugwort." Though her smile remained, her eyes sharpened to serious. "I'm pleased to meet you. Your FamWoman has a question to ask you."

Still gnawing, and appearing totally disreputable, Felonerb looked up at Tiana. He burped. *What, FamWoman?* His green eyes were wide . . . and also totally trusting. Yes, she had the help—whatever that might consist of—and the supportive love of her Fam.

Matching his gaze, she said, "We are being offered the opportunity to live in the Turquoise House."

His pupils enlarged. *WE ARE! I will be the only Fam!*

Tiana winced. "Quieter, Felonerb, we can hear you. And I think I heard there are feral Fams that live outside and that the Turquoise House takes care of."

But he was standing, tail thrashing in glee, bone forgotten on her lap. *I will be the only Fam In The House!*

"I believe that answers your question," the High Priestess murmured. She took a business card that could turn into a three-dimensional holo portfolio from the folder and a folded packet of papyrus. "Here is Mitchella D'Blackthorn's information and the lease documents."

Most of the last day Tiana had been in reaction mode. A fairly good thing when dealing with superiors you wanted to eventually replace, but now it was time to take charge of her own actions. She nodded to the High Priestess. "I'm sure I will work that out with the Turquoise House."

D'Sandalwood's lips curved. "I'm sure you will." She waved her hand. "You are dismissed for the day to settle into your new chambers here and move into the Turquoise House."

YAY! A new place of OUR own. Our very own House! Felonerb jumped from her lap and did a tail-twitching cat dance around the room.

Tiana and the High Priestess laughed. Then the woman sobered and inclined her head. "And, of course, you must draft . . . *help your mother* . . . draft an appropriate Intersection of Hope ritual."

The elder Priestess's brows lifted and fell, just as her husband, the High Priest, would have rubbed his hands at this moment.

Felonerb disappeared behind her desk and Tiana got the impression he was sniffing her shoes, but Tiana had to concentrate on D'Sandalwood's words.

"I must admit I am looking forward to being a participant in someone else's very different ritual." The High Priestess's expression turned thoughtful, a line digging between her eyes, her lips thinning before she said, "We shall see who of this Temple agrees to take part, and who of the FirstFamilies. I'm sure the High Priest and I can persuade the entire Blackthorn Family to come, Antenn's father and mother and siblings." D'Sandalwood glanced at the pretty timer on the wall. "I need to update all the FirstFamily Lords and Ladies regarding the ritual and invite them. Before the conference with the newssheets and viz reporters." She reached for her old-fashioned but elegantly cast silver scry bowl and pulled it in front of her. Tiana took the motion for the dismissal that it was, and rose. Felonerb pranced out from behind the High Priestess's desk.

Without looking at Tiana, the High Priestess tapped her fingers on the folded packet. "You will need to review and sign these papyrus and take them personally to the GuildHall. The City Property Clerk handles all of the Turquoise House's rentals for it. A glider is waiting for you. Please use it today."

A glider, too! I looove gliders. Felonerb nearly bounced to the door, then stood outside its range and scrunched up his muzzle, and the door opened.

"Thank you, High Priestess," Tiana said, and took the thick papyrus. "Thank you, Felonerb." So very odd that her life had gone off in another direction once more within a few minutes.

She slipped from the room even as D'Sandalwood's fingers skimmed around the edge of her scry bowl, initiating the communication spell. As Tiana turned to close the door, the High Priestess looked up at her with a straight, serious gaze. "FirstLevel Priestess Mugwort, you *will* use your influence on your friends D'Hawthorn and T'Hawthorn to attend the Intersection of Hope spellshield ritual, yes?"

Tiana swallowed but said the only thing she could, despite the fact that she hated asking her friends for favors. "Yes."

I will ask Brazos and Mica to come, too. Felonerb lifted his lip and revealed his broken tooth. *They will listen to Me. All Fams are afraid of RatKiller!*

D'Sandalwood's lip twitched and she murmured, "I wonder what T'Ash's Zanth would say to that."

Tiana didn't even want to contemplate a confrontation between Felonerb and the legendary Zanth.

Zanth is ooooolllddd. With one last tail flick, Felonerb exited the office.

And though Tiana supposedly had the day off to move, and the High Priestess might think that was the largest job for her today, Tiana knew that writing the ritual between now and tomorrow morning would take time.

She'd better use the glider for travel around the city while she had the chance. She'd go to the GuildHall, then to the Turquoise House.

We get to ride around in a glider again! Felonerb strutted alongside her.

"Yes."

Fun. It is Very Fun being your FamCat.

"Thank you."

As she headed toward the entrance, she saw Lucida Gerania walking along the opposite side of the curved corridor, stormy of expression. She glared at Tiana. Gerania must have heard of the ritual then. Of course the ambitious priests and priestesses who worked in the Temple would attend the Intersection of Hope spellshield ritual just to please the Sandalwoods, but that wouldn't prevent Gerania from thinking the whole thing was low-class.

Her gaze swept Tiana from top to bottom and her mouth curved and her hand smoothed the fabric—the more expensive fabric and more flattering and better-tailored tunic—over her hip. Then she seemed to notice Felonerb, and she simply stopped and stared.

Though the back of Tiana's neck heated at her forever-scruffy Fam, she kept her face tranquil. She'd get over being embarrassed by her Fam . . . just another feeling that needed to be excised. Through love, that should happen soon.

Tiana reached the entryway of the east door of the Temple before she had to greet her rival with a brief courtesy. Then she exited . . . the unspoken insult to her clothes and reminder of her poverty was just another thorn of hurt she'd gathered this morning. Her head began to throb and she knew she'd have to stop at one of the HealingHalls, too, or perhaps the Turquoise House had some good medications. He should be well stocked; he'd hosted Tiana's sister, a Healer, for a while.

Felonerb sniffed. *I saw that woman. She is snotty, like some other Fams I know. I will leave her a rat—*

"No, Felonerb, you don't have to do that." Tiana paused. "Do you know where she lives?" Tiana had a vague idea.

She does NOT live in the famous Turquoise House, Felonerb said with satisfaction as the door to the glider lifted and he hopped in and made himself comfortable. *WE do!*

Tiana's heart gave a solid thump in her chest. "I suppose we do." Then she pulled out her scry pebble and contacted her mother, asking for her help with the ritual, and got an agreement. Good.

*A*ntenn *saw GraceLord T'Equisetum as he left the press conference.* None of the spiritual folk seemed to have noticed the guy had stood in the back of the room. Antenn didn't bother to nod to the man as he had to others.

They both exited the building through the back door and were in the paved courtyard, surrounded by bare trees and prepared garden beds a short garden pathway to Antenn's own office.

"Well, if it isn't the fake Blackthorn kid. The Downwind slum kid who wormed his way far into T'Blackthorn's house," the man sneered, with a good emotional jab that caught Antenn straight in his gut.

He tucked his hands in his pockets so he wouldn't swing at the guy, eyed him, and said, "You're older, and yeah, maybe you're in prime shape." He studied the man insolently enough to make the GraceLord flush. "And maybe you could whip my ass."

"No *maybe* about it," T'Equisetum snapped.

"But probably not." Antenn settled slightly into his fighting stance and the man didn't seem to notice. He shook his head. "Probably not. Because, after all, I train with the best, and at the best place, with the Hollys at The Green Knight Fencing and Fighting Salon. I've been a member there since I was fourteen, and I've never seen you there."

T'Equisetum snorted. "Expensive and overrated."

That made a real laugh push from Antenn's chest and let him see the guy for what he was . . . pitiful. "I sure would like you to say that to the Hollys," he said, amused.

The man showed him teeth, not in a smile, but in a predator's grimace. "And you know what I'd like to see, younger brother of Shade the murderer?" T'Equisetum gestured widely, then pointed at Antenn's office. "I'd like to see you invite all of the FirstFamilies to dine with you right there, in your business back courtyard. Not at T'Blackthorn Residence or the Clover Compound where they'd feel obliged to come. No, *your* Moss place." He smiled and rolled on. "Those FirstFamilies who had loved ones that your brother murdered with a firebombspell that could not be stopped and burned them to death."

Antenn's spine chilled at the thought. He kept his fingers from bunching. That would show the GraceLord he was getting a reaction. Antenn thought back to the morning's talk of the mob and what he recalled. "Interesting that *you* brought up firebombs."

To Antenn's surprise, T'Equisetum went from red to white, and Antenn stared. Interesting and disturbing.

After a breath through his nose, Antenn jerked his chin up and said, "I'll leave a guest pass at The Green Knight Fencing and Fighting Salon, if you ever want to try the place out with members of your own age group."

"Pup," the GraceLord snarled.

Antenn took his hands from his pockets and, keeping his Flair and senses focused on the man behind him, strolled with all the casualness he could muster to his office. Once there, equally casually, he glanced back. He didn't see T'Equisetum. The Lord had either teleported away or moved quickly to the front and a glider on the street.

Antenn hadn't made an enemy of the man; the guy had just been revealed to be one. Antenn rubbed the back of his neck and studied the courtyard behind his office. Yeah, it could hold a table for the FirstFamilies' Lords and Ladies and their spouses. The image tightened his gut. As far as he knew the FirstFamilies were deeply divided regarding his existence. His friends liked him; everyone else, especially of the older generation, hated him.

How would that affect the cathedral? Would it?

He set his jaw. He wasn't giving up that project.

And he couldn't ever see himself taking the chance of inviting the FirstFamilies to a meal here.

He wasn't that brave.

*T*iana *missed the press conference and announcement of the building of* the cathedral as the glider took her and Felonerb from the Guild-Hall to the Turquoise House. She'd have to watch the viz, read all the newssheets, and keep her ears alert for general reaction.

The glider pulled up by the side of the road; a pair of fancy greeniron gates opened, then the vehicle was banked by formal garden beds. The gliderway was only a couple of lengths of a large vehicle before it opened into a flagstoned courtyard. Before the glider stopped, Felonerb had thinned his window and leapt out. Tiana gasped, and then as the vehicle stopped so her door was parallel to the entryway she just blinked and blinked.

The House *glowed*, a vibrant, shiny turquoise. It was a modified U shape with small angled corners instead of sharp ones. On either side of the U were additional room-blocks that appeared to extend from front to back.

Then the glider door lifted and cool spring air flowed around her. The morning had alternated sunny and cloudy, rather like her life at the moment.

Before she exited the vehicle, she said, "GreatCircle Temple glider, please wait, and disregard any orders by my Fam, Felonerb RatKiller, unless I confirm them." She sure could have used the vehicle yesterday.

"Yes, Priestess," the automatic voice of the glider responded.

The black-tinted wooden door opened and she walked into the entryway of the House.

"Greetyou, FirstLevel Priestess Tiana Mugwort! I am pleased to meet you. I like your sister, Artemisia, and your brother-in-law very much and am glad you are here," the House said.

Good thing she was accustomed to talking to a Residence . . .

another blessing she needed to keep in mind. Lower Nobles such as her
Family didn't often live in sentient Houses, but she had for years, and
perhaps that was why the Turquoise House was being so generous.

"Thank you, Turquoise House. I am pleased to be here," she
said, and it wasn't even a fib. She glanced around the entryway,
which held built-in closets and plush cushions on enclosed benches
set against the pale gold walls, along with a couple of wardrobes.

"Please call me TQ. I am large and beautiful; please tour me and
choose your rooms. I would recommend the MasterSuite or the
MistrysSuite that is attached . . . I have a lot of space for an office
and a den and a library and a mainspace or *two* or a playroom . . ."

"You overwhelm me." Tiana's breath had caught at the very idea
of having all that space—a whole *House*—to herself. Mind boggling
enough that she didn't realize for a few seconds that her Fam was
nowhere in sight.

"Felonerb!" she called, and her voice echoed in emptiness and a
trace of panic surged through her. She'd never lived alone. She gasped.

"Your heart rate has increased," TQ said. "What is wrong?"

"I–I–"

"Felonerb, your FamWoman needs you!" TQ sent the demand
through the House. Tiana thought she heard windows rattle. She
sank onto the bench. "I've never lived alone."

"You have me," TQ pointed out.

"Yes."

Felonerb shot through the corridor doorway at the far side of the
room and skidded in front of her, then leapt to the bench, her lap,
her shoulder. *You have ME, too. This is a WONDERFUL place.*

"What rooms would you like?" TQ asked.

"Ah, a bedroom."

We have a bedroom and another room at home, Felonerb said.
*And two rooms at GreatCircle Temple, too! My FamWoman got a
promotion the day she got Me, too. It was a WONDERFUL day.*

Tiana yelped and rubbed her temples.

"What is wrong?" TQ asked.

"I have an incipient migraine," she mumbled.

"I have a fully stocked medical closet," TQ said with pride. "Come, look at my rooms. Most are empty of furnishings since I changed my mind about redecorating after your sister and her HeartMate left last year. I decided to repurpose my chambers, move inner walls and the like."

"Oh." Tiana rose, stretched long and hard to release tension. This time Felonerb stayed close and began sniffing around the baseboards.

"But we will be able to choose what you like and make the rooms what you want!" TQ said.

"Sounds great." Now she did some strong, rhythmic breathing. These last two days were shredding her calm in more ways than one. "But I don't know how long I'll be here."

"I do not know how long it takes to build a cathedral, do you?" TQ asked.

"No." She managed a smile. "Another question I didn't ask." She thought a little. "Though the Chief Ministers of the Intersection of Hope might have said in their talk with the newssheets this morning."

"I will review that as you look around!"

"You can do that?"

"Oh, yes. I have combination scry-viz panels in most of my rooms. Here you are at the main corridor; the old MasterSuite and MistrysSuite is to your right. To your left are areas that can be mainspaces or the library or the playroom or a den or—"

"I understand. Where is the medical cabinet?"

"In the MistrysSuite waterfall room. You should look at it first, perhaps."

"That sounds good."

I know where it is! I will show you! Felonerb angled into the corridor and to the right.

Fourteen

*S*he listened to both TQ and Felonerb as she walked through the House and checked out the rooms. Some were obviously guest bedrooms; others could be anything.

"I am very pleased with my new MasterSuite and MistrysSuite. They compose one of my short wings with views of the courtyard and the south side gardens," TQ said.

Standing in the MasterSuite—a bedroom with a sitting room on one side and a waterfall room that was as large as her bedroom in BalmHeal Residence, then a dressing room—she decided it simply was too large for her, especially since there was probably another whole set of rooms like it.

"This is made for a couple," she said.

"Yes," replied TQ. "But you are very welcome to have it. You will be comfortable here."

Felonerb hopped onto the one piece of furniture, a massive bed, kneaded it, grinned. *We are a couple.*

"It's made for a human couple. And, so far, you've liked to sleep in your own space." She wasn't sure whether she wanted that to be different or not.

Easier to come and go without waking you. He tried to appear innocent.

"That expression doesn't work on you, Felonerb. I will never mind if you come and go as you please."

TQ made a noise that sounded like a human snort. "All of my outside walls can accommodate a Fam door of several sizes. I have learned the art. Though currently I have small cat doors." There was a *swish* and Felonerb sped from the bed through the door in the wall into the gardens.

"The medicine cabinet is in the MistrysSuite waterfall room. You enter the MistrysSuite through the dressing room." Now it sounded uncertain . . . so far TQ had a wide range of expression, and Tiana abruptly recalled that an actor had read for the House when it was younger and given it his voice.

Her turn to ask, "What's wrong?"

"I anticipated that you would like the MasterSuite. The Mistrys-Suite doesn't have even a bed."

"No worries," she managed. Her headache began to pound in earnest. "A bedroom and sitting room will be fine with me."

"You need a private waterfall room, too. I have found that my ladies prefer this."

"All right." After going through the masculine dressing room to the bare MistrysSuite dressing room and finding herself in a beautiful waterfall room staring at a huge tub, the large waterfall enclosure of beige marble with threads of brown, she agreed that a private waterfall room was necessary. Against one wall stood a built-in cabinet of many drawers. The piece looked a lot like a cabinet in BalmHeal Residence that her mother and sister used. She swallowed and headed straight to the drawer that might hold her migraine herbs. "My sister set this up?"

"Yes, and stocked it. I do not have a stillroom, but I could make one! Would you like a stillroom?"

"Thank you, no." She drew out the drawer and there was a small dissolvable envelope that contained her migraine herbs, and she said a quiet blessing. "Thank you, *so* much, Turquoise House. With this, I should be able to make it through the day." And all the night that she would be working on a ritual for the Intersection of Hope.

"There is a full no-time in your—the MistrysSuite—sitting room, and a beverage one in your bedroom. I believe those herbs go into a mixture that I have in both no-times."

"Wonderful." She moved from the waterfall room to the bedroom, saw one of the panels of the room open and the no-time extrude, that door opening, too. Moving fast, she grabbed the hot mixture in a tall pale-blue mug, dumped the herbs in, said the spell she knew, and sent Flair to the whole thing. She added a blessing and a prayer and barely waited until it was cool enough to drink.

Then the migraine receded, which was good, because when the catfight erupted, she was ready.

Yowls, cat screeches. She jogged through the suites back to the corridor and the south door. The minute she opened it a ball of spitting cats rolled in, Felonerb and a long-haired gray. "Stop!"

They didn't listen. Too bad her cup was empty.

But she'd gotten her second wind and snapped her fingers above the combatants and drew water from the humid atmosphere to spray down on the cats.

With a shriek Felonerb jumped to her shoulder, arched, and growled, *You are a common Cat. You are not a Fam!*

The gray cat hunkered down and hissed, his nose bloody.

"Easy," Tiana soothed, sending waves of calm toward them, wondering if such Flair would work.

With a low, rumbling growl the cat inched back toward the open door, ears flat, eyes darting as if watching every centimeter for threat.

"Turquoise House, is this cat one of your ferals?" Tiana asked.

"Yes, Tiana. I have five who live on my grounds and whom I feed." The House's voice hardened and echoed through the corridor. "Felonerb RatKiller, I am *not* pleased with you. I consider my land neutral territory for all animals."

Felonerb hissed loudly in her ear.

"Stop that," Tiana said. "We are guests here and we will abide by the Turquoise House's rules." She paused. "Unless you'd like to return home while I stay here. Or, I could ask the Licorices who live in CityCenter to put us up. Of course, you wouldn't be the primary *indoor House* Fam."

Grumble-growls sounded in his throat. The other cat reached the threshold of the door and bolted.

Felonerb sat up straight. She felt something wet soak through her tunic. Blood. Great. She was going through clothes at an alarming rate and only hoped that the Whirlwind Spell had included a little protection.

I will accept moving to your other friend's Residence, T'Hawthorn Residence.

"Because you know you can intimidate—so far—the Hawthorn FamCats?" Tiana asked. "I don't think so. T'Hawthorn Residence is far in Noble Country, and the reason we are here at all is that I need to be available if the Chief Ministers have questions. So your choices are here or at the Licorices'. And I want you to respect the cats who are not Fams."

Felonerb jumped off her shoulder in the direction of the main part of the House. Tiana turned to watch as he sashayed, tail up. *I am going to find My OWN room.*

"Just as I thought," Tiana said quietly. "You really don't want a companion, just a warm home."

That seemed to electrify Felonerb. All his hair stood out and he literally hopped in a half circle, spattering droplets of blood in an arc, and raced toward Tiana. That he didn't teleport meant that he was running low on his Flair, too. *Nooo!* he wailed. He jumped straight at her and she caught him. He snuggled in, even as he nipped her arm. *You are MY FamWoman.*

She wondered how long playing the guilt card would last, probably just once, though it wouldn't have worked at all if she hadn't felt exactly the way she said.

A long-suffering sigh. *I will stay here and in a closet near you.*

"Perhaps a connecting room," TQ said.

"Yesss," Felonerb verbalized.

"Family is very important," TQ continued. A creak came. "And speaking of homes. I would like a good, solid home for my feral cats in the far corner of the yard. The winter was hard on them. But it must be designed so they will accept each other."

Swish! The floor where Felonerb had been showed no blood. TQ continued, "Maybe we can find someone to plan and model it for me?"

Tiana petted Felonerb. "If it helps territorial disputes, I'm all for it."

Flair hummed in the air as TQ muttered, "Perhaps a multilevel structure with exit and entrance holes."

Ramps, too, Felonerb said. *Some of those cats can't teleport.*

"Ramps," TQ said. "You'll help me with this, Tiana? If you will look out the MasterSuite sitting room, I will show you where I want my ferals' house."

"All right." Still holding Felonerb, she went to the back window and stared at the far corner of the property, delineated by a nice wooden fence with artistic holes for Fam—no, just animal—entrances and exits.

"You will help?" asked TQ.

"Of course."

A long creak that sounded as if he were considering something, and then TQ said, "You asked a question earlier about the length of time you might spend with me. I have reviewed a bit of the press conference of the Intersection of Hope Chief Ministers and the High Priest and High Priestess and the architect."

Tiana pulled herself away from watching the cats outside move in some status patterns. "Yes, what did the FirstLevel Architect say?"

"He could not say exactly for raising such a large structure, but the range he gave was from three to seven months."

"Seven months!" So long living alone, away from her Family.

"I have reviewed the materials I have on Earthan cathedrals. Most took many years, at least a decade to build, one or two a century. Of course that is Earthan centuries, which are shorter than ours because we have longer hours and days due to our planet's rotation around the sun." A pause, and TQ's voice came back rougher. "I was unaware that Antenn was contemplating such a project."

"You know him?"

"He was one of my first tenants," TQ said proudly, then added in a softer tone, "Though he was only with me for a short time."

"Oh."

"I never decorated for him, though. Mitchella was the one who had all the ideas and has mostly designed me through the years."

"Antenn's mother, GrandLady D'Blackthorn."

"Yes. Now which rooms do you want?"

"Ah, I *would* like a small suite. Perhaps a guest suite with bedroom, sitting room, and waterfall room." An image came to her mind. "In my sitting room, I'd like a desk set against a window that looks out to the gardens."

"Perhaps you would like the northeast corner suite? There are rooms that face the back grassyard and the flower beds on the north side of the House and my hedgerow and trees?"

"I'll look."

The end of the hallway showed a polished wooden pointed-arch door. She opened it, and the soothing dimness of the light appealed to her more than the brightness of the MasterSuite, or the MistrysSuite with the large windows on all sides, and the main one facing the front courtyard.

This room was larger than she needed, nearly as large as the MasterSuite at the opposite end of the House. "Open the north wall paneling," TQ said, and Tiana gasped as the narrow slats of the wall folded back to reveal a simple sunroom with long sections of glass angling downward, then curving at the top and forming a straight wall.

"Oh."

"Is that good or bad?" TQ asked.

"It is wonderful."

Felonerb jumped from her arms and began to sniff around the room, rubbing his nose now and then on the glass, leaving smears that had Tiana wincing.

TQ said, "I had the room made from a porch. The porch on the opposite side of the House is used for storage of food and items for the feral cats."

"Yesss," hissed Felonerb, grinning and staring at a couple of the cats peering at him from low bushes. *And I am the only Cat here in THIS room! Mine, mine, mine . . .*

Before he could finish the possessive claim of six "mines," Tiana said, "Ours."

"I'm glad you like it," TQ said. He hesitated. "BalmHeal Residence has boasted of his conservatory."

"Yes, the conservatory is large and very . . . intricate, lacy iron and glass. I like this room much better. Is the glass armored?"

"Yes, and I have the very latest in spellshields!"

Tiana wasn't surprised, now. This House-becoming-a-Residence was a real gem. "I'm honored that you have accepted me as an occupant."

We will be wonderful occupants, Felonerb said. *WHERE IS MY ROOM?* he shouted telepathically.

"I will remind you, cat, that I can hear your mental voice quite well. No need to shout," TQ said. "You may have the room next door to this sitting room. It is large for a Fam companion's den . . ."

I am a SPECIAL Fam.

"So all cats believe," TQ said. "But I think I might have a wall inserted and make you a very cozy room *just* for you."

"You'd do that?" Tiana asked.

"Absolutely. Tiana, I am pleased that you accepted my offer. I have not designed the sunroom space yet, with raised plant beds, though I do want a small fountain. Do you wish to plan the chamber, or have me ask Mitchella or maybe Antenn?"

A whole room for her to design, a garden room. But the sitting room she was in was bare, too, and showed an open door to the waterfall room, also bare, and she reasoned that the bedroom beyond would have no furnishings like most of the House. Plenty of rooms to decorate, make herself comfortable in.

Still staring at the sunroom, she said, "I would like to make that room a combination garden room and office area. I can't think of a more lovely space to work. Surrounded by the smell of lush plants, the scent of flowers."

"What flowers do you like?" TQ asked.

"I'm a simple person. I like roses," she said.

"Hmm. I will contact Antenn's office about what landscaper he uses for his architectural business. To work on this room, and see if we can do roses, and perhaps the rest of my grounds, too. What do you think about them?"

"Your gardens are nicely landscaped."

"I think they are too . . . regimented. Yes," TQ said with a little more determination. "I want something different."

"All right." She cleared her throat. "You know that I have an assignment to write a ritual for the Intersection of Hope that would include our Celtic priests and priestesses?"

"That's you? Such a thing was mentioned on the viz interview. You are doing that, making a ritual that all can take part in when raising spellshields on the foundation?"

"Do you have Flaired security spellshield chants in your library?"

"Yes!"

"Can you, ah, transfer that information to recordspheres for me?"

"Of course. Please go to my library. It is down the hall to your right, with windows looking out on the courtyard."

I will look at My room, Felonerb said, trotting with her only a short ways and stopping at the first door on her left, looking at her to open it. She did and saw a room larger than the sitting room and sunroom she'd just left.

"I can give the Fam a nice, small room," TQ said.

"Gracious of you," Tiana murmured, smiling at the thought that TQ would not be a pushover for Felonerb.

"Yes," TQ agreed.

She stopped at the right door and paused to listen to the loud purr coming from her Fam. "What I wanted to say was that I will be relying heavily on my mother to help me write the ritual and"—Tiana's voice caught—"I think it would be a real treat for her to design this sunroom, if you permit." She paused for a breath because she'd teared up. "She hasn't been able to make a room entirely her own since we lost our home." And, maybe, just maybe, Tiana could get her mother out of the sanctuary and across town for more than a couple of septhours. "I know that whatever she would design would fit me."

"I do permit. I will also give you the dimensions and a blueprint of the room on a recording sphere," TQ said. There came a slight vibrating creak that sounded like a chuckle. "I will boast to my friend, BalmHeal Residence, that Quina Mugwort will be making a very special room for me."

"That could work to encourage BalmHeal to allow Mother to change some chambers in that Residence. Thank you, Turquoise House."

She opened the library door and went in. A large window showed the courtyard. As she studied the landscaping, she admitted it appeared to be more formal than she liked and especially what she was accustomed to. Only four of them lived in the large secret sanctuary, and there was a limited amount they could do on the estate, so she was used to wild gardens.

All the other walls of the room were lined with bookshelves, books, vizes, recording spheres, and even memoryspheres, real actual thoughts and experiences, probably from TQ's previous occupants.

"I sent my library and important documents and spheres to the PublicLibrary to store so they would not be destroyed as everything else was after the medical experiment with the Iasc plague. After I chose this room as the new library, I had them returned." Once again pride throbbed in his voice.

"It's beautiful." She swallowed. The shelves were the same wood as had been in her lost childhood home. BalmHeal Residence's bookcases were a different, paler wood. So many times in the last couple of days she'd been reminded of the wrenching change in her life.

A drawer opened from one of the bookcases, with a large data sphere, a smaller recording sphere no doubt containing one ritual of the Intersection of Hope, and a piece of papyrus. She crossed to the opening and took them all, putting them all in her large sleeve pockets. The pockets were bespelled not only to protect and lighten objects within, but to appear flat.

Chimes sounded.

"I have visitors!" TQ trilled. "Come to see you and me!"

Tiana heard the rapid thumps of Felonerb running, saw a streak of brown-gray through the open door as he shot down the hallway.

Fifteen

Antenn had sloughed off T'Equisetum's words. Mostly. A few had gotten under his skin and dug in . . . or maybe they'd traveled to his brain and took up space in the back of his mind. In any event, he had a cathedral to build. The notion just plain thrilled him.

He stopped in his office to change from his professional tunic and trous to work leathers. Sturdier clothes in which to supervise the digging of the deep foundation trenches. Glancing at the timer, he saw he could just make the small, private, and sacred ceremony the Chief Ministers planned for the groundbreaking.

Like Tiana Mugwort's mother, a spouse of one of the Excavation Earth Mages belonged to the Intersection of Hope Church. The Excavation Earth Mage and her sisters had given Antenn and the Chief Ministers a good deal on the trench digging. They would handle the excavation only.

The ministers used people connected to them if at all possible, and others who fit into their budget. Unfortunately that did not include the best in spellshielding, a FirstFamily woman. But with a ritual composed of many, the shields should be plenty strong.

Even though Antenn had worked with these mages before, he

needed to be there to supervise. *No one* in his lifetime had undertaken such a massive project.

And from now on, he'd have to walk the site every day to keep the detail in his mind for teleportation purposes . . . and he needed to set up teleportation areas complete with signals and a glider parking lot.

At the last minute, he thought of T'Equisetum's sneer and Vinni's warning and belted on his sword and blazer.

*B*eing at the *Turquoise House* was too distracting: too many people came and went, just checking up on Tiana or checking out the House itself.

Then the Sandalwoods had shown up, and Tiana had accompanied them around the House as TQ gave them a tour loaded with attention and detail and added the outside back grassyard and garden.

Meanwhile the minutes until the deadline for her to present the new ritual to the Chief Ministers ticked off in her mind, the time waning ever scarcer.

MidAfternoon Bell rolled around, and the steady stream of visitors continued . . . priests and priestesses, friends, who'd heard of the cathedral and the upcoming ritual, and the Turquoise House—who'd apparently been very exclusive the last couple of years. And the inner pressure of hard *important* creative work instead of interacting-with-people work scraped on Tiana's nerves.

As soon as she was between visitors, she closed the House and, apologizing to it for her desertion for the rest of the day but promising to make it up to the youngster later and that she'd be back early the next morning, she left for BalmHeal Residence.

The rest of the day and past dinnertime, she studied reports, old and new, regarding the Intersection of Hope religion, and the materials TQ had given her. She'd reviewed her own notes on the rituals she'd done for her mother over the years—fewer than she'd recalled.

Sitting at her desk, she massaged her scalp to hopefully stimulate her brain. What she really, truly needed to do was to find the absolute kernel of commonality between the two religions, a spiritual basis shared by them both.

Kindness, compassion, and love for their fellow beings as all progressed on their lives' journeys.

Simple might be best. And simple and inclusive . . . and here she was thinking inclusive again . . . might not work for the Chief Ministers. Her mother was a Healer and loved her HeartMate and children, who followed the traditional Celtic religious path . . . so Tiana's mother probably accepted flexibility in her rituals where the ministers would not.

Tiana scrapped another idea. She stood and stretched and paced her small sitting room. She'd have liked to go down the stairs and walk into the night, but that would arouse the Residence, who preferred everyone inside his walls once dark fell. The estate attracted the desperate, allowed afflicted beings inside for sanctuary, but nothing in the spellshields prevented the evil or insane.

True, the evil and the insane didn't often remain that way . . . the sanctuary gave them surcease from their pain and they Healed. Or they died. Or they left. But the Residence guarded his people jealously. Another of the reasons why her parents had remained inside the estate . . . to soothe the first Residence that had become sentient on Celta . . . and then had been abandoned.

BalmHeal Residence *liked* having people who didn't leave the estate to work in Druida City as Tiana and Artemisia and Garrett did.

So Tiana was stuck inside, though the fresh cold air outside of winter turning into spring would refresh her. Her sitting room was too small for pacing.

After the last couple of days, she didn't dare teleport outside the walls or outside the estate. Lately, she'd needed all her energy, physical, spiritual, and Flair, to just get through her workday.

Finally she threw out everything she had and decided against a circle. She liked the circle work, being connected with others, feeling the variety of others' energy, Flair, *personality* flowing around her, through her . . . But that was not the way of the Intersection of Hope folk until the very last of their ceremony.

Those who could not set aside their own preferences and prejudices to take part in a spiritual experience—even if it was a decidedly *different* spiritual experience—did not need to attend. She began to draft explanations to her fellow priests and priestesses as she worked on the ritual.

In an Intersection of Hope ceremony, one chose an end of the arm of the cross from which to enter the sacred space—as the childlike self, the guardian spirit, the adult full of vitality, or the very mature and accepting person. Of the four of her Family, when they'd taken on the aspects, Tiana had always written herself in as the guardian spirit and had planned on being part of that line of celebrants in this ritual. Perhaps, with the recent experience of her interviews with the High Priest and Priestess, it was time to reconsider.

Going to the meditation corner of her sitting room, she folded into a seated position, let her shoulders drop and stress flow from her into the floor, and closed her eyes. Just as she whiffed something odd, a bony cat hopped onto her lap and began a rough and rusty purr.

She smiled. "Felonerb," she whispered.

I am here. He sniffed, and it wasn't as lush and wet as that morning. She petted his knobby spine.

We will fatten you up, she sent telepathically.

His purr increased and she relaxed further.

I ate much today. Regular meals!

He sounded thrilled, and her heart simply squeezed with the aching at what he'd already suffered.

He nudged her hand with his head. *That is all over. I have found My forever home.*

"Absolutely," she murmured.

Another sniff. *Your Dam and the grumpy old House made me sit in a spot and blew smoke over me.*

Probably to clean him and make him smell better. Since her mother hadn't said anything at dinner about having to clean up his vomit, they'd all been spared that. Tiana said, "Smoke is better than a wet bath."

A series of sniffs. *Yes. And I saw Gwydion Ash! And he saw Me! And looked Me all over and petted Me and tickled Me inside and out and We played and I felt warm and hot, and then fine, Fine, FINE!* Felonerb's lashing tail thwacked her. Sounded as if he'd needed Healing and had received it. Tiana breathed a prayer of thanks to the Lady and Lord.

Then I joined you. It was a good day. A pause of a heartbeat. *Are We going to sit here long?*

She chuckled, felt the simple joy throughout her body. "No. I have to talk to my mother."

A rumble sounded in his throat as he hopped off her lap and onto the bedsponge. There he curled up and draped his tail over his nose, sniffed again in a disgusted manner, and muttered, *She SMOKED Me. I do not want to see her again soon.*

Tiana laughed. "All right." She went to her desk and swept up the three simple rituals she'd drafted. None of them had triggered her Flair, as often happened when she created. So they were far from perfect.

But if she worked with her mother, she'd find which was the best, and anything that might alienate the Chief Ministers.

Tiana *did* know that when all four lines of celebrants met in the center of the space, they formed a square and connected with each other by holding specially consecrated rope ties they wore as belts. That time would be nearly the same as a circle in her own religion . . . and the moment that they'd use Flair to raise the spellshields. She needed to ask her mother's opinion on chants and incenses.

Tiana wasn't sure how long it would be until the ritual was scheduled but thought it would have to be within a few days. The sooner she had copies of the chants to distribute to the High Priestess and the High Priest so they could study their parts, the better.

She walked down the stairs and to the conservatory where her parents were sitting together in the dark before they went to bed, as was their custom. Her father saw Tiana and rose and stretched, lifted his HeartMate's hand, and kissed her fingers. "Later, beloved."

Tiana's mother's smile was soft. "Later."

With a wave of her hand, Tiana set a spellglobe over the table in the middle of the room. She breathed deeply of the humid, plant-rich air, paused to listen to the trickle of a tiny fountain, and settled into real peace that had escaped her for most of the day.

Her mother kissed her cheek and drew out a rough wooden chair that matched the table, and Tiana did the same, sitting on a bright red cushion.

"What do you have, dear?" Quina asked.

Tiana sat and gave her mother the rituals she'd worked so hard on.

Quina Mugwort read the three rituals in detail, frowned, and made Tiana stand and act them out. With a wave of her fingers, Quina translocated several small *real* papyrus books. A couple of them Tiana had seen before . . . an antique one she and her Family had purchased for her mother's Nameday. Chants and spells.

Then came a long silence as Tiana's mother stared in her general direction but with her eyes focused on a vision in her head or something more distant. After a moment she shook herself, then met Tiana's gaze. "You know the words and the prayers, my darling, but you don't *feel* it, don't have the spirit in your heart." She put her hand between her full breasts.

Tiana nodded. "No, I wouldn't. I believe in something else." She lifted her arms, centered herself, closed her eyes, and called to her Goddess. Felt her spirit rise to meet that Female Essence that flowed and enveloped her, enriched her life, touched her mind with wisdom more than Tiana could comprehend. A tang of duality slipped through her, too, the touch of the more aggressive male energy, that called out to that small bit she carried within. She stayed in the refreshing state of bliss for an eternal instant, then exhaled a long breath as the Lady left.

When she opened her eyes, she saw silent tears sliding down her mother's face.

"That was beautiful. And special. And I am proud and happy for you in your faith," said Quina, her voice clogged. "But it is not my faith."

"No. But I love you and your faith, and the joy you have in the journey of your spirit," Tiana said.

Her mother banished her tears, swallowed, and tapped her forefinger on one of the rituals. "This one is the best." She laid her hand atop the books and smiled with that joy that was one of her essential characteristics. "I think if we stick to some of the very first chants and spells that were written, the Chief Ministers would be surprised and pleased. I don't believe some of these have been used in centuries, perhaps not even after we landed here on Celta." She lifted her chin. "They'll be impressed, too, with my wonderful daughter."

"With the ritual mother and daughter make," Tiana said.

"Yes." Another gesture and a carafe that smelled of hot, black, potent caff appeared on the table, along with a couple of green, herbal pills. Tiana knew what that meant. "We're going to be here for a while."

"Yes."

A couple of septhours later, when her mother finished with her additions, Tiana took a clean piece of papyrus and began writing the first part of the ritual for the childlike self, as those choosing that godhead processed through the arm of the cross that would be dedicated to that portion of the journey that the Intersection of Hope praised.

Her Flair sparked and the words flowed, and she could *see* the ritual, the rising of crescent twinmoons blinking white and streaming light over the black horizon beyond the plateau.

Chanting came in the rhythm and the beat she now wrote to, voices singing and praying and lifting bass to soprano in the song she penned. She smelled the incense she'd recommended for the ritual, the drifting fragrance of sage and sweetgrass, the light perfume of violet, the darker note of cedar. She walked in a line—not a circle this time—with bodies before and behind her. This was not a *true* foreseeing of the event, but a total immersion that seemed real. That was what she told herself and others.

The procession of those celebrating the childlike self met and flowed, intersected with the other three lines, strode on and spread out. They stood close to the low jutting walls outlining the cathedral. Night had fallen with a gauzy haze over the night sky that let only the most brilliant stars shine through. The mass of voices fell silent and Chief Minister Younger spoke the spell she wrote . . .

As always she lost herself in the vision as she worked, lost track of time, only knew the experience of the ceremony.

She came to herself, dizzy yet buzzed with creative delight, when her mother touched her arm and quick static electricity snapped between them. Tiana's brain settled and she blinked at her mother.

"It's done," Quina Mugwort said softly. She gestured to the sheets of papyrus before them on the table. "You've written all four parts and the spellshield. Put the writestick down now, Tiana, love."

Without waiting for an answer or movement, Tiana's mother plucked the writestick from Tiana's fingers. Shaking her head, Quina said, "Your Flair always amazes me, and I can see this fulfills you. I don't know why you'd want to do anything else."

"Like be the High Priestess of Celta?" she said lightly, and found her mouth had stretched in a strange smile.

"Like that." Quina stood. "I'm going to get you a drink with cocoa so you'll sleep well and deeply for the short amount of time you have."

"I'd rather have a cocoa square."

"No. Go up to bed." But Tiana's mother stroked the papyrus. "Even your writing is beautiful when you do this, so easy to read." She met Tiana's eyes. "It will be a very special ritual. I'm proud of you."

"I couldn't have done it without you."

"No, it wouldn't have been right without me, but that is because I am a member of the Intersection of Hope and believe in the journey." She leaned down and kissed Tiana's forehead. "For your own faith, your rituals are deep and true."

*   *   *

The day had been crammed with events. Almost enough to distract Antenn from the kiss he'd shared with FirstLevel Priestess Tiana Mugwort. A *priestess*. The kiss itself hadn't been too carnal, but the effect on him had been. He'd barely gotten his body under control and his mind nailed to the project by the time he'd had to stand in front of a bunch of newssheets people and explain the cathedral. Then the others—the religious folk—had done a little group telepathy and decided that talking was less exciting than showing, and he'd been front and center with models of the structure. He'd had to do some quick translocation and it was a damn good thing that the briefing took place a few doors down from his office.

There'd been a lot of interest and questions since nothing like the cathedral had ever been built on Celta. He'd done a little spiel about old Earth.

In the end, everyone had seemed satisfied and the Chief Ministers had formally accepted his bid and signed the contract. The only anxiety he'd felt with regard to the project was from Tiana.

Antenn returned home to T'Blackthorn Residence late in the evening after the free melee at The Green Knight Fencing and Fighting Salon among his age group. For some reason—no, he was *not* thinking about the sexy priestess—he had a lot of energy to burn off. And after the fighting, he'd treated his friends to a round of drinks at a social club. While he discreetly rambled about the cathedral, he watched his friends—most of them Nobles. Even the Clovers who'd been commoners like him when they'd met were now Nobles.

None of them seemed like they'd have a problem with the Intersection of Hope building a large place of worship. Vinni T'Vine said nothing about security or threat. Relieved, Antenn took his business glider home, letting the vehicle proceed on automatic as he relaxed and muttered some minor pain spells that would ease the aches of being thrown around the floor of the fighting salon. He'd managed to be one of the last five to go down, a personal best.

Good day and evening all around.

He entered T'Blackthorn Residence by the door on the end of one wing. As the oldest and first child adopted by Mitchella and Straif, he got the preferred rooms closest to an outside exit. His suite itself was a little cramped and consisted only of a small bedroom and sitting room and a tiny waterfall room.

The minute he opened the door to his rooms, he saw his father on the stool by the drafting table looking at the holos of the cathedral.

Sixteen

*A*ntenn's stomach knotted, even as he <u>knew</u> he hadn't done anything that would have disappointed his parents and resulted in some fliggering father-son chat. Though he reckoned he'd never grow too old for that, and what a damn shame.

"Helluva project you've got here." Straif swiveled on the stool to face Antenn. "I heard congratulations are in order."

Antenn let his shoulders sag a bit. "Yeah. Got the approval and contract today. Started the excavation mages on it."

"Beautiful building," Straif said, tapping the table and bringing up the three-dimensional model.

"Yes, it is."

"You do me—us—proud. Not sure I've said that lately."

This was just getting weird. Antenn cleared his suddenly tight throat. "I appreciate hearing that."

Straif waved toward the holo. "You know if you need any help we can give, you've got it."

Slinging his jacket on a coat stand, Antenn said, "I'm not letting Mitchella decorate it. The Intersection of Hope Chief Ministers have already chosen an interior designer for the rugs and chandeliers and pews and stuff."

"Pews?"

"Wooden benches." The Celtic religion used huge pillows in a circle if sitting. The Intersection of Hope used benches lined up in squares.

"Odd." Straif stretched out his legs. "Rumor has it in the First-Families that you'll be wanting some folk to take part in a strange ritual to raise spellshields for the building."

"The cathedral," Antenn corrected.

"The cathedral," Straif said amiably. "I'll go, and your mother is avid to see the space."

"Thanks. Where do you think those rumors started?" Antenn dropped into a black leather chair.

Straif shrugged. "Dunno. Might be from the High Priest or Priestess?"

Antenn grunted.

"Might be from Vinni T'Vine."

Antenn grimaced.

"Might even be a round of whispering through the network of Residences. Don't know."

"All right."

"And speaking of Residences, that's why I'm here," Straif said.

Straightening from his lounge, Antenn said, "What? Does our Residence finally want a little upgrade, maybe in the paneling?" His mind whizzed with old ideas, reevaluated, revised.

"No. The Residence is perfectly happy with the renovations we did before I wed Mitchella." A slight smile curved Straif's lips. The man was remembering that time, years ago, and pleased. "I'm happy with the Residence as is, too."

"So, what does it want?"

"I was asked if I minded if you slept in the HouseHeart tonight," Straif said, in his I-am-a-FirstFamilies-Noble-GrandLord tone. "Naturally I replied I did not. So, the Residence and the House-Heart want you to spend the night there."

"Why?"

Straif raised a brow. "I was not informed." He rose, flicked a hand at Antenn. "I didn't ask. Just passing on the request."

A request Antenn couldn't refuse . . . not that he wanted to. "All right." He stood, moved close to Straif, and hugged the man. "Thanks." The guy smelled like the only father Antenn had known.

Claws of memory of *before*, when he'd been a child running with his older, crazy brother and a gang, raked Antenn, and he held the man close and harder for an instant before letting him go. Straif patted his shoulder, avoided meeting his eyes; maybe his were damp, too.

"See you at breakfast," Antenn said.

"Right."

With the loose and silent tread of a tracker, Straif left the room, and Antenn let his breath whoosh out. Memories were a bitch.

A quarter septhour later Antenn slipped through the secret door and descended the tight spiral stairs cut from the bedrock of the earth beneath T'Blackthorn Residence to the HouseHeart, chanting ancient Earthan Words of a special blessing. All of his adopted father's children had equal access to the HouseHeart.

And though Antenn *was* adopted by Mitchella and Straif Blackthorn, at their behest he kept his birth mother's name, Moss. Neither he nor his lost brother Shade had known their fathers. He remembered his mother, and men sleeping with her, and her death.

The day he'd been hauled before the SupremeJudge and Mitchella had taken him under her wing had been the very best of his life.

Remained the best day of his life.

The day his small cat had managed to expand his consciousness and become a Fam—something Pinky still didn't speak of—had been the next best.

Sort of sad that his best days were so far in the past. Well, becoming a Master Architect, being designated as FirstLevel—those had been great days, too, but he'd been aware of all the damn toil he'd put into making those grades. He'd been sweaty with nerves awaiting the results of the various tests.

Come to think about it, he'd been covered in cold sweat as a child when he'd been in JudgementGrove. And he'd been so worried about Pinky . . .

Huh, all the best days of his life had been accompanied by sweat.

Today the Chief Ministers had signed the contract with him to build the cathedral. That had happened just before the press conference. So, yes, it had been the most successful day for his career . . . so far. And not so much sweat, except for the morning when he'd awakened from a sweaty, sexy dream.

Just the word *sex* got him thinking of Tiana Mugwort. He both wanted to work with her and feared working with her, and the attraction between them.

He'd reached the HouseHeart door, also carved stone and nearly blindingly white, with intricate carvings of an infinite Celtic knot. He'd said the chant by rote and had finished the last Word, but stood and caught his breath and admired the door, as usual. Some distant Blackthorn had been Flaired with stone.

Antenn studied it. Would the Chief Minister like something like this for one of his doors? It echoed their culture, sure, but wasn't overtly religious. There had to be some ancient Earthan Celtic knotwork that showed an equal-armed cross. If the Chief Ministers didn't have such art, Antenn could make another visit to the starship *Nuada's Sword* to mine its history and art data.

He placed his hand on one of the portions of empty space in between the lines and received the typical small jolt. Because he didn't have any true Blackthorn blood in him. Nope, he was as common as . . . Moss. No knowledge of his MotherSire or MotherDam, or other antecedents. Never any father, FatherSire, or FatherDam in the picture.

When he shucked his clothes and folded them, he wondered, as he often did, whether his cuzes, of a minor Blackthorn line, felt such a shock or not. He knew his sisters and brothers did.

The door swung open silently and the voice of the HouseHeart, some wise-old-woman-type voice, said, "Welcome, Antenn Blackthorn-Moss."

With his first deep breath, he smelled the scents that meant *HouseHeart* to him . . . ingrained incense, a mixture of blackthorn blossoms, birch leaves, and St. Johnswort. Harmonious, powerful. The sound that pleased him most wasn't the crackling fire but the bubbling of the round tiered fountain.

This room was circular. He wasn't sure how many HouseHearts were, and as he'd experienced one after another, he'd been surprised how many were rectangular or square. The Celtan religion celebrating the Lady and the Lord tended to prefer round and curved and even digits. He wasn't quite sure what the Cross Folk preferred . . . one times four? An individual moving through four stages of life? A spirit divided into four parts?

Tiana Mugwort would know. Might even have a bit of that knowledge deeply embedded in her mind, since her mother was Cross Folk.

Greetyou, Antenn. You have much on your mind?

Uh-oh, please, not another lecture session. He cleared his throat, bowed to the ring of clear and polished cabochon quartz crystals. Some Residences could "see," and it was wise to believe all could. He thought this one could. "My apologies, T'Blackthorn House-Heart. My mind was elsewhere."

Your mind so often is, the sentient being, the core being of the Residence, said indulgently. It—she—preferred to speak with him telepathically. He thought she might also be monitoring his brainwaves somehow but hadn't been rude enough to ask. After all, he wasn't a real Blackthorn.

You are Blackthorn enough! Scolding, now. *Bonds of love are more important than bonds of blood.*

Yeah, that's what his parents always told him. He answered aloud. "Let's face it, bonds of blood can last longer. A man or woman with the Blackthorn blood in his or her veins will always be welcomed by you. And they might not get shocked by the door, either."

"What!" The woman's voice actually echoed through the room and pulsed against his eardrums, raised from mature calm.

He turned over his palm and showed his slightly red skin to the crystals.

I am appalled. I must check the door. Place your hand in the fountain and I will add a Healing balm to the water to cure your small burn.

"Thanks." He walked over and held both hands under the water . . . and realized that the effervescence he felt came near to equaling when he touched Tiana Mugwort. He continued, "And all of us adopted children would appreciate it if you did something to the door." This close to the fountain, the tiny spray of droplets from the fountain coated his skin and added to the natural humidity of the room, offset by the dry, hot air pumping from the fire. He glanced at it. Unlike the rounded oven of the restaurant and tearoom, Darjeeling's HouseHeart, this one was near bonfire proportions in a large square fireplace. Perhaps it made so much more impact because of the square against the curved wall, which continued to curve up into a domed ceiling. The room was half a sphere.

The thick grass represented the element of earth, lovely to swish through, nice enough to sleep on, but deep within himself, Antenn yearned for a moss floor. Somewhere. Somewhen. He could have made one in his rooms . . . but this was T'Blackthorn Residence.

There! It's done! said the HouseHeart with satisfaction. *My door will no longer harm any of my people, Blackthorn blood or no. And your burn is Healed.*

Antenn supposed so. He pulled his hands from the fountain and went toward the airshaft announced by a tinkle of small, melodious chimes. Obviously the early Blackthorns who'd built and modified the HouseHeart felt more in tune with the fire and water elements, even liked earth, but didn't care much for air. Still, the warm breeze dried his fingers. He found a spot an equal distance between the fireplace and the fountain and lowered himself onto the plush grass.

I heard the congratulations of the Family for you, Blackthorn son.
"Blackthorn-Moss," he corrected.

It is honorable that you do not forget your mother's surname. The older woman HouseHeart persona approved. So Straif T'Blackthorn had told Antenn when he'd wanted to ditch the name. No great honor attached to Moss. In fact, great dishonor did, with the deeds of his brother Nightshade. Not that Shade had gone by any other name than Shade.

And it was obvious where Straif T'Blackthorn had come by his standards. His father probably would have said the same thing, as taught by this being here . . . ad infinitum back to the first colonist who'd funded the starship and called himself Blackthorn.

Let me also say how proud I am of you.

He flushed. "Thank you."

We are VERY interested in having a cathedral built! She sounded more than interested, thrilled.

"We?" Was it thinking of itself as the HouseHeart *and* the Residence . . .

We, the FirstFamilies . . . and other . . . Residences, the Public-Library, the starship Nuada's Sword.

He shifted uneasily. "Oh, yeah, I'd heard that you all talk to each other now."

We have a circle.

He wasn't sure what that meant and repeated, "Oh."

You can call on all of us or any of us for information. I will be pleased to relay it to you.

"Thank you." He'd sort of thought he'd have a nice meditation session here during his allotted septhours in the HouseHeart today. Guess not.

Will you be building in a HouseHeart? she asked.

His throat got clogged again. "That's very confidential."

I will not tell anyone who is not directly involved.

Antenn figured that since he knew little about the entities involved, that promise left a few loopholes. This time he answered mentally, too. *Yes, a HouseHeart chamber has been designed.*

Good! T'Blackthorn HouseHeart sounded satisfied. *We will be pleased to welcome him to our ranks.*

"Him?" Antenn asked aloud.

Though two of their spirits are considered female, or gender-neutral, the Cross Folk tend to be male dominant, the HouseHeart stated.

"Ah." Antenn hadn't thought that through.

So the cathedral will likely take a male persona.

"Oh." The word slurred from his mouth. Tiredness began to press upon him.

You should slee—meditate, the HouseHeart said.

"Mmm." He heard a faint hissing, from the air vent? Or maybe it was an extra sound from the fire . . . or the fountain . . . and there was another, nice fragrance wafting around him.

I did want to speak to you of something, the HouseHeart said in an ultrasoothing, lilting tone. *Antenn Blackthorn-Moss, son of the Blackthorns by love.*

He smiled. "Mmmm?"

One time, long ago, you put a lockspell on your mind and emotions in regard to your HeartMate.

HeartMate. That word had always been fraught with pain, with danger, with fear. So why wasn't he feeling much now? Nothing much more than a sleepiness, a drifting into a trance.

You asked my help to make that spell, and I agreed, and we did it in a trance rather like the one you're falling into now. Her voice pattered.

I sort of re . . . re . . . r'mem . . . ber . . . that.

You are an adult now. Not a fearful boy. A man. We do not think it wise that you keep such a lockspell.

Several words and phrases there that should cause alarm, and didn't. And, like, who was this specific *we*?

He slipped into an odd space—mental, emotional, he didn't know. There was a sense of floating, of complete peace . . . nothing he had to do, nothing he had to worry about . . . though he knew who he was, and that the cathedral project could be all-consuming. Didn't matter.

And then, then, his body bowed as the sound of flesh hitting flesh came, *smack, smack, smack!* He felt nothing, but his mind reeled because what had been gray mist all around him now flashed bright colors of the spectrum, iridescent, holding huge worlds in each droplet.

The mist became a waterfall and cascaded through him until he didn't know if he was more than rushing water. He pooled and emotions whirled through him. Need.

Lust.

"It is done now. I will withdraw," said the HouseHeart.

And, yeah, he recognized her voice, was all the way back in his body, with skin sensitized so that he felt hot, moist atmosphere enveloping him. His face was wet.

The tiny brush of flowing air scraped at him, as if he had a virulent sunburn. More, his favorite muscle was rampant.

What the fliggering fligger had the HouseHeart *done* to him? Scowling, he thought back to its—her—words. Removed a lock on his emotions . . . the HeartMate thing he'd been so scared of experiencing at odd times in his daily life. He'd had more Flair than he'd known, triggered more and expanded more when he began living with Straif. His life had turned inside out and upside down and he'd struggled, especially during Passages—the dreamquests that freed his Flair.

After second Passage, which had been unusually lengthy and featured a long term of flashbacks, he'd asked for and been allowed the HeartMate block. It had been removed during his time of Third Passage, then reinstated.

Now, apparently the lock was gone and whatever HeartMate yearnings or connection might have withered was back.

He was sure he could have done without it—forever. HeartMates weren't for the likes of him, a stray who'd run with a gang Downwind. They were for Nobles or people who had exceptional Flair—no, just for Nobles. He didn't like the idea that some *force* would drop him in the lap of some woman and make him googly-eyed and love-daft over her.

Though, right now, contemplating his cock, he wouldn't mind having a woman dropped into his lap.

"Sleeeeppp." That was a hushed word in a genderless voice and it occurred to him that septhours might have passed, maybe even most of the night, while the HouseHeart was tinkering with his mind and his emotions and *himself.*

Another fragrance wafted through the chamber, and this he recognized as a sleep aid. He stretched a little and winced, even the soft grass chafed under him. Might as well let that bank of darkness flood him, take him.

The next thing he knew, he stood in the dark on a solid stone terrace overlooking what had been old Downwind. The FirstFamilies had moved in and rehabbed the place more than a decade and a half ago. No more shanties . . . most of the gangs had broken or had moved to the countryside and tried their hands at banditry and then were killed or dissolved . . .

He shifted his feet, stopped. That would have gotten a reprimand from his old fighting trainer. Hell, would have him singled out for practice and demonstration at The Green Knight now. But he felt great. He was naked, but that didn't bother him and the granite under his feet made him proud. This terrace had been built just last year, and he had designed it. Before him wound parks that looked lush and green even in the night, along with a few creeks that had been hidden by rickety structures. Now all was beautiful.

He descended the stone steps to the park and began walking on the path. The area was so very changed, yet he knew, in his very bones, where his mother's lean-to had been, where he'd grown up before she died. He'd never been back. Had shuddered to think of it.

He walked, more like floated, to the place, and found himself in the center of a small garden, hedges around him. Blackthorn hedges. Straif must have seen the place in Antenn's mind.

As he turned, his feet scuffed thick, lovely moss, and the scent of rich earth and thick greenery came. The inner space wasn't large, four meters at the most, and in the center stood a sundial on a pedestal. Pretty.

"It's lovely," said a woman's voice behind him, and before he could turn, she wrapped her arms around him and he stiffened, and flushed. She was naked, too. Her breasts flattened against him.

"I've wondered where you were. And it's here. But I don't know where here is." Her voice was husky, the essence of woman, any woman, all women.

But he knew who she was. His HeartMate.

Seventeen

He couldn't seem to care that his HeartMate had found him. Probably because she'd moved a little and her hand had closed around his shaft.

Fabulous.

His eyes had closed, and his mouth had opened. He'd thought he was going to say something, but all the words had fallen out of his head and he only breathed harshly and rapidly.

"Lie down with me," she whispered, and then he did, atop soft moss cool beneath his back and his butt. She sat beside him, a fascinating shadow, and he thought of blinking to bring her into focus, but . . . didn't want to.

Her hands brushed his hair away from his face, trailed over his forehead, each of his features, and he began to tremble. He *knew* what she wanted, breathed that knowledge in with her scent. She wanted to touch him, head to toe.

At least.

Yes, he trembled.

Her fingers traced his brows, stroked his cheeks again, explored the angle of his jaw, feathered down his neck to the hollow there. Then she swept her hands along the curve of his collarbone, and for the first time in his life he thought of *himself* as a structure, bone and tendons, muscles and skin, the container for his thoughts, his emotions, all that he considered his self. His soul.

But she'd put her hands around the curve of his right shoulder, felt it, kneaded his biceps, and a groan cracked from him.

"Ah, lover," she said, leaning forward and kissing his mouth, her soft lips sinking against his own that felt plush, too. Swollen from need. All of him throbbed with need.

She nibbled at the edge of his mouth, then kissed under his ear, tasted his jaw, his neck. She shifted and lay beside him. He thought she'd propped herself on one elbow, but his gaze had fixed to the magnificent spangles of the stars.

Her hand went to his chest, teased his light hair, measured the breadth of his torso, angled downward to his hip, to his thigh.

He dug for and found one word only. "Please."

"Yes. I will please myself, and I will please you," she said, and touched him. One long stroke and he was gone, shattered, thrown to the stars, sinking into the earth, floating away in the air.

But when his wits coalesced again, he found her lying atop him. His first deep breath moved her breasts against him, her soft stomach against his, and his sex stirred again. His hands went to the globes of her butt, muscle covered with smooth skin, perfect texture against his palms.

Her head lay against his shoulder and her legs intertwined with his, though her feet . . . all of her . . . wasn't as long, as tall as he. His muzzy mind couldn't judge how tall she might be if they stood together, though when she'd been behind him, her chin hadn't reached his shoulder, and he wasn't a tall man.

His breath had barely begun to ease, his shaft to harden, when she moved. Now she lifted her head and he felt her hair skim across his skin, caressing him in a completely different way than her mouth and her fingers. Another moan tore from him and evaporated into the air like a sigh.

She slipped downward and his hands fell away from her derriere, and then her tongue touched his right nipple, licked it, and it beaded and he panted, tried to raise his right hand but had no strength. The woman was over him, shifting along him, warm, supple, graceful, overloading him with a barrage of sensations. Under him was soft and cradling moss. He couldn't move.

Then she feathered kisses to his other nipple and he heated; fire shivered down his nerves and he shuddered but could do nothing but experience.

Her mouth vibrated against his skin as she spoke or chanted or sang, and he felt the unknown words sink deep into him, coat the inside of his bones. Her lips caressed, her tongue tasted, and he *ached* waiting for her to get to his shaft.

He reached and his arms worked and his hands closed and his fingers caught her hair that slid silkily across his palms and escaped. His legs widened and she knelt between them and touched his straining cock again and he jackknifed, caught her under her arms, drew her up until her damp sex slid along him. Changing his grip to her hips, he lifted and she moved with him and then she was atop him and then he was *in*!

Exquisite paradise. Nothing, nothing, nothing in his life had been as good as this. She sheathed him warmly, wetly, tightly.

Now he went blind. Their joining encompassed his world.

They rocked together. Rose and fell. Slow, but the pulse of his blood beat in his ears, through him, through *her* setting the rhythm of their mating. Until they spun together outside the world, outside time. Only the joining necessary.

Faster. Harder. *Now!*

Sensation swamped him and he drowned in it, in her scent and her crooning and her enveloping self, sex and arms and throbbing emotions.

The brightly colored starbursts behind his eyelids vanished and the blackness took him.

*E*ons later Antenn awoke, head pounding. *"Wha—? What's that?"* His dry lips formed the sounds, and they emerged as questions.

The HouseHeart said, "It is time for you to prepare for work."
And those sounds made sense, too, and the pounding turned out to
be a pattern of melodious, soft chimes. He sat up and it felt like the
grass under him abraded his skin. Pressing his fingers to his eyes, he
yelped.

What is wrong, Antenn? asked the HouseHeart.

"My skin—I dunno—*all* of me feels scoured or like I have a
really deep sunburn."

What was probably a small hum from the HouseHeart buzzed
in his ears like ten thousand bees. He clapped his hands over his
ears, and that had a cry ripping from his throat.

"Hmm," the older-woman voice said.

"Too loud!" he shouted, but it was the barest whisper.

*I believe that removing the emotional lock has left all your
senses extremely, ah, sensitive.*

"Yeah, got that," Antenn answered hoarsely. He didn't want to
move. He felt just as bad as before . . . he fell into the sexy dream.
Well, he supposed his inner self, his nonphysical self felt pretty
damn good, but his body . . .

Let us consider our options, the HouseHeart said.

"*Our* options?" Antenn snapped.

I will help you if you will let me, son of the Blackthorns.

He began to grit his teeth, stopped that in a hurry. Fliggering
fligger, even his *teeth* hurt.

You can teleport to a HealingHall, the HouseHeart stated.

"Naked?"

They're Healers, Antenn.

"No."

Slowly, carefully, he stood, stretching each muscle millimeter by
millimeter. One step on a raw foot and pain-sweat drenched his scalp.

*Please, wait. I was not aware that this problem could occur. I
am consulting with other sources.*

"All right." Antenn looked at the fountain, wished it were big
enough for him to submerge himself in it. As it was, he figured a

droplet hitting his skin would bring him to his knees, which would end him entirely.

We have decided to try a combination of things, the HouseHeart stated, an odd resonance to its voice as if it were not a single being.

"Yeah?"

You can clothe yourself in illusion—

Antenn closed his eyes. It didn't hurt. In fact, he felt better with his eyes shut; everything had been too bright. "No. Absolutely not. I am not walking around naked."

Ah. We can have your mother prepare a very good potion that should ease your sensitivity.

"Take it away?" He perked up.

Not exactly. It seems to us that the most problematic of your senses is touch—your skin. The potion can, ah, adjust your sight, hearing, smell, and taste, but your skin will remain as if you have that bad sunburn.

"Great."

It should wear off during the day.

"I hear you. And what am I supposed to wear?"

Your mother is also taking care of that.

"Well, if anyone knows clothes and fabrics, it's Mitchella."

She will be down shortly.

"All right."

We suggest that along with the potion, you subsist on liquids until the sensitivity fades.

"Wonderful."

We are sorry this happened to you; however, we would like to point out that had you not had the emotional lock on so long, the effects of its removal would not have been so dire.

Nerving himself, he said a short after-sex cleansing spell that every gentleman who cared about himself and his partner knew. By the time it was done he was curled over with hands braced on his knees, head down.

A perfunctory knock and his mother walked in. She had some

opaque tissue-thin fabric draped over one arm, and in her other hand she carried a tall tube of murky brown liquid.

"Drink this first."

He took it and heroically swallowed the nasty stuff and threw the tube in the reconstructor. Watched narrowly as his mother snapped the sparkly white film of cloth out and saw it was some lame, all-encompassing robe.

"Put this on," she said.

With a pained glance, he shook his head and she gave him that stern-mother I-am-not-going-to-accept-refusal look. "It is a very expensive robe. You *will* wear it."

He opened his mouth to continue to disagree and she stabbed a finger at him and he shut it.

"The robe is imbued with several spells." Now she raised that perfectly manicured index finger. "First, once the robe is on, though the fabric is light and breathable, barely touching the skin, it will *look* like whatever you want it to. As long as you aren't in the company of a null who kills spells, *no one* will sense that it is any different." Another finger went up. "Second, if necessary, it has a slight no-contact spell, and I have started that. No one will get close to you. Not close enough to touch you, which is what you want, right?"

"Yes, Mitchella."

She nodded. "You might also want some sort of an additional spellshield for backup, but I don't have the Flair for that. I do have this garment." She held it out.

He took it, shrugged it over his head, and let it settle, without too much pain, over his body. It felt a little like a dressing gown.

"Now visualize what you were going to wear today."

Even though she'd taught him about dressing professionally, he rarely decided what to wear until he looked in his closet after his morning waterfall. Today would probably be meetings with his clients, so that was preeminent on how he needed to present himself. Probably a talk with Tiana Mugwort.

The trenches for the foundation had gone in yesterday, and he'd

supervised that, but he'd need another go-ahead from the Chief
Ministers to actually begin the real building of structure . . . the
final cutting of the massive stone blocks from the quarry and translocating them to the site. He wasn't sure how quickly they'd authorize that, so he wouldn't dress for fieldwork today. Despite
everything Mitchella said, he wasn't sure he'd trust the dressing
gown to the elements sweeping across the plateau.

"Antenn?" she prompted.

So he visualized not his best tunic and trous, but one step down—
simple and brown and with embroidery on his cuffs that showed the
plants that gave him his name: blackthorn leaves and moss clumps.

Mitchella said, "At full strength, the no-contact spell should last a
good half day, then will gradually diminish. The cloth-transformation
spell will last a full month."

He looked down at himself and though he *felt* a dressing gown,
he saw boot liners, trous, and tunic. He pinched the fabric on the
sleeve and his fingers touched good-quality cloth. Different on the
inside than the outside. He shrugged. That was Flair for you.

With an intricate spell verse, he conjured up a spellshield. He'd
used that one in grovestudy when he didn't want to fight bullies
who insulted him with his brother's crimes. It had been a while
since he'd summoned it, but it came quickly and was solid.

Mitchella walked around him. "Looks good. Otherwise, how
do you feel?"

The brightness of the light, of all the colors of the room, of his
mother's hair, had faded to normal. She was speaking in a low voice
but not a whisper, and the sound didn't spear his eardrums.

"Well enough."

She nodded. "That's fine." She stepped closer, stopped and made
a face, then retreated a pace. "The garment works, but I wanted to
give you a hug."

He put on his most disappointed face but flinched inwardly.
"Tonight, Mitchella."

Air-kissing, she said, "Yes. I'll expect you for dinner."

"I'll be here."

"And you can tell us what your clients and the High Priest and Priestess want from us with regard to the ritual in more detail."

"Sure. Thanks."

"You're welcome." She opened the door and glanced over her shoulder. "Blessed be."

"Blessed be," he replied.

She shut the door and the HouseHeart said, "There is an incoming scry from the Chief Ministers of the Intersection of Hope. They would like you to meet them at the building site in a septhour." The no-time against the wall opened. "You can eat breakfast here, first."

A rough tongue licking her cheek—not *the tongue of her lover, which* she hadn't tasted since she'd been more interested in other things— dragged Tiana from sleep and she stared into Felonerb's green eyes. His breath wasn't nearly as bad this morning. Not great, but . . . bearable. Or maybe she was just getting used to it.

Still, she'd rather linger on the dream sex than whatever her Fam wanted to say.

He smiled his ingratiating smile. *High Priestess called ME!*

She sat up and rubbed the back of her neck. Spring-night chill remained in the room, but her clothes stuck a little to her body . . . from love perspiration. She must have finally connected with her HeartMate . . .

Holy Lady wants to see the ritual before you give it to other holy guys.

Eighteen

Of course the High Priestess wanted to see the ritual before Tiana gave it to the Chief Ministers. Tiana rubbed her scalp, her head. Luckily it didn't seem like another migraine threatened.

She switched her thoughts back into regular channels of work and superiors. Why hadn't she anticipated that the High Priestess would want to see the ritual? Because Tiana doubted the woman knew much at all about Intersection of Hope rituals . . . except what D'Sandalwood brushed up on in the last few days.

Irritation bloomed. Tiana and her mother had worked hard on this ritual, and both agreed it was good. Now she had to run it by D'Sandalwood? Adding another stress-element to the day, and cutting short any breakfast time Tiana might have squeezed in.

But the High Priestess was her boss. She huffed out a frustrated breath, flicked the fingers of her hands to rid herself of the negative energy. She was tired, and, yes, she should have anticipated this. If she had, she wouldn't have been caught by surprise.

Felonerb rubbed against her side and purred. She petted him. His fur felt better after even one day of care. "Thank you for waking me up."

You are welcome. He sat and lifted his muzzle so she could scratch under his chin, so she did. *Holy Lady wants you at Temple quick.*

Tiana sighed, knowing another Whirlwind cleansing and dressing spell was in her future, and teleportation to the Temple. Not one minute to think of other things, like meeting her HeartMate in a sex dream. "BalmHeal Residence, will you lower your shields so I can teleport from my sitting room to GreatCircle Temple, please?"

"Yes," he grumbled with creaking wood. "It's good that you are moving out. Rush, rush, rush. Do this, Residence. Do that."

Tiana pressed her lips together to stop a comment that would escalate the annoyance of them both. "I will be back sometime today, to pack some of my belongings and move them to the Turquoise House." She hoped.

"I can pack your clothing," Tiana's mother said from the door. She must have knocked, but Tiana hadn't heard her. After the long night and little sleep, Quina looked a whole lot better than Tiana felt.

"Thank you," Tiana said.

Her sister showed up behind her mother. "If you can spare a couple of minutes to show me what you want, Garrett and I will take some boxes into town for you and leave them at the Turquoise House. I heard that you'll be gone for a couple of months, at least."

"That's right."

"How are you feeling?" both of them asked together, love emanating from them.

"I'm fine. I drank an additional migraine potion at TQ's yesterday." She smiled at her sister. "You stocked the medicines?"

"I did, yes."

"We'll make sure you have replacements, too," Quina said.

"What time is it?" Tiana asked, slipping from the bed.

"About an hour and a half before WorkBell."

Holy Lady said come as soon as possible. Felonerb licked his front paw and smoothed it over his ear. *I will stay and supervise the packing.*

"Don't go near my good work robes," Tiana said. She closed her eyes, summoned her energy. "Whirlwind Spell standard professional tunic and trous." Keeping the image in her mind, she initiated the spell and suffered through it, dry cleansing that never felt as good as a bath and made her squeak as it removed any traces of the dream loving.

Then she stood, panting and staring at her relatives. Artemisia was boxing up her favorite little items from the top of her bureau. "Will you want your pillow?" her sister asked.

"I don't think so. TQ will have new ones."

Artemisia smiled. "He'll have pretty much new everything. Last time I was there he'd even moved some walls around."

"New will be nice," Tiana said, lifting down the drawing on the wall. "I want this with me."

"That is *my* frame," the Residence said.

"All right, I will pay you for it," she said stiffly.

A creaky grumble. "You may have it. But it is made of wood from one of *my* Earthan trees."

The Residence considered the whole estate his, though he couldn't monitor anything outside his walls.

"I will treasure the frame," Tiana soothed, taking time for the oldster she didn't think she had. "And I'm sure the Turquoise House will, too." Two breaths and she made an impatient gesture. "I have to go."

She was enveloped in soft hugs from her mother and sister. Her mother kissed her hair. "The ritual is wonderful. Have no doubt about that."

"I don't," Tiana said, and it wasn't exactly a fib. When she wrote rituals in a Flair trance, they were usually special. "I must get my materials." She went to her desk in her sitting room. Thank the Lady and Lord she'd made six clean copies of the rite. Four for the ministers, one for herself, and one for Antenn Blackthorn-Moss. She hesitated, then put the two most important books and all her drafts into a large portfolio, slipped all but one of the copies inside. Best to have them in case she had to revise. She raised a hand to her mother and sister, then teleported away to the pad in the atrium outside D'Sandalwood's chambers at GreatCircle Temple.

The spellglobes in the small room were night-dim and no one sat at the reception desk.

Please come in, the High Priestess sent to Tiana's mind. *I am in my inner office.*

Not the less formal sitting room. Composing herself, Tiana walked into the suite and saw the High Priestess behind her large but elegantly carved desk. Tiana placed the rite on the table and stood until D'Sandalwood gestured to a chair.

The High Priestess scanned the ritual, brow wrinkling. At the end, she looked up. "This is a very basic ceremony, and, ah, slightly stranger than those I've perused in our archives."

"My mother and I discussed the whole matter and created a rite that harks back to the first celebrations of the Intersection of Hope faith, reflects its very roots." She met the High Priestess's gaze. "I think that anyone who believes in the Lady and the Lord should also be able to celebrate this rite with those of the Intersection of Hope . . . no matter that the chants are to four instead of two, and that there is a specific procession and the final shape is a square instead of a circle."

D'Sandalwood inclined her head. "Yes, it will be slightly uncomfortable for we who worship the Lady and Lord, the Lord and Lady, but . . . seems invigorating." She set the papyrus aside. "Neither my HeartMate nor I should have problems with this, and the chants and responses are easily learned."

Easily learned for someone who memorized such things all the time. Tiana fully expected that any FirstFamily Nobles who showed up, such as T'Blackthorn and D'Blackthorn, might have trouble recalling the odd words, the times to occasionally bow, turn in another direction, and bow again, the special gestures.

D'Sandalwood said, "I congratulate you on a job well done."

"Thank you, High Priestess."

There was a pause and the woman tapped her forefinger on the papyrus, staring past Tiana. "After the joint press conference yesterday, I was surprised to be contacted by some council members. Some of those involved in the Traditionalist Stance movement."

More silence, and she didn't elaborate who of which council had scried her—the Commoner Council, NobleCouncil, or FirstFamilies Council.

Shaking her head, D'Sandalwood said, "They had . . . concerns . . . about the Intersection of Hope building this cathedral. Rather baffling." Her brows went up. "And actually asked whether I and T'Sandalwood truly approved." She sounded less than calm when she reported this, and her lips thinned.

Her gaze met Tiana's. "We have asked you to keep us apprised of the project." The High Priestess hesitated. "Though we don't anticipate any trouble, we do want you to report any problems, no matter how slight, with regard to this matter. And understand that you can count on our support."

"Yes, High Priestess."

Again the woman's gaze swept the short and simple ritual once more. "I think this is very well done."

"Thank you."

D'Sandalwood waved a hand. "Go see to your chambers here and your new quarters at the Turquoise House. I noticed that they are not yet furnished and ready."

Tiana had barely had time to do anything other than what she'd accomplished. She dipped her head and withdrew.

She hurried to her two rooms and began to arrange the items in her office, set up her simple desk and a plain but beautifully thin china old-fashioned scry bowl. She poured bespelled water into the Flaired-tech bowl and ran her finger around the rim to start the working, and both the bowl and her perscry pebble sounded an incoming call.

Chief Minister Custos's face beamed at her when she answered. "Greetyou, Tiana."

"Greetyou, Chief Minister Custos."

"We would like you to meet the four of us at the site of our cathedral so we can read and block out the ritual you wrote."

"My mother and I wrote," Tiana corrected, not falling into the trap. "I would not presume to create a ceremony for you without her help." And if she'd thought she could yesterday morning, this morning she knew the folly of that. "We think you will be pleased."

"Will SecondLevel Healer Quina Mugwort also be joining us?" His brows arched.

"Not today, she has other duties."

He dipped his head. "We will welcome her whenever she returns to share celebration with us."

"Thank you, I will let her know that and fervently hope that she will join you in the future."

"We would especially like her to take part in the ritual she crafted," Custos said.

"I will do my very best to persuade her."

"And your father and sister and brother-in-law?" Custos continued smoothly.

"I cannot speak for them, but I am hopeful they will be present." Artemisia would come just because she was Artemisia, a kind soul. Garrett would come because he was endlessly curious about everything.

Someone called to Custos, and Tiana couldn't make out the words. "We'll see you shortly," he said.

"I'll be right there. I'm taking a Temple glider," Tiana said, not even having to check with the High Priestess to know one would be awaiting her.

This time she enjoyed the luxury alone and actually missed her irreverent Fam, though she did notice that when the vehicle passed through the southern gates of Druida City, the guards stared at her with considering expressions.

Everyone, now, knew that a big spiritual structure was being built on the open area of the plateau. A tingle settled between her shoulders. She wasn't a warrior, or a detective, but she was a counselor and when she got that tingle, it meant trouble. Now that she thought about it, that tingle had been with her for the last couple of days and had begun again when she'd listened to the High Priestess this morning.

And when she stepped from the glider to see the four Chief Min-

isters and Antenn Blackthorn-Moss, it felt a lot like the first morning she'd been there, including the chill wind . . . and then she
understood that the wind was warmer, but the atmosphere, a warning carried on the wind, invisible, to her ears, to herself, contained
a vibration of wariness, and danger. More than just the wind, a tiny
drift of a smoky smell made her nose twitch.

Her eyes widened when she saw the deep trenches that outlined
where the walls of the cathedral would go.

The ministers and Antenn gathered around her and she handed
out the papyrus with the ritual, kept her last-messy-draft herself.

Grumbles came from Foreman and she tensed, but the rest had
good comments, though she sensed there would be some discussion
about the choice of chants and spells and incense. She hadn't
included the mixture with pylor.

"Let's try this out," Custos said.

"It's going to take a septhour!" Younger protested.

"The sooner we begin, the sooner we end."

Younger wiggled his shoulders. "I don't know some of the chants."

All the other ministers stared at him. Elderstone looked appalled.
"You should have them memorized."

Tiana whipped out the chant book she'd used from her portfolio
and handed it to him.

"Thanks."

"To our positions, Excellencies," ordered Custos.

As the Chief Ministers went to their stations outside each end of
the arms of the cross, she and Antenn were left in the center. The
architect held himself a little stiffly, as if he'd been injured and not
quite Healed. A spellshield surrounded him. "What's wrong?" she
asked. "Are you hurt?"

"Nothing's wrong," he said. His jaw flexed.

She knew he lied.

The ministers read, and walked, and chanted through the ceremony, and Tiana caught her breath at the solemn beauty of it. Simple.
Awesome. Standing here, it seemed as if she could *see* the inside of the
building form around her, towering columns, beautiful stone floors,

incredible stained-glass windows . . . and then she realized she was picking up the images from Antenn's mind as he visualized the rite taking place in the finished cathedral.

When the men formed their square in the center of the cross—the intersection—she caught Antenn's eyes and hummed along with the chant and responses. From the ministers' gazes, she thought that they, too, were swept up in Antenn's vision.

With a last Word that echoed on the wind, sped away from the four quarters to the rest of the world, the ministers fell silent, the illusion of the building thinned to nothingness.

Foreman clapped his hands. "Good." He smiled at her. "Excellent. I don't think it needs any tweaking. Your mother and you are to be commended."

Tiana curtseyed. "Thank you."

Custos checked with the others, then turned to her and Antenn. "Before we leave, we wish to give you something," Custos said. Each of the men reached into a pocket of his tunic, then handed her thick papyrus envelopes sealed by his ring. One of the missives had her name inscribed on it in fancy handwriting; two others were addressed to High Priestess GrandLady D'Sandalwood and High Priest GrandLord T'Sandalwood.

Chief Minister Foreman stared at her with a hard gaze. "Formal invitations to the ritual, though we're still discussing the exact day and time, but soon." As he said that, she felt an irritation rise in the ministers and knew the discussion might have been, or was, heated. "We wish you to hand-deliver these."

Tiana nodded. She'd hoped to translocate them to the proper desks and head straight from the plateau to TQ to move in. Plush glider or not, her energy and Flair were being depleted by this job, and she was ready to rest a little and settle into her temporary home.

"Let's be off." Foreman moved to a spot that Tiana recalled from the vision would be a small teleportation area for staff and held out his large, workman hands to the others. They arranged themselves around him and linked hands.

Just before they teleported away, an inner *push* forced Tiana to say something. "I . . . I . . ." She didn't know whom they'd hired to do the spellshields, figured it wouldn't be the best since that was a FirstFamily woman . . . and felt it *should* be the best. They all stared at her and she ended up saying, "We need to make sure all is safe."

Only the architect stiffened with offense, which was good, the others just nodded or shrugged and disappeared.

With a scowl, Antenn turned to her, opened his mouth, shut it, and gestured shortly to her glider. "I teleported here and would appreciate a ride back to the Temple with you. I can get to my office from there."

She didn't know how much Flair it took to keep up his unusual aura spell but agreed. During the trip, he kept his distance in the backseat of the glider. He didn't say anything, but she believed he was thinking hard . . . and simmering.

The glider swept through the Temple grounds and up to the northern portico. She and Antenn exited.

Still scowling, he asked, "Just what do you think you were doing back there?" He waved in the direction of the cathedral. "Are you trying to delay or kill this project?"

Nineteen

*S*tepping aside as the glider cruised away to the garage, Tiana turned toward Antenn. "What I said wasn't that bad."

"No, but there's a pattern of negativity on your part."

She flung her arms wide. "I've done everything I've been asked. I took the job as liaison, I've *been* a good liaison. I worked with my mother—all night—to create the ritual I gave to the Chief Ministers this morning. I've moved out of my own home to live here where I'll be 'more available.'" She ended with enough bitterness in her tone to make her eyes widen.

"You've done what you were asked," he repeated flatly, his expression closed. "But only what you were asked. Admit it, your superiors pressured you into this job. You didn't—don't want it."

"I *do*! Wasn't *I* the one to offer a solution to that problem yesterday morning?" Waving her hands, she said, "There's just something in the air."

He seemed to vibrate with tension. "Building this cathedral is a priority for me. *The* priority, the most important thing in my life right now. It's a big commission and a boost to my career, but more, the cathedral will stand long after I'm gone. Designing this shows that I am a contributing member of our society—" He stopped, took in a breath, but his darkened gaze remained fixed on hers. "The Chief Ministers yearn for this, as do the members of their church. The High Priest and Priestess want this." He opened and closed his hands. "I want this."

She squared her shoulders, lifted her chin, and spoke a few revealing truths of her own. "My goals aren't that different from your own," she said. "You are judged by your brother's murderous reputation. I am judged for my mother's religion—a religion that was also supposedly associated with the murderous. I want to be judged by my own actions."

"You're wrong."

"I beg your pardon?"

"And don't use that freezing voice on me." He pointed at her, rudely. "Our situations aren't the same. My brother *was* murderous. He killed. He died. Your Family were only accused of being murderous, and weren't in fact." He paused, stepped back to lean against one of the fluted stone pillars of the portico, and crossed his arms. "And what are you going to do about it?"

Her mouth fell open. "What?"

"You've let that fligger GraceLord T'Equisetum get away with ruining your Family. For years. Shouldn't you be doing something more active?"

She'd planned on it . . . once. Even though her father hadn't wanted to press the issue, and no one else in the Family seemed to care once they'd been offered the custodianship of the secret sanctuary. What had happened? Had she accepted what the man had done?

Her breathing went unsteady. "What am I going to do about it?" she repeated softly, more to herself than him. "No, I haven't accepted what he did to my Family. That he influenced the Noble-Council to condemn us, take our title and wealth and estates away." She whispered under her breath, "That he had someone rile up a mob against us."

His eyes narrowed and she didn't know if he'd heard that or not. In a stronger tone, she said, "But I've put it behind me." She rubbed her temples, met his hard gaze "Revenge is not something a priest-ess is supposed to yearn for."

"What about justice?"

Chin jutting, she answered him. "Yes, I want justice. But my father, who was a judge, didn't want to go after it . . . there were reasons . . ." Each and every one of her Family had promised not to reveal the location of FirstGrove and the BalmHeal Residence, and it they'd been questioned, *where* they were staying would have been asked and they couldn't answer without breaking a vow. Nor had they wanted Lord T'Equisetum's hatred following them to Balm-Heal, endangering the special place.

"I had my career to think of," she said, instead. She'd started with the Temple that same year, been accepted into the charity pro-gram and moved into a full apprenticeship after she'd proven herself.

Antenn rolled a shoulder. "Um-hmm."

Standing straighter, she said, "I put it behind me, only wanting to prove—"

"That you were as good as everyone else. Yeah, that we have in common."

Did his lip curl slightly? She was trained to read nuances; was he disgusted at the *events* that had shaped him? Or at himself? Or *her*?

She couldn't help it, she felt that expression was aimed at her. That he judged her inaction.

"We were firebombed out of our home! We—I—had to recover." Just as she was being given too little time, now, to recover from all the recent changes in her life.

He gave her a crooked smile. "Now there we have something in common."

She gasped. "You were firebombed!"

"That's right."

Goggling, she backed up to a bench flanking one side of the double doors and let her knees fold under her, dropping her with a little jolt to the marble seat.

He pushed away from the pillar and crossed to stand in front of her. His smile had faded to lips set in a compressed line, his brows angled low, and his whole aspect seemed darker. "How'd you get out in time?"

"I . . ." She gasped again, couldn't seem to catch her breath, as fog clouded her mind. Another person had lived through what she'd gone through! Someone not her Family who could understand the crash of glass, the whoosh of fire, the horror, the fear, the—

He hunkered down in front of her, stretched out his hands, and then dropped them. "Sorry. Forget about the question."

Her brain gave her one word and her lips formed it. "You?"

"Years before you, when I was a kid, younger than you. We . . . Pinky my Fam, me, and my cuz Trif Clover, retreated to a corner of a room. I curled around Pinky, and Trif—she was bigger than me then—covered me. Straif T'Blackthorn and T'Ash saved me."

"Trif Clover. Circles and circles," Tiana whispered.

"What?"

"She was kidnapped by the Black Magic Cult, the cult *they* said my mother and other Intersection of Hope members belonged to."

He shook his head in a rueful manner, stood, then sat beside her. "Yeah, odd how life circles around."

Tiana took a shuddering breath and shook her head. "I can't forget about your question. You're right. We should have demanded justice. *I* can demand justice."

"Can you prove GraceLord T'Equisetum riled up the mob against you?"

He'd heard her!

Her scalp had heated with all this thinking. Her heart quivered in her chest with all the feeling. She lifted her hair from her neck, sifted her fingers through it. "I don't know. I think . . . I'm sure T'Equisetum made speeches in the NobleCouncil against us, even went down to the Commoner Council to vilify us."

"Because pylor, the paralytic drug that was used against the Black Magic Cult victims, was found on your premises."

She couldn't read his tone, either. Something about this man skewed all of her senses. She said, "Incense with pylor was found in our house, yes. You've seen yourself that such incense is a part of

Intersection of Hope rituals, and not in any amount that would hurt a person. How would a minister do his job if he was paralyzed? And at that time, pylor was an ingredient in many incense sticks that most people had in their homes."

"So the case that you were part of the Black Magic Cult was—"

"Never made. We, my mother, was never charged, but the ruin was done all the same."

He cocked his head. "Why?"

She chuffed a breath, glared. "Because my father is—was—a judge, and my mother was—is—a SecondLevel Healer. Both professions demand a pristine reputation."

"You think?"

"Yes. I know."

Again he shrugged. "Rather like a priestess. Yet here you are."

She'd sat up straight and tense and hadn't even realized that had happened, had lost the sense of her body, and not in a good way as in a meditative trance. "You're right."

"And you can still fight for justice. If you want. I can't. I can't even fight for mercy for my lost brother." A short, jagged gesture. "He's dead. His memory is defiled by his angry deeds, his murders."

Her jaw set. "Yes, I can try to get the estate back . . ." She blinked away stinging tears. "We didn't have a Residence, and we teleported away as soon as we could, and those watching through the windows saw us, so they left the place alone." She gulped. "I haven't been to the house for years." Swallowing, she continued. "I think GraceLord T'Equisetum had plans for it to be given to a . . . friend . . . of his."

"An ally."

"Yes."

"Huh." He stared off in the distance a moment as she gathered herself to turn over the idea of how to go about seeking justice at this late date.

Then, slowly, he said, "And if you follow up on what you just said, getting justice against him for his past hurt of you and your Family . . ." His breath went out; he paused, inhaled, and said,

"You could occupy T'Equisetum on another front than the cathedral, distract him from our project."

"What?"

"He's a member of the Traditionalist Stance movement, and already murmuring to his friends about the cathedral. Started immediately after the press conference. Straif has heard that. Equisetum might even call his own press conference."

Shock rattled through her. "Your cathedral. You did say it was your highest priority."

"I think I just laid that out." He frowned. "Not my cathedral. *The* cathedral." He shrugged a shoulder. "I told you it was my priority."

"But my bringing up old wrongs by GraceLord T'Equisetum would distract him."

"Probably." Antenn shrugged. "But it would be good for you, too."

She vibrated with rage. "You're using me for your own ends." She found that her hands trembled, so she stuck them in her sleeves and sank into her balance, grounding herself.

"What! No." He appeared confused. "Not really."

"No? Or not really?"

At that moment Lucida Gerania strolled up, glanced at them. Her lips curved in a half smile, her brows lifted. "Problems?" she purred.

Spine straight, Tiana said, "The Temple teaches us to be serene." She managed not to spit it out, knew that under her flash of rage was a deep hurt, a wound that shouldn't be so deep but was. And now here was her rival to see her struggle with her temper, but she ignored Lucida though anyone with training would feel the vibrations of her outrage. Since Antenn scowled, she thought he might, too. Her fingers cupped her opposite elbows too hard and she loosened her grip, her mind already sliding into a mantra to settle down . . .

"The Temple also teaches us to let the Lord and Lady deal with those who have harmed us . . . because they *will* be dealt with, and to focus on the now and the present." She turned to Lucida, modulated her voice. "Isn't that so, FirstLevel Priestess?"

Lucida flushed a little and stood straighter herself, the smile wiped from her face as if embarrassed to be caught enjoying Tiana's discomfort. She inclined her head. "Yes."

Slowly Tiana inclined her head to Antenn. "I must deliver the envelopes. I'll see you later."

Much later, as *later* as she could humanly manage. She walked away from him, through the doors, and didn't look back.

*A*s *she finally put the items she had in her office to rights, with some* help from her in-Temple friends, she brooded until she made a decision.

The architect had angered her, but his words were the truth. It had been easier for her just to live as an example, be passive, than to work to clear her Family's name. Though she also recognized another truth: the Priests and Priestesses of the Celtic religion on this planet should be as whole and stable as possible, so they could counsel others. And she'd aimed for that.

But she *did* have a pocket of inner fury, one she'd thought she'd worked through and drained off during the years but had really just tamped down . . . Well, she *must* have drained some of it off, but unfortunately she found too much anger remaining.

Because there had been no justice.

Because the person who'd caused her Family harm had not, in turn, been punished. And she realized that she wanted her society to punish him for his greed, his envy, his hubris.

Because GraceLord T'Equisetum had never said he regretted his actions . . . Well, he couldn't, could he? He couldn't admit that he'd wanted that position that her father had also wanted and T'Equisetum had manipulated others' fear to smear her father and be appointed. He probably couldn't even say he was wrong to hate the Intersection of Hope. He certainly couldn't admit that he'd been behind the instigation of the mob that had firebombed the T'Mugwort estate. That was simply criminal.

According to all she believed, that hatred should have eroded his

soul. His misdeeds should have come back upon him by three . . .
spiritually, physically, emotionally.

But she hadn't seen or heard that it had. And, apparently, that
was a problem for her.

The man who'd ruined her Family had not suffered as they had.
Perhaps he hadn't prospered, but he was still wealthy and respected.

No, she hadn't been able to forgive, and the High Priest and
High Priestess had seen that flaw in her and it had been a detriment
to her career, not only her soul.

So, if, in her innermost being, she thought that *she* would Heal
from lingering childhood wounds better if she pursued a societal
justice, that was exactly what she should do.

And that was what she should admit to her superiors that she
was going to do. She didn't anticipate that the conversation would
go well, but she'd already been through all the counseling and rituals to root out the unforgivingness in her and they hadn't stuck.

The rest of her Family seemed to have worked through whatever
fear, anger, and resentment they held at their ruination better than she.

She grimaced at that notion, but she was human, and apparently, in this one matter, she carried a grudge that couldn't be banished just by meditation and journaling and all the other tools she'd
already used.

Even when the Lady had touched her in ritual, when the Goddess had flowed from Tiana, there yet remained a kernel of ire that
she couldn't root out.

Time to work for change, then, for justice.

And she *did* know the difference between justice and revenge.
She *could* be satisfied with justice.

She also knew the first person she should approach—her
brother-in-law, the man who *felt* like a true brother, her sister's
HeartMate, Private Investigator Garrett Primross.

Tiana had never been to Garrett's office, but she scried him and
asked for an appointment.

"I think I know what you want to discuss, and it's about fliggering time someone in your Family talks to me about it," he said with a predatory smile.

"Oh."

"I don't have any appointments today, and my current caseload is full but not urgent, so come on by. Public Carrier number five stops just a block from the building." He gave her an address and she nodded. As she left GreatCircle Temple by the east door she saw the number five going in the right direction on the street bordering the wide grounds. Other people stood at the plinth. "I'm on my way!" she shouted to Garrett on her perscry.

She ran, recalling that she might not have to do this alone. She had a Fam. *Felonerb, I'm going to Garrett Primross's office. Want to come?* She hoped he did and sent the visualization of the public carrier she was jogging for to him.

I do not like being inside a common glider box, he replied, but sounded a little distracted.

There was not a creature more common than Felonerb.

I can teleport later. After I GET him.

She sensed him wiggle his butt, in pounce mode.

Get who? she asked automatically, then rather wished she hadn't, as a bloody mess of rat along with the intention to KILL was sent to her by her common Fam.

There is a rat hole in the wall of the house next to TQ. None of the cats here have been able to GET him, her Fam sneered. *I will! He is not TOO CRAFTY for FELONERB RATKILLER!*

See you later, she sent as she hopped onto the carrier and took a seat, blocking any more images and bloodthirsty communications from her Fam.

Twenty

♥

$\mathcal{A}$ quick ride later Tiana was in a shabbier part of town and walking up a short set of steps to a reinforced door set in a brick building, so square and minimalist that she didn't think it could inspire Antenn the architect.

Several cats watched her from the stairs and she had to step over them. A week ago she'd have thought them scruffy. All of them appeared sleeker and better cared for than her poor Fam.

Bloody thoughts or no, she must give Felonerb her best. She sent him a spurt of love and received one back from him.

Smiling, she walked up to the door then *through* it as the illusion over a spellshield thinned.

Garrett awaited her outside his open office door, a few strides down the nondescript corridor. "Come on in." He turned into his office.

When she entered the small chamber he was behind a large, scarred wooden desk but sitting in a brand-new comfortchair. She closed the door behind her and smiled. He looked good in his place of business. Seriously competent.

"Sit," he said.

She did and realized his two client chairs might look old, but the cushions were plump enough under her . . . better than her own patron chairs.

He leaned over the desk. "You want me to look into the fire-bombing of your house when you were a kid."

She stiffened. "That's right. I want to hire you for that. I can pay—"

"There is no payment among Family members," he said gruffly. He swiped his hand across his desk and a folder appeared. A fairly thick one with caff stains on the red, red cover. Red for fire? Tiana swallowed.

"As you can see, I've been checking it out myself, but a lot of years have passed. No mob members came forward after the fact, of course, for either the harm to your house—which was the worst case—or the other two homes firebombed."

"Of course they wouldn't come forward," she snapped.

He grinned. "Not sounding very compassionate and priestessly."

"I get irritated when I think of that."

"I'd get infuriated, myself." He opened the file. "The guards found some leads but couldn't prove who might have been in the crowd. 'Rumors' from what the Air Mages heard when they arrived on scene to put out the small blaze in your house, and from the guards who came and only saw fleeing folk, stated that there was an in-person instigator who led the mob to your home."

She looked at Garrett Primross across his desk and shook her head. "You've done some work on this."

"I opened a case file, yeah. Did you really think I would let the wrong to your Family stand? That I hadn't already begun to investigate that fliggering incident? But I've come to a tangled web, haven't been able to prove who was in the mob that night and whether anyone had ties to T'Equisetum. Who you once said you thought had caused it. You stated T'Equisetum also denounced your father in NobleCouncil during the Black Magic Cult hysteria. That was proven." Garrett's voice lowered, softened. "But why do you think T'Equisetum is involved in the riot and firebombing, Tiana? *You* are the only one who believes that."

She flinched. "He made speeches against us."

"He, like many Lords and Ladies of the time, emphatically railed against the Black Magic Cult murders and got caught up in the rampant fear that lasted a few days. After all, their children were targeted for human sacrifice."

Scowling, Tiana explained, again. "When the information that pylor incense was being used in the murders leaked from the guards—"

"Or was planted by one of the Black Magic Cultists," Garrett reminded. "Evidence showed."

"Well, T'Equisetum denounced the Intersection of Hope religion . . . because they used it. He set the guards upon us, searching our home because my father had more influence than he, because my father was going to be considered for an important appointment! T'Equisetum used my mother's religion to ruin us." Her hands had clenched and her voice had risen. Oh, yes, the quickest way to blow her tranquility to smithereens was to recall that night. No, she had not worked through all of the pain, obviously.

"And how did he ruin you?" Garrett pressed, though he must know . . . not that the Family often talked about the past.

"He cast doubt on my mother, my father . . . just dark enough and just for long enough that he got the appointment instead."

"All right." Garrett inclined his head, leaned back in his comfortchair, and linked his fingers over his flat stomach. "So that's a matter of record in the NobleCouncil. And Councils and such take away rights and privileges a whole lot easier than they grant or reinstate them. But why do you think Equisetum's behind the mob, too?"

"Because he's a hater, a fanatic . . ."

Garrett looked thoughtful. "Or he's . . . thorough."

Her shoulders sagged. "I suppose. It's hard to deal with such people. Those who have one idea of right and wrong in their head, and that idea might not correspond to reality, but they won't change it, *can't* change it without wreaking their worldview. Emotional dissonance. It's difficult to counsel such individuals. Though T'Equisetum is the worst of that bunch that I've met."

"Is that all you have against him?"

"He was behind the mob!"

"How do you know?" Garrett shot back.

Flashes of orange and yellow. Flickering sheets of fire seared in the vision of her memories of that night. She put the heels of her hands over her eyes and pressed to get a clearer picture. "I . . . I . . . saw an employee of his . . . one of his lesser relatives who worked for him . . . that night."

Garrett's chair whooshed forward, pushing him upright, nearly across his desk, definitely into her space.

"Are you sure? Who?"

"Someone who worked in his office." She still huddled in on herself, trying to remember, to *see!*

"How did you know the person?"

"The man."

"How did you know the man?" Garrett was relentless.

Her mouth opened and closed. "I was at home one day when the . . . that man . . . came to the door . . . to pick up a formal papyrus decision with regard to a case of Father's to take to Lord T'Equisetum." She found herself whispering. "I think I saw him in the mob. You must know, we are a small Family, and we didn't have staff. I remember him, and others, from the mob. GraceLord Galega . . . who died later that year. I remember."

"All right."

"We were minor Nobles and our house was not a Residence . . . though it might have had stirrings." She'd tried not to think of that. "I hope if it did, its new Family treated it well." Tears pressed behind her eyes and she blinked hard to keep them back as she straightened. "If the house is coming to sentience, it would think of *that* Family as its own. Not us."

"A great deal was taken from you. And in the murders and the outcry, I know why you didn't press for redress at the time."

"Terrible." Tiana swallowed. "That time sent fear into the very bones of my parents. My mother couldn't worship as she wanted . . . *we* couldn't worship as we wanted. You know that the hiding crippled Artemisia's Flair when her Passage came. She should have FirstLevel Flair, but we repressed it."

"The mania passed quickly," Garrett said, and though his face didn't give much expression away, he was her brother now and she knew he kept a tight rein on his temper. He picked up a coin and sent it rolling back and forth across his fingers.

"Yes." Tiana gulped, murmured a spell couplet to banish the tears. "I think that the next morning, those people who'd been in the mob were ashamed of themselves."

"Can you remember faces?" he pressed.

She shuddered. "Yes."

"But you did not prosecute."

"We had *nothing*! My father's judgeship was stripped from him, given to another, as had been the appointment . . . and T'Equisetum holds grudges. And the HealingHalls were too . . ." She stopped herself from using curse words. Cursing showed a lack of control. ". . . self-righteous to accept my mother back into Primary Healing-Hall. She occasionally worked at AllClass HealingHall, but she did not disavow her religion and other Healers didn't want to work much with a person of the Intersection of Hope. Our Family reputation was ruined forever."

"A mistake to run instead of fight."

"Like fighting a mob is easy! Or honorable. Or right." Anger flashed through her. "You're a fighter. I know that." She angled her chin. "We had Flair, no weapons. If we used our Flair to fight, we would have further stirred the mob. What would have happened when we ran out of energy? We'd have been killed."

A short nod from Garrett, who still frowned. "You escaped."

"We escaped," she said softly. "And those Lords and Ladies in the NobleCouncil who had believed the lies that people of the Inter-section of Hope had conspired with the Black Magic Cultists stated they were wrong." Her smile felt more like a grimace. "They didn't, quite, apologize, but they admitted they were wrong. All except T'Equisetum. I don't know what twisted in him, if he thought repa-rations might be made to *us* if he didn't stand solid against us. Or whether he was twisted in the first place, but he stood his ground that the Intersection of Hope members were evil."

"He lost his influence."

Tiana couldn't stop her lip from curling. "He lost some of his influence . . . and no rational person really likes a fanatic unless they are of the same hue as the fanatic . . ."

"And there aren't many of the same hue."

"Thank the Lady and Lord, at least not that darkest hue. But he belongs to the Traditionalist Stance."

Garrett flipped the coin, snatched it from the air, and grunted. "Like insisting on no change to the current councils is going to work when people are gaining more Flair all the time, when Walker Clover, a former Commoner, will someday be Captain of AllCouncils."

She let a breath out, sat back against the chair. "*Different than you* does not mean evil."

"It doesn't even mean worse than you. Just different," Garrett said. Now the silver coin disappeared into his palm; he waved and it was gone, and then it appeared in his other hand. No Flaired tricks, all manual dexterity. "And, after your year of—"

"Poverty."

"After a year of poverty you landed on your feet." He smiled. "More, you . . . thrived."

Garrett wouldn't—couldn't, because of a confidentiality spell—mention FirstGrove and BalmHeal estate.

Tiana nodded. "We found a new home. Artemisia was accepted at AllClass HealingHall and began to rise in her career . . . under the name of Panax." Tiana jutted her chin.

"You were accepted as an apprentice in GreatCircle Temple."

"Yes. Artemisia and I are doing relatively well. Mother practices her craft on those who . . . find her . . . office."

"It's an open secret that your father writes cogent and well-respected articles for legal journals."

"Yes."

"So T'Equisetum didn't keep you down."

Pure fury flashed through her. "That doesn't mean what he did was right. My parents—"

The silver coin spun and flashed in Garrett's fingers. He set it on the desk. "You're damn right. Your parents have hidden for too long. This wrong needs to be righted. Now. But I can't accuse the man without evidence, though I'd love to confront him with a formal complaint about his actions. After all, he harmed my woman, my HeartMate—he set events into action that crippled her Flair—I, we, can't prove it yet. If we do, a complaint would be better coming from you."

She saw her career vanish before her eyes.

"If you're strong enough and gutsy enough to do it." He paused. "And I don't think, with this new Intersection of Hope cathedral, that T'Equisetum will remain quiet. You know that he brought up the matter in the NobleCouncil and was quashed by others, don't you?"

Tiana wet her lips. "I think Antenn Blackthorn-Moss mentioned something. I hadn't heard specifics."

Garrett nodded. "A man who hires others to rile up mobs to hurt or kill a rival cannot be allowed to prosper." His gaze locked on her. "Your mother and father won't prosecute. Artemisia is happy with me and our life." A slight smile. "But you . . . you want justice, don't you?"

She narrowed her eyes at him. "You want something more like revenge."

He shrugged big shoulders. "Sure, I want him ground into the dirt and never able to raise himself out of it. I want him banished from Druida City, Gael City, and public life. I want his title stripped from him, and reparations *times three* paid to you from *his* wealth. I'd like to beat him until he's bloody and begging."

Her mouth dropped open at the list Garrett had obviously put a lot of thought into. "Oh."

"But I'm not a priest. I can allow myself revenge." Again he picked up the coin, staring at it as he made it disappear and reappear through his fingers of both hands. "And, I think, you might be the one who observed most that terrible night." When he looked up, his stare pinned her. "Didn't you? You looked out the windows, saw the people surrounding your house?"

Her breath caught, then came out creakily. "Yes. I watched the fire. Horrified and fascinated." She squeezed her fingers tight as she slipped back into memory. "I saw faces."

"And your parents?" Garrett asked quietly.

Tiana felt the blood drain from her face. "They were running around . . . teleporting to gather things we might need, translocating items—"

"Making sure their children were safe. Artemisia?"

She glanced at him. "She stayed in the middle of the room, the long ResidenceDen in the back of the house, under the desk where they told us to hide."

"But you didn't. You went to the window and looked out."

"More than one window. All. All of them, front and back, all the ground-floor rooms." Her fingers twined together. "I couldn't help myself. We were surrounded."

"And you saw. Faces. People."

"Yes."

"All right." He slapped the desk, pulling her from the near-trance. "I'm going to arrange for some people to witness you as you go into a trance and remember that night, record it on a memory-sphere."

"I've done that before."

His brows went up.

"Did you?"

"Yes. The priestess who counseled me requested I do that. Years ago. Within a week of the incident . . . as soon as I was accepted into the apprenticeship program . . . my application had been before the Temple, but was approved quickly after the . . . incident."

Garrett's smile was slow. "Good. Then we can compare the two. They'll be excellent evidence."

A sigh came from the bottom of her gut.

"I know it's going to be hard. But you can do it," he said.

"Yes." She set her feet under her, made sure her legs would support her, and rose. "You think we can really obtain justice for my Family."

"Oh, yeah." He smiled and there was an edge in it that made her wary. With a flash of insight she thought that if legal means didn't work, the man in front of her might . . . use his influence? Call in favors? . . . to ruin T'Equisetum.

She should have felt bad about that.

She didn't.

Garrett stood, too, came around his desk and tucked her hand in the crook of his elbow. "I'll walk you to the front door. I think I can get everything set up for your session in a couple of septhours with several witnesses, including a guard. Who has your previous memorysphere?"

"High Priestess GrandLady D'Sandalwood."

"Ahem." Then he shrugged. "I'll scry her . . . or her assistant."

"I should do that, authorize that." With relief, Tiana recalled that the High Priestess was busy with a small wedding ritual in two septhours. She pulled out her scry pebble and requested that a verified best copy of the memorysphere be forwarded to Garrett's office cache.

"With you being a priestess and all, you won't need anyone to talk you into a trance," Garrett commented.

"I can handle that myself," Tiana agreed, tucking the tiny scry pebble back into her sleeve.

The front door thinned, revealing Antenn Blackthorn-Moss sitting on the stoop and petting one of the feral cats.

Twenty-one

*A*ntenn *glanced up, and it seemed to Tiana that his automatic smile* brightened when he saw her.

"Blackthorn-Moss," Garrett acknowledged.

Antenn stood and nodded to Garrett. "Primross."

The ginger cat sniffed Antenn's boots and sauntered down the steps, and Felonerb bounded into sight. A low growl emanated from the cat and he flicked the tip of his tail as if demonstrating to Tiana's Fam that he *had* a tip to his tail.

FAMWOMAN! Felonerb said. He leapt straight for her, trusting she'd catch him. So she did. He licked under her chin . . . his breath was bad but not the hideous odor of when he'd killed and eaten prey.

He snuggled in her arms, twitched his whiskers, and said, *Hello, Antenn. You see how much My FamWoman loves Me?* Felonerb cocked his half ear at Garrett. *Hello, Garrett. You see how much My FamWoman loves Me?*

Antenn laughed. "I do."

She asked Me to come with her and I did!

"A little late, cat," Garrett said. "But it's good that you'll be with her when she recalls the firebombing of old T'Mugwort house

in two septhours." Garrett looked at Antenn. "You're here and con-
venient, and don't have any personal tie to the Mugworts, so you'd
be a good witness. What do you say?"

A flush darkened over the architect's cheeks. He glanced at
Tiana. "I asked Felonerb where you were, and I came to say I'm
sorry I prodded you to do this."

"No. You aren't."

He grimaced. "You're right."

"No personal ties to the Mugworts at the time of the Black Cult
murders," Garrett repeated.

"My cuz was nearly a victim!" Antenn shot back.

"Just so," said Garrett. "And you *do* have an interest in keeping
T'Equisetum under control."

Antenn stared aside. "I had a run-in with him yesterday morning." Worry lines showed around his mouth. "He is not a pleasant
person." Then Antenn's head came up. "I also just checked out
what he said yesterday in NobleCouncil with some friends of mine
who attended. The man needs to be stopped," Antenn said. "Yes,
I'll witness."

"We three agree about stopping T'Equisetum," Garrett said.

I think he is a nasty man, Felonerb stated.

Tiana petted his fur, still rough and matted in places. She'd have
to be more diligent in grooming him.

I can groom myself just fine, Felonerb said telepathically, and
she thought it was only to her. He wiggled and she let him jump
down to the stoop, where he sat on one corner and preened as if he
owned the whole building.

"Have you even met GraceLord T'Equisetum?" Garrett asked
Felonerb.

No, but he makes FamWoman tense, so he is a bad man. He
aimed his muzzle toward the building. *Are we going to stay here?*

"I'd planned on going back to GreatCircle Temple," Tiana said.
She had some lunches left in her personal no-time there, and the
public carrier line was a straight shot. "I'm not finished arranging
my new chambers." A couple of friends who had chosen to move to

their own Temples told her that she could take their extra furniture. There'd be enough to make her sitting room and office look cozy, not barren. She thought the quality of the items might be better, too.

Garrett rolled his big shoulders, frowned at the building. "I was planning on using the conference room here, but I suppose we could do this at GreatCircle Temple." He didn't sound thrilled, but he'd had his own deep counseling session there.

Tiana flushed at the thought of hosting people in her rooms, counting people in her mind: Garrett, Antenn and another witness, a guard . . . and whoever might be interested enough to drop in . . . which several of her friends might want to do. Even with the donations, she didn't have enough chairs. She didn't even have enough floor pillows, yet.

Let's do it at Turquoise House! Felonerb said. *The House can be a witness, too. He would like that.*

Now both Garrett and Antenn flinched.

"I understand if you don't want to revisit the place, Garrett," Tiana said softly. "You did live through the plague there, after all."

But everything is new and clean and smells goood! It's not like it was when you was sick! Felonerb grinned at Garrett. *I saw you there when you needed Healing!*

Garrett bowed stiffly at the Fam. "Thank you for the energy you sent me. You must have been with the other feral cats."

For a while. You needed everyone on that one night. Felonerb licked his paw and rubbed his ear.

"I suppose," Garrett said. He looked at Antenn. "That all right with you? Turquoise House in a little less than two septhours?"

"I can make it." He seemed to grit the words through his teeth.

"Fine." Garrett nodded. "Later." He went back through the door that solidified into spellshield-with-illusion behind him.

A long sigh Tiana hadn't known was trapped in her lungs whooshed from her.

Antenn raised his brows, rocked back on his heels, and considered her. "This event . . ."

"Going back in trance to the night the mob surrounded our house and firebombed it."

He winced, tugged at the collar of his tunic as if he needed to breathe better, and she recalled he'd said he'd been in a house that had gone up in flames, too. His hand dropped and he shook out his whole body. "Firebombs, the weapon of choice of criminals on Celta." His curved lips were not a smile, especially since his eyes looked tragic. "Including my brother."

She *ached* at that and said the first thing that popped into her head to distract him. "As an architect, can you tell by looking at a house from the outside whether it is sentient? Or becoming intelligent?"

Interest sharpened his gaze. "Maybe. Sometimes. What do you have in mind?" He descended the steps, held out a hand to her for a second, and then dropped it.

She paused and stared at him for a couple of breaths. His brown hair gleamed in the sun and his hazel eyes appeared even darker . . . though that might be because he was gazing at *her* with admiration. Perhaps the reason he affected her more each time she met him was that he seemed very interested in her.

Could he have been the man in her sex dream last night? Her HeartMate? Her breath caught . . . she was forgetting the dream and her lover already! Too many emotions had crammed into her this morning; too many memories, too many thoughts had blurred the nighttime sex. She bit her lip to stop an incoherent protest at this *new* memory fading—when she could remember the old so well. Surely dream sex with your HeartMate was as life-changing as a firebomb.

But it couldn't be Antenn, could it? In the back of her mind, foggy as it had been last night during sex and the mind-twilight before waking, she'd thought that the man must have just come to town, that distance had kept him from claiming her until now.

She was confused. She had a lover, a HeartMate. But he hadn't wanted her until now and she didn't know what might have changed. If that had changed. He still might not want her, just be unable to suppress the sex dreams.

And *this* man was attracted. As no man had been in years. Feeling the weight of his regard, she descended the steps . . . her body moving in a more graceful manner than she was accustomed to. And then she was close to him, nearly touching . . . and felt a tiny static-shock-fizz as she hit his spellshield. She blinked and stepped back.

He flushed. "Bad sunburn." Then he coughed. "Potion took care of the color, but skin's real sensitive."

She thought he lied but said nothing.

Where ARE we going now? Felonerb asked. He hopped down the stairs and wove between their legs. Antenn nodded to her.

"I thought . . ." She glanced at Antenn.

"I'm with you." He grimaced. "I scried the Chief Ministers for their approval to start the real work, laying the huge blocks of the foundation, and was informed they aren't available. Probably still discussing when the spellshield ritual will be. But I'm not taking the next step without authorization. So I'm with you."

"Oh . . . all right." She spoke around a new lump in her throat. "I'd like to look at the old Mugwort Family estate. My childhood home."

Felonerb sniffed. *Bo-ring. Past is past. I will tell TQ of Our decision. HE is our present and future.* Her Fam slid her a sly look. *Time for lunch and better food at the Turquoise House.* The cat stropped her ankles, then 'ported away.

Now Antenn's smile faded and his expression went blank. "Are you sure you want to go to your old home?"

Tiana made a moue, thought about walking away from the man and to the public carrier hub. She still knew what carriers went past her old home.

But she stayed instead. A bit of understanding trickled through her. She trusted him. "My reviews pointed out that I have not progressed as well as I—or others—believe I should in getting over my childhood trauma."

Her next swallow was more of a gulp. "I haven't been back to look at hom—at the place—since a couple of weeks after the event."

He reached out toward her hand, then stopped and turned the movement into a gesture. "If you feel you have to do this—"

"I do."

A shrug. "All right. Do you think you remember enough of how the light streams at this time of year and day and all the rest to teleport?"

The question took her breath in an emotional blow and tears sprang behind her eyes. Dammit! She didn't want to wobble in front of him. She cleared her throat, blinked hard, and used Flair to banish the tears. "No. I don't recall enough." She thought she did, saw her old home in her mind's eye, but couldn't risk their lives if her recollection was wrong.

He grunted in an almost absentminded fashion and she thought that under his manner she felt a twisty hurt from him. She opened her mouth to ask what was wrong, then decided he didn't want to talk about whatever pained him.

Gesturing to the street, he said, "I have a glider right around the corner." He led the way.

It was one of the new, small vehicles catering to the professional class and could seat four instead of a whole Family. He lifted the door and seemed to step away reluctantly as she slid in, then he closed the door and went to the driver's side.

When he was in, he asked, "Address?"

She stated it and the glider nav system engaged and the vehicle began to move.

"Nice area," he said, and angled toward her on the bench, his demeanor easier.

"Yes, it was. Is." She returned to her main concern. "Do you know if any houses in that area are becoming sentient?"

"No, I don't know." His inhalation was audible. "Do you know who's living there now?"

She frowned. "Whoever paid the NobleCouncil the most gilt, I think." She paused. "T'Equisetum had some hanger-on lined up to receive the estate, but the NobleCouncil quashed that, at least."

"Still sound bitter."

Gritting her teeth until they hurt, she grabbed at the sidebar in the door, sent her anger and bitterness through it . . . and gasped when she felt her energy being *stored*.

"Great feature, huh?" Antenn said. "GreatHouse Alder really knows how to combine Flair and tech."

"I suppose," Tiana said dubiously.

"Energy is energy," Antenn said.

"I know, and I shouldn't spend energy on negative emotions, especially with regard to the past. Even my FamCat knows better than me about that."

"And I suppose that you spiritual types figure you can order your emotions. And maybe you can. To me it sounds natural that a bad past could haunt you."

This time she truly felt that grinding hurt in him. Once more she hesitated to speak, and then the glider pulled up outside the tall, spiked greeniron fence now standing around what used to be her old home and front grassyard and garden.

Silently Antenn raised the vehicle's doors. He got out first and Tiana reluctantly followed, her stomach squeezing. Now she was here, she wasn't sure she should be.

Twenty-two

Sticking his hands in his trous pockets, he studied her old home and rocked on his heels. She crossed to stand next to him and swallowed more tears, cleared her throat, and managed to say, "We didn't have the greeniron fencing when we lived here."

"Or the spellshields coating them, either, I bet."

"No."

"Nothing to prevent a mob from storming the place."

"No. We're . . . were . . . a very minor GraceHouse Family. Minor nobility."

"But an old Family, and well respected."

"Not well enough."

"Minor enough that your enemies could take you down."

"Yes . . . and I'm not sure that my parents even realized they had enemies, or that T'Equisetum is . . . was . . . is the kind of man who would use any means to get what he wanted."

Shaking his head, Antenn said, "None of the FirstFamilies would be so unwary. Even the old T'Ash Residence that was burned had spellshields that had to be circumvented. By the way, have you spoken to T'Ash about your circumstances and justice? They're rather like his and he could be a great support—"

"Absolutely not! I don't know him or any of the Ash Family. Like you said, they're of the FirstFamilies. I won't approach him."

"Hmm," Antenn said. He slowly turned in place to look at the modest estate, the road, the neighboring houses and those across the street. Tiana followed his gaze since she'd avoided actually looking at her old home and wanted to nerve herself just a bit more. She found herself comparing this neighborhood to the one that TQ was in. The original status of the Families was about the same—minor Nobles with titles nearly three centuries old.

But the houses here were not as close together as in TQ's neighborhood, and the area felt slow. The part of the city surrounding the Turquoise House had picked up in popularity, gave off a more sophisticated vibration. One she thought she liked better.

Antenn moved to within centimeters of the gate. "House doesn't look as if it was too damaged in the past." He squinted. "Its aura is good. Solid. Whole. No smudging of past harm."

Tiana goggled. "You can see a house's aura."

His shoulders hunched a little; his face took on color.

"What a lovely, strong Flair." She infused her voice with admiration.

He glanced sideways at her. "You think?"

"One of the reasons you're a top architect, I think."

Inclining his head, he said, "Thank you. Yes, I can see auras around buildings." His hand brushed hers; static shock again, and they both stepped aside. "You haven't looked at your old home. Would you rather leave?"

Emotional support flowed from him. She said, "My question remains. Is it becoming sentient?" After a deep breath she *did* focus on the house through the gates. Pale-yellow grass and garden beds turned to show rich earth ready for spring. There were curved flower beds that weren't the same shape as when she'd lived there. More garden and less grassyard.

Another big breath. The house of rough-cut gray stone blocks looked . . . not the same. She blinked in surprise and, with another slight wash of tears, frowned as she stared, then understood that

the tiled roof was no longer dark rust-red but black. It gave the
house a more forbidding aspect.

Especially compared to the bright turquoise enamel exterior of TQ.

"Black door and shutters," she murmured, still frowning. "It looks
so stern."

"I believe that's mostly external. There's a warmth and a feeling
of lighter colors inside. The house itself is . . . content. Intelligence
slowly budding, I think," Antenn said.

"Good. That's good." She found her shoulders had risen, her
back tightened, and she deliberately relaxed them. Then she turned
away. "It isn't the same. It shouldn't be." She walked back to the
glider and he kept pace with her. She must put the past aside; time
had streamed on since she'd been here last. She shook her head.
"There really is no going back."

He grunted a response, and when she looked up at him his eyes
were distant. She'd missed that his hurt was back and enveloping
him—hard and aching emotional pain. A flash of a wooden lean-to
missing planks flickered before her vision, and she knew she'd connected with him more than just a brush of auras. The sound of high
voices came, boys, and worse, the scent of sewage.

Suddenly her brain clicked in on what must be bothering him.
She'd been mourning a home lost to her.

He hadn't even had a childhood home, but had lived with other
boys in a decrepit lean-to, with *nothing*.

A breath shuddered from him and he leaned against the glider
and looked at the house. "It's worth fighting for."

"I can't get it back. We can't, our Family. We've moved on."

"I don't know—"

With a wry smile, she stated a simple truth that she felt and
acknowledged. "This estate is really in the past for us Mugworts."

He glanced down at her and nodded. "All right."

She studied the house, remembered it as it once was, then looked
at him consideringly. "Would you have fought the mob?"

He froze, mouth turning down. "I was part of a mob."

She gasped. "You torched—"

But he cut her words short with a sharp gesture. "No, I was part of a gang. Ran with them. Did close to moblike behavior."

"You would have fought in our place."

"I would have ripped the house apart and rained stone and roof tile on them," he stated flatly, then went to the passenger side of the vehicle and tapped the door to rise. "Which would have damaged everyone, the people outside, me being punished for hurting them, and the house."

She reached out and hit static again, stepped back. "We weren't and aren't a violent Family."

His face had set in clean, firm lines. "I had a violent childhood, then a little time with Mitchella and the rough-and-tumble of the Clovers, then the fighter training of a FirstFamily son. Different than you." His eyes had darkened, pupils dilated because of the clouds that had rolled across the sun, the pain of his past, because he liked looking at her or all three—though she liked the last reason best.

His eyes lingered on hers. "Though the Clovers and the Blackthorns and the Mugworts have something in common, I think. We believe in justice."

"Yes." Her shoulders were stiff and tight again, sheer anticipation of a battle, perhaps a war, to come. "And it's time we demanded that."

He moved close to her, just outside the range of his spellshield, though she could feel the crackle of it between them. She wondered if it bothered him like it did her. She'd wanted to take that hand of his earlier. Link fingers. Give him the support of touch.

Just wanted to touch him.

But, of course, he didn't feel the same. He'd have dropped the spellshield if he had.

On her side there *was* a building sexuality for him. Again she wondered if he might be her HeartMate. She gazed into his eyes. "Ah . . ." Should she mention last night?

FAMWOMAN, ANTENN, TQ thinks you should come eat! Felonerb blasted into her mind.

A not quite amused smile flickered on and off Antenn's face. He gestured for her to get in the glider. When the doors closed, he said, "I'll drop you off at the Turquoise House. I have a lunch date."

That didn't sound truthful.

He gripped the steering bar. "Another session with a Healer."

More confusion buzzed in her mind, trying to sort out his words and actions. She caught a quick glance from him, a flash of yearning, of hopelessness—what!—in his eyes.

"I understand."

"I'll be back to witness." A pause. "You can count on me."

"I'm sure."

Just before they turned off the block, Antenn stopped and thinned the window in his door as they slowly pulled away from the house that formerly belonged to the Mugworts. Tiana could *feel* how he strove to lighten his own mood.

He shook his head.

"What?" she asked.

"The contrast between this place and the Turquoise House is amazing."

"Yes." Again she experienced the flash of the wooden lean-to but kept that to herself, since she didn't feel like she could bring up his past.

A childhood that was so very different, so very much worse than her own. Was that why he'd withdrawn from her? Because his past somehow presented an unspoken barrier between them?

She'd let it go, for now. Perhaps forever. Did she want a lover in her life now? One she might work with on a daily basis? Too much was happening. She'd been swept along by a flood of events and needed to find her footing to *direct* them.

One last time she considered whether Antenn could be her Heart-Mate. She slid her gaze toward him. His hands were on the steering bar, so he'd disengaged the automatic system and was driving, seemed to be concentrating on that as if it were a moving meditation.

No, he could not be her HeartMate. He sensed the auras of buildings, a strong and unusual Flair. He was a FirstLevel architect, as she was a FirstLevel Priestess, as her father was a FirstLevel judge, and her sister should have been a FirstLevel Healer.

Among people with such great Flair, HeartMates connected in dreams. And most particularly during at least two dreamquest Passages that freed their Flair. Though she'd experienced Passages, no sex dreams had come to her. Until last night.

She didn't know what to make of that, and just thinking of how passionate she'd been, how free, made her blush, and she sure didn't want Antenn picking up on that. So like other issues in her life— apparently riddling her life—she tucked it away to deal with it later.

She had a lot to deal with later . . . and hopefully those concerns would *stay* tucked away and not explode through her at the worst possible moment.

*N*ow it was *Antenn's turn to ignore a House. An extremely glowing* House, not only from the spellshields that made the Turquoise tint bright and shiny, but from the glow of the aura of the House itself. Flashing blue-green. Very pleased with itself.

He left Tiana with a wave. Pulling away, he thought the aura dimmed. Imagination. He told the nav system to take him home— with just enough time to dress in real clothes and grab a bite to eat and return—then slumped back in the seat and closed his eyes.

He didn't know what had gotten into him. He'd seen Tiana and all these feelings had tangled inside him. Was she his HeartMate? Surely not. She wouldn't have acted so . . . so . . . like the woman had during the dream sex.

The remembrance of which he'd tried to shut down. Again and again.

Throughout the day, he'd set his jaw and concentrated on the cathedral. GraceLord T'Equisetum threatened his project. The cathedral *must* remain Antenn's first priority.

It was the most important structure he'd ever design and build and would stand as a monument to his hard work. Proving he was now, and forever, a contributing member of his society. People would look at it and respect him.

He shifted as that notion itched in his mind and his body. Yeah, he knew he did this to gain respect . . . And he also knew that no matter what he did, his reputation wouldn't change a thing for a lot of people. Like T'Equisetum—or the FirstFamilies who'd suffered at his brother's hands.

But it had been his *brother*, not him. He'd do his best and they'd still condemn him. Dammit, yes, he wanted respect.

He let his anger flow out on a long breath. Focusing on the cathedral was good, and by doing so, he'd managed to stay a little emotionally distant from the priestess. Sympathy for her losses, a feeling of having a lot of things in common, were just natural. Anyone would have been empathetic in the same circumstances. Thankfully the spellshields on himself and his robe kept him from touching her very appealing self.

Letting himself into his suite at home, he took an easy waterfall that didn't sting, much, and dressed in the clothes that the illusion robe had mimicked. He translocated the robe to his mother's sitting room so she could do whatever had to be done to cleanse it.

Then he ate a quick sandwich and suddenly Pinky appeared, ready to be friendly and munch with him. Antenn gave his Fam some chopped furrabeast—very lean and a smaller portion than usual.

Pinky smiled, then lowered his head and began snarfing it down. *You are very odd today.*

"Yeah?"

The HouseHeart made you weird.

"Uh-huh."

And you wore a sparkly white robe.

Antenn froze. "You could see that?"

Pinky paused to look at him and snort. *Of course, Cats have wonderful vision.*

Neck burning, Antenn wondered about the ferals he'd petted near Primross's office and Felonerb RatKiller, *and* whether Tiana's Fam would comment on Antenn's garb to her.

After a deep burp, Pinky sat and looked at Antenn. *Where are you going now?*

"To the Turquoise House." He picked up his plate and utensils and dumped them in the dish cleanser. "You can come if you want."

Another belch. *I have heard that TQ has a special cat.*

"He has several ferals. And Felonerb RatKiller is living there."

Pinky hopped to all paws, flattened his ears, and hissed. *I do not like him. Why is he there? Is he living INSIDE?*

"Yes, he is the new Fam to FirstLevel Priestess Tiana Mugwort."

Tail thrashing, Pinky lifted his nose. *She has poor taste.* Without another word, he sauntered over to one of his pillows—the one in the sun—and curled up.

Antenn stopped in the rectangle of bright light shining through the windows himself and took a precious minute to just *be*. Maybe a little of Tiana's serenity was rubbing off on him. Though he was pretty sure he'd soon find out how deep that calmness of hers went as she reexperienced the firebombing of her home. His gut tightened. He wasn't looking forward to this. Nope, worse than that, he *dreaded* it.

A soft snuffle came and he glanced at his plump, light-beige cat and some of his tension eased. He crossed over to stroke his Fam's stomach. Pinky didn't awake, but stretched, and Antenn gave him a couple of more pets. The fur remained one of the softest things he'd ever felt . . . and Pinky . . . one of the great gifts of his life.

Odd how a cat had kept him sane . . . and his brother had gone mad.

Twenty-three

Tiana ate a beautiful, tasty, and healthy lunch and alternated between nerves and calm . . . that is, she'd feel the nerves, then worked at being peaceful.

The Turquoise House informed her that her mother had sent over a plan for the sunroom and he'd implemented it. When she looked at the space she'd been stunned at the staggered garden beds filled with thriving plants, a pond the length of the room, and a small fountain. A fan-backed wicker chair with colorful cushions stood in the room—TQ stated he'd put out several chairs within his chambers.

After lunch, once again nervous about the upcoming regression, she decided to occupy her mind with arranging her few belongings in the House. She set her small personal treasures on the top of a bureau that had appeared that matched the bed, and hung her clothes in a bedroom closet, though TQ had offered a variety of free-standing wardrobes from the simple and inexpensive to what appeared to be elegant heirlooms.

Finally she unwrapped the architectural drawing of TQ and hung it on the bedroom wall. The map in multicolored ink fit perfectly.

There was a sound like a gasp from TQ. "That is *me*! That is my floor plan!"

"Yes." She stepped back and admired it. "It looks well in this spot."

"But how did you get it?" Some creakings. "I only have my floor plan filed in the GuildHall with a request that it be *private*." His tone took on a slight haughtiness. "Like the other intelligent Residences."

"It was a gift." She enjoyed the lilt of emotions in his voice, sensed the avidity of his interest, and decided to spin out the story a bit. Sinking down onto the bed, she continued. "Yes, it looks very good."

"A gift! From whom?" In her mind she saw a young man hopping from foot to foot, perhaps even a boy. The Turquoise House might think he was a mature adult, but he simply wasn't. Not in human terms and especially not in sentient dwelling terms.

She leaned back on a pillow.

Tell me, tell me, tellme! The excited demand shot to her mind faster than words could be said.

"I was given the piece by the Fam, Mica. Camellia Darjeeling's Fam, before Camellia married Laev T'Hawthorn."

"A *Fam*!" TQ's voice was back and a near squeak. Tiana hadn't spent much time in the company of Raz Cherry, the actor who'd given TQ his voice, but she'd never heard him squeak like that. Hadn't ever heard a grown man squeak like that. Maybe TQ needed some remedial voice lessons . . . but, oddly enough, right here and now, sitting in the sun on a wonderful bed, she didn't want to share the House with her Family . . . not even her best friends.

Right now, this moment, she was alone in a House as she'd never been alone before. No other resident—human resident—living with her. And she liked it. Who knew?

"You are telling me all this too slowly," TQ grumbled.

"I'm teasing you a little."

"Oh."

"And where your floor plan came from originally is a mystery to me, too. Now settle yourself in patience and I will continue."

"All right."

"I was given the gift not quite a year ago by Mica, who found it for me when my friends and I attended the Salvage Ball—that party where one brings items one doesn't want and leaves them for others as a price of admission."

"Ooooh!" TQ said.

"Mica found Camellia a carved cat, gave my friend Glyssa a beautiful leather wallet engraved with gold, and showed me the scroll of a floor plan that was revealed to be yours."

"A cat sculpture that had once been made by Laev T'Hawthorn to Camellia Darjeeling. A wallet created by Jace Bayrum for Glyssa Licorice, and *my* floor plan to you." Now TQ's spoken words reminded Tiana of a pounce . . . and the thread of logic was a little scary. Camellia had married Laev, and Glyssa had wed Jace. "Mica said it smelled, or felt, or something, like me." Tiana stood. "I mounted and framed it for my sitting room at—"

"BalmHeal Residence," TQ ended. "I know *all* about that."

"What?"

"It was here within my walls that it was determined that Balm-Heal had awakened and needed a Family of caretakers."

"Really? I never knew that!"

"Yes. I was BalmHeal's first House friend!" Pride throbbed through TQ's voice, and once again Tiana couldn't help but compare him to that other intelligent Residence. She'd nearly had to beg for a wooden frame for TQ's floor plan from BalmHeal. Then she'd had to refinish it. This morning the Residence had wanted it back.

BalmHeal Residence had always loved Tiana's sister, Artemisia, the best.

Looking out the window at the modest land around TQ, Tiana ached in homesickness for FirstGrove, but not so much for the Residence itself. TQ was so very accommodating.

"It is a wonderful item to have on my walls," TQ said with satisfaction. "Thank you. You seem pensive. Would you like more to eat or drink?" A small click came and a no-time door opened from the wooden cabinets next to her table in the sitting room.

"Cocoa?" asked TQ.

The smell steamed and had her mouth watering. Cocoa in the middle of the day, easily obtainable, easily offered.

"You are rich, indeed."

"Yes. I have been lucky in my friends and in my occupants."

When Tiana crossed from bedroom to sitting room to get the large pottery mug full of the beverage and topped with white mousse, a floorboard creaked under her foot.

"Yes, TQ?"

"I would be very grateful if you performed some rituals in my HouseHeart. I have not had renewal rites like the other Houses and Residences for some time."

"How long?" she asked as she went back to the corridor and moved through the House, opening the doors and leaving them open, a smile spreading on her face as the notion of pure freedom filtered through her body. The doors were always closed at Balm-Heal Residence, and she liked them open . . . and hadn't known that until now.

"Ah." There came a tiny creak. "Sixteen years."

Tiana simply stopped, staring out the window to her left that looked out on the back grassyard. "Sixteen years!"

"Yes." TQ rushed into speech. "Naturally I had the Sandal-woods from GreatCircle Temple come and do rituals before and after the medical experiment, but they have not been in my House-Heart for years. I wanted . . . I was waiting . . . I wanted someone special."

"Oh. I'm honored that you consider me special."

"You are *the* best priestess."

Tiana gasped. "Me!"

"You live in BalmHeal, who is My Good Friend and Mentor. He loves you."

"Not as much as Artemisia."

"That is because BalmHeal has always been a Healer household," TQ said.

"And you?" she asked, amused at herself and TQ and the whole conversation.

"I have had many tenants, and I have let several people into my HouseHeart, and Artemisia has been my Fail-Safe person to know of my HouseHeart. Before."

Tiana frowned. "Before?"

"Before you. I want you, a priestess to be my Fail-Safe person until my Family comes."

All she could do was to repeat what she'd said with all the depth of feeling that she had. "I am honored."

Felonerb appeared, smelling incredibly bad. He pranced around. *I got it. I got it. That terrible sewer rat. I got him and I killed him and I ATE some of him and left the rest for the ferals, to show that I am STILL RATKILLER!*

"Fabulous," Tiana said, breathing through her mouth. It didn't help a lot.

"Yesss," her Fam said, trotting with pride. She studied him. He left little bloody smears and tiny bits of . . . stuff . . . fell from his claws as he walked. But as she watched, the floor seemed to absorb it.

Perhaps you would like to clean yourself in the HouseHeart, TQ offered.

The cat stopped in his tracks; his ears pricked straight up, his eyes went large. "Yesss." This time it sounded like a soft, hesitant breath.

You are almost to the staircase into my HouseHeart. I would like to show it to you.

Tiana hesitated. "How much time do we have before the witnessing?"

"Sufficient, I believe," said TQ aloud, then went back to telepathy. *I will alert you when it would be good for you to begin your cleansing waterfall. My HouseHeart will soothe you, and I would love for you to see it.*

I have never been in a HouseHeart! Felonerb said, then actually emitted a squeak of delight. *I NEED to see one.*

I would like to see it, too, Tiana said. This would be her second, for she'd been in BalmHeal Residence's, of course. She thought of Antenn Blackthorn-Moss and the ones he'd experienced, and wondered if TQ's had been one of them.

Look! TQ said, and a piece of the carpet, the entire floor, lifted. *My stairs. My entry room is very large and now has a standard illusion. I am thinking on its final configuration. My Family MUST have something especially made for them.*

"All right," Tiana said out loud. She reached the stairs, a tight stone spiral like nothing she'd ever seen before, and on one side darkness and depth loomed. No railing.

Ooooh! RatKiller exclaimed, and zoomed down the staircase.

Tiana summoned a bright spellglobe to illuminate her way and took the steps slowly. Once down, she stepped into a summer's day in a deciduous wood, with tall, thick-boled trees and sunlight slanting through them, dappling lower bushes, the occasional flower, and leaves that covered the ground in a thick layer. She dissipated her own spellglobe.

"I had a cave with stalactites and stalagmites," TQ said. "But I outgrew it."

"Oh."

I LIKE this. Felonerb took off, slithering between the trees.

TQ said, "It is beautiful, isn't it? I copied it from several vizes and records of Earthan forests that the Ship *Nuada's Sword* sent me."

"Very pretty. From Earth, you say." She took a deep breath but smelled only woods and green growing things.

"Yes."

"And there is a path to your HouseHeart?" She squeezed sideways between a couple of trees and swore bark scratched her skin. "How large is this entrance area?"

"Yes, there is a trail. You are smart, you will find the path! And the moles got carried away."

"The moles."

"They helped me with my HouseHeart. It was originally small, but they wanted to teach their pups to communicate telepathically and work with other sentient beings, and I volunteered." A pause. "Most of the other Residences were too stuffy."

"I understand." She *had* found a track, probably from Felonerb's passing, and tramped down it.

"As I said, this is mostly illusion."

"It's very well done, including all the senses." She heard birdsong she didn't recognize that was probably Earthan, too.

"Thank you. I liked making the spellglobe sun. I tried several different sizes."

"Um-hmm."

"I have an entrance rhyme that must be chanted nine times," TQ said, and told her it. So she began the chant.

Felonerb raced back to her, grinning. *Follow me!*

She was glad to do that.

"Will you want me to do a ritual in this space?"

"No, I think in the HouseHeart, and upstairs in the MasterSuite or MistrysSuite, and perhaps you will celebrate some rituals and holidays in my back grassyard."

"That sounds fine."

"The High Priest and Priestess say you are *the best* at writing rituals."

"Thank you," she mumbled, irritation flickering that she'd be treasured for a desk job instead of leading circles.

"You can always write rituals for me and celebrate them here," TQ said.

I am a Fam now, I get to go to human rituals. They will let me in special holiday circles when accompanied by a human. I like those. They have food.

Tiana laughed. "Yes, mostly they do."

Do you have food in your HouseHeart, TQ?

"Yes, FamCat."

Ooooh. Special food!

"Some is special, some is regular," TQ said. "I have a most beautiful HouseHeart and most modern."

"I'm sure," Tiana murmured, then saw a large rectangular metal door a few paces before her, and she hurried and followed her Fam in.

The first thing she saw as the door closed behind her was a large holo mural of Maroon Beach, surf ebbing and flowing in ceaseless wondrous pattern. So she faced west. Good to know.

"If you will sit on the hearth, Felonerb, I will waft some cleansing smoke at you."

Felonerb hissed.

"And we will feed you," Tiana said, removing her shoes and liners, unsurprised to see that thick and richly patterned Chinju rugs layered the floor. Light emanated from the walls in a dim and comforting glow.

"My cat-smoking cleanser is a new tech and well regarded."

Her Fam sidled toward the thick sandstone slab of the raised hearth.

"It has several scents," TQ continued. "Including lavender, sage . . ."

A sniff. *I don't like those.*

"And some herbs that might not smell nice to a cat, but attract prey, such as celtaroons."

Felonerb's eyes widened. *REALLY?*

"Yes," TQ said.

The tom hopped onto the stone, kept to the edge as fire flickered into flames.

Tiana said, "I think Felonerb, who just kill—triumphed over great prey, should not need any celtaroon pheromones or whatever, right now, TQ."

Her Fam scowled.

"I'll need your support in a while," she said. "I'd prefer to have you pleasant smelling."

Felonerb lifted his nose, twitched his whiskers. *For you, I will have a different smell.*

"Thank you."

"I have a range of fragrances," TQ said. "I shall demonstrate."

They settled on the scent of flatsweet dough. While TQ billowed the cleansing smoke smell over Felonerb, Tiana took the time to scrutinize the room. Roughly six meters square, murals graced two walls. The north showed a lush jungle garden with thick-trunked trees and ferns growing around a turquoise pool fed by a narrow waterfall over rock. As she stared, figures moved in the trees and came to face her, raised hands as if greeting her, and either lingered at the side of the mural or walked back into the tree shadows.

People she'd seen at GreatCircle Temple now and then such as Mitchella D'Blackthorn, Tinne and Lahsin Holly showed up. She blinked when her sister and brother-in-law, Artemisia and Garrett, sat on a stone bench near the pool, smiling at each other, then at her.

A boy peered at her from under shaggy hair, expression stormy, keeping close to a fern frond as tall as he was.

Tiana stared. "That looks like Antenn Blackthorn-Moss, but much younger."

"Yes. He has not come back for a long time. But he'll be here today. In under two septhours!" TQ's voice lilted with pleasure. "I'll be glad to see him."

"I'm sure." The sight of the boy hurt her inside. Surely he'd been here at TQ not long after he'd lived in the slums Downwind. He looked distrustful, wary. Needing love.

Had her image been taken at the same age, she'd have been happy, sure in the love of her Family. And despite all they had lost, they hadn't lost the love they held for each other. She was truly blessed in that.

She glanced at the wall with Maroon Beach and the surf again, the mural of the garden—surely somewhere in the southern continent—then looked at the wall holding the door, walked over to touch the pale-yellow silkeen wallpaper, smooth under her fingers. The pattern showed curving lines of light-green leaves and stylized crownlike blooming flowers of blue with two red lower petals. The same pattern as a room in BalmHeal Residence. Near each corner stood weeping willow trees.

"I have a Fam here, too," TQ said. "Look closely."

Twenty-four

Tiana did and saw a small gray and white tabby with black stripes painted on the wall, though there seemed to be an added holo dimension to it. It was difficult to see since it blended with the wallpaper.

"A cat!" She slid into a cross-legged position on the floor. "How pretty it is!"

"She," said TQ. "She lives off my energy, but I have enough to spare for her, and with all the visitors yesterday, she has enough to move a little, see?"

A tiny "mew" came, and then her right ear angled slightly.

"Oh, lovely!" Tiana cooed and reached out and touched the green spot between the cat's equally green eyes. A tingle brushed her fingertips with Flair, but she sent some of her edginess to the cat and *almost* thought she received a vibration of appreciation in return.

Felonerb harumphed from his place on the hearth and leapt toward Tiana with a draft of sweetness. "Do we have sugar flat-sweets here?" she asked.

"Of course. In my no-time as part of the altar."

Her mouth watered, and she got one. When she turned to ask Felonerb if he needed more food, she saw that he sat a few centimeters from the cat on the wall, tail flicking, staring at the small gray tabby. *I think she needs some imperfections*, he said, jealousy rippling from him, surprising Tiana. She'd thought he'd treasured every scar of his.

"No," said TQ. "She is as perfect and beautiful just as she is. When we have enough energy for her to come out of the wall is soon enough for her to look different. I like her very well as she is."

Tiana's Fam stood and ostentatiously turned his back on the cat, walking toward the no-time.

She has FLOWERS tinted on her, Felonerb said.

Tiana thought she saw the wall cat blink.

Felonerb sat on Tiana's foot and purred loudly.

"She likes her red and blue and green and yellow tinting," TQ said. "*We* like her tinting. You are not to be listened to in this matter."

I will have some shredded furrabeast steak, the tom said.

Tiana stared down at her. He grinned, then added, *Please*.

"TQ?"

"Of course Felonerb Mugwort can be fed. But he is not allowed to disparage my Fam."

"No. You understand, Felonerb?" She got out a small dish of food.

He stood and his back rippled. *I will say nothing bad about stup—about Wall Cat.* He began to gulp down the food.

The interchange and the wonderful ambience of the place relaxed Tiana so she stilled for a moment. Lived.

Moved by the sound of the surf, the tinkle of wind chimes, she drifted to the center of the room and grounded herself, breathed deeply, cleared her mind, and let her cares fall away, her body ease.

Here, between quiet breaths, the slight tease of whirling air, she felt the Divine. So she lifted her arms and uttered a quiet, peaceful prayer, drawing in energy from that which was greater than she, and releasing it into her surroundings, to enrich the atmosphere and sink into the Turquoise House.

Felonerb rumbled a purr, and when she opened her eyes, his eyes appeared brighter, his fur slightly sleeker, his bones less prominent.

A low humming permeated the air, and she understood it came

from the House itself. On a whisper of a wind chime, TQ whispered, "Thank you very much. I have not often had such an experience. You blessed me."

She had. "The One who came through me, blessed you."

"Yes." Breeze soughing through trees—the trees of the murals? The ones outside the door? Archetypical trees?—replaced a sigh from the House. "I thank you now, and I thank you for all the rituals you will perform for me in the future." TQ hesitated. "I am sorry to say that you have twenty minutes before beginning your ritual cleansing for the regression."

Just that easily, she found her teeth clenching. "Thank you." Scooping up Felonerb, she hustled out the door, threaded through the woods and up the stairs. She lay down on the new bed for a quarter septhour and relaxed every muscle she had in sequence until the timer rang to tell her that she must prepare for her ordeal.

After a quick waterfall infused with the best herbs TQ could provide for cleansing and calming, Tiana stood under a skylight streaming sunlight to naturally dry her—faster because of a spell in the glass. Wonderful luxury. She could become accustomed to these extravagances all too easily.

When she sent the last of her anticipatory concern from her body into the grounding mat beneath her bare feet, she opened her eyes, completely tranquil, and hoped to keep that state until she was regressed to the terrible night . . . keep emotions at a distance, something to observe but not allow to influence her.

She saw Felonerb hunched over with narrowed eyes and bared teeth, staring at the waterfall enclosure, and smiled. Such an archetypical cat she had. Yes, she finally understood that was why he was sent to her. Primal cat.

His eyes shifted to meet hers. *You will not put ME in ANY water at ANY time.*

"No," she agreed, shaking her head and sending, perhaps, two droplets flying.

"Eeeek!" Felonerb leapt to his feet and backward, straight out of the waterfall room, using Flair.

"It didn't hurt you," Tiana said, drawing on a white robe, embroidered in white, that she used for summer rituals. The simple garment would do well for the Intersection of Hope ceremony, too.

"Phhpptt." Felonerb stuck out his tongue. *This flatsweet smoke smells tasty but it is NOT.*

"Hmm," said TQ. "We should consider taste, perhaps—"

No more smoke now! Maybe I will try. Later. I am clean now.

"Tomorrow, then."

Maybe.

Another exchange that amused her, wrapping her in cheer. Yes, positive emotions were even better shields to walk into this experience than serenity.

"Are you going to stay with me and help me when I regress, Felonerb?"

He sat straight. *I am your Fam. Yes. I will be with you.* His tail lashed. *You do not need to worry. I will protect You!*

Pleasure at his loyalty seeped into her. Yes, archetypical cat, and archetypical Fam.

"Just memories. Let's go."

Felonerb lifted his muzzle. *I am your FamCat. I am with you.*

"Thank you."

*A*ntenn's muscles tightened again as the glider passed through TQ's gates, and though he didn't hear them close behind him, in his mind they clanged shut with the force of thunder.

Wisps of the mental redesign of the inner cathedral columns vanished as he focused again on Tiana.

He'd definitely been roped in as a witness to more of her distress, to the worst night of her childhood, probably the worst night of her life.

And here he was at the Turquoise House. The glider stopped, and he locked the stands but continued to sit in his vehicle. The small stone courtyard held a Temple glider and a Healer's glider but nothing from the guardhouse. Yet.

Here he was. After years. At the Turquoise House, which pretty much corresponded to a major change in *his* life, and the most roiling emotions.

He'd met Mitchella Clover here, papyrus in hand, to ask her to adopt him. He'd been all too aware of his past as a gang member . . . if there'd been a status below Commoner, he'd been it.

The Turquoise House, glowing so boldly, had seemed just like him . . . the lowest of the low in Houses. He'd thought that he and Mitchella Clover would live there, her brokenhearted from walking away from her HeartMate, him not *quite* a "real" Clover kid. He'd been struggling to define himself, *become*, quickly, a different boy. Grow.

They'd moved to the Clover Compound; he'd been accepted into the huge Family and had worked in and with the infant Turquoise House for only a few weeks. Straif T'Blackthorn had come around, married Mitchella, and taken them both to T'Blackthorn Residence.

Now Antenn'd finally returned, and the bright shine of the place to his eyes and his mind continued to symbolize that explosive and fearful period of his life.

A glider parked beside him and he looked over to see his cuz Trif Clover Winterberry's HeartMate, Ilex Winterberry, now the Chief of all the guards of Druida City. Hiding a wince, Antenn undid the safety web, lifted his door, and went around to hug the man whom he hadn't seen for a few days. Ilex pounded his back, and Antenn was deeply grateful that his burn was better and that he'd have Family witnessing with him.

"How much do you know about this?" Ilex asked as they walked to the door.

"Probably not as much as you do. Garrett Primross is running the show. I happened to be at the wrong place at the wrong time."

"Do you know FirstLevel Priestess Tiana Mugwort well?"

"I met her two days ago when she was assigned to me and the Chief Ministers of the Intersection of Hope as a liaison to GreatCircle Temple."

Ilex grunted. "All right, we'll go through this whole rigmarole of oaths, et cetera. You can witness."

"You sure? Maybe you should dismiss me?"

Ilex's cool blue-gray gaze met his. "If I must do this, you must do this."

The door swung open. "Greetyou, Chief Winterberry. Greetyou, Antenn," TQ said in the smoothest of tones. The last time Antenn had heard the House, it had been speaking with Mitchella's voice. Big difference.

"Greetyou, Turquoise House," he and Ilex said at the same time.

The entryway appeared larger and was minimally furnished, along with the sitting room beyond.

"Please take a right at the corridor and go to the end and turn right once more. I have set up and furnished a temporary meditation room for this event."

Antenn's steps had slowed. He recalled the layout, of course, and the outer walls hadn't changed, but he believed that most of the non-load-bearing walls had been moved or removed all together.

Ilex opened the door and went in first. This particular chamber had no windows outside, but the walls had holo murals that appeared like they were in the center of GreatCircle Temple and the dome had been opened to let in the fierce rays of the summer sun and the deep infinite blue sky. Within a pace, Antenn's foot bumped against a thick bedsponge that covered the floor. He stopped and pulled off his shoes and liners and stepped up. His toes curled under and he glanced around.

High Priest T'Sandalwood sat cross-legged and straight-spined on a fat floor pillow made of a carpet in rich shades of brown and gold with an ornate pattern of black. Though his expression appeared impassive, Antenn sensed the man was not pleased with the situation.

A young journeywoman in Healer green whom he didn't recognize sat in the farthest corner, wide-eyed and excited, nearly rocking on her green pillow-seat.

With a grunt, Ilex went to a pillow at right angles to the empty

crushed red velvet pillow in the middle—Tiana wasn't there yet—
and Antenn grabbed a blue pillow against the wall and sat close to
his cuz-in-law.

Garrett Primross sat on the bedsponge on the other side of the
velvet pillow.

"Since we are all here, shall we conclude the formalities before I
inform FirstLevel Priestess Mugwort that it is time?" TQ asked.

They went through the long and tedious process of stating their
names and swearing that none of them had been involved in the
events of the night in question—except Ilex, who had arrived on the
scene to investigate after the mob had dispersed.

They also stated their current relationship with Tiana, and only
T'Sandalwood, who was one of her immediate superiors, and Garrett Primross, who was her brother-in-law, were considered "close."
To Antenn's surprise, TQ sounded a little disappointed to be named
as an impartial witness.

The door opened and Tiana walked in, dressed in a simple, flowing robe of white, her long hair unbound and damp and feet bare.

Antenn's breath simply stopped. Here in this room, with no outside influences, her serenity glowed in her aura, even under these
circumstances.

She was gorgeous. And perfect.

She greeted everyone with a curtsey, then took her place in the
middle of the room. Glancing up at the illusion of blue sky and
white sunlight, she smiled, then lay down, her torso angled against
the red velvet pillow. Felonerb trotted in behind her. It didn't look
like he'd done any cleansing at all. He took his place atop the pillow, close to her head, purring rustily.

"Ready?" asked Garrett.

The private investigator and Ilex had consulted and Ilex had
given the Garrett the job of asking a list of agreed-upon questions.

"Yes," Tiana said.

"Would you like me to count you down into your trance?" said
T'Sandalwood in his High Priest voice.

Antenn noted the hint of disapproval of this whole matter and flinched inside. *He'd* started this chain of events, and it might cost her more than he'd imagined.

"Yes, please, count down for me."

"Five, four, three—"

Tiana's eyes closed on three and Antenn sensed she'd plummeted deep into a trance state. A whole lot faster than would happen with him.

"Hello, Tiana," Garrett said.

"Hello, Garrett." She sounded completely calm, and her voice lilted with affection for her brother-in-law.

"I love you like a sister, you know."

"Yes, I know, and you're a good brother, too," she approved.

"I'm glad you think so. Now we want to go back, far back into your past."

Her body tensed, then eased after a second as if she used all that practice she must have had in her career.

Sexy priestess. The dichotomy hit Antenn squarely, and he accepted that he liked the contrast, his desire for lusty physical relations with a woman who dealt daily with the spiritual.

Not that the Lady and Lord weren't lusty, too. Physicality and sexual relations were celebrated, especially at certain times of the year—in private—but like most people he thought of the priests and priestesses as focused on more elevated matters.

He thought Winterberry's gaze stopped on him as the guard scanned the room, and Antenn began breathing in a more calming pattern himself.

"I will count you back," said T'Sandalwood, "to the last night you spent in the old Mugwort home with your Family."

"The night of the firebombing," Winterberry added.

Her face crumpled.

"Are you listening, Tiana?" asked the High Priest. The edge in his gaze wasn't reflected in his mellow voice.

"Yes."

"You're regressing. You can do that."

"Yes."

"I am counting down from three. At one you will be there. You will not—"

"You *will* experience the events exactly as you did," Winterberry insisted. "So that we might bear witness to what happened that night." He slipped a glass sphere into her palm, curved her fingers around it. "This is a memorysphere to record your experiences. You understand what to do with it."

"Yes," Tiana's voice sounded distant.

"Three, two, and *one*," T'Sandalwood intoned.

Twenty-five

❦

$\mathcal{T}$iana sat reading a papyrus book about the building of GreatCircle Temple when an odd noise caught her ears. She looked up, but no one had moved like they'd heard anything. She smiled at her parents and sister, all of them gathered around the fire in the ResidenceDen.

Papa was working on an old-fashioned lap desk with papyrus and writestick. He was a respected judge and they were a Family that prized traditions. Mama and Artemisia—who was *almost* an adult since she was seventeen and her Second Passage would come soon—sat together on a twoseat. Both bent over an old diary about Healing herbs.

Tiana glanced at the pile of presents ready to be opened on Samhain, New Year's Day. The book she read said Samhain had once been called November first by their Earthan ancestors. An interesting word. She mouthed *November.* Contentment welled through her . . . or she should have been . . . no, she *was* happy . . . but there was some mar to her—

Glass broke, then *Boom*!

She screamed and jumped to her feet.

What? asked a voice in her head.

Who are you?

A friend. Tell me what's wrong.

She shook her head, staring. "Something came in the window and exploded and there's fire on the carpet. Papa's putting it out." She clapped her hands over her ears, weeping. "I hear more, more of them in other rooms. Here's another one!"

It arced through the smashed window, a softleaf burning in the top of a glass bottle that broke. Fire flew. Artemisia screamed.

"Oh, no! Noooo!" Tiana shrieked. "Artemisia!"

What's wrong with Artemisia? The voice snapped and she heard fear in it. Fear that pounded in her, making her throat dry. Making her tremble. Making her freeze when she should be doing something.

What? It—he, it was a he—demanded.

"Artemisia's scalp is cut, and her hair is on fire!" Tiana keened.

"Stop that," Mama ordered, face pale.

"Yes, Mama," Tiana said, above the loud voice in her head ordering her to tell her everything that was going on, in detail. She also felt a cool glass sphere in her hand, waiting for her to stuff it full of all her emotions, everything she saw—fire!—and heard—loud voices, yells, shouts, pummeling her ears from outside—and touched—the wood of the top of her chair cracking under her fingers—and tasted—smoke, smoke, smoke!

So she told him everything. And his voice made her less afraid, like this wasn't the end of the world, and she felt a rumble in her ears, too, a nice sound, that also helped.

"Mama is helping Artemisia Heal and Papa isn't here. He's running from room to room, putting out the fires, but he says he is using Flair and spells in the walls to make it look like the house is still burning."

Canny man, your father.

"Yes. Yes. Artemisia is Healed and Papa says this room, under the desk, is safest and she's hiding under there while Mama is getting our things to take with us before we all teleport to Papa's office. He says he's read about mobs like these and they don't give up. They will come in and hurt us. So we will go somewhere else." Tiana panted, glad her fear had lessened because her voice didn't squeak as much. "Papa is getting stuff, too, and scrying the guards and doing other things."

Panting, Tiana said, "I think we will be okay." She crept to the window, keeping to the side, stood, and looked out. "There are a lot of people out there," she whispered. "Why would they be screaming and throwing fire at *us*? They look like they hate us." She shuddered and began counting them, each of them, their faces upturned in the bright flickering light engraved on her memory.

What are you doing?

"I am looking at them. I am counting them. I will never forget this. I won't! I will remember and know them." She ran and thought someone's hands tried to stop her and flung them off and didn't listen to the man as he said, "Easy," again, but kept on running. "I am looking out every window downstairs. They are all around us! Why are they doing this to us?"

You're looking out the windows?

"Yes! I told you, again and again and again for years and years . . ." Her voice broke and she shook her head, confused. "Artemisia is hiding under the desk, but I can't. I *can't*. I have to see who would hate us so that they threw a firebomb in our house. Who?"

And you can see faces, just confirming.

"*Yes!*"

Which room are you in now?

"The mainspace in front. They are all around the house. I need to check everywhere! Oh, oh, *oh*! Why is he here, why? The others— I don't know them except old GraceLord Galega, who hates everyone."

Who are you talking about?

"He is the man I saw a month ago. The man sent from GraceLord T'Equisetum for a written decision from Papa on a case he'd adjudged." She moved closer. "Yes, I am sure that is he! An Equisetum. I don't remember his name. He's standing in the back, but yelling, 'Burn them out! Burn them out! Fliggering Cross Folk!' But . . . but . . . he doesn't look mad. He looks *mean*. And he's tossing a bottle and rag back and forth in his hands! He threw it!" She ducked, wrapped her arms around herself, sniffling. Her throat felt raw from screaming, her eyes and nose hurt from the smoke. Her heart just plain hurt.

"Mama and Papa are calling me. I must go back to the Residence-Den. Here's Papa. He is calm, but pale. Mama has a trunk. Artemisia is crawling out from under the desk. We're holding hands and Papa will give us the coordinates for his office at night. He says some bad things happened in NobleCouncil today, and after what happened tonight, he isn't going to fight, and his office isn't his anymore, but no one will look for us there. Then we can go to Mama's relatives, at least for the ni-ight." She curled in on herself and cried and cried.

One last thing, the voice said.

"What?"

How long has it been since the first firebomb?

She looked at the timer on the fireplace mantel. "Twenty . . . twenty minutes," she said.

Sucking in a deep breath—air with no taint of smoke—Tiana shuddered and fell back into the present. She opened her eyes to see a blue sky, with dim shadows around her that moved. Felonerb crawled into her lap and she stroked him and felt his rumbling purr vibrate under her palm, sending loving through the rest of her.

The first face she saw after she blinked away leftover tears was Antenn's, paler than any time she'd seen him before—strained, too.

Then Chief Winterberry, face set in a grim expression, moved into her sight. He plucked the memorysphere from her hand and put it in his trous pocket. "I have a viz of people we believe might have been in the mob at your home that night. TQ will access the pics, along with miscellaneous other people as blinds, and flash them against the wall, and I'd like you to tell me who you saw." His voice dropped. "You remember, don't you?"

"Yes. The ones I saw well. Some were blurred or stayed in the shadows or were overshadowed by others."

"I understand."

"Does this have to be done now?" asked Antenn.

Everyone stared at him.

"It's best," said Garrett.

Tiana nodded. "While the memories are fresh. Though I think both this memorysphere and the previous ones I recorded should also be fine."

"I witness that I regressed FirstLevel Priestess Tiana Mugwort to the night of the firebombing of her childhood home, and I heard everything she said while she was in the trance, and no one and nothing influenced that experience," the High Priest said heavily.

Tiana sat and twisted to see him. He was all stiff and formal and again her spirit sank that she was doing this—no matter how necessary it seemed—and it impacted her career. It appeared as if the process had affected T'Sandalwood, too, and not in a good way.

Something she'd think about later, since guard pics began to appear on the wall, four at once. She jolted at the first image, that of a middle-aged woman who was also one of the first faces she'd seen when she'd peered from the broken window of the mainspace. In the pic, she smiled. In Tiana's memory her round face had been flushed, her eyes glazed with frenzy, and so Tiana described.

Tired, she went through them as quickly as possible, though sometimes she hesitated and said that she *thought* one or another had been there, had seen his shadowed features. GraceLord Galega was there, but she'd known he'd died before that very winter was over, years ago. She also figured that some innocent people were mixed in the viz, recognized people whom she knew but who *hadn't* been in the mob that night.

She recognized instantly the relative of GraceLord T'Equisetum, and Chief Winterberry stated the man's name was Arvense Equisetum.

Finally it was done and she slumped on the pillow.

High Priest T'Sandalwood rose heavily to his feet from the floor, moving more ponderously than she'd ever seen him outside death rites of a friend. His gaze connected with everyone but hers, and he said, "This is very disturbing information indeed regarding GraceLord

T'Equisetum. I need to meditate on this, consult with the High Priestess." His gaze latched on Winterberry. "But first I would like to speak with you in my office. If you would be so kind to accompany me to talk about what actions should be taken, small and large, and the procedure?"

Winterberry bowed stiffly, then turned to Tiana. "I strongly advise that you file a formal complaint against GraceLord T'Equisetum and his relative who incited the mob. They owe you reparations. As does the whole NobleCouncil. The actions of that body must be scrutinized. At the least, the title must be returned to your parents, your sister, and you. You've all done work in contributing to Celtan society for which you haven't been paid your annual NobleGilt."

"We at the Temple have been paying Priestess Mugwort the standard salary for commoners who are on our staff." T'Sandalwood sounded offended.

"But even commoners usually have Family members with other sources of income," Winterberry said.

Garrett said, "The Primary HealingHall hasn't been as generous to my HeartMate Artemisia, and I guarantee that GraceLord Mugwort and GraceLady Mugwort provide great services to Druida City and our society, for which they have received no remuneration for over a decade."

"That must be remedied," T'Sandalwood said.

"Agreed," Winterberry said.

"But this is a sensitive matter with wide ramifications," T'Sandalwood stated.

"We can approach T'Ash to lead the charge on this," Antenn said.

The older men stared at him.

"T'Ash is wealthy, Noble, of the FirstFamilies. Formidable," T'Sandalwood replied.

Just throbbing silence.

Antenn gave a little cough. "Scary. And *he* had to fight to get his title and estate back after an enemy fired his Residence and killed his Family. That might be a long time ago to some, but"—Antenn swept a hand to Tiana—"like Tiana, he's never going to forget that night, those moments. He'll be solid on wanting justice for this, and he'll be persistent. He won't quit until things are right."

T'Sandalwood's brows dipped as he scrutinized Antenn. "You, young man, are absolutely correct."

"T'Ash will never give up on this." Winterberry nodded slowly. He turned to Tiana. "You will have a very strong advocate." He paused, took the memorysphere from his pocket, looked at the High Priest. "Can we copy this for T'Ash and ask him to join us if he is available?"

T'Sandalwood closed his eyes briefly. "Yes. Let's hammer some ideas out first." With an admonishing nod to Tiana, he said, "I would prefer that you fill out the legal documents in GreatCircle Temple and stay there until you are done, so you are available if we need you."

She nodded.

"After you are finished with the forms, if you have not heard from us, you may consider your day done." He sighed heavily. "It has been a—challenging—experience for you."

"Yes, High Priest T'Sandalwood," she said.

"I will have complaint forms translocated to the Temple for Priestess Mugwort to fill out." His expression was absentminded as if focused on the meeting with T'Ash. "Surely you'll feel more comfortable working on them at the Temple."

Everything moved so quickly! As if she'd dropped the pebble of her memory of the night into a lake and it rippled clear across, affecting others as it went. T'Ash on their side! Though Antenn had mentioned the man to her before. She slid a gaze toward him, saw that his focus was on the older men. Then, as if he felt her study of him, he turned his head and winked at her.

With an additional rush of pleasure at his support, her knees went wobbly and Garrett stepped up and steadied her with a hand under her elbow.

"Tiana needs to recover a little first," TQ stated with authority. "I have several restorative drinks in my medical room. Antenn, please follow my instructions to get them. Garrett, please settle Tiana in the chair in the mainspace."

"Whatever we do, this is going to be a long, and perhaps ugly process," Garrett said.

Winterberry shrugged. "Maybe, maybe not. Once you have a FirstFamily Lord or Lady involved in something, things get done fast." He looked at Antenn. "I'll need you to fill out a witness statement immediately, too. Please go to the Temple so you are at hand if I wish to consult with you. I'll translocate some there."

Bowing to T'Sandalwood, Winterberry said, "High Priest, if you would offer to teleport me with you to your offices, we can get this process rolling. I'll send my glider back to the guardhouse."

T'Sandalwood held out his hand and Winterberry clasped the man's fingers, and they were gone.

Meanwhile, Antenn had slipped from the room, and Garrett led her from the chamber—which she didn't think she'd care to see again—to the left.

"I have two areas that might be mainspaces now, Garrett," TQ informed him. "But on second thought, I believe Tiana would be more comfortable in her sunroom."

"Fine." Garrett kept his steps as small as hers and his pace slow, staring at her thoughtfully.

"What?" she asked.

He took a coin from his trous pocket, then sent it running through the fingers of his free hand, appearing and vanishing. "You spoke in the tone of a girl."

She shrugged. "That's not unusual when a person is regressed to a younger age, you know that."

Nodding, he said, "That's true. But it affected every man here. Every one of them will fight for justice for that child who was ripped from her home."

"Oh." The back of her neck heated along with her cheeks, and she knew she flushed. Then she let a long sigh out. "That will be good."

"I think so. You know that Winterberry was the guard the First-Families called on when any investigation needed to be handled? He knows them. Not sure how well he works with T'Ash, but Antenn

Blackthorn-Moss is right. T'Ash will go after the NobleCouncil to make sure you Mugworts get what you're due with blood in his eyes. They can't just ignore this like they have for years." Garrett shook his head. "And I think Winterberry and the FirstFamilies are shifting all investigative business onto me. Winterberry is the Chief of all the guards now, and the FirstFamilies seem to want someone not . . . tied into the legal system. Though, obviously, in this instance, he can help a great deal."

They'd reached the end of the hall, and Tiana touched the door latch, which she'd closed and locked since it was the portal to her personal rooms, and the door swung open. The sitting room still looked stark, but they walked through it to the sunroom.

That door swung open for them, courtesy of TQ, and the humid scent of green and growing plants, the small rush of a fountain, wafted over her like a balm.

"Nice," Garrett said, glancing around at the tiers of beds and plants, the long pond, and the fountain in the corner. "That the Mugworts hold the BalmHeal estate and run the secret sanctuary is not well known," Garrett said slowly, "but I'm sure some FirstFamilies know."

"Like my friends the Hawthorns."

"Yes. And there isn't a more influential man in the younger set, a wealthier one, than Laev T'Hawthorn." Garrett paused, raising an eyebrow in a question toward her as he settled her in the wicker chair. "Unless it's Vinni T'Vine?"

She sat. "If you're asking me whether GreatLord T'Vine has ever visited FirstGrove and the sanctuary, I couldn't tell you, not even here."

"Aww, Tiana," TQ said.

Garrett jolted a little.

"I'm accustomed to keeping secrets. But, actually, I don't think T'Vine has been—where I live."

"Lived," TQ said firmly.

"Where I lived." She sighed and leaned back against the pillow of the chair and let the tangled, tired emotions within her subside as she considered the places she'd lived. Her childhood home, which had been budding with intelligence and now was firmly in the past. The series of rental apartments during that year her Family hid, blessedly fading from her memory. BalmHeal Residence, who had tolerated her, and who housed her loving Family, but hadn't ever quite felt like a real home to her. And now here, with the cheerful TQ.

Antenn appeared with a tube that showed thick orange-brown sludge, green bits, and a sprig of mint. He stared at it doubtfully and handed it to her.

She opened the top with a grateful sigh, swallowed some down. The restorative would give her energy and also contained a small spell to deflect a headache, though she didn't feel as if a migraine loomed.

Antenn glanced at her. "Better you drinking that stuff than me."

"My sister Artemisia stocked the medicine room here, and this concoction is one of my mother's. It's not bad and I'm used to it."

Antenn nodded and went back to studying the sunroom. "This isn't quite finished, either, is it?"

"None of my rooms are all the way finished," TQ said. "I want my—Tiana to make it the way she prefers."

Tiana sighed. "That's very nice of you, TQ."

The fountain splashed an extra-happy burble.

"I have a message for you, Garrett," TQ said. "The High Priest and Winterberry want to talk to you and for you to fill out the witness statement immediately. I have already done mine," TQ ended with pride.

Garrett grunted. "I don't know the light well enough in Great-Circle Temple to teleport there."

"You can take the Temple glider T'Sandalwood came in," Tiana offered. "And I'll go there with Antenn in his." She'd seen the vehicles through the courtyard windows as she'd walked to her rooms.

"Fine. See you later." One side of Garrett's mouth kicked up. "Glad this thing is finally being taken care of. The Family can use the gilt." He left.

Antenn paced the length of the sunroom and back. With the

plant beds, it was narrower, barely big enough for two to walk side by side. "You know, TQ, if you're still working on the beds, I'd recommend multicolored stone instead of just gray." He stopped at the corner. "And I think the fountain is too small and uninteresting. It doesn't fit. You need a fountain especially shaped for a corner. Red granite rock at various angles would look good."

"Do you know where to obtain such a fountain?" TQ asked.

"Yeah. I'll order it for you."

"Thank you, Antenn."

The architect took out his perscry pebble and, eyeing the corner, did so.

"Charge me, Antenn," TQ said.

"It can be a housewarming gift," Antenn said gruffly, not looking at Tiana.

"Thank you, Antenn," TQ said.

"Thank you, Antenn," Tiana echoed.

He shrugged. "'S nothing." When he turned to her, his face was pleasant but unrevealing. "How do you feel now?"

Twenty-six

Tiana rose to her feet, crossed into the sitting room, and put the tube into the reconstructor. Taking a softleaf from her sleeve, she wiped her lips and crossed to the door, then noticed Antenn standing in the middle of the room, hands on his hips. "You haven't chosen a color scheme for your rooms yet?" he asked.

"Ah, no." She hadn't thought to, was too accustomed to deferring to others.

"What would you like?" Antenn and TQ said at the same time.

"Ah—"

With narrowed eyes, Antenn said, "Warm tones. I think you appreciate warm tones. What's your favorite color?"

Tiana glanced around the sitting room. "I think I'd like peach in here."

A grunt from the architect. "Then you can have a rich cream for your bedroom." He paused. "Or pink."

"Not pink, a rich cream sounds good," she said.

"Layers, subtle swaths," Antenn said. "It's old-fashioned but it works. Cream and pale yellow and slight peach, shaded all together." He nodded. "That would work. See to it, TQ."

"Yes, Antenn!"

"You might want a contrasting wall in here, or a full mural. Think about it."

"Sounds lovely."

TQ said, "I know Avellana Hazel, *the* three-dimensional mural artist. And I've had lots of wonderful murals on my walls. The ocean at Maroon Beach . . ."

Antenn flinched.

"The great labyrinth through the seasons," TQ continued to gush. "FirstGrove."

"FirstGrove?" Antenn asked. "FirstGrove! You know someone who's been to FirstGrove? The secret sanctuary, BalmHeal estate?"

Tiana kept a casual smile on her face and refrained from tucking her hands into her opposite sleeves, a nervous gesture that might clue Antenn in.

"I am on good terms with BalmHeal Residence," TQ said haughtily, as if to make up for his mistake. "All us sentient Houses and Residences have links, you know that."

"But you'd need a person with a recordsphere to viz FirstGrove," Antenn pushed.

A slight sighing of the House around them, little wood creaks, air drafts. "Antenn, I have had desperate people within my walls."

"Oh."

Tiana's perscry lilted a formal processional march. She plucked it from her sleeve. "The High Priest is calling." Answering it, before the man with lined brow could speak, she said, "I—and witness Antenn Blackthorn-Moss—are on our way."

T'Sandalwood nodded. "Good, that's good. By glider?"

"Yes, the guard glider."

"Your memorysphere has been copied. The complaint form is on your desk in your office." He rubbed his forehead. "T'Ash is here. I'll see if he needs to speak with you."

Her stomach clenched and she felt the blood drain from her face. T'Ash. As Antenn had said, a very formidable man, one she'd never spoken to. "Very well," she said, her voice high.

The High Priest shook his head. "These FirstFamilies Lords and

Ladies . . . too curious for their own good. All of them." His lips firmed. "I will see you shortly, FirstLevel Priestess."

"Yes, sir."

"Antenn Blackthorn-Moss's witness statement has also been translocated to your desk. You can ask him if he needs a private meditation room to fill it out."

"I'll be fine working with the priestess," Antenn said, and Tiana liked that idea; it both relaxed her that she wouldn't be alone and pleasantly stroked her nerves.

"Shortly, then," the High Priest said. "Blessed be." He grimaced. "I hope this whole matter resolves to blessings upon all of us . . . and receiving what we deserve." He signed off.

Tiana found her palms pressing together in a reflexive gesture.

"Justice balanced with mercy, I suppose," Antenn said.

*The glider ride to GreatCircle Temple passed in quiet, Tiana too preoc-*cupied to converse with Antenn. It had been another long and emotionally strenuous day. And she could only see those continuing in the future.

Sooner or later she'd have to confront GraceLord T'Equisetum.

When they reached her chambers, she was pleased that though they weren't as elegant as her rooms in TQ, the furnishings were comfortable and of a homey shabbiness, not threadbare from poverty.

She led him into her office, which held a desk in the back corner that she'd use mostly for writing reports . . . and drafting rituals. The desk had been assigned to her as an apprentice when she'd entered the Temple for training years ago, and she'd kept it with her. Not at all an impressive, intimidating piece of furniture. Or one she used to show her status as a FirstLevel Priestess.

Antenn glanced at it and flicked his fingers at the light-spellglobes in the corner that lit with a full-spectrum daylight glow. He said, "When you receive the NobleGilt due you as a contributing member of our society, you'll be able to purchase a better desk." He frowned.

"And a more comfortable chair for sure. I can get you a discount with Clover Fine Furniture."

"Thank you," she said coolly, and went to the desk where two stacks of papyrus lay. Her stomach jittered from his words—he was sure the NobleCouncil would recognize its mistake and give the Mugworts back the gilt it had confiscated, acknowledge them as a Noble Family again. She wasn't so sure. In her counseling experience, it wasn't easy getting a person who felt entitled from birth to admit they'd been wrong—let alone a whole Noble body.

The other thing that dried her throat was the "Formal Complaint against a Noble" that lurked on her desk. Was she really going to do this? Perhaps jeopardize her career by stating that GraceLord T'Equisetum had wronged her Family, and her?

It could be a big, public, acrimonious mess. Just what the Sandalwoods would like one of their FirstLevel Priestesses to become involved in. Just what her colleagues would look at askance.

Antenn joined her at the desk, scooped up his stack titled "Witness Statement." "You're not going to back off now, are you?"

He stared down at her, hazel eyes questioning, and other feelings unfurled in her. She didn't want to be seen as lacking in any way by this man.

Her shoulders went back. "No."

He grunted and walked to a small table placed against one of the curved windows looking out on the gardens. "This will do well enough as a desk for me." Gaze locked on hers, he said, "We first met the day you had your reviews and received a promotion and the cathedral liaison project. I could tell the reviews bothered you. Are you worried about the High Priest and Priestess because of this complaint and petition mess?"

Her breath stuck in her chest and she nodded, then managed to say, "Yes."

"One trait all honorable people aspire to is justice."

She stared and a flush showed under his skin. His jaw set, and then he continued, "The Lord and Lady must prize justice also. And for the

High Priest and Priestess to lag in supporting one of their own in seeking justice would be seen as a failure, wouldn't it? Not only as members of the Noble class in failing to protect someone weaker from exploitation, the honest from the dishonest cheat, but also spiritually, wouldn't it? A failure of a spiritual nature." He gestured awkwardly. "A weakness or something?" He ended, brows down, frowning.

His words, the concept behind them, calmed her. "Yes. You're right. The three of us might not discuss this at all, if they take that point of view." She pressed her lips together, released them. "Though I do not think of myself as weak."

He slanted her a look. "Not in courage, or . . . grace . . . with the Lady and Lord, I suppose, but T'Equisetum has more status, gilt, and influence than you, for sure." Antenn paused. "But not nearly as much as T'Ash."

"Who is a force to be reckoned with, as are all the FirstFamily Lords and Ladies. Such as your father," she said.

"Such as your friend, Laev T'Hawthorn."

She used Antenn's words. "I suppose."

He jerked a nod and turned away to the small table, actually seeming to see it: graceful tapering pillar legs, multiwood inlaid top. "This is nice."

"A gift from a friend who doesn't need it in his chambers."

"His?" Antenn's expression, which had lightened, clouded again.

"Leger Cinchona. He moved from chambers here to his newly refurbished Temple in Apollopa Park."

"Oh." Antenn nodded as if no longer interested, set the papyrus on the table and squared the sheets, then sat and translocated a writestick from *somewhere* with such ease she knew it was a daily occurrence as with her, too, and began to study the first page. His face soured.

She went to her desk and sat and read the top sheet of the complaint. Her mouth dried and her heart beat faster, but she took her own writestick and began filling it out carefully. All the people who looked at the complaint would analyze her handwriting and what it indicated about her and the issue she brought before JudgementGrove.

The standard questions were easy to answer, and she snuck

looks at Antenn. Even just sitting she felt a wave of attraction moving through her.

Oddly enough, she finished both the complaint against Grace-Lord T'Equisetum and Arvense Equisetum and her portion of the Petition to the NobleCouncil for Redress of Wrongful Action—which Garrett would also fill out, since his HeartMate had been affected and therefore he had—before Antenn stopped writing his Witness Statement. He seemed to be noting every detail.

Then his scry pebble sounded, and he fished it from his trous pocket and glanced at her. She nodded.

He frowned. "It's a three-way call with Chief Minister Elderstone, Winterberry back at the guardhouse, and me. They probably want you, too."

Probably, since she was the official liaison of the Temple to the Intersection of Hope. She gestured to the scry panel on the wall, something the Temple provided to a FirstLevel Priestess if she couldn't purchase her own, which she couldn't. Better for conference calls than her scry bowl. "Please forward the scry to here."

Antenn nodded and flicked the pebble with his thumb, sauntered over and took a chair in front of her desk, and set a foot across his knee, which did interesting things with his trous, and she yanked her gaze away.

She raised her voice. "Open scry from Chief Minister Elderstone of the Intersection of Hope Church, and Chief Guardsman Ilex Winterberry." A moment later the panel swirled like the water in the old scry bowls, shades of blue, and both men showed up on her screen.

"Better if you came and sat next to me," Antenn said gruffly.

Tiana flushed a little, then joined him in her other client chair; his aura seemed to envelop her and she liked it. She waved and had the screen rotating and tilting to show them both.

"Greetyou, Chief Minister and Chief Guardsman." Tiana inclined her head.

"Greetyou, Chief Minister, Priestess Mugwort, and cuz," Winterberry said. He sat behind a larger and more authoritative desk than her own, appearing guardlike and serious.

"Thank you for joining me for this conference," the Chief Minister said. "My colleagues and I have been discussing the security situation of building the cathedral."

Antenn sat up straight; his face went expressionless, though every muscle and sinew of his body seemed to have tightened, and she *knew* he was concerned the Chief Ministers might have canceled the project. That radiated painfully from him, though his mouth curved in an outwardly easy smile.

Could the Chief Ministers cancel the job? Weren't there contracts? She didn't know, but the architect wouldn't worry over nothing.

"Naturally the building of our cathedral is preeminent in our minds and we have had long and continuing discussions of all the ramifications."

Antenn relaxed, his face set more naturally.

Chief Minister Elderstone paused and his face seemed to sag into new lines. "We have decided that we will have the ritual tomorrow night at twinmoons rise." He sighed. "Please inform those from the Temple of that."

Twenty-seven

*T*omorrow! *That's hardly time to learn the parts,"* Tiana said.

Antenn said, "I think you will have more participants of the FirstFamilies if you wait."

"Will we?" Elderstone's expression solidified into austere. "There are rumors going around that our rituals are lesser—not different, but *wrong*—and we should not be supported by anyone who truly loves your Lord and Lady and the many aspects they take. In fact, we have heard that one of the proponents of the Traditionalist Stance political movement that has been coalescing in the last few years, GraceLord T'Equisetum, will be giving a press conference, and that he will be hinting that our faith is not acceptable."

Tiana made a noise; that man had dominated her thoughts for the afternoon and she didn't like it. Antenn's gaze slid to the witness form that still lay on the table but kept his face unrevealing. Winterberry appeared inscrutable.

"Yes, FirstLevel Priestess?" Chief Minister Elderstone asked.

She had to say something. "He is a . . . negative man. One who dislikes change."

"And who *hates* people who don't believe the same as he does?"

Winterberry asked, as if he hadn't been there as a witness and considered T'Equisetum's motivations, as he would.

She shrugged.

After a silence of a few heartbeats, Elderstone continued, "Tomorrow evening will be a good day for our ritual, on one of our holy days, and our members will turn out." He bent a look at Antenn, at Winterberry. "So you will know if people start targeting them."

"I will participate myself, sir," Winterberry said.

Elderstone's brows rose in surprise, and then he nodded. "Good." He turned his gaze back to Tiana. "Do you know your part?"

She shifted. "Of course. I wrote the ritual and it's still in my mind."

"And all of our parishioners will know their parts because the ritual is simple, it includes our oldest chants and responses, and"— he raised a finger—"we will allow papyrus prompts for those who are not members of our belief system but who wish to attend. Will you make copies of each of the four parts for our guests, FirstLevel Priestess?"

"Yes."

"I'll be there," Antenn said in a rough voice.

The Chief Minister nodded. "We expected you. We toured the area again during our discussions this afternoon and concentrated on the trenches instead of the ritual. They are, as required, eight meters deep for the great foundation blocks. We did a spot check here and there to ensure they were level, and all are."

"Of course," Antenn said stiffly.

"Excellent, efficient work."

"Thank you," Antenn said.

"You have our authorization to proceed with setting the foundation. You stated the first blocks could be cut, translocated from the quarry by a specialized Earth Mage company, and set within a ten-septhour time span?"

"Yes," Antenn said. His jaw flexed. "We can start tomorrow morning at dawn, but it *will* be pushing the work to finish by sunset. I will have to notify the mortar makers today so that they may begin their batches."

"We must have at least the first blocks down and solid so we can infuse the spellshields into the basic structure. Can we count on you for that?"

Antenn's fingers twitched, and she got the impression he wanted to run them through his hair. He scowled, then nodded and said, "Yes. Twinmoonsrise might give us just enough extra time to finesse any problems that might arise." Antenn stood and bowed as if to a FirstFamily GreatLord. "If you will excuse me, I need to speak to my subcontractors." He paused. "And to all whom I might be able to persuade to join us in this enterprise."

The word *enterprise* flicked an image of Laev T'Hawthorn into Tiana's mind. "I'll speak to the Hawthorns." She already had a stack of formal invitations ready on a side table, but face-to-face by scry or in person would be best. Her eyes met the Chief Minister's. "I cannot promise that they will compose part of your—" She stopped because she'd thought *circle* and that wasn't correct. "—ceremony," she finished.

"We thank you. Now, we, too, must practice. Since it seems we will be viewed by those of great status and influence of Celta, we must be as perfect as possible. May your day's journey be sweet." He cut the scry.

Winterberry stayed on the screen. "One moment, Antenn. Whom do you approach?"

"My Family, the Blackthorns. All of us who can be there." He paused. "I'm sure my mother and father will come, my siblings and my cuzes Draeg and Vensis, who are living with us. By extension, I'm pretty sure that Del and Raz Elecampane might come. Raz, as an actor, would find it interesting." He paused. "That's how I'll be spinning the experience, interesting and unique. Once-in-a-lifetime, maybe."

"Good idea," the Chief of the guards said. "I will contact the head of the Clover Clan, Walker T'Clover." He smiled. "If the Clovers come en masse, they might confuse prejudiced onlookers as to who are serious Intersection of Hope adherents."

"You think there might be trouble, then," Antenn said.

"I think I'm paid to make sure there won't be . . . and I've heard the circulating rumors, too."

Antenn's jaw clenched. "Worse than I thought, then."

"Well, there isn't any panic like there was during the Black Magic Cult murders, but there's distrust of the Intersection of Hope people, and, I think, malice toward them."

As they watched a guardswoman came and whispered in Winterberry's ear. He nodded and dismissed her, then said, "I've been informed that GraceLord T'Equisetum has called a press conference to speak with the newssheets and viz reporters about the new Intersection of Hope cathedral. Tomorrow morning, a septhour before WorkBell, when folk might be watching."

Antenn said, "He's gone to the public, then." The architect rolled his shoulders as if releasing tension. "I don't know if that means his influence with other Nobles and in the NobleCouncil is not as much as he wishes—others aren't listening to him as much and he wants more support—or that he's consolidated support and has a good base and wants to become even more popular."

Winterberry looked straight at Tiana. "As a liaison between the Temple and the Intersection of Hope, don't you think you should be there?"

"Where is he holding the press conference?" Tiana asked.

"T'Equisetum keeps a business office near the GuildHall. He handles the selling of some food crops." Winterberry paused. "Especially those of his cuz, Arvense, to whom he gave a valuable estate just after the firebombing of the homes of the Intersection of Hope during the fear of the Black Magic Cult." The Chief looked straight at her. "You can decide whether to hand GraceLord T'Equisetum your complaint, as an injured party. As soon as you transmit the complaint also naming Arvense, one of our guards in the north will serve it upon the man." Now Winterberry smiled, showing teeth. "I think that Arvense will lose that estate, and justly so. Please finish that complaint as soon as possible and translocate it to the clerk of all JudgementGrove. I'll ensure that a copy of your memorysphere is available for review upon request from the clerk."

Her mouth dried, but she forced words out anyway. "I will. Right now. As for the press conference, I'll plan on attending," Tiana said. "I must send out the invitations to the Intersection of Hope ritual to my friends and Family." She closed her eyes at the rush of it all. "Tomorrow night. At twinmoons rise."

"Later, then," said the guard. Tiana opened her lashes to see the scry panel go dark.

The instant the scry flicked off, Antenn was on his own perscry speaking to a woman who apparently ran a mortar mixture shop. Antenn's and the mortar maker's conversation was brisk and seemed to end on a satisfactory note.

Tiana skimmed her complaint, hesitated, then copied it the requisite five times and sent it to the JudgementGrove system's chief clerk. They hadn't moved fast enough to stop T'Equisetum from maligning the Intersection of Hope ministers.

Antenn rubbed his pebble again with his thumb, scried the quarry that would cut the huge stone blocks for the base of the cathedral, and gave them the go-ahead to begin work.

She listened a little to that, then went to the stack of invitations she'd penned and placed her fingertips on them, concentrated on imbuing the time and date into the bespelled space she'd left in each one, and then, with a snap of both thumbs and forefingers, translocated them to the mail caches of each person.

With bare patience, Antenn scried the Earth Mages' company, Apex Mage Builders, twice, but was forced to leave a message in their cache. When he looked up from his calls and saw her watching him, he flushed. "Forgive me for using your office as my own. I'm finished for now."

She inclined her head. "Events move apace."

"Yeah."

They gazed at each other. Now they were alone again, and looking at each other, and, not focused on anything else, the atmosphere throbbed with the attraction between them. Every time they spent a little time with each other, the connection got stronger.

She grabbed at the first passing thought. "If you can get me a count of the people who might participate in the ritual, I'd be grateful."

"Yes?"

"It would be best if I ensured there are sufficient copies of the ceremony for all. The Chief Ministers will expect that of me. I'll walk you to the main teleportation pad." As if he didn't know, but she needed to move.

"All right, I'll get you my list." His lips quirked up. "And thanks for the escort." Antenn paused at the door and held it open, but in such a way that their bodies brushed. His spellshield was gone and she hadn't noticed. She *did* notice how she enjoyed the slight contact. Even though they were both clothed, she thought she could feel his strong, tough body.

They didn't speak as they walked through the busy Temple and to the teleportation pad. Once there, she offered her hand. "Merry meet."

Instead of shaking it or gripping her arm in a more businesslike greeting, he began to bow, took her fingers. Lightning sizzled through her; she did more than tremble, she *shook*, and knew to the marrow of her bones that she touched her HeartMate.

They stared at each other, and Tiana thought his expression was just as aghast as her own.

His hand slid from her fingers up to her wrist, circled it, and desire swamped her.

Her mouth formed *HeartMate*, but she couldn't get the word out.

"No. No!" Antenn said. But he didn't release her. He swallowed. "It's just . . . just . . ." He coughed. "Just, ah, passion." He gazed at her as if he wanted her to agree, then added, "I can't have a close, a deep personal relationship right now. Career too important."

That ruffled her ego, but her brain, which had gone blank, started working again and she nodded. "The cathedral is a priority."

He was her *HeartMate*. Here! Standing right in front of her! She wanted to fling herself into his arms. She wanted to pull him down to the ground. Right. Here.

She wanted to smack him.

Acting on any one of those three needs in her workplace, in the view of all levels of priests and priestesses, visitors, people who came to the Temple for counseling or otherwise, would completely destroy her career. She sucked in a breath and took a step back, breaking his grip, though his fingers reluctantly gave way.

She looked around her to remind herself of where she was, and curled her toes in her shoes and sent sexual heat into the floor of the Temple. Like many buildings, it had a storage area for excess Flair. She thought she heard it hum approvingly in her mind.

She hoped that neither of the Sandalwoods was so tied to the Temple that they could feel what she'd done.

Career. He was right. Both of their careers—that they'd both spent years building—were on the line in this project. Though the Sandalwoods had given her this assignment with the Intersection of Hope, most of Tiana's peers thought it was a low-status situation, and a step down from the level she should be working at. This would always be remembered among her set after the Sandalwoods retired. She didn't need any more negative impressions associated with her priestesshood.

Antenn jammed his hands in his pockets. "I don't have time—" he began roughly.

"I don't have time for this," Tiana said at the same instant.

"We don't have time for this . . . for . . ." he started, and stopped.

She nodded, meeting his eyes. "Anything major."

"That's right." He paused, and they looked at each other for a solid minute. "Would you like to have dinner with me? Privately? At T'Blackthorn Residence?"

Her blood beat fast and hot and her mind struggled to understand that he wanted her—wanted to do more with her than have sex.

Not HeartBond, of course. Not. But be with her.

He stared at her and she couldn't break that gaze. Didn't even want to. She swallowed. "Not T'Blackthorn Residence. Come to TQ," she said on a whisper of breath.

He bobbed his head. "Yes. Right now."

"Yes. Right now," she agreed.

He grabbed her hand. "Let's hurry."

"Yes."

"Damn, I wish I knew TQ better so we could 'port," Antenn said.

"Yes." Catching her breath, she said, "GreatCircle Temple, may I have the use of a glider to the Turquoise House? It can automatically return."

"Of course, FirstLevel Priestess Mugwort. There is one available at the east door."

She trembled at the fire heating, heating, heating her blood, and walked quickly toward the east exit and out.

The glider door rose and Antenn slid in first and Tiana followed. "To the Turquoise House," she gasped to the autonav. The door descended and the glider accelerated away.

Antenn tugged on her, sliding her across the long bench close to him. With a hasty Word, she used Flair to retreat to the length of their arms, though their fingers remained clasped.

"Wait, wait," she said, breath still coming too quickly, desire flooding her so that her mind swam in it, barely functioned. "This is a *Temple* glider." Her eyes met his and saw his pupils wide with need, too. "I . . . I have no willpower with you."

He grunted. His mouth formed words that she couldn't read. "I understand," he croaked. "Glider, go as fast as possible, just below emergency status."

"Speeding up," the glider's mechanical voice said.

This time the ride seethed with tension. Their hands had clasped, but otherwise they stayed as far apart as they could. Tiana *felt* the cycling heat of their passion. Her mind wanted to consider the ramifications of finally meeting and having—soon to have!—her Heart-Mate. But her body was readying for sex, her breasts tightening, feeling heavy, her core dampening. From just a touch! The touch of her HeartMate, the man made for her.

He'd been here in Druida City all the time and she hadn't been able to sense him, a puzzle she'd think about later. Much later.

"Thank the Lord and Lady," Antenn mumbled as the glider halted before TQ's front door. He dragged Tiana out of his side of the vehicle and around it heading straight for the entrance. "Open the door *now*, Turquoise House!" Antenn demanded.

The front whisked open. "Please tell me there's a bed in your bedroom, Tiana. A couch. Large body pillows. Anything."

"At least a bed," she muttered.

"There is a bed in Tiana's bedroom, of course," TQ said. "And one in the MasterSuite and the MistrysSuite, and I can have—"

"That's enough. Privacy mode, TQ." Antenn and she ran lightly through the rooms, the corridor, heading straight for her chambers. Obviously he had a great memory.

"Privacy mode?" Tiana asked.

"He won't watch or listen or record our bodily functions such as heart rate, breathing, whatever."

"Lady and Lord," Tiana said. "Thank you for privacy mode, TQ."

"You are welcome. I am withdrawing from your bedroom," the House stated.

"Good. Great," Antenn said. "Thanks."

"Felonerb RatKiller is exploring beyond my environs," TQ said.

"Thank you," she repeated, a little dazed. She hadn't spared her new Fam a thought; instead images of what Antenn might look like naked rolled through her mind.

Antenn gave a snort of laughter.

"What?" Tiana asked.

"He'll be back at dinnertime."

"Oh. Yes." Then the door was there and it didn't open. Tiana stopped and set her palm on it, undid the spell lock, pushed it open, and stared a little at the peach-yellow-cream walls. Warm and welcoming and beautiful.

"Your bedroom to the right or left?" Antenn asked.

"Ah, to the left."

"Can't wait. Gotta get my hands on you." He picked her up and the feel of being carried, being *held*, against him, the scent of him, that windblown plateau smell, whirled in her head.

Lord and Lady, she wanted him. His arms were warm, strong behind her back, under her knees, and she became all too aware that she wore nothing under her dress but skin.

Then he grunted as he opened the latch to the bedroom door and they were through. Here, too, was a rich cream with a tinge of yellow.

He lowered her to her feet and her eyes widened at the new huge bed with light-colored wood lattice corners and top with live plants twining around them, and buds of some flower that already graced the air with a light fragrance even before blooming. Or maybe that was the leaves themselves. She didn't know.

Didn't care because Antenn stood before her, looking down at her and what was important was seeing him, the softened expression on his face, the brown of his hazel eyes darkening, the flush across his cheekbones. Surely that meant his desire flamed as high as her own.

Twenty-eight

*H*er hands lifted to his shoulders, felt the curve of muscle under well-woven cloth. "You have too many clothes on," she said, then blinked that the words came out of her mouth. She hadn't been too sexually aggressive before—except for that one dream they'd shared, just last night. It seemed eons ago, yet her body recalled the exquisite release and her head tilted back in provocative surrender. "I want your kiss."

His mouth opened on a moan and his breath caressed her and she more than wanted his kiss, she ached for it, the taste of his tongue, the probing of her mouth that would prelude his shaft driving within her.

Yes, all of that.

But he didn't move, held completely still.

So she broke her stare from his and pressed her fingers against his shoulders again, said a throaty Word and smiled from under lowered lashes as the bespelled tunic and shirt fell away from him. Lifting her hands, she took a half step back, not too far, still within the tingling caress of his aura—his non-spellshielded self—so she could see him.

He was lean, and probably would never have the height or the bulk of a man who'd been well fed and cared for as a child, but was subtly muscled. Strong. He'd thought nothing of carrying her. He'd be a fencer, a duelist, if necessary. That's how the FirstFamilies settled some of their problems with each other, by calling feud.

She—her father—her Family could have called feud on T'Equisetum. Her mind blurred at the impossible thought, and she threw it out. Much nicer to stroke Antenn's smooth chest, feel him tremble under her fingertips.

Another moan, and his hands twitched by his sides, but it appeared to her that his brain had just turned off.

He lowered his head and rubbed his cheek against her hair—for that particular sensation? To memorize her scent as she had his? Her hands settled on his hips, the leather of his belt, the sturdier fabric of his trous. His flanks were muscled, and she'd noticed his butt was prime . . . but the front of his trous showed a thick, long bulge that her fingers itched to touch. Another goal surfaced in her mind. To make him move. To snap his control. To drive him mad.

Touching his belt buckle, she nibbled on her lips. It had been a long time since she'd undressed a man. Couldn't, right now, even recall her last lover.

"Undo," she whispered, and the belt flicked open and slithered from the loops and fell to the floor; the trous dropped, too, but caught on his boots. Something she didn't notice at first because she was staring at his loincloth.

Seeing him ready for her had her dampening more. Her nipples beading and nubbing against the front of her dress.

"Mine," he said roughly. One of his arms came around her and fisted behind her back and he arched her, then lowered his head and brought his mouth to her right nipple and began sucking at it through the cloth.

Her hands fell away from him. The only thing in her entire universe was the feel of his lips, the edge of his teeth on her breast. Her nipple being laved, the damp cloth rasping against her.

Then he trailed kisses that blazed through her bodice to her other nipple and began to suck on that one. Her breasts moved against the dress with her panting whimpers and her fingers went to his biceps and felt the tensile strength of him beneath smooth skin, and her body bowed. And yes, yes, she surrendered to lust, to passion, to him.

He lifted his mouth and said, "Dress *off*!"

It fell from her.

"Lady and Lord," he cried, like a prayer. "Mine. Must have. Now!"

He lifted her and swung and tossed her onto the bed and she sank into the puffy comforter and her legs parted and the air between them cooled the heat of her sex and she *throbbed* there, needing him.

"Boots gone!" he said gutturally, and leapt after her and then he moved up her and he thrust within her and again went completely quiet.

They gasped in unison. His smooth hair had tufted out around his strained face. His neck, chest, arms dampened.

And he felt incredibly wonderful inside her. Filling her just right. Completing her.

But his arms braced on either side of her, his face, his body, was so beautiful. The feel of his lower body against hers, his legs around hers, the slight slide of his skin dazzled her.

Hot.

He was inside her, and heat filled her and burned through her from her veins to her nerves to the outside of her skin. All was heat and desire soon to tip into madness, and not just his. Hers. Theirs.

"Want to wait," he said through gritted teeth. "Can't." He pulled back, nearly out of her, and she moaned at the wonderful sensation, and the loss of him, and her *need* of him. Then he thrust into her and her body ruled. She wrapped herself around him, feeling the flex and release of his muscles, letting the blood pound through her, arched and curved herself, and they spiraled upward as passion seized them, and he shouted and she cried out and she exploded into sizzling fireworks with him.

Her senses worked oddly. Darkness when there should be afternoon light. Thrumming heartbeats racked her body. She thought she heard wind chimes. Or it could be clashing sword blades. She smelled herbs released from the comforter as it cleansed automatically, Antenn, maybe a lingering fragrance of the soap she'd used in the waterfall.

A groan? Did she do that? Coldness as weight left her and breath came into her lungs. She discovered she could open her eyes and the light, all mellow and pretty, nearly dazzled.

Rolling onto her side, she stared at the man who was her Heart-Mate. She'd found him sexually attractive but now scrutinized his face, his body. "You're beautiful," she said.

His eyes opened, greeny-brown and looking startled, a flush flowed under his skin. "No."

She nodded and the smoothness of the linen under her cheek pleased her, too. "Yes, you are."

"It's the . . . the *you know* talking."

"The HeartMate connection? Perhaps." And at that he tensed. She continued conversationally, "I didn't see anything like the golden HeartBond that is supposed to be there for us."

He leaned up on an elbow, scowling. "By the Lady and Lord, we've really only known each other for a few days."

She nodded. "I suppose that makes a difference." Keeping all judgement from her tone, she said, "I was sure that my HeartMate wasn't in Druida City because I couldn't feel the connection with him—with you."

Flushing even redder, he dropped flat onto the bed, put his arm over his eyes, and then removed it, as if thinking better of hiding from her. And, yes, she was receiving input from their bond. A small but strong link between them.

HeartMates newly met.

She breathed steadily, making sure any tiny thread of resentment that he hadn't looked for her was far from the bond. In truth, the sex had been so incredible that she felt more relaxed and easy about her whole life than . . . for weeks. "So why didn't I feel you?" she prompted.

"The first days of my Second Passage to free my Flair were horrible," he said. "So we—my parents and I—knew the whole term of both dreamquests would probably be bad, too."

She frowned. "I think I *did* feel you a little during your Second Passage, though not much during my own. Did you make me a HeartGift?"

He glowered, then turned and stared up at the ceiling, which had no mural or anything interesting. It was white.

"Yeah," he said. Snuck a glance at her. "Did you make one for me?"

"Yes. Do you want it?"

"No!"

"All right. So why couldn't I find you when I looked?" Now the shadow of old pain lurked in the back of her mind. She wouldn't, didn't think she dared let it out.

He rubbed his face. "It's a long story."

"Um-hmm." She sat up. "Would you like something to drink? I think there's a beverage no-time in here. Juice?"

"Yeah, sure. Water."

She nodded and studied the walls, the bottoms of which were paneled, and decided she didn't want to break privacy mode with TQ.

Antenn pointed at a handle that appeared to be the same color as the cabinet, and she walked over and opened the no-time. She got tubes of water for both of them, turned, and lobbed his toward him. He caught it at the last minute and laughed. He'd sat up and was staring at her with appreciation.

Opening the top, she settled next to him and drank a few sips. "So, HeartMate, go on with your long story."

His frown returned. "Even after Mitchella and Straif adopted me and the Clovers and Blackthorns welcomed me into their clans, life wasn't . . . easy." He chugged some water, staring at the tube. "Mostly because of my vocation. SupremeJudge Elder assigned me—the second time—to the Cang Zhus to study under them as an apprentice and journeyman. They liked the gilt I brought in, but all the other students were relatives. And they didn't appreciate my Fam, Pinky."

"Hmm," Tiana said.

"And when the parents took me to FirstFamilies events, I wasn't exactly welcomed. Because my brother had murdered some of those high-status Lords and Ladies."

"You are not your brother. If you weren't different from him, you wouldn't have been adopted by good people."

Antenn angled his water tube at her. "You have a point. But it's not something I've ever been allowed to forget, not during my years before I tested and passed my FirstLevel Master status, and not at social gatherings." Another gulp or two, then he met her eyes. "My situation was especially bad in my seventeenth year, when I became an adult as I suffered another horrific Passage. I was in no shape to connect with a HeartMate. Furious. Rebellious. Barely skimming through my studies. We talked. By the Lady and Lord, did we *talk*. My parents. My employers. SupremeJudge Ailim Elder. T'Blackthorn Residence. All my friends of my age group. Lord and Lady." He wiped his arm across his forehead to remove beaded sweat she hadn't noticed. "All of those and me, in all the different combinations you can imagine. I hung on to human decency by a microfilament." A huge sigh escaped him and he stared at the shuttered northern windows that showed bars of moving shade from the trees outside. "I had constraints put on me, on my behavior, some I agreed to, some I fought bitterly." He turned to face her fully. "No one thought me finding my HeartMate at that time would be a good thing. Not for me, and especially not for you."

She was some years younger than Antenn and was forced to inwardly agree that she couldn't have dealt with an angry teenaged boy.

"But you should know that it was my decision—when I was slightly more sane—to have the lockspell to suppress our link placed on me. My decision that I rarely thought about and didn't regret."

"So what happened recently?"

He finished the tube, got up, walked over to another panel and opened it to show a reconstructor, and flung the tube in. The sight of his excellent backside nearly distracted her from the question.

"T'Blackthorn Residence said it was time to remove the lock-spell, and it did."

"Hmm."

He turned and put his hands on his hips and, of course, her eyes went to his sex and that was even *more* distracting. "You've hummed a couple of times. Just what does it mean?"

Tearing her gaze from the most interesting part of him, that was doing equally interesting things, she met his stare . . . which lifted from her breasts.

"It means that when the High Priest and High Priestess discussed my promotion, being a HeartMate was briefly mentioned. And the fact that destiny might be catching up with me."

"You seem fairly calm about all this," he said. He didn't move from his spot.

"Perhaps right now." She smiled. "And after amazing sex. And knowing I won't have to go on a quest to find you, which, it appeared, I might have to do. I have enough projects I need to fulfill right now."

"The complaint against T'Equisetum and the petition to the NobleCouncil are your priorities."

"Along with working with the Intersection of Hope as they build their cathedral." She lifted her chin. "My career is as important to me as yours is to you." She pressed her hand between her breasts. "But I think, in a while, I'll be angry with you for that lockspell. Surely you haven't needed it for years."

He shrugged, and that gesture *did* rile her.

"I wanted to get my business established." His lips firmed. "I will never be able to forget that I am brother to Shade the murderer."

"Are you going to let his actions define you?"

Antenn laughed shortly. "My brother's murders *have* defined me, all the time I've been growing up. There are people in the First-Families who will never look at me without seeing him first, no matter what. Powerful people. Only my father, T'Blackthorn, and my Clover relatives make me acceptable. If I were disinherited tomorrow, say, I would not live to the next day."

Shock at his words pulled a gasp from her. "You mean that."

"Oh, yeah. And if old T'Yew or his daughter, D'Yew, had lived, I wouldn't be here today. I'm sure I'd have had an unfortunate accident." Antenn's mouth twisted. "And that's one of the realities of my existence that I had to accept." His gaze burned. "And something my HeartMate will have to accept."

Her hand went to her throat. "I had no idea."

"Of course not." His lips curved in a sardonic smile. "I am not good for you, Lady. Not only because of my personal problems, but the external ones of my existence that I carry with me." Another shrug. "I don't dwell on it. Live in the moment. And once this cathedral is built, I'll have proven my worth once and to all."

A calendar sphere popped into the air. "Dinner with the Family," it said in a voice that Tiana now knew was Mitchella D'Blackthorn's.

"I must leave. I'll take a waterfall at home." Antenn bowed to her, and when he straightened his expression seemed vulnerable. "We, uh, are all right for now?" he asked.

"You mean just having sex?" she asked.

He laughed. "Oh, yeah, I'm fine with that."

"For now," she said austerely.

His shoulders straightened. "Being up front with you. I don't want much more than that. Not right now when we have this cathedral project and the controversy going."

"I can't imagine HeartBonding with a man I've barely known for three days. Not at all wise."

"Well, no."

She decided to say something before he did. "And I'd rather keep the fact that we're HeartMates to ourselves. I'm not going to say anything to anyone, not my Family, not even my closest friends."

Hurt passed over his face—the reason she wanted to put it out there, so she wasn't the one being hurt by those words, and that was low . . . and human—and he nodded, raised a palm. "I won't say anything to anyone, not my Family nor my closest friends."

"We understand each other then."

"For the moment," he said, pulling on his underwear and trous, studying her. "It's a good thing that you're a priestess, compassionate, forgiving. Lord and Lady know I have problems. And faults."

"I'm sure," Tiana said. Looking inwardly at their bond, she saw it wasn't thick, but it did link them, emotionally, even physically, perhaps. But spiritually? She didn't know. She would keep it open, observe it. Without the lockspell she didn't think he'd be able to block it.

He finished dressing quickly, then walked over to her, eyes gleaming. He picked up her hand and kissed her fingers, placed her palm on his chest, then leaned down and brushed her lips, including a small stroke of his tongue. Then he kissed her brow. "We will have to make time to be together, and not only in dreams; though that was great, *this* was *the best*. Later."

Before she could reply, he was gone.

Twenty-nine

She got up and threw her empty water tube in the reconstructor, then opened the bedroom door and walked to her waterfall room. Already she felt chafing of skin that hadn't experienced a man's body in a long while . . . and the strain of muscles she'd used enthusiastically.

TQ creaked and she became abruptly aware that she lived in a sentient House.

"I trust the interlude was pleasant?"

"The interlude was magnificent."

"Good. That's very good."

"I certainly thought so."

TQ chuckled.

"By the way, when Antenn is here and we are in my bedroom, I wish to always be in privacy mode."

"Yes, Tiana. By the way, I have not received any more of your belongings," he said. "No trunk or two have been sent to my mail cache."

"I have everything," she said, a little stiffly.

A long pause, and then TQ said in a near whisper as if not wanting to offend, "They aren't much."

She shrugged. "I don't have much, and don't really need much."

"It's lovely to have nice things," TQ said in Mitchella Clover D'Blackthorn's voice, and Tiana understood the House teased her. She laughed and realized that she'd tensed up again, the back of her mind turning over those words of Antenn's about enemies. A good waterfall would ease her again. She bit off a sigh as she stepped into the enclosure and let the water stream down. So much had happened these last days that her life had been thrown off the course she'd plotted.

The greatest event and hopefully the best was discovering her HeartMate.

She hoped. Then she let her mind blank to another pleasure, liquid sluicing her body, herbs she loved and could name released in the steam that rose around her and suffused her muscles, loosening them. When she was finished, she dried herself the old-fashioned way with fluffy towels and donned a very old, very soft robe—one she only wore privately in her rooms at BalmHeal Residence.

But she was totally alone here, an extremely odd feeling. She had never lived alone, and worked in a busy building. She'd liked the extreme privacy before, but now she wasn't sure about all this very quiet personal space.

She did know one thing. "TQ, your heat seems to be a degree or two too cold for me. Can you raise it, please? And do you have the energy to keep it that warm?"

"Oh, yes, Tiana. At once!"

"Thank you."

"I am a wealthy House. I have received gifts and gilt and I have invested them well. You will lack for nothing within my walls," he said, and it sounded like a vow.

"You're wonderful," Tiana said.

"Thank you. I wish to furnish the mainspace and would like your opinion on furniture."

"All right."

"Here are some chairs, which do you like best?" He showed her vizes of chairs against the walls—fancy carved wooden chairs with elegant fabric backs and seats, leather wing chairs like those in BalmHeal Residence but newer. Her breath caught.

"Which one, Tiana?"

"That big, fat cushioned one. The one with the round arms and back that could hold two of me." For some reason just looking at that chair made her feel wealthy . . . and free. She could sit sideways with her back against one arm, legs hanging over the other, not at all a position her mother or BalmHeal Residence would approve of.

"Ah. I have only two of those in my basement storage room; shall I translocate them so you can examine them?"

"You can do that?"

"I am also a powerfully Flaired House and I have had some humans teach me such spells."

She wondered who, but said, "That's great."

"Please go to the north mainspace that looks out on the back grassyard."

Felonerb turned the corner of the hallway, burping, then said, *I have heard we are getting new furniture.* His claws clicked on the polished wooden floor.

"You will *not* scratch at *my* chairs," TQ said.

The cat's ears went down, then his expression changed from peeved to pitiful, with the big, pleading eyes Tiana didn't believe for a second.

"I have found that cats particularly like to rip at wall panels of sisslerug," TQ said. "I will put such panels in any room you designate, Felonerb Fam."

"Oooh," Felonerb said. *Thank you.* His whole posture changed, head and tail up as he pranced ahead of Tiana to the rear mainspace.

There stood two chairs, one in subtle stripes, one a very feminine, pastel floral. She wondered what it said about her that she loved the floral one. She'd never thought of herself as that girly. Antenn might find it uncomfortable to live with that chair. But as she contemplated it, she thought of what she knew of the Blackthorns—Straif extremely alpha-manly, a tracker. Mitchella, an interior designer. Antenn might already live with extreme girly. And, after all, Tiana was pleasing herself here. For the first time ever.

"I like the floral one."

"I can change the tint from the background of powder blue to dusky rose or cream or pale green . . . Mitchella told me the pattern is called chintz." TQ varied the background. It amazed Tiana how different the chair looked when just the base color changed. Obviously Mitchella Clover D'Blackthorn knew her stuff. "I like the blue," Tiana said. "And could the room be close to that color or complementary?" She waved a hand.

"Certainly. These were sample chairs given to me some time ago, but I believe that Clover Fine Furniture has other pieces in this suite."

"Oh." Tiana didn't even know that a bunch of pieces of furniture was called a suite.

"And I have all of Mitchella's decorating plans and holo models with regard to myself. She decorated a mainspace of not quite these dimensions in this style."

The air wavered and Tiana seemed to be standing in a different room—walls blue as she'd envisioned but a different, better hue. An illusionary chair like the real one was there—except it didn't have Felonerb bouncing on its seat and arms in a frenetic pattern. There were also sturdy wooden side tables and another fat chair along with an equally overstuffed couch in a deeper shade of blue.

Her breath caught again, behind her fingers that had pressed to her mouth. "Oh. It *is* lovely, but, but—" She frowned, scraping her brain for what would make the vision perfect.

"Yes?"

For an instant Tiana was distracted by Felonerb's Flaired leap to the other chair; he sniffed it and began rolling around on the seat. "Ah. Maybe the wood is too dark for my taste? Or maybe it should have more of a reddish tint?"

The tables cycled through colors until her pleased noise had TQ stopping at a lighter, redder hue.

"So good!" Her own furniture, to her own tastes, for the first time in her life! She cleared incipient tears from her voice and said, "I'm so sorry that I can't help you pay for this."

"Furniture, in the long run, is not important," TQ said. "Much will come and go in my lifetime. Having you here and happy is important. Even with so short a time as you've spent with me, you bring peace and tranquility to my walls. I am better for them."

"Thank you."

Felonerb rubbed her ankles, front and back. *I'm hungry!*

"Naturally," she said.

Before her eyes, a simple dining room table of a deeper reddish wood, gleaming with polish, appeared by the window that looked out on the back grassyard and the gloom of early evening as the sun sank on the opposite side of the House. With another couple of faint thumps, two matched chairs with tapestry seats and backs sat near the table.

"Wow," Tiana said.

Felonerb leapt for the chair, landed, and sat straight up, turning to grin at Tiana.

"You really want to sit at the table to eat?"

His ear cocked. *I can stand on the table—*

"No, you can't."

Muzzle wrinkling, he said, *I would like to eat inside here where the ferals can see Me.*

"No doubt." She sighed. But as she watched, a sturdy tray extruded from beneath the windowsill.

"You can sit there, FamCat," TQ said.

Felonerb hummed in pleasure. *Thank you, Turquoise House.*

"Your behavior has been acceptable today, so you get a small privilege. If it continues to be acceptable, you will accrue more privileges. Should you backslide, privileges will be removed. You understand?" TQ asked.

"Yesss," Felonerb vocalized. His expression grumpy, then calculating. Tiana had no doubt that he'd push the limits too far and find the exact line of how unacceptable his behavior could be without losing privileges. That would be interesting to watch over the coming days and months. It began to sink in that she'd be living here, with only Felonerb, for a considerable part of the year.

"Tiana, there are formal table settings—"

"No, thank you."

"—and some that are more casual. I am coming to know your tastes. I think if you say, 'Casual yellow,' you will enjoy the results."

"Casual yellow."

The atmosphere over the table blurred with Flair, and then two place mats of woven butter-colored cloth and cream-colored plates with one yellow and one turquoise stripe sat on each mat.

"Sorry," TQ muttered, then ordered, "Single."

One setting disappeared, clinking.

"It has been a while since I had a single renter."

"No problem," Tiana said lightly, but her mind went to the cheerful dinner her Family would be enjoying right now.

Or maybe not so cheerful, because Garrett would be recounting his day and her decision to file a complaint against GraceLord T'Equisetum and his decision to co-file a petition with the NobleCouncil.

A relieved breath poured from her. Yes, much better to remain here, tonight. Eventually she would have to discuss the complaint—*everything*—with her parents, but the later, the better.

"I'm not sure what I want to eat," she said. "I'll look in the kitchen no-times." She turned to leave the room, and Felonerb, who'd been making faces at the feral cats outside the window, jumped down to follow her.

Dinner passed happily with conversation with her Fam and TQ, and she sat at the table until the window glass reflected herself against the dark night.

"Would you like me to turn on one or several of the back grassyard lights?" TQ asked.

"No, thank you." She moved to the chair and found that a side table and a lamp had appeared when she wasn't looking. She sat and sighed, not quite ready to consider all that had happened that day, the events, the conversations. The sex with her HeartMate.

She didn't know much about the FirstFamilies, not even much

about being Noble, as she hadn't passed from childhood to adult-
hood as a noblewoman. Though, like everyone else, she knew the
highest Nobles were intertwined in webs of alliances that often
opposed. And occasional feuds popped up to settle matters.

"Turquoise House?"

"Yes, Tiana?"

"I need some deeper background on Antenn Blackthorn-Moss."

"Of course, Tiana."

She rearranged herself in the big chair with fat arms, making
sure not to hit Felonerb where he lay sprawled on one of those arms,
paws up, sleeping in utter abandonment. Yet she felt as if questioning TQ wasn't quite right, especially since she'd seen Antenn in the
mural in the HouseHeart . . . but if she limited her questions and
stuck with facts, she shouldn't be violating his privacy too much.

And he'd thrown that verbal firebomb about him having enemies
that would like him dead—and her, as his HeartMate, too.

"I don't recall who of the FirstFamilies Antenn's brother Shade
killed." And, what with everything, that notion of a verbal firebomb wasn't good. Too many memories for herself.

TQ took on a lecturing tone. "It was a firebomb*spell*," he said.
"That GraceLord Flametree had developed and the Rue Family
used on the Ashes."

"Oh, dear."

"Unlike the ones you experienced, the spell could not be stopped
by regular Flair. Once it began to burn a person it could only be
extinguished by the null who suppresses Flair, Ruis Elder."

"And he saved people in the FirstFamilies Council."

"Indeed, he did."

"But some died. Who? And some were HeartMates, weren't
they?" The HeartBond was so strong that once a couple had one, a
HeartMate only lived for a year after his or her spouse died.

"Five people of the FirstFamilies died; of those only one was a
HeartMate, T'Rowan."

"So D'Rowan died within the year."

"Within two months," TQ said.

Tiana shuddered. "Terrible." She cleared her throat. "Does Antenn have deadly enemies?"

"He has enemies. How deadly they are is unknown."

"Certainly his being a son of the Blackthorns and a relative to the Clovers helps protect him," she said. Antenn had been right.

"Surely. But will you let that stop you from HeartBonding with him?"

Thirty

$\mathcal{Y}$ou know we're HeartMates!"

"There is a certain aura present in HeartMate couples that I can sense, and I did so when you came from GreatCircle Temple this afternoon."

"Oh."

"Enemies of Antenn, and of you, are not pleasant subjects, especially not for your first night surrounded by my walls. I suggest a comedy viz. I have one featuring Raz Cherry Elecampane, who gave me his voice. I have *all* of his work. You will laugh and retire to bed in a more positive mood."

"That sounds wonderful." So did the purring of Felonerb as she stroked him.

Late that night, after she'd already gone to bed and was sinking into sleep, a soft chime drew her awake and TQ said softly, "Antenn Blackthorn-Moss requests entrance."

"He is always welcome. You may note that for the future."

"So noted, and thank you. I like him very much and am glad I have permission to always let him in. Do you want me to turn on the lights?"

"No." She smiled, recalled that she'd left her door open, and listened to his soft footfalls down the uncarpeted corridor. With each step she recalled their loving that afternoon and she began to ache, her body dampened, her lips plumped.

Without a word, he came into her bedroom; she caught his scent, heard him disrobe. Then he slipped in behind her, naked and ready for sex. His hand went to her breasts . . . and she let passion flood her, ebb and flow, and erase everything else but craving for her HeartMate.

*A*ntenn *left in the middle of the night. Her heart twinged when he* slipped from bed, but he kissed her temple and whispered, "Sleep," and the small Flair spell he'd put in the Word slid her back into dreams.

When she woke again—Felonerb jumping on her—as soon as she sat up and grunted, TQ said, "Antenn said I was to tell you that he needed to conduct some business this morning before dawn if the foundation of the cathedral is to be built today in time for the ritual tonight."

"Oh. What time is it?"

"A septhour and a half before WorkBell. I understand from your calendar sphere that you must attend the press conference of the current GraceLord T'Equisetum."

"Current?"

"He will not be allowed to keep that title when it is revealed how he plotted to kill you Mugworts."

Her chest tightened. "I think he only wanted to do what he did—discredit us and scare us. The firebombs could have been worse."

"We shall see. But he is guilty and will be found guilty by a judge."

"I hope so." She stretched.

"Do you think someone will be viz-recording the building of the cathedral? I would like to see that. And the ritual tonight, too." TQ sounded wistful.

"I'm not sure the Intersection of Hope folk will permit cameras during their ritual, but I'm sure the construction of the cathedral

will be vized. You might contact the PublicLibrary or one of the
Licorices. They're fully as curious as you and committed to recording history. Including the ritual."

"That is a good idea."

Felonerb gave her what she believed *he* thought was a winning
smile. At least he looked healthier already, and he smelled . . . unex-
ceptional.

After dinner the previous evening, Antenn checked with the mortar
maker, went to her business and had an excited conversation with
her and checked all was on track there. Once again they discussed
the mixture, spells, and Flair. Something he was quite sure interested a very limited number of people but fascinated the both of
them.

He teleported to the quarry and watched the granite blocks pre-
cisely cut with Flair-tech lazers. Again, he and the quarry overseer
discussed the cathedral animatedly. *Everyone* he'd hired as subcontractors was excited about building a unique structure that would
last for centuries.

Afterward he did another walk around the cathedral site and
inspected the trenches. The FirstLevel Stonecutter said he'd spoken
with Apex Mage Builders, the Earth Mages who would handle the
construction as opposed to the excavation, that day about the
project, but they still hadn't scried Antenn.

He woke early, in Tiana's bed at the Turquoise House—and that
entity wasn't as obnoxious or needy as Antenn recalled. He'd been
needy, too, as a boy, and stunted in sharing his emotions and
love . . . for a while.

Even now, curled around his HeartMate, fear that he'd let her
down, do something for her to abandon him, gnawed at him. The
HeartMate deal—which looked good on the outside, but which he
doubted when applied to him—had already turned into a strong
link. He couldn't deny the sex was great. He liked being with her,
too. She made no judgements.

It was still dark, but he had to *move* on the project. Make sure everything lined up for the day. Just thinking of that tightened his gut.

Carefully, carefully he lifted his arms from embracing Tiana, scooted away so her butt didn't snuggle against his front, dressed, and when she stirred, he sent her back to sleep. He glanced at his timer. A couple of septhours before dawn. Time for a waterfall, then he could contact Apex. They'd worked dawn-to-dusk jobs together before.

Absently, he thanked TQ for his hospitality, left a message for Tiana, and headed into his office.

This time when he scried Apex Mage Builders, GraceLord T'Pulicaria, the senior partner, answered himself, grimaced, and said flatly, "We can't take the job."

Antenn should have listened to his gut the day before. Always bad when he didn't pay attention to it.

Keeping a stone expression, Antenn said, "We have a contract."

The guy cleared his throat; his gaze went past Antenn. "Uh, that contract. It's, uh, invalid due to, uh, 'unexpected danger.'"

"What danger?" Antenn demanded. "Everything we spoke of before I hired you continues to remain true. The land is sound, the materials are top-of-the-pyramid with no expense spared."

The man's jaw clenched. He shrugged. "People don't like it. Won't support it going up. Not a good project anyway."

Anger sparked through Antenn. He'd figured out that the people who didn't like the project were GraceLord T'Equisetum and his ilk. Maybe GraceLord T'Pulicaria listened to T'Equisetum.

Or did the rumors going around include whispers of firebombing? As a mob had done to Intersection of Hope homes before?

"Very well," Antenn said. "Since you can't explain this 'danger' that will keep you from working, I accept the resignation of your team. However, I will not pay any outstanding gilt. And you can be sure that I will file a complaint against your firm with the GuildHall."

"No!" T'Pulicaria sputtered. "You can't—"

Antenn raised a hand and cut him off. "No. I will not listen to excuses. You are supposed to be a top-rated building firm and I

know you've handled dangerous projects before. Since you don't
care to detail the danger, I believe you to be in violation of your
contract, and furthermore, you bid on a job you couldn't fulfill.
That is grounds for a complaint to the GuildHall. I will never use
you again, do you understand?"

The mage made a disgusted noise, jutted his chin. His lip curled.
"No great loss."

"No? You've just thrown away a project that will stand for centuries."

"Won't be built." The man chopped his hand.

"It *will* be built. The financing is there. The contractors."

T'Pulicaria shook his head. "Not us. Good luck getting a company as good as we are. You can't. Won't be built."

Bile rose in Antenn's throat, searing it. "I will not let you stop
this project. There *will* be a complaint filed against your firm. And
I think my mother—"

"Adopted mother," the man corrected.

So he was one of those. Antenn hadn't known. The guy thought
nothing of Antenn as a man, as an architect, as a builder. Only
responded to status. Yeah, this man threw in his lot with the Traditionalist Stance people. Time to let him live up to his beliefs and
take the hit his beliefs brought him since he wouldn't honor his
contract.

"My adopted mother, you say?" Antenn gave the man a shark
smile. "I can only say that she loves me like a son. She's a FirstFamily GrandLady and a decorator and recommends firms. All sorts of
firms in the business. You will not be on her list."

"I don't think—"

"No, you don't, or didn't if you think that your political beliefs
won't cost you if you disgrace yourself. Know this, I have friends in
the FirstFamilies, and they will hear of your dishonor—"

"You can't."

"I *will*. As you know, I am also working with the liaison of
GreatCircle Temple."

"The Mugwort Black Magic Cult member bitch."

Antenn's head nearly exploded with the surge of pure fury. He braced himself against his desk, gripping the edge so the rage shuddering through him wouldn't show. "We're done. And I'll make sure that the High Priest and High Priestess of Celta know of your opinion of their FirstLevel Priestess. I'll be contacting the entrepreneur Laev T'Hawthorn about your work—"

"Not T'Hawthorn—"

"And T'Vine. And, of course I'll mention this to my adopted Family, the Clovers . . . who continue to expand their compound. Don't consider submitting any bids to them."

Now the man had gone white. "I could be ruined."

"We. Are. Done. I don't know what it is in you that cannot work on a building of spiritual significance. That is between you and your soul, though your priest or priestess may consider you in need of counseling."

"What!"

"This cathedral *will* be built. My name as primary architect will be on it, to be seen for centuries and by generations to come. Neither you nor your team will be remembered." He stared at the man who seemed to be sweating as much as Antenn himself. "Be glad that I am not the head of my own household so that I could call feud on you."

"You're overreacting."

"It is good that you're gone. The Intersection of Hope cathedral should not have your hatred, your negative energy, besmirching its stones." He ended the call and let himself just plain shake. Anger.

And desperation. He would not be making any gilt on this project after all. It could even bankrupt him if he put his own gilt into it . . . which he would.

He was right. He did not need negative people on this job . . . but, damn, Apex Mage Builders was a good company. *Had been* a good company. He didn't think it would continue, and it had had a bad structural fault in its foundation.

Better move as quickly as possible. His first scry was to the GuildHall, canceling his contract with Apex, stating no gilt was owed to them and filling out a brief complaint form that he indicated he'd make more formal within the next two days.

Holding his breath that it wasn't too early, he scried Captain Ruis Elder of the starship of *Nuada's Sword*. The man actually answered. Antenn made an appointment to see Elder in a half septhour.

The starship was known to have city-building machinery . . . hell, the colonists had constructed most of Druida City, anticipating a bigger population of their descendants than had occurred, and most of their work still stood. Antenn could only hope that Captain Elder could help. A year back, the man *had* given a demonstration of razing a tottery warehouse and rebuilding it.

Antenn had kept the machines in mind, toying with building the simple ministers' quarters outside the cathedral with the old tech . . . now it looked as if they were his last resort. If he was lucky, one of the other partners from Apex might contact him. He had a gut feeling that Pulicaria had spoken for himself and not his team . . . and probably had spun a pretty story about the lack of consequences for breaking the contract. Perhaps thought Antenn wouldn't call him on it, or that Antenn would accept the excuse.

Wrong.

The guy had obviously not considered that Antenn might spread the word that Apex Mage Builders couldn't be trusted. Antenn was a younger but rising architect; he was a Commoner who'd grown up in the slums. Not born equal with GraceLord Pulicaria. Politics. Status. He *loathed* those.

But not as much as sheer stupid prejudice. Whether it was aimed at him for his birth, or his brother's actions, or at a group like the Intersection of Hope.

No, Antenn had—or had had—a relatively easy-going reputation. He'd never wanted to be as stuffy as the old firm he'd apprenticed and learned with, the Cang Zhus, though he was as proud of his reputation as the CZs.

That he would use his influence and his Family and friend connections hadn't seemed to have occurred to Pulicaria. But Antenn would.

He finally knew what this was. This was a war against prejudice, against hatred.

Lord and Lady knew that Antenn himself had weak spots, pockets of envy and resentment, but he didn't think he hated a person, a
group, for who they were, where they came from, what they believed.

Not GraceLord T'Pulicaria, not T'Equisetum.

He could not give in, and, yes, he had to continue to move fast.
Not only on the foundation that had to be done *today* for the
spellshield ritual tonight. The weather was good this week, the
building *had* to progress, not only to keep his deadline but to show
everyone that he would not accept failure . . . that he wasn't a
failure.

Antenn called Chief Minister Custos and was thankfully put
through to his message cache. He stated that Apex Mage Builders
were no longer acceptable and that no invoices presented to the
Intersection of Hope instead of Antenn should be paid. He also said
that building would begin shortly.

The spring dawn wasn't warm, and the starship *Nuada's Sword*
blocked the wind from the Platte Ocean beyond the cliff it was built
on, but Antenn sweated. He'd stared at the clothes he'd learned to
keep in his office closet. He didn't know, exactly, what to wear, but
decided to be conservative. After all, Captain Ruis Elder was a
member of the FirstFamilies Council.

It had been a while since he'd been in the Ship. He'd contacted it
for historical research, and had interacted with Dani Eve Elder, but
like most folk with strong Flair, being in the presence of people who
negated psi power, like Ruis and Dani Eve, made Antenn extremely
uncomfortable.

The Captain himself met Antenn, a tall man with reddish-brown
hair and aristocratic features. They clasped arms.

"Good to see you again, even at this time of morning. Would
you like breakfast?"

Antenn drew in a deep breath, steadied himself. This was a man
equal with the FirstFamilies, and he should show minimal distress . . . at both having his Flair suppressed and his circumstances.

Elder probably knew more than Antenn supposed about his circumstances since the Captain was wed to the SupremeJudge of Celta. They probably knew of the upcoming complaint Tiana would file.

"No breakfast, thank you," Antenn said.

Elder inclined his head. "Come to my office, then, and we'll talk about what I can do for you." He smiled briefly but sincerely. "Ship will be listening in."

Thirty-one

*A*ntenn *knew that of the two beings, the starship demanded the highest* fees. His skin began to itch at the lack of Flair, his mind clouding. He ignored the feelings.

They walked through the Ship, their boots clicking on the metallic floor, then went through an equally metallic door that opened in the center as both sides slid into the wall.

Captain Elder sat behind a wooden desk that appeared centuries old. Antenn took an equally antique wing-backed chair of leather other than the standard furrabeast.

"What is the problem?"

Antenn gritted his teeth and made himself spit it out. Hopefully in a conversational tone. "I am here because Apex Mage Builders refuses to work on the Intersection of Hope cathedral. We had the foundation blocks scheduled to go in from the quarry to the site today. A ritual has already been scheduled by the Chief Ministers of the Intersection of Hope to place spellshields on the foundation. Tonight at twinmoons rise."

"Yes, I received a courtesy invitation." The Captain shrugged, smiled lopsidedly. "I don't—can't—go to spellworkings."

After a deep breath, Antenn continued, "I believe the head of the team, GraceLord T'Pulicaria, illegally canceled our contract because he is prejudiced against the Intersection of Hope, and a member of the Traditionalist Stance political movement."

Captain Elder slowly straightened his spine from the lounging position he'd been in to sit erect. His eyes flashed. "Is that so?" he asked quietly.

Antenn nodded. If any man in the recent history of Celta had been an outcast, it was the null before him.

Captain Elder said, "I am sure the Traditionalist Stance allies would prefer *not* to see a null as Captain of this starship. Would, perhaps, wish to replace me. Worse, deny my daughter, also a null, her birthright, the Captaincy of this Ship."

"We will not allow them to do that!" the Ship spoke in a multiple-toned voice. "And we have weapons."

"Quiet, Ship. They won't be able to unseat us." Elder sounded amused. "There could be a FirstFamilies Lord or Lady who belongs to that movement." He considered. "Maybe two. But I don't think the rest of the FirstFamilies Council will allow the party to get much purchase. Most of them are pleased with the increasing Flair."

Because they had the most Flair to begin with, Antenn knew. And if Flair increased across the board, the people with the most might continue to receive the most. So far there had been more Flaired prodigies in the FirstFamilies than any other strata.

"We—the FirstFamilies Council—are prepared to let a Commoner-Raised-to-GrandLord, Walker Clover, become the Captain of All Councils. Members of the FirstFamilies are finding and marrying HeartMates outside their circle. And T'Yew and D'Yew, the most conservative members when I rose to the Captaincy, are gone." Then Ruis Elder grinned. "And we have weapons."

"And the will to use them," Antenn said.

"That is true. However, in this instance my—our—machines are at your disposal," Elder said. "We will have to consult the plans to see what we can do."

"I have the plans," stated the Ship. "We can do it all, the building of the foundation and flying buttresses and the entire stone cathedral. We also have machines that can do all the embellishments as noted in the plans. If necessary." There was some sort of sound that Antenn couldn't place but sounded close to a human sniff. "We Celtans must not forget our history, that we left our home planet because of prejudice, of mobs against those with psi power."

And the Ship's championship further soothed Antenn, almost made him smile. "Quite so." If there was any being on Celta that could be said to have been Earthan, it was *Nuada's Sword*. Just as the Turquoise House was pure Celtan.

"Can you get the foundation set today within the time period?" Antenn asked bluntly. "There is also a problem with the transport of the blocks. They are cut—"

Ship interrupted. "Since I am interested in this structure, one based on information I provided to you, I have had my satellite keep track of the progress. I have the latest data with regard to the trenches and the quarry." A short hum came, then, "Dani Eve has been experimenting with a transport system called a mass driver that could be installed this morning from the quarry to the site. We have heavy-duty anti-grav sleds that can be used instead of Earth Mages to translocate the blocks, and large machines to lift and place the blocks. Yes. We can get this done by the deadline this evening if we start quickly. I will notify Dani Eve—"

"Wake her up," Ruis Elder said, winking at Antenn.

"She will be excited to prove to all that she, and I, can still contribute to Celta," Ship said.

"Seems to be a goal all around," Antenn murmured.

"Ship, you see to everything," Elder said, his sharp gaze on Antenn.

"I will. I have programmed the sleds and they are on their way to the quarry. I am waking—"

Captain Elder said, "Give me a time when FirstLevel Architect Antenn Blackthorn-Moss needs to be at the site—the quarry or the cathedral."

"A septhour."

"Good. Please continue to supervise. I'd like to talk to Antenn without interruption."

"Very well," Ship said, and though Antenn knew the being was as curious as any creature, it—he—they, sounded distracted.

Captain Elder rose. "Let's proceed to the southern entrance, a good walk."

Antenn stood, too, noting the slick of sweat of his shirt. Of course the spell wicking it away to the atmosphere and leaving a nice herbal smell did not work. He rested his hand on the back of the chair, leaned against it an instant, and closed his eyes. Said a prayer of gratitude to the Lady and Lord. Opening his eyes, he bowed to the Captain. "Thank you for your generosity."

"Oh, we'll charge you," the man said, then named a price a quarter of what had been earmarked to pay Apex for the foundation.

Antenn lowered his head, again closing his eyes. "Thank you." He breathed deeply, then met the man's inscrutable gaze. "I must tell you that if I find another Earth Mage building company, I will hire them."

"Instead of using ancient Earthan machines." Ruis Elder gestured and the door opened. "We understand, but the machines remain viable for work." He turned right and began walking down the long, long hallway. "We don't mind proving ourselves several times. In this particular instance, we know the ultimate clients are the Chief Ministers of the Intersection of Hope, and though the notion of having colonial machines build their cathedral will please them a little, they, too, will be wary."

"Thank you for understanding," Antenn said.

"The Ship's lifetime is even longer than ours, and it will see this as unexpected progress sooner than anticipated on its timeline."

"Ah," Antenn said. He matched pace with the Captain, though the man was taller than he by a few centimeters. Still, though they didn't hurry, they didn't saunter, either.

Quietly, Ruis Elder said, "We have never spoken about Shade, your brother. I knew him fairly well."

That stunned Antenn. He stared at the Captain for several steps until Ruis Elder glanced at him. "Your brother was a very damaged person, mostly because he'd bonded with two other boys in a triad and they died."

Flickering memories slashed through Antenn's mind of the triad, their glisten-metal coated incisors that showed they belonged to each other. The other two for whom his brother had abandoned him . . . until the three let him tag along in their gang. He didn't care to remember that time . . . couldn't remember that much, and thank the Lady and Lord for it.

"I liked Shade," Ruis Elder said. His eyes met Antenn's in a simple glance. "He had potential." The Captain looked away, and Antenn saw grief.

Antenn could actually share grief at the loss of his brother with this man. He'd never considered that anyone but himself remained who'd known Shade.

"The . . . timing . . . of the events when our lives tangled together was poor; if Shade had been given a little more . . ." Ruis shrugged. "He might have redeemed himself. As it was, through his acts, he let *me* redeem *myself*. He wasn't totally bad. But he hated and that hatred killed him, and had him killing others. If there's anything we must fight, it's poisonous hatred of others. In our own selves and by not allowing it to flourish when we can step in and say that hatred is wrong."

They walked along in silence until they came to a cart, and Ruis gestured Antenn to get into it. "I know you're anxious to get to work. This is programmed to head straight for the southern door." The Captain offered his arm again, and this time Antenn took it and kept the clasp for a good half minute.

"For your brother, and for yourself, count me as a friend," Captain Elder said. He smiled. "You are always welcome here."

All Antenn could say was, "Thank you."

Then the cart sped him from the Ship, and he teleported to the cathedral.

*T*iana took the public carrier to GraceLord T'Equisetum's business address . . . which was close to the Intersection of Hope's city office and Antenn's architectural firm. Perhaps the proximity irritated the GraceLord.

Her pulse beat fast. She'd filed the complaint and Garrett had filed their petition. The NobleCouncil Clerk would have processed the petition and sent it to the NobleCouncil. Had word of her complaint gotten to T'Equisetum's ears, yet? Only a matter of time. She'd been advised to hand it to the man herself, as a victim confronting one who'd harmed her and accompanied by witnesses. The other option was to let an impartial guard take care of the duty. She hadn't quite decided what to do.

She walked into a medium-sized room full of people from the newssheets and the new viz channels. GraceLord T'Equisetum stood behind a tall lectern. Just looking at him caused her stomach to roil. Though lines of dissatisfaction—hate and bitterness?—had carved deep in his face, he appeared invigorated by the thought of fighting the construction of the cathedral. She studied him from the back of the room. Yes, the passing years showed more on his visage than on her father or mother.

"Your attention please, Lords and Ladies, GentleSirs and GentleLadies," said a slender man of about Tiana's age, no doubt GraceLord T'Equisetum's current assistant, and a member of his Family. He shared features with that man.

"Greetyou, all," GraceLord T'Equisetum said. "As I said when I called this newssheet conference, we of the Traditionalist Stance do not want a Cross Folk *cathedral* near Druida."

"It's out of the city," someone pointed out.

"I've seen the plans, I very much like the idea of such a structure, another large sacred space like our GreatCircle Temple and the Great Labyrinth in the north," a man who sponsored the arts—and spoke about them in viz reports—said.

"How can it be sacred if it is not of the Lady and the Lord?" GraceLord T'Equisetum asked.

"How can the Traditionalist Stance movement be acceptable if it is not accepted by all Nobles, and so new?" someone else fired back.

"I will speak of the Traditionalist Stance movement in a moment."

The GraceLord leaned on the lectern. "Why, this building will be larger than our GreatCircle Temple."

Tiana just couldn't stop her tongue. "So what?" she asked. "It's only men who believe larger is better."

That got a laugh from the press. The people in front of her moved to the side, leaving an aisle for her to walk toward the podium where T'Equisetum sneered.

"Ah, it's the little Cross Folk lover."

There was a short gasp from someone in the crowd at the rudeness.

Tiana lifted her chin. "Yes, my mother practices the Intersection of Hope faith, and I deeply love my mother." She turned to face the room, blinking when she saw Chief Minister Younger dressed as an innocuous journeyman. Letting her glance graze over him, she scanned the rest of the people.

And Younger's mind brushed hers. *We have decided that we don't care for the name Cross Folk. We would prefer "Hopefuls"; can you offer that name now?* His gaze had sharpened and Tiana suppressed a sigh. It appeared as if everyone continued to test her.

She lifted spread hands. "You know, Cross Folk is such an old nickname. We're in the third decade of the fifth century. New Flair techniques are being developed every day, some of which I'm sure the FirstLevel Architect will be using in this structure." She smiled widely, and, she hoped, disingenuously, noting that most of the people there were more her age than GraceLord T'Equisetum's. Because he didn't rate the older reporters? "I think we should call the Intersection of Hope people 'Hopefuls.' I know it's a quality that my mother has."

"Hopefuls," someone said.

"It is a stupid label," GraceLord T'Equisetum said.

"As opposed to 'Traditionalist Stance'?" Tiana asked. " 'Hopefuls' can be a shortened form of 'Intersection of Hope members.' 'Traditionalist Stance'?" She shrugged and spread her hands.

"I will explain the Traditionalist Stance movement," GraceLord T'Equisetum said in a condescending tone, staring at Tiana. "We must maintain the high standards for admission into the Noble class. With the onset of greater Flair by everyone, the Testing standards must be raised—and any unusual Flair must be scrutinized."

"I think you might have a hard time convincing T'Ash, who does the best Testing, of that," someone drawled.

GraceLord T'Equisetum flushed. "We of the Traditionalist Stance have members in the FirstFamilies households—"

"Does that mean that everyone currently in the NobleCouncils, such as yourself, will be *re*-Tested? To make sure you meet the new standards?" someone asked.

The GraceLord's mouth opened and closed. "That is not necessary. The current Nobles should be accepted as is."

"In perpetuity?" someone else questioned.

"Yes, *as is*." T'Equisetum glanced down at his papyrus of prompts and stated, "Another item we wish to institute to provide stability in our society, in our Councils, is that Lords and Ladies should be required to follow our majority religion that our ancestors crafted for us, the duality of the Lady and the Lord."

Several people gasped. Then a man stood up and pointed a finger at the GraceLord. Tiana recognized him as Majus T'Daisy, also a GraceLord, who liked a fiery debate in his newssheet.

"Are you bringing up that old lie that the Intersection of Hope people were involved in the Black Magic Cult murders? Everyone knows that's not true."

"Is that so?" GraceLord T'Equisetum murmured.

GraceLord Majus T'Daisy rocked back and forth on his heels. "Well, I tend to believe the statements and interviews of the guards involved in the investigation. Or do you not believe the guards?"

"I think the guards might be mistaken."

"In that particular matter?"

"Yes."

"As opposed to all the other matters since you voted to increase the percentage of gilt going to them from the gilt the All Councils disperse to various governmental entities."

"We need a strong guard."

"All right." GraceLord T'Daisy scratched his head and Tiana got the feeling he disliked GraceLord T'Equisetum personally. She didn't keep track of Council politics, but there had to be bad blood between T'Daisy and T'Equisetum.

"Hmm. You think those who govern us"—he winked at the rest of the reporters—"or those of us who govern should all believe the same way, in the Lady and Lord."

"Yes."

"The way you believe."

"Yes."

"That's interesting, too, since no one has seen you at a public ritual for some years."

"What?"

"Why is that?" GraceLord T'Daisy set his feet as if he prepared to roll out a speech, and began. "Is it because of the fact that your intolerance had the High Priest and High Priestess refusing to allow you to participate in rituals that an ordained priest or priestess conducts? Because the High Priest and High Priestess don't believe that *you* show the compassion they expect in a person who spiritually accepts the religion our ancestors crafted? Just *what* religion *do* you believe in? And, you know, this whole string of shit you're handing us today just reeks of intolerance. Me? I think I'd like people with compassion and mercy in my life more than I'd like rigid rules."

"That's because you have a ThirdDaughter who wishes to Test to establish her own NobleHouse," GraceLord T'Equisetum snapped.

GraceLord T'Daisy flung out his arms. "Yeah, that's right. Unlike you, I'm hiding nothing. My ThirdDaughter is hiding nothing. She was counseled by GreatCircle Temple to be ambitious and strike out on her own. I'm very proud of that. Because, you know, she *can* Test and show she is worthy to make her own House, and be accepted as a GraceHouse, too." Daisy rubbed his chin. "Sure would like to see your most recent Testing."

"That is not the issue here," GraceLord T'Equisetum said in freezing tones.

"Yes, let's get back to the original reason for this show," someone said. "The cathedral."

GraceLord T'Equisetum jutted his chin, lips quirking in a smug smile. "Oh, I don't think it will be built."

Younger tensed, glanced at Tiana. She shrugged. She didn't know any more than he.

Thirty-two

Oh, wow. Oh, zow." *A boy of about twelve bolted into the room and up* to GraceLord T'Equisetum. "FatherSire, you told me to watch the cathedral foundation being laid? It is *so* fascinating."

"What!" barked T'Equisetum.

"*Nuada's Sword* sent city-building machines. Really, really old ones. They are *so* interesting. Half of Druida City is watching, and all of my GroveStudy group! Gotta get back!" As quickly as he popped into the room, he zoomed out.

"*Nuada's Sword*," GraceLord T'Equisetum snarled.

"Something not going according to plan?" GraceLord T'Daisy asked trenchantly.

"This conference is over." GraceLord T'Equisetum picked up his notes and marched toward the side door.

"I certainly hope so," GraceLord T'Daisy said. "I hope your whole 'movement' is over. We don't need people who hate some folk making rules for all folk." He hitched his trous up over his substantial belly. "'Cuz, you know, if you hate Commoner Joe on the weekday of Mor according to your own personal rules, how do I know you aren't gonna hate GraceLord T'Daisy on Twinmoonsday? And use everything you got against me until I gotta cry 'feud' on you?

277

Myself, I'd like to go with folk like the High Priest and Priestess and the Chief Ministers of the Intersection of Hope who love Commoner Joe on the weekday of Mor . . ."

Laughter rippled through the room as GraceLord T'Equisetum stormed out.

GraceLord T'Daisy beamed. "By the way, colleagues and friends . . . well, colleagues. I am writing a nonfiction book on the Black Magic Cult murders . . ."

More laughter at his promotion.

Tiana tipped her head at Younger and, still smiling, left and took the public carrier back to work.

When she walked into her chambers at GreatCircle Temple, she faced the accusing gaze of Felonerb. *You left Me alone in TQ. Who smoked Me AGAIN! I had only kilt three little mousies outside in a stinkbush.*

"I *did* tell you when I left for CityCenter."

He grumbled, *No glider today.*

"Not yet." Though her stomach tensed at the idea she might be assigned one to serve her complaint.

Now that the ordeal of the press conference was over and the complaint yet to come, hunger spiked through her and she went to her near-empty no-time. She might have to eat a meal placed there to share on a holiday ritual altar, but she needed a snack.

She opened it and gasped. It was full. Every section. And she had no idea who'd stocked it, since, like many, she didn't keep her chambers or the no-time locked. If anyone—priestess, priest, or visitor—needed a place to sit and think, or food and drink, they were welcome to hers.

Staggered, she pulled out a piece of dense brown bread and butter that she believed would soak up any remaining acid in her stomach nicely, put it on a plate, and indulged in hot cocoa with white mousse.

Felonerb, meowing at her feet, got a steaming plate labeled "Protein for CatFams."

As she munched, she studied the Intersection of Hope ritual set for this evening, reading the praise and prayers so she could commit them to memory. Simple enough.

She'd just put the two dishes in the cleanser and had taken her seat again when great Flair washed her way.

GreatLord T'Ash and GreatLady D'Ash stood on her threshold. He was big and swarthy with startling blue eyes; she small and brown-haired. Both radiated intensity.

At his slightest glance, Tiana found herself rising.

He had a piece of rolled and wax-sealed papyrus in his hand. "Your complaint has been approved by the general clerk of all the JudgementGroves as pertinent." He stalked forward and laid the scroll on her desk. "We think that the best strategy in this action would be for you to present the complaint to GraceLord T'Equisetum at NobleCouncil this morning."

"We?"

T'Ash scowled as if unaccustomed to being questioned. She hadn't had any interaction with him but had heard that though he was a very tough man, he wasn't unkind. Anyone who grew up in the slum Downwind wouldn't have a sense of entitlement. That included T'Ash as well as Antenn Blackthorn-Moss.

"Me, Winterberry, and T'Blackthorn, whom I consulted."

"SupremeJudge Ailim D'Elder, whom *I* consulted," Danith D'Ash said.

"Oh." Tiana gestured to her two patron chairs. "Please, sit."

He inclined his head and lowered into the one closest to the door, and Tiana got the impression it was a fighter's move to guard her and his HeartMate.

"I am pleased to help you in this matter," he said gruffly.

"And I am honored," she replied, curtseyed, and sat again.

T'Ash's face looked carved from stone, expressionless, but eyes hurting. Whatever else he felt had his HeartMate, Danith D'Ash, moving from her chair to his lap.

"I understand losing everything to a firebomb," he said.

Tiana spoke gently, trying to move him from that hideous moment in his own past. "But you saved your Residence and rebuilt your home, and have a loving HeartMate and four children."

His stiff form relaxed. "Yes."

Then he smiled, a feral one. "After I followed the Vengeance Stalk, killed most of the Flametrees and the Rues." He shrugged his massive blacksmith shoulders. "Got the rest of them sterilized and banished from Druida City for life." One jerk of a nod as if he liked the job he'd done.

Again his stare met hers. "And I know what it feels like to have a Family member not fight for you."

"My parents—" she began, but he stopped her with a raised palm.

"Even though she was a HeartMate, my mother chose to die with my father instead of live for me, help me for a year, her child."

D'Ash made a little noise and hugged her HeartMate tighter. "I can't say—"

He stroked her hair. "She wasn't as strong as you are. You would never have abandoned a child of our own. And you would have fought for his title, his wealth, his estate."

This was not going at all the way Tiana thought it would.

T'Ash said, "I will fight for you, for your estate, against the stupid politicians and sly enemies who took it from you. I will be there to back you up when you file your complaint. We will meet you at NobleCouncil in half a septhour." He stood, his small HeartMate cradled in his arms, nodded at Tiana's openmouthed, wide-eyed self, and strode out of her chambers. She thought either he or D'Ash opened the doors with Flair. Her mind scrambled at the thought of actually taking the complaint approved by the general Judgement-Grove clerk and handing it to GraceLord T'Equisetum.

The time had come.

Before she'd caught her breath, Antenn propped himself against Tiana's doorjamb, tucking his thumbs in his trous pockets. "T'Ash makes a statement."

Tiana squeaked. That wasn't what she'd tried to say. Reaching for her cup that held a last swallow of cocoa, she slugged some down since her mouth was still open.

Felonerb jumped up on her desk and sat purring, a grin on his face. *We are allied with the great ZANTH! I will go tell him.*

Choking, and risking her fingers, Tiana grabbed her cat by the scruff of his neck, seeing blood in their future if she didn't restrain him. "No! You know how, uh, prideful Zanth is. He challenges new toms he meets . . . and, uh, you are, uh, *RatKiller*. Leave the old tom—"

Antenn rolled his eyes, no doubt knowing Zanth personally, but Tiana continued fast-talking. "—alone. He is no match for you and it would be pitiful to watch his defeat."

Felonerb preened. *Very well. It's time for My morning sitting in sun, anyway. There is some sun in the other room.* He strolled into her sitting room and Tiana heard a plop and grunt.

"Nice save," Antenn said. He stared at her and she wanted to be alone with him, back in her bed in TQ.

But what he said was, "You're allies with T'Ash?" His voice held incredulity.

"I, uh, yes, I think."

"You, personally. Not your Family."

She rubbed her temple. "I don't know."

Antenn pushed against the jamb, walked into her office, and took the chair D'Ash had been sitting in. "It will all shake out," he said.

"I *do* feel shaken. Things are moving so fast." She wanted to just sit and stare at this man who was her lover—would be her lifelong mate—but this was work. "How's the cathedral coming? I heard that the starship *Nuada's Sword* lent machinery."

His jaw flexed. "Touch and go this morning when Apex Mage Builders backed out." His gaze bored into hers. "I think GraceLord T'Pulicaria is with GraceLord T'Equisetum and the Traditionalist Stance folk." Then Antenn's gaze went to the window and one side of his mouth lifted. "I listened to a report of the press conference. Good job."

"I didn't say much. I didn't have to."

His eyes flicked back to focus on her. "Good job."

"Thank you."

He glanced at his timer. "We're working hard to get the foundation in. We'll have some stone blocks of foundation ready to cast the spellshields on by the time the ritual starts this evening."

"Good, though I haven't often done spellshields."

"I have, my father has, the other FirstFamily Lords and Ladies, and even lesser Nobles have raised them, as well as the professional whom the Intersection of Hope hired to do the spell. He's not too pleased with the idea of taking part in a ritual, but he'll do it. And he wants a copy of the ceremony, now."

"So you came to pick that up," Tiana said, reaching for a papyrus from the stack to her left and handing it to Antenn.

He smiled. "No, I came because I haven't been able to get you out of my head and I needed to see you. Otherwise I'd've asked TQ to give me a copy, or the Temple itself. You had them both make dozens."

"Yes." Her exhalation was shaky, this time due to rising desire.

Taking the sheet, he stood. "I can't stay here. I can't touch you, or all reason will drain from my head."

"Thank you."

"Yeah, yeah. After you serve that complaint on T'Equisetum, come look at the foundation going in for a little while. It's a beautiful day and it'll take your mind off the man."

"I'll think about it."

"Later." But he walked around her desk, bent and brushed her cheek with a kiss, and vanished. Leaving her aching for him. But their bond had grown in circumference and strength. A regular mental, emotional bond. *Not* the HeartBond. She'd known him for only three days and wondered how long it would be before they *would* HeartBond.

Probably before she knew all his flaws.

Or he learned hers.

A scary thought, that they might be propelled by fate into linking their lives together without good consideration.

She stood and picked up the complaint, weighed the thick, rich papyrus in her hand, stared at the red seal. A move she couldn't take back. Like learning who her HeartMate was.

But she'd already committed, had filed the petition, had *T'Ash*, of all people, at her back. Lady and Lord.

Felonerb trotted in, let out a belch, and said, *Let's go to see the nasty man. I will bite him. On the ankle. Maybe on the ear. Is he a tall bad man?* He shook his head. *No, not the ankle. I do a mighty LEAP and bite him on the ear. Claw his head. Maybe go for his nose. No, his EYES. Yes, yes, YES!*

She stared at her wonderful Fam—her wonderful *violent* Fam— and nodded. "Yes, I would very much like you to come with me and support me." She sucked in a big breath, through her teeth even, with a rude noise, but no one but Felonerb could hear, and he stared at her in admiration. "We'll go, and perhaps you can stay outside the door—uh, guard it in case he might escape."

YES! I can do that! I am EXCELLENT at sitting at micey-holes! He grinned widely and she saw that his teeth looked better. With one of his mighty leaps he landed on her shoulder, settled his still-bony rump, gave *her* ear a lick, and said, *We go now. D'Ash is waiting for us. I like looking at her.*

"Ah," Tiana said. D'Ash was the animal Healer in Druida City, a rare trait, and the person who usually assigned Fams since they were drawn to her, no doubt by the Flair that even influenced Felonerb—a free spirit if there ever was one. Tiana didn't see him changing much as her Fam companion.

Though she believed, to the recesses of her heart, that her Heart-Mate and she would change each other over time and naturally, as all well-married people changed. She sniffed. Felonerb smelled better. He'd been accepting smoke and other cleansing. Not because he cared, but because she did. So she was wrong to think he wasn't changing.

She'd been, too. She stared at the complaint, balanced the large papyrus on her palm. Would she have filed this last week?

Before her review and promotion? No.

And even if she lost any upward momentum in her career . . . the High Priestess and Priest had been right. She'd wanted to prove herself because of what had happened that night in her childhood home. Handling it in a different manner might ease that inner need.

She turned to the door, minding her step so she wouldn't jostle Felonerb unduly, and saw High Priestess D'Sandalwood studying her. Her gaze dropped to the complaint Tiana held.

"We haven't spoken to you about the ramifications of this action," High Priestess D'Sandalwood said.

Tiana braced herself.

"Which we, all of us, your previous counselors, the High Priest and I, have seen as a failure on our parts."

Tiana stared, then lowered her gaze.

"We have little excuse for not helping you sufficiently, though it appeared to us that since your Family . . . ah . . . seemed to have recovered well, we did not understand the weight it had on your heart and your emotions. And you have learned serenity well, are an excellent priestess and counselor yourself, so we ignored the damage your past might have inflicted on you." She sighed, and Tiana looked up again.

"We three—you, me, and the High Priest—will have some heavier sessions in the future, but not until the Hopeful cathedral project is done."

Holding the complaint up, Tiana said, "I think that this action will resolve some of my issues." She was sure none of them wanted more heavy counseling sessions.

"Perhaps. And perhaps we should have encouraged you to file that complaint the first year you were with us." The High Priestess shrugged. "But that is in the past." Slowly she smiled. "Your transport to the CouncilHall awaits at the eastern door."

We must go tell the bad man he is bad, Felonerb added. *See you later, Holy Lady.*

The High Priestess chuckled. "Yes, later." She stepped away from the door and Tiana curtseyed before she walked through, then picked up speed as she nearly ran to the eastern entrance. Once there she stopped, felt her mouth simply drop open. People crowded around a huge and empty FirstFamily glider. With T'Ash's arms on the side.

The vehicle chimed as she neared, and then the back door rose. Flushing, Tiana slid into the glider, feeling underdressed. She skimmed her gaze around but didn't see Lucida Gerania. Though it appeared that Tiana's status might have shot up among her colleagues in the last few minutes.

Felonerb squealed with delight and hopped around the benches in the glider as the door closed and the vehicle accelerated. *I smell him. I smell Zanth. And other Cats and a fox!*

Throughout the short drive to CityCenter, Felonerb continued to jump around, sniffing. Tiana watched his every movement in case he contemplated marking the vehicle. Apparently, rubbing his head against the floor and the benches was sufficient. That took her mind off the trip until the glider pulled up to the new CouncilHall and the portico that could handle large gliders like the Ashes'.

The response at the CouncilHall wasn't quite as goggling as GreatCircle Temple, but a few people stopped to see who emerged from T'Ash's new Family glider. Felonerb swaggered out, crossing to the huge armorglass doors, tail up and waving. Tiana thought she heard suppressed laughter. Wanting to hurry, but knowing, as always, that she wore priestess robes, she remained calm outwardly, not harried or rushed. With a soft smile, she left the glider and entered the hall.

Her nerves returned when T'Ash and D'Ash flanked her, and sweat from her palm sank into the complaint she held. The walk down the long marble halls, past the doors to the Commoner Council chamber to the NobleCouncil, passed in a blur. None of them said anything.

Then T'Ash curled his fingers around one of the door handles and nodded to her, ready to open it at her gesture.

Danith D'Ash picked up Felonerb and he purred outrageously. "You will stay out here, right?"

To guard the door in case he tries to escape. Yes! Tiana's Fam said.

T'Ash snorted. "We'll prop the door open with Flair to watch." He glanced up and down the corridor. "Guards are coming to witness and for other legal reasons I don't know." Then he rolled a shoulder and opened the door.

Tiana took a big breath and walked in.

People stopped talking—arguing whatever was on the agenda of the day. All gazes of the Nobles sitting in the tiered seats turned to her, and Tiana used all the calm she'd gathered over the years of her career to proceed in a serene manner and without flushing.

"Greetyou, FirstLevel Priestess," stated a man behind an elegantly carved heavy wooden lectern, no doubt the Captain of the Noble-Council. She should know his name but her mind had blanked.

"Greetyou," she said, continuing to move toward him, and then she realized that GraceLord T'Equisetum was in the front row, behind another lectern as if he'd been speaking on a matter. Well, the timing hadn't been hers, after all, T'Ash had finessed it—or another person told him.

"What is your purpose here?" the Captain of the NobleCouncil asked.

She dipped a slight curtsey to him, turned, and did the same to the rest of the chamber. "I am FirstLevel Priestess Tiana Mugwort, of the once GraceNoble house of Mugwort. I am here to deliver a criminal complaint—*my* criminal complaint to GraceLord T'Equisetum."

"A criminal complaint!" GraceLord T'Equisetum bridled, then strode from behind the lectern. "What am I supposed to have done to you . . . *illegally*, little Mugwort?"

Rude, confrontational, forceful, but none of that ruffled her as it had that morning. She'd been staring at him from the moment she'd entered, and she tried to sense him as she would a person to be counseled. His spiritual health seemed . . . very off . . . as if he couldn't access his inner self who could connect with the divine.

Continuing to assess him, she tilted her head. "GraceLord T'Daisy was right about your Flair this morning, wasn't he, about how you might fail for a Testing as a GraceLord in Flair? And I've been wrong all along; I did not trust the Lady and the Lord. Those events you instigated years ago, here in the NobleCouncil and with your cuz Arvense, *have* worked on you, threefold, haven't they?"

She offered the complaint. He ignored it.

With narrowed eyes, she said, "Your Flair is suppressed. Quite odd."

She pitied him. He saw it and lashed out.

He struck her.

Thirty-three

T'Equisetum *sent Tiana crashing into the lectern, then suddenly* Danith D'Ash had her arm around Tiana's waist, helping her stand. Sucking in a breath, Tiana put her hand to her aching face and drew off the heat and the pain, murmuring a standard Healing spell. Occasionally people she counseled became violent, and she knew what to do.

Danith D'Ash stepped up to T'Equisetum. "So you're a proponent of the Traditionalist Stance movement, are you? You wouldn't let people like me Test and rise from Commoner to Noble anymore, huh?" She tilted her head. "Well, since you don't think my Flair is acceptable. I guess I'll take your Family off my list of people to receive animal companions. Not that I would give one to a man who'd strike someone weaker than he."

T'Equisetum bared his teeth, lifted his hand again.

The hiss of a sword being drawn froze most. T'Ash stalking in with an unsheathed blade immobilized everyone else. Tiana smelled fresh urine.

"Bad enough that you strike a priestess, for *nothing*, T'Equisetum," T'Ash growled. "Wouldn't want to be you when High Priest D'Sandalwood shows up at your door for some penance ritual you can't refuse. Don't you use that hand on my HeartMate or you will lose it. Now take the lady's complaint, 'cuz Lady and Lord know, you are guilt—"

"Stop, T'Ash," Danith said. "Legal rules. He is innocent until proven—"

T'Ash grunted, his gaze still fixed on T'Equisetum, who, though motionless, flushed bright red.

"Bad health. Nasty temper." Now Danith tsked. "Yes, this one needs counseling. Or punishment, though from my point of view, I can see the rule of three has acted upon him. His misdeeds have come back thrice."

She turned to face the other Nobles in their tiered seats. "Just who among you is of the Traditionalist Stance and saying I'm not good enough to sit in this chamber if I wanted to? Because you have the right to your beliefs and the consequences thereof. And I have the right not to place Familiar companions in the hands of stupid, shortsighted, idiot—"

"Danith." Her name was spoken softly. The same voice said, "T'Ash, please put the sword away. We don't want any feuds called in hotheaded impulse." A tall, scholarly-looking man who carried himself with authority strode up and put his hand on T'Ash's shoulder.

"Hi, Walker!" Danith beamed at the rising star of the Noble-Council, Walker Clover, who'd been a Commoner like her.

"Merrily met, Danith," Walker said, smiling and giving her a short bow. He glanced at T'Ash, who sheathed his weapon. "Always interesting times when the Ashes are involved." Walker's gaze swept the assemblage. "I suggest you all remember that. Now, T'Ash, you are here to witness the proper service of the complaint?"

An unbending and a muscular presence, T'Ash said, "I support FirstLevel Priestess Tiana Mugwort in her claims."

Walker Clover's jaw flexed. His eyes cooled as he stared at T'Equisetum. "Ah. I suggest you take the complaint, GraceLord."

"No," T'Equisetum said between choppy breaths.

"Guards," Walker Clover said.

Two guards in uniform strode in. One was Chief Winterberry.

He paced up and stood next to T'Equisetum, facing in the same direction. The other man, who looked as if he usually had a cheerful manner, came up and ranged himself beside Tiana.

He nipped the complaint from her fingers, cleared his throat, and stated in a voice that rolled through the chamber, "I, as a duly sworn member of the Druida City Guard, a subsidiary of the Celtan Planetary Peace Keeping Force, do stand as proxy for Tiana Mugwort, who has a complaint vetted and approved by a legal clerk of JudgementGrove against Hyemale T'Equisetum, do serve this upon that person—"

"GraceLord T'Equisetum," said the man, his color fading to pink.

"—such complaint." He offered the papyrus to T'Equisetum. Who didn't take them.

"I, as a duly sworn member of the Druida City Guard, a subsidiary of the Celtan Planetary Peace Keeping Force, do stand as proxy for Hyemale T'Equisetum and accept—" Winterberry began the litany.

"Just give it to me." T'Equisetum took the papyrus packet and crushed them in his fingers. "I deny all charges."

Winterberry nodded. "So noted. It would be helpful if you, and your cuz Arvense Equisetum, voluntarily share your memories of the night that mobs firebombed GraceLord T'Mugwort's home and other Hopefuls' abodes."

T'Equisetum shrugged. "I can't recall that particular night."

Tiana thought she heard a lie, and from the glances between the members of the Lords and Ladies in the first row of seats, they had, too.

Winterberry, face expressionless, said, "It's done." Nodding to Tiana, he asked, "Do you need a Healer, FirstLevel Priestess?"

"No. Thank you." Again she touched her cheek where only a lingering sting stayed . . . more due to memory than actual bruising.

"Good," T'Ash said. A click came. Tiana realized that he'd snapped the cover over his blazer, then shuddered a little that he'd been ready to use *two* weapons. She wasn't the only one who trembled.

"I don't know about you, Tiana—" T'Ash began.

She jolted at her name on his lips.

"—but Danith and I want to go look at the machines from *Nuada's Sword* building the Hopeful cathedral. Our glider is out in front. We're taking all the children for the educational experience," he said indulgently, "and Laev T'Hawthorn, too. Camellia D'Hawthorn made us—and you—a picnic lunch."

Danith D'Ash linked arms with Tiana. "Come on, let's get out of this stuffy old place," the GreatLady said with the disdain of a person with great Flair and of the highest status.

Yowls and roars came from the open doorway to the marble corridor.

"Catfight!" someone shouted.

"Zanth!" T'Ash bellowed.

"Felonerb." Tiana sighed.

*T*iana and Felonerb ended up being transported to the cathedral site on the Varga Plateau in a GreatCircle Temple glider once more assigned to her. Eventually she'd learn the light and venue well enough to teleport there, but it would take daily visits. She didn't think anyone except the Chief Ministers, Antenn, and perhaps some of his crew could teleport there now.

She stood a few minutes in awe with other newcomers and just stared at gigantic machines oddly silhouetted in black and gray and green and rust against the bright blue sky. Lifting huge blocks from a line of cut stones that just appeared due to some sort of ancient Earthan all-tech transport system. *Fast* transport system, as fast as a Flaired thought. Machines trundled or glided the massive stones to the trenches, delicately placing them. Then people would swarm down and measure, have them adjusted in tiny ways she couldn't distinguish, and continue on.

Soon her training—and her desire to be near Antenn, *help* Antenn—kicked in and she hurried over to see him explain something with gestures that he'd already used five times on different groups. She listened to him, and he seemed to calm when she showed up, and then he referred them to Dani Eve Elder or Captain

Ruis Elder. The group rarely trudged over to the two nulls, who would suppress any inherent Flair they had. And even less rarely approached one of the Intersection of Hope—Hopeful—ministers.

After a few minutes Tiana understood the construction process and led informational tours, including speaking to the Chief Ministers. After a while, her good friend PublicLibrarian Glyssa Licorice Bayrum appeared and helped her.

Whenever anyone expressed interest in the ritual that evening, Tiana handed them all four papyrus sheets—and if she saw a page fly across the plain in the wind, she snatched it back.

In the late afternoon, two trios of Earth Mages began to work in concert with the machines, and after WorkEnd Bell sounded in distant Druida City, a flood of people who hadn't been able to attend during the day showed up to watch.

By sunset, two full tiers of granite blocks, with the special mortar between, had been laid along the entire outline of the cathedral. They didn't reach the lip of the trenches but were sufficient that all the First-Family GreatLords and Ladies who'd deigned to visit had told her the stones would hold a strong spellshield. This would be just the first spellshield, and particular to the granite. When the limestone and foam metal girders—that came from the starship *Nuada's Sword*'s storage—were placed, there would be additional security spells.

Everyone felt that there couldn't be too many since GraceLord T'Equisetum, as a member of the Traditionalist Stance movement, had denounced it and the Hopefuls.

*S*o. *Lucky.*

*A*ntenn had been so lucky that day, and every time he'd had that thought he muttered a prayer to the Lord and Lady. Laying the foundation had gone more smoothly and quickly than he'd even originally scheduled.

Both Captain Ruis Elder and Dani Eve Elder worked with him

on setting up the even flow of the transport of granite from the quarry and the careful placing of blocks in the trenches. He sweated now—and his bespelled clothes absorbed the sweat and negated any smell—just thinking about the whole thing. The Elders had treated him with respect, and they knew their stuff—the workings and capabilities of their machines.

Most of Druida City, including about half of the FirstFamilies Lords and Ladies—twelve of them—had turned out to watch the colonists' machines that had built their city in magnificent action.

At first he'd been pestered, by the Chief Ministers with whom he had to smooth over the absence of Apex Mage Builders, then by every Lord or Lady who had a nodding acquaintance with him.

Tiana had shown up and been an amazing help as a liaison in every way with every group. Glyssa Licorice Bayrum had pitched in.

Then two subcontractors had shown up, impressed with the machines and the Elders and wanting part of the action. One had been a firm Antenn had called in desperation near dawn, the other three were partners that had split from GraceLord T'Pulicaria and Apex.

Antenn had crossed his arms and let the two underbid each other for the day's project. Both of them wanted contact with the Elders, wanted to be considered for any other jobs the Elders and *Nuada's Sword* might get from this demonstration. In the end, Antenn had been able to hire them both.

Lucky.

Now the sun dipped under the horizon and he was going back to the Turquoise House, who admired him, with his lover. His HeartM—no, he couldn't think of that right now. He couldn't afford to let any great emotions overwhelm him at such a thought.

He checked the temporary, very minor alarm spellshield he'd set around the perimeter of the trenches, went over their duties with the six private guards he'd hired to patrol the area before everyone returned for the ritual. Then he called to Tiana, Pinky, and Felonerb to take her glider back to TQ with him.

If his luck continued to hold tonight, he'd get sex and food before returning in a septhour and a half to participate in the ritual.

Their Fams' meeting had been brief and bloody, with each cat pretending he'd won the fight, though Antenn and Tiana had separated them. To everyone's surprise, both Fams knew the rules laid down by Danith D'Ash at sharing a home and their persons . . . and neither Pinky nor Felonerb wanted to break those. Mostly, Antenn thought, because Felonerb hadn't gotten a special Fam collar from his FamWoman and Pinky wanted a new one. Whatever worked.

He and Tiana sat in the glider with Felonerb and Pinky between them, but hand in hand. The cats ignored each other and the sexual tension between himself and his HeartMate rose higher and higher. He drew circles on her palms with his fingertips, unable to help himself.

When they reached the door, the cats shot around the House to the back grassyard and he and Tiana bolted for her bedroom. Again.

Then he just stood, framing her lovely face with his hands and staring at her, letting all his emotions show, especially his need.

His craving.

He had to look at her, cherish this watching of her as the sun slipped away and shadows contoured her beauty.

"I'm dusty," she said on a quiet breath.

"So am I. Don't care." He drew her close, close, close, so he could feel her body against his, the softness of her breasts and belly against his chest and shaft. The most wonderful sensation since he'd left her that morning.

Wrapping his arms around her, he held her tight. His. As no woman had ever been his. A dangerous feeling, almost threatening, that could rip him into pieces. He disregarded it.

She hugged him back and the lifting of her arms, the arching of her body caressed his sex, and he fought to say words through ragged need. "Gotta have you. Now. Terrible day. Lucky day. Cave of the Dark Goddess, it was strange."

"Yes."

He vaguely recalled he should ask her about something but couldn't think of it. Could only manage his thick fingers undoing the tabs in her clothes and kissing her neck where her essential fragrance tempted him.

"Sorry," he said gutturally. "Gotta be quick."

"Yes."

"And hard."

"Yes."

Thought evaporated. This time he couldn't let go of her, of her skin under his hands as all their clothes fell away, not even to throw her on the bed. Instead he walked her back, nibbling up her neck along her jaw. When she ran into the bed he pushed her back, took her mouth, and as her legs opened, he thrust inside her.

Wet. Ready for him. A whimper of delight from her.

Fabulous. He groaned, long. His cock thickened.

Couldn't talk. Knew he wouldn't last long, wanted to give her tenderness. He rose to look her in the eyes. Hadn't ever cared about seeing a woman as he had sex with her.

But not sex, now. More. Not love. Not yet. But more than sex.

The bond between them throbbed strongly, red with desire. With a jolt that cleared his brain a bit, in his mind's eye he saw the famous golden coil of the HeartBond! Couldn't be, could it? So soon? Too soon!

She shifted under him, lifted her legs and wrapped them around his waist, and that was it.

Only plunging inside her, again and again. Looking at her eyes that watched him. Gazes locked. Bond pushing feelings back and forth, passion.

"So. Good," she said.

And his control snapped and they moved together, strained together, whirled through a cyclone together. He saw her eyes go wide. His own blurred and only the rocking slide of skin against skin, the pulsing bond, mattered. They broke into ecstasy, holding each other.

Long minutes later, she murmured a couplet and they rolled, but he kept his grip on her. They settled against the pillows at the top of the bed. He couldn't say anything. Didn't want to say anything. That she didn't need to fill the silence with chatter pleased him.

He didn't deserve her, though he felt the cycling of their emotions as if they were true equals, meant for each other.

Most emotions. He frowned, considered her. Some of her emotions seemed thready. What—?

His perscry pebble alarmed in obnoxious pulses. He jerked to sit. "Damn. That's the guard at the cathedral site."

Thirty-four

She hopped to her feet. *"Lady and Lord."* That was a quiet moan. "Not another Whirlwind Spell."

The thought hadn't occurred; he *hated* those. Most men didn't bother with them. But he'd learned it. Because his mother was fussy Mitchella D'Blackthorn.

"Right. Block scry. This is Blackthorn-Moss."

"Better get here, Boss. Got an interesting situation."

Not something any man wanted to hear from a guard. "On my way." He cut the scry. *"Whirlwind Spell, twinmoons ritual robe!"* Damn, damn, damn, *fligger*! Rasped clean, skin stinging, especially the skin of his favorite part of his body, then a soft loincloth wrapped a little too tight. A heavy blue robe draped around him.

Between gritted teeth, he said, "I don't like that."

She sighed, looking perfect and immaculately groomed in a bright yellow gown, hair falling simply to her shoulders. "No one does." She took his hand. "You can teleport?"

"Yeah. Privacy off. Turquoise House, can you send the Temple glider to the cathedral site?"

"Yes, Antenn."

"Tiana and I are leaving now to deal with an urgent situation."

"Good luck," TQ said.

"Thanks. On three." Antenn took her hand, counted down, and then they were there, in one of the two designated teleportation areas.

Three guards holding three men stood only a few meters away.

Antenn strode up. "What's the problem here?"

The burliest guard jerked his chin at the man he held. "Perimeter alarm went off. We came running, found these fliggers." The guard's gaze went past Antenn. "Beg pardon for my language, FirstLevel Priestess."

"Not at all," Tiana soothed.

"They *said* they belong to the Traditionalist Stance movement," one of the other guards added. He snorted. "Don't know whether or not that's true, but they had their privates outta their trous and looked like they was trying to pee in the trenches."

Tiana gasped. "Desecrate the Intersection of Hope cathedral?"

"Yes, FirstLevel Priestess."

"That is . . . that is . . . just so wrong."

"Call for backup to take your place, then take them to the guardhouse and file complaints against them."

"Hey, man, wait. It was just a little fun. Nothing to be concerned about. Just the Cross Folk church. Nothin' special!" one of the men whined.

The biggest one broke away, pushed at the guards and Antenn. Hot blood flooded Antenn's veins. A different kind of release for this day tempted. He waded into the general melee, and in a few minutes, guards and violators were gone.

He'd just risen from the dust and flashed a grin at Tiana, who'd calmly watched the fracas, when the four Chief Ministers teleported in.

It was later than Antenn thought.

Tiana went to intercept them and she and the ministers dropped deep into conversation. Religious professionals discussing *their* business . . . ceremonies. Slowly, the five of them began circumnavigating the cathedral, as if none of them had been there that entire day.

Antenn guessed the number of onlookers had cramped their style when considering all the details that the rite might have.

Before they'd returned, he'd briefed the newer guards, and participants in the rite began to show up.

Tiana joined him, holding stacks of the papyrus prompts for the four different parts and appearing distracted.

Then Chief Minister Custos sounded a gong, letting folk know that the ritual would begin in half a septhour and a familiar voice hailed them, and Antenn turned to smile at Vinni T'Vine and Vinni's fiancée and HeartMate—Antenn swallowed at the designation—Avellana Hazel.

The gong brought Tiana from last-minute memorization of her part to scan the goodly amount of people—perhaps a hundred and twenty—who'd shown up to take part in the Intersection of Hope's ritual to set spellshields in the foundation. People only—the Chief Ministers hadn't allowed Fams because none of them *had* Fams.

She recognized GreatLord T'Vine, the prophet, walking toward her and Antenn. She thought he was near in age to Antenn, but he appeared older—especially his expression and the shadows in his eyes. A young woman accompanied him, fingers intertwined with his.

"Greetyou, Antenn," T'Vine said, then smiled at Tiana. "A pleasure to meet you again, FirstLevel Priestess."

Tiana had been introduced to him a while back when she'd still been a ThirdLevel Priestess.

T'Vine said, "May I introduce you to my fiancée, Avellana Hazel?"

Avellana inclined her torso slightly. "Greetyou, FirstLevel Architect Blackthorn-Moss."

Antenn bowed. "It's been a while."

In a colorless voice, Avellana said, "Yes. Muin says the plague is completely eradicated from Druida City and won't come back. He's allowed me to return."

"And this is FirstLevel Priestess Tiana Mugwort," Antenn said smoothly.

Turning to Tiana, Avellana curtseyed. "Greetyou, FirstLevel Priest-

ess Mugwort. It is an honor to meet you. And I thank you for inviting me to such an interesting event."

"I'm glad you're attending," Tiana said, "and I'm sure the Chief
Ministers are also. The more people who participate in the ritual,
the less confusion and ignorance there will be about the Intersection
of Hope faith in those hearts and minds."

"Also, the spellshields will be stronger," Antenn said.

T'Vine inclined his head. "Always a consideration." He scanned
the area like a nobleman checking to see who of his allies had come
and who had not shown up, and Tiana thought he'd used his influence to draw people to the ritual. Nerves about her work crawled
under her skin.

"Looks like a good showing—" T'Vine began.

"Please hush, Muin," Avellana interrupted.

He did. Tiana looked at her and noted that Antenn's gaze had
slid to her, too. Avellana let go of T'Vine's hand and dipped her
own into one of the long rectangular sleeve pockets of a formal
gown that cost about five times the amount of Tiana's best. The
young woman drew out four sheets of unfolded papyrus, copies of
the four parts of the ritual. She fanned them out, stared at Tiana,
and gave them a little shake. "I understand that you wrote this ritual, FirstLevel Priestess Mugwort."

Tiana nodded. "Yes, along with my mother, who is a member of
the Intersection of Hope Church."

Avellana looked down at the uppermost and read the first line
aloud. "I am a wayfarer on a great Journey, a hopeful innocent
child toddling into the bright light of my future." She slipped that
page to the back, squared the papyrus, and read the next opening:
"I am a mature adult strong in my vitality, master of my intellect,
my emotions and my Flair, striding along the path of my Journey
with the knowledge I am guided." She flipped that to the back, took
the third. "I am the guardian spirit ever present in each wayfarer on
this hopeful Journey, touchstone for each." Finally, Avellana read
the last. "I am the eldest approaching the end of my Journey, full

of light, knowing I have done my best, hopeful for whatever comes next."

Brows down Avellana stared at them, from one to another. "*This*"—she fanned the papyrus again—"*these* concepts make sense to me."

"Avellana?" T'Vine's voice rose, and Tiana understood that unlike most situations in his life, this was unforeseen and had jarred him with surprise.

The young woman pressed the pages to her breasts and repeated, "This makes sense. Life as a Journey. *This* is right." She smiled with radiant beauty that lightened her serious expression.

"The Intersection of Hope faith was founded by the generational crew during their centuries on the starships. Of course they would think of life and religion as a journey," T'Vine said reasonably.

Avellana sniffed. "That doesn't make the faith any less viable." Shuffling the papyrus, she said, "I will take the part of the innocent child tonight." She glanced at Antenn. "Which is the proper entrance for those of us who are innocent children?"

"The southwest," he replied.

T'Vine reached out and touched her fingers. She clasped hands with him again.

"I thought you'd walk with me down the guardian spirit path," T'Vine said.

She gazed up at him and said, "I don't feel much like a guardian spirit yet." She sounded younger than she should have and must have been very sheltered.

Then Tiana stilled her face in a pleasant expression, remembering that Avellana Hazel's brain had been damaged as a small child. So she might sound young, but Tiana sensed great Flair . . . and will . . . and determination and a bright mind.

Avellana offered GreatLord T'Vine the appropriate papyrus and slipped the other two sheets back into her sleeve, then tapped the back of her head. "My guardian spirit part hasn't unfurled itself yet. It's still a little cramped. But you go ahead." She looked at Tiana. "Muin makes a very good guardian spirit."

"I usually take the role of guardian spirit," Tiana said, "but this evening I will be walking along the southwest aisle, as the innocent child, too. We can proceed together."

"I'd like that," Avellana said.

"The space between the foundation blocks is wide enough for four abreast," Antenn said.

"And I'm pleased that two such Flaired women are walking together," T'Vine said. He bowed to Tiana. "Thank you."

"I will go as the vital adult," Antenn said.

"And that surprises no one," Tiana said, with humor in her voice.

"All my focus is on this project," Antenn stated.

The four Chief Ministers took their compass points at the end of each arm of the outline of the cathedral.

"Greetyou," Custos said, his voice augmented with Flair and loud enough to carry to everyone. "Welcome to the sacred site of the cathedral of the Intersection of Hope. Please gather at the indication of the doorway of your chosen pathway."

A small gasp came from Avellana, and Tiana, Antenn, and T'Vine glanced at her.

"What?" asked T'Vine.

Whispering, Avellana asked, "Those are the four High Priests of the Intersection of Hope?"

"The four Chief Ministers, yes," Tiana answered.

Even lower, Avellana said, "They are all men." She paused. "That is *not* right."

"Something to think about," Antenn said. He reached out, took Tiana's fingers, and bowed over them, and her whole body clenched in pleasure at his touch, in remembrance of their coming together sexually, physically, and the emotional bond resonating between them. "Later," he said.

"Yes."

She glanced around and saw her Family, all of them stationed at the door for those participating as the guardian spirits, and she thought her father had persuaded Garrett and Artemisia to do so as protection for Tiana's mother, the true Intersection of Hope member.

Father is a little nervous, Artemisia said to Tiana telepathically.

We have arrived late and will teleport home the instant the ceremony is over. Then we'll eat and talk and discuss everything. Blessed be.

Blessed be, Tiana returned.

The High Priest and High Priestess stood with Elderstone at that minister's outlined entrance, another surprise for Tiana since she'd thought they'd be with Antenn and Chief Minister Foreman. They nodded to her and she felt their appraisal . . . and approval, and let out a little sigh.

As Tiana progressed to the correct area with Avellana, T'Vine sent her a grateful smile, but it only made her wonder what danger he might have foreseen.

Each Chief Minister held a hand gong and Younger struck his first, followed by Foreman, Elderstone, and Custos, and the ritual began.

"I am a wayfarer on a great Journey, a hopeful innocent child toddling into the bright light of my future," Tiana said in a measured way with everyone else in her area, about thirty people, only five who might be Intersection of Hope faith followers. By the end of the sentence those reading and those reciting had caught the rhythm. Echoes of the other three parts came to her ears, in a different beat . . . Foreman's slightly slower and more forceful, Elderstone's much slower and contemplative. By the time everyone reached the inner end of the equal arms of the cathedral, the chant would be the same in words, rhythm, and tenor.

Avellana Hazel had glanced at her part, and though she continued to hold the sheet, she didn't refer to it. And as the ceremony progressed, Tiana fell into a moving meditative state and got little peeps into the young woman beside her so Tiana *reached* for her aura, found it slightly odd, but caught Avellana's attention and blended that aura with hers, sinking again into a light trance and bringing Avellana along with her.

Everyone met in the center, lined up and sang the simple blessing, then bowed and curtseyed to those around them and continued straight down the opposite arm. With the last quatrain, they stepped from the "door."

There they joined hands and each minister took the lead in gathering the Flair of his group—Avellana's great but mostly untamed—and linking together with the other ministers and those who knew spellshield chants. Then they raised a golden dome, stories high, over the area.

Then the cathedral itself showed in glowing golden lines, like an architectural drawing. Gasps of awe rose in the night air. Antenn must be doing the visualization and projection and Tiana looked to where he stood, linked with his father, T'Blackthorn, and other members of his Family, most with a large amount of Flair.

"Ooooh," Avellana said, staring at the airy construct. "So, so beautiful. Do you think they would be interested in holo artists?"

Since Avellana was the daughter of a FirstFamily and *the* holo artist of the age, Tiana said, "Absolutely. You can speak with any of the Chief Ministers or Antenn Blackthorn-Moss." She paused delicately. "I'm sure they would love any donation you might give them."

Avellana's smile was dazzling. "Oh, I would have to do something for the space and the ambiance of the cathedral."

"Of course."

Avellana said, "Time to join in the spellshield chant again. *Not* as beautiful as your ritual. You should think of revising some old spells and giving them new vigor," Avellana said, then frowned and bit her lips as she funneled energy to Chief Minister Younger.

Narrowing her own eyes, Tiana strove to *see* the spellshields, both physically and with Flair. She *did*, glossy silver layers coating the stones, hopefully threading through them, too.

With a last sustained Word, the spell ended and people dropped hands.

Tiana turned to look at her Family, but they were already gone. Head tilted, she *sensed* the atmosphere and was pleased at the shrouded quiet of people who'd been drawn emotionally into a rite . . . or experienced a spiritual uplift. One by one, couple by couple, or Family by Family, people winked out like stars, teleporting home. A lesser number of celebrants walked to gliders.

When GreatLord T'Vine came up and took Avellana Hazel's

arm, she said, "Thank you so much for inviting me to this wondrous ritual." She curtseyed deeply to Tiana.

"You're welcome."

"My Family should have come. I think they will regret not doing so."

"Merrily met, FirstLevel Priestess Mugwort," T'Vine said.

"Merrily met," Tiana responded, and knew she *did* feel joyful, her spirits lifted from the ceremony.

With a last nod, T'Vine vanished with Avellana.

Then, as at the end of the workday earlier, there were only Antenn and her and the Chief Ministers—who had sent the guards home, confident in their spellshields. As they should have been. More than half of the twenty-five FirstFamilies Lords and Ladies had attended and given their strength and Flair to the spell. As many as often worked together in the important quarterly rituals to shape Druida and Celta in GreatCircle Temple.

With a formal bow, in unison, the Chief Ministers said, "Thank you for aiding us on our journey; may yours be sweet tonight," and left.

Antenn slipped an arm around her waist. "Yes, my thanks." He cleared his throat. "The ritual went well?" he asked.

She stared at him. "You tell me how *you* felt about it."

He considered, nodding slowly. "Really good. Not as connected as I am in the best of the rituals at GreatCircle Temples, when I sometimes experience the Lord, but . . . really good."

"Excellent."

"My parents and siblings and cuzes were impressed." Antenn kissed her on her cheekbone. Not an asexual buss. "Let's go back to TQ."

"Yes." The breath had gone out of her with anticipation.

"I saw a fabulous bedsponge in the MasterSuite, bigger than the one in your bedroom, brand-new and top-of-the-pyramid. Let's try it out."

Her mind fogged with the images coming from him of various sexual positions on that bed. "Yes."

During the quiet glider ride they cuddled together. Tiana let all the loveliness of the ritual, the small buzz of anticipatory sex swirl through her, exhilarating her senses . . . until her hand accidentally brushed the front of Antenn's lap as she shifted closer and found him thick and hard. All her focus narrowed to passion and her blood ran fast and hot. She took his hand and his fingers linked near violently with hers. His face showed strain.

She began to tremble from the inside out and the familiar yearning for him, his hands on her body, his thumbs rubbing over her breasts. Him inside her, surging with her to explosive release.

Yes, she trembled. But she savored the moments that seemed strung like glittering beads, one after the other, precious.

The glider halted and let them out, then left for GreatCircle Temple. Pinky and Felonerb met them, sniffed around their feet as they walked, and then the Fams shared a look and, without one mental word, ran around the House to the back in opposite directions.

Wrapped in each other, she and Antenn looked at TQ.

"It's a beautiful House," Tiana murmured.

"Yeah. Looks good. Great personality," Antenn said in a distracted voice.

"Thank you, Tiana. Thank you, Antenn," TQ said. "Please come in." He opened the door.

Thirty-five

*They walked together, arms around each other, and it wasn't awk-*ward, through the door and the entryway and turned right toward the MasterSuite. Her body swayed, brushing his, teasing him and herself.

The moment the MasterSuite bedroom door closed behind them, her whole being seemed to expand. Free. She turned to him. If she knew anything, it was the construction of ritual robes. She touched the tabs at the top of his shoulders, flicked at the seams of the garment made with Flair, easily dismissed the spells.

His robe fell away, lay in folds at his feet. She should send it to the wardrobe to hang well. She didn't care.

A sleek man but as she ran her hands over his chest, down his arms, she felt the strength . . . and his slight perspiration under her palms. She slid her hands to his hips, touched his loincloth, and it dropped, too. Looking down at him, large and thrusting, she smiled, all of her body warming and flushing, preparing for sex. She loved the way he made her feel, this burgeoning weight to her body, to her blood that would release in orgasm.

Freedom.

No constraints. Not here in the bedroom.

Not with Antenn.

"Tiana," he whispered hoarsely, put those callused palms of his on her face, urged her to look at him . . . as she'd stared at him throughout the last time they'd made love. His eyes had widened, showed vulnerability again that she reveled in. She thought he masked himself as much as she did herself. She reached down and circled his sex with her fingers, stroked him. He closed his eyes and shuddered, his hands curving around her shoulders as if to hold on to her.

She liked that. Loved the urgency of their coming together. No polite little dance as sex had been for her before.

His head angled and he nibbled her earlobe and it was her turn to shudder, letting the full sensuality of every action vibrate through her. His hands went from her shoulders to feather down her sides, lift and caress her breasts, her nipples.

"Tiana," he whispered—like no other, that catch in his voice, that lilt or huskiness or pure emotional resonance. "So perfect," he murmured, playing with her hair. "I don't deserve you."

The sentiment bothered her, but she didn't stop to correct him, since his fingers had gone between her legs and he was stroking, stroking until pleasure washed through her and he enlarged in her fingers and she didn't want to be vertical any longer. With one last caress, she let his shaft go and took his hand and led him to bed.

Softly, lingeringly they explored each other, with hands and mouths. His tender and slow touch freed her again, to take, then to gasp, then to give. Minutes slowed and only the next skim of his fingers, the next taste of his skin under her tongue mattered.

Seduction, both of them. She wouldn't have thought it of him, but the once-street-boy knew how to give, and she pleased them both in returning his gift, showing him her need for him, and that he fulfilled her.

She drew him over her, free to express the sweet craving for him, free to be gentle and vulnerable and utterly true to herself. And they joined, so naturally, so wonderfully that she knew no other lover, no other love would match this.

Again, they linked gazes, and hands . . . and emotions through their bond. They moved together, giving and taking, each second fluttering exquisite sensation through her. No rough demand, awful need now, but winding tension that flung her to the stars, burst through her, and then he peaked and they spiraled down on a drift of starfire back to the bed and slipped into sleep, still entwined.

The Turquoise House's Family was here. Again for the night. Two in a row!

They were sleeping now, and the privacy rules had been lifted. Because they weren't in Tiana's bedroom. A small detail, but a vital one.

He liked feeling them within his walls, sensing their breathing and their heartbeats. They were together under his roof.

Maybe it was time for a nudge. He could send them subliminal visions and suggestions that might be incorporated in their sleep, but that wasn't allowed. But he was allowed to . . . whisper quietly to them, he thought. He checked the Residence Ethics. Yes, he *could* whisper. So he did, as they slept in each other's arms, as they dreamed—perhaps of one another. They *were* HeartMates; a nudge should be fine. Everyone would say so. Especially all his other Residence friends.

"You want to HeartBond." He sent the barely humanly audible words to them, lilted them in the voice he knew people paid the most attention to, along with an airy tune that also caught humans' attention.

Tiana frowned, but held Antenn tighter.

She floated in a dream with her HeartMate. Finally found. Finally lost to him. And she wanted to HeartBond. The beautiful golden rope lay in coils near her, ready for her to send to Antenn during sex.

Reaching out, she found him, glided her fingers over him until he became erect.

Yes, the HeartBond was there, ready for him to accept. Would he? She didn't know.

And she hesitated, too. Everything moved so fast lately. She didn't feel ready to bond for her whole life with someone she barely knew. Or was she wrong, *was* she ready? To tie him to her forever? She let her fingers fall away from him, confused.

Antenn's dream turned from a simple stream of pure white happiness, to lying next to his HeartMate. He knew her now, was learning her body, celebrated mating with her. Sex. Loving.

He looked at her in his dream, studied her, picked up the Heart-Bond to send to her once he slipped inside her again. Then he saw she wasn't whole. That jarred him from feeling into thinking.

Within the dream, when she slept, he could scrutinize her as never before.

Yes, there was a barrier between her and some seething fire of emotions. Easier to see, and he understood her well enough that he could sense her down to her foundation. Her serenity wasn't false, but she'd built that block over something he was sure needed to be released. Strong, such a strong lady, his Tiana.

Should he touch that block? Dared he?

Dare, yes, he'd dare anything for her. But he'd already prompted her to demand justice for the crimes against her Family . . . and done that not only for her, but for himself.

All the thinking woke him up. He rolled onto his side and propped himself on his elbow and looked at his HeartMate. Still gorgeous. Still outwardly perfect. Still inwardly better than he was. He didn't deserve her, but he wasn't sure he'd tell her that again. A flaw.

He could still see that blockage . . . as dark and heavy as the granite cathedral foundation. Surely she, as a priestess, would want the block gone.

Her eyes opened. She smiled, stretched lingeringly, then stared at him with puzzlement on her face, lifting her finger to touch the knot between his brows.

"What's wrong?"

Despite himself, he said, "I'm not deserving of you."

Now his frown transferred to her. She sat and gave him a stern priestess look, and said crisply, "You're still reacting to the fact that Shade did terrible things and you're his brother and responsible for them, too. That's just wrong."

Oh, yeah, that stung. He jutted his chin. "The fact is, some people will always judge me by him, FirstFamilies people."

She tilted her head, considering him as he had her. But he was awake and didn't like it.

"How do you know?" she asked. "You assume that, but how do you know those people are so unforgiving?"

"They're FirstFamily Lords and Ladies, not known for their flexibility."

She sniffed.

"And their careers, unlike yours, don't include being forgiving." But he shifted uncomfortably, sat up himself. Her words had echoed T'Equisetum's the day before, though their motives were directly opposite. Antenn ran his hands through his hair, scrubbed his scalp, gave her a sideways look. "And maybe you think I lack a trifle self-confidence."

"I do."

"But I'm not the only one with flaws here."

She jerked as if she'd been struck, and he winced. "I didn't mean it—"

"I think you did." Her lips compressed before she spoke again, "I never said I was without flaw."

"No. You didn't."

"So?"

"So, what?" he asked.

"I gave you an unwelcome truth. You can tell me one."

He took both her hands, and the thing was, he could now *feel* that lid she had on her emotions, the solid door she'd locked them behind, the block she'd squashed them under. Whatever image he thought of it, the thing was real. And irritating, and would be that way until one of them fixed it.

The flow between them came haltingly on her part. He dragged in a deep breath. Yeah, he was prepared to remove it for her. He thought he could do that, though he wondered what the explosion might do to him. He could deconstruct as well as design and build.

He stood and she rose at the same time and they faced each other. He settled into his balance and matched her irritated gaze and said, "You don't give all of yourself to me, Tiana, and I want it."

Her eyes widened and her mouth dropped open in outrage. "I certainly do give you everything I am!"

"No. You don't. I want all of you." He scanned her from top to bottom. "Despite all your serenity, you've blocked a part of yourself off." He coughed. "Like I did when I put a lock on the HeartMate connection between us."

She stared at him, scowling.

"That barrier might never shift, might never crack or break . . . but you won't be living a full life if it doesn't, will you? And if I've learned anything from this whole situation, I know that I want to experience every moment of my life, and treasure every instant with you."

"You must be wrong."

"I have a bond with you, my lady. I can sense your deepest self." He paused, then said deliberately, "And it is not serene."

He heard her teeth grind. She jerked her hands away, her fingers fisted, and then she took a deep breath and her hands uncurled.

"No!" he snapped. "Don't do that. You don't have to be careful around *me*. You don't have to suppress what you feel around *me*!"

"I . . . I . . ."

"All the time since I've known you, you've been trying to 'work through' this crap. Like you've 'worked through' it for years." He swore he could see flashes of Flair lightning through her eyes, and some might be directed at him. So be it. He went on. "Maybe it's better that you just let it all out."

She hunkered down, her back curved a little, her head thrust forward. Good, he was getting to her.

He smiled a charm-the-client-smile he'd practiced for hours when an apprentice.

A growl came from her.

His smile widened. "Good, good." He tilted his head, lifted his hands, and wiggled his fingers in the bring-it-on gesture. Even she, who wasn't a fighter, would recognize that.

She did.

Narrowing his eyes again to check her inner self, he saw there was a crack in that barrier—like a stone flooring. "Come on, darlin', tell me what's botherin' you." His voice lilted with a patronizing note.

And that was all it took.

Boom! Not an audible sound, but an emotional one that hammered through the atmosphere. And that rush of fury crackled out in huge sheets, nearly searing him with the real and heartfelt heat. He caught the edge of it and the power of her Flair shoved him into the closest wall, which he banged with his shoulder.

He grunted, felt her surprise, her hesitation.

But he wouldn't let her stop. Not now. This needed to be *done.* His mind scrabbled to grab on to the *reason* behind her anger, and he settled into his balance and gave it to her.

"You are angry at your parents." Yeah, that surprised him.

"No!" she nearly shrieked.

"Yes, but—"

"No!"

The barrier had blown up and away now. "Yes. You are." He frowned. "Why?"

She just shook her head, but they were well connected and the huge rage had begun to dissipate in her. He could sort through her turbulent emotions. "Yes. You're angry because they didn't fight when your home was firebombed."

"We might have hurt people if we—"

He flung up a hand. "You don't need to mouth any excuses to me. Your folks didn't fight then, and they didn't fight afterward. And that angered you."

Her lips and chin trembled.

"And it's understandable . . . both that you were furious and what your parents did—or failed to do. Your Family is gentle and pacifists, so you copied their behavior and accepted what was. Your training helped you squash those feelings."

"I . . . I . . ." Tears coursed down her cheeks. "I thought I'd gotten through these issues."

"Probably some, but not all. Not the underlying basic stuff." Cautiously he stepped forward and closed his hands around her upper arms. He dug down for a tone of command he rarely used. "Why are you mad at your parents?" he snapped.

"They took my home away!" She shuddered now. "No—"

"Yes. They took you away from your home and you never got to go back . . ."

Her shudders turned into full-body shakes.

"So you're angry at them. Let it out."

"Yes, I'm furious with them. They didn't *try* to fix things. To get back what they lost." She wrenched away from him, flailed her arms as she stomped around, tears pouring down her face. Then she pounded her chest with a fist. "That *hurt* me and I was a child and couldn't do anything about it and—"

He nodded. "I understand."

She flung out her arm, pointing. *"And YOU!"*

"Me?" He blinked.

"You are my HeartMate and you HID from me. I couldn't find you. Why, why?"

"Not my fault—"

"Shut up! You! You could have had that spell taken off at any time. You didn't let me help you, either. You didn't have faith in yourself or me."

Thirty-six

*T*hat's not true," he protested.

"It *is* true." Her stomping had turned into striding. "I'm angry at *you*, too."

"I can see that."

"You hurt me, too." She swallowed hard and the tears, which had paused, began again.

"I'm sorry."

Her eyes lit with a wild ferocity he'd never seen in them . . . far, far from her usual tranquility. She sure was letting it all out.

"*Years* I endured thinking you didn't want me because of the scandal. Because you might have believed the original lies about me and my Family."

He rocked back on his heels. "So you can understand some of what I went through—go through—too. Not being good enough for you."

"Not *feeling* as if you're good enough for me. Tcha!" She paced up to him, stabbed a finger in his chest, flung out her arms again. "Blood doesn't determine who I love."

"Easy for you to say," he muttered. "You're a priestess and supposed to be nonjudgemental." He squared his shoulders, letting her words actually sink in. "So you just thought I was cowardly and stupid," he said evenly, his own temper beginning to simmer at how dismissive she'd been of his concerns.

She tossed her head. "Stupid in a different way."

"Right. Great. Just what a man likes to hear from his lover."

Narrowing her own eyes, she corrected, "HeartMate. And you were the one who started this. *Yes, I'm carrying a lot of anger from my past. Ire at my parents for just abandoning our life. I'm . . . peeved . . . at you for your stupid spell, and for thinking the way you did. The way you do!*"

"Oh, yeah?"

"Yes."

Before either of them could say anything else, Felonerb RatKiller appeared, hissing. *You all big mad!* he said to Tiana, then whirled to face Antenn, all his fur on end. *He hurt you! You said so. I will BITE him.* He leapt for Antenn.

"Wait!" Tiana *pulled* at her Fam and he landed into her arms. Her expression tightened to stone. "You *did* hurt me." Her breath came out less explosively, and Antenn reckoned she was winding down. "All those years I couldn't find you, even if I'd tried."

"Which you didn't." He discovered *he* hurt, too.

"I tested the link between us often. There was nothing there," she said. "I don't care who your brother was or what he did. I don't care who your father is or isn't. I want my HeartMate. And if you wanted me to reach my full potential, I want the same for you. Accept *yourself*, Antenn. Value yourself."

"Ah, Family?" TQ asked tentatively. "You are affecting my emotions and those of the ferals around me." He cleared his throat. "There are fights."

"Oh," Tiana said.

Antenn snorted. "Oops."

"It's not funny," she said.

"I suppose not. Maybe you should discuss this matter with your parents and clear stuff up."

"I can do that."

"Of course you can," Antenn said.

She glared at him as if she thought he was being sarcastic. He wasn't.

Felonerb jumped from her arms onto the bed and she strode over to a dresser, yanked a softleaf from a box and used it to wipe away continuing tears, then blew her nose. "I *will* discuss this with my parents. And my sister."

She looked at Antenn, then flushed. "Fighting, I've caused fighting between innocent animals."

Felonerb, kneading the comforter on the bed, belched.

"You've made me understand how much you hurt me." She put her hand on her heart. "I don't know when I'll want to see you again."

"We have to work together."

"Perhaps."

"Perhaps!"

Pressing her hands against her head only emphasized how flushed she was and her tear tracks. "I can't think. I'm only feeling." Biting her lip, she shook her head. "I don't know what I want with you." She flung on her clothes, then walked over to a corner that held a teleportation pad.

"Wait—" She shouldn't leave him. Couldn't. Desperation fired through him, making him wave his arms jerkily. "Wait! I didn't mean to—"

But she left.

Felonerb hissed at him.

"I don't have to stay here, cat. And I'm not." He wouldn't go home. His mother and father would want to talk about the ritual, the cathedral, and Tiana. His Betony-Blackthorn cuzes would—

His cuzes Vensis and Draeg would be at The Green Knight Fencing and Fighting Salon. Tonight was an all-night melee for charity, the continuation of the refurbishment of old Downwind.

Antenn had paid the entrance fee for the fight and pledged more besides but had disregarded the event when the Chief Ministers had set tonight for their ritual. He kept a locker and fighting robes at the salon. All-night fighting. *Damn* good release.

Surely others would have arrived late. Or the rounds of competition were over now. He didn't know, but yearned for a good bout.

"TQ, thanks for your hospitality. Good seeing you again."

"Antenn, it's all my fault—" TQ began.

He didn't hear the rest of that, and didn't need to, because Antenn knew damn well whose fault it was. His own. As he changed in the Men's Locker Room, he understood that the disaster he'd been flirting with all day had finally caught up with him.

And losing—for now and who knew how long?—Tiana's affection sliced worse than if he'd lost the job. He didn't want to contemplate how tough it would be to work with her on the cathedral. She'd probably retreat behind that perfect priestess exterior that he found difficult to affect. Or maybe she'd go icy. Either way, he didn't like the results of what he'd said and done.

Needed to be said and done, but maybe he should have put it off until later, until they knew each other better.

But he'd never been one to let a faulty foundation stay.

When he stepped into the main salon, Tinne Holly nodded to him and strode up. Though Antenn was sure the man would have been in several fights by now, he appeared unharmed, unmussed. He clapped Antenn on the shoulder. "Greetyou, Antenn. Sorry the Holly Family couldn't be at that ceremony of your cathedral tonight, but we'd already set this up."

"I understand."

Antenn's cuz Draeg, who spent most of his time at this place when he wasn't prowling the city streets looking for trouble, pummeled Antenn on his opposite shoulder. Draeg was taller, broader, and hadn't been starved for food in his childhood. He said, "It was a good ceremony. Unusual since it was not to the Lord and the Lady, but intriguing, all the same. I liked it. Like the look of that structure you're building, too. Didn't expect to see you here tonight, though. Guys with new, hot lovers can find better things to do than fight."

Draeg and Tinne laughed, and Antenn said, "Let's fight." He poked Draeg, who could take him down three out of five times, in the chest.

"Trouble so soon?" Draeg shook his head. "Sad to see." He scanned Antenn up and down. "Just sad."

Antenn growled.

Tinne raised his voice. "Change of plans! General melee in *two* minutes."

"Fine," Antenn said.

"Fine," Draeg said.

*T*iana *dropped onto the teleportation pad in the mainspace of Balm-* Heal Residence. She'd been a little off, but was lucky her emotions hadn't influenced her 'porting even more. She'd have liked to have blamed *everything* on Antenn, but of course she couldn't do that. No strong person could, let alone a priestess. All he'd done was prod her to reveal—spectacularly—the understandable but awful emotions lurking inside her.

She must *still* be broadcasting great distress because her mother ran in. Her mother and father had probably been spending time in the conservatory, talking about the ritual, which seemed years ago instead of a couple of septhours.

Quina appeared anxious. "What's wrong?"

Tiana wobbled over to a twoseat, not her regular chair in the Family grouping, and collapsed. She translocated the crumpled softleaf in her hand to a cleanser, pulled another one from her sleeve, and wiped her face. She couldn't stop crying . . . better not to stop crying.

Sinjin! her mother called telepathically. *Artemisia! Garrett!*

Tiana wanted to say Garrett didn't need to be here, but that was her own cowardice speaking. He'd understood her before, but he loved her sister and her parents. He wouldn't be on her side now.

Tiana's father jogged in, expression concerned, followed by Artemisia. Maybe Garrett wouldn't show—

There was a quiet swish and the man appeared on the teleportation pad, face tense. Like her father, he went to his HeartMate and put his arm around her waist. Tiana wanted to think that she and Antenn would be like that, but they hadn't meshed.

She wanted all the pain to go away, all the anger that still spurted through her, all the exhaustion and confusion. She wished to bury her head in her hands, but until she faced the situation, life wasn't going to get better. So she lifted her hunched spine bit by bit and faced her Family.

"What's wrong, honey?" asked her father, who sat next to her. Her mother, still linking fingers with him, hovered close.

Tiana gulped because she was afraid she'd scream at him, as she'd screamed at Antenn. Absolutely no rein on her emotions.

"I . . . I . . ." A gulp of air, this time, not swallowing tears. She pressed her flattened hand above her breasts, close to her heart. "I have this rage inside me I didn't know about."

Her eyes had blurred again and it was good because it distanced her a little from the world, from whatever reaction she would see in her father's eyes when she told him the truth. "I am angry." Her voice shook and now she couldn't tell if it was only anger, but fear of hurting her parents, or embarrassment at losing control or what-all-ever.

Stumbling, she let it out. "You just . . . we just . . . we left our home during the mob firebombing and we never returned. We abandoned it and everything!" The words tore from her.

Her parents shared a glance. To her absolute surprise, her father lifted her and set her on his lap, and then her mother took Tiana's seat, crowding her. That was fine.

Artemisia and Garrett drew up their regular chairs.

"How could you do that? Leave our home?" Tiana cried.

Her father held her close and rocked her. "There was evil out there. An evil man of the Black Magic Cult had left clues implicating us—your mother as a member of the Intersection of Hope—as running that murderous cult. Everyone, Commoners and Nobles alike, went through a time of panic."

"But afterward, you didn't try to get things back, did you?"

She felt his heart pound faster in his chest beneath her cheek. "I presented document after document, petition after petition. Clerks lost them. Nobles never heard of them. People who we thought were friends didn't speak with us. People I sent messages to said they never received them."

Garrett nodded slowly. "Nothing shows up in any official records that you tried to get your home and holdings back."

Her father shrugged. "I tried every avenue I thought of to file such petitions."

"Then I panicked," Quina said. "We were disenfranchised. Nobody. Easy prey for those who might want us to disappear—all of us, even my babies. No one would care. So I took another name and worked at AllClass HealingHall. We moved often. We stayed beneath notice of anyone who might pursue us.

"We decided to leave Druida, change our names, and move to a smaller town," Tiana's father said.

Her mother lifted her chin. "Healers are always useful."

"Then came the offer to stay here, to mind the estate, and to care for the Residence."

And I thank you, said the Residence. *You have been a good and true and honorable Family.*

Tiana leaned back and stared at her father's worn and lined face, met his steady eyes. "You did try."

"It was my home. I loved it. Yes, I tried. But I failed."

"You never told us."

"Who likes admitting they're a failure? And there was plenty to do here. There was nothing for us outside in the city."

She was nearly too distraught to phrase things correctly. "I need to know. I needed to know then."

He nodded. "I guess you did. Your counselor and I spoke about having you help with the petitions, but I was against it. She was in favor." He grimaced. "I was wrong then, too."

"So you worked for a year on the petitions . . ."

He shifted under her. "For about five months. I was angry and impatient, too. I pushed when I should have waited. My Family home . . ." He shook his head. "Then we were preoccupied keeping you children safe and hiding and just surviving. Then this place . . . such a boon, such a blessing." Meeting her eyes, he said, "I gave up."

"All right." She'd learned what she needed about the past. It wasn't what she wanted to hear, but it wasn't as bad as she'd believed.

Garrett cleared his throat. "Did you keep copies and notes of the petitions you filed, or handed off to someone? Maybe we can find out, even at this late date, what went wrong."

Her father's face went stony. "Of course I kept them. But—"

"Tiana and I filed a petition today. I didn't tell you, wasn't sure you wanted to know because you have withdrawn so much from the world. But your previous notes can help. There's a good chance we can get your title back. Probably not the estate, but the title and your wealth and the back NobleGilt."

Garrett stared at Tiana and said in her mind, *You look wiped. You want me to tell them about the witnessing and complaint and everything?*

You haven't told anyone?

Nope, busy day, not even Artemisia. I'll handle this and let you rest.

I should not let you do this for me.

You look wiped. Rest. Nothing you can say about the complaint that I don't know. Garrett jerked his head toward the doorway. "Come on, all, let's confabulate, plan our attack."

Tiana's father squeezed her tight. "Life here has been good, easier than battling. But this must be done."

And that brought Tiana back to the notion that they should have fought when the house had been firebombed and mobbed. But they didn't know how to fight, or how to fight effectively and with minimum casualties. If they'd been the Holly warrior Family . . . but they weren't. And here they would never have to fight, either. The best spellshields on the planet took care of that concern.

Her father slid her to her feet and rose himself, took a step to stand next to his wife. Tiana finally noticed that though her own tears had dried, they now trickled down her mother's face, silent tears. Quina took her HeartMate's hand and they looked the way they did when they were communicating telepathically.

They both bowed to her. "We ask your forgiveness for not being candid with you, for unknowingly causing you hurt, and for not being able to Heal you from that hurt," they said in unison.

New tears spurted from Tiana's eyes and she wiped them away. "You're forgiven."

"Thank you."

"Are you staying the rest of the night, dear?" asked her mother.

"I don't know. I'll sit here a while."

Her mother kissed her temple. "It was a lovely ritual. Thank you for that, too."

Tiana nodded.

Before she could settle in, BalmHeal Residence grumbled at her mentally. *I suppose you're going to return to that upstart Turquoise House. What a name. All this coming and going, teleporting in and out. I don't like it. YOU don't need to do it.* The Residence gave her a little mental jab, one she was accustomed to . . . and she caught her breath.

That wasn't the first nudge she'd felt from a sentient House tonight! She remembered now. Recalled the HeartBond she'd visualized, the whisper in her mind that she should HeartBond with Antenn. She'd withdrawn from that notion.

And immediately afterward awakened to see Antenn examining her. Had TQ prompted him to do something, too? She gasped, fury whooshing through her like a cyclone. "Yes, BalmHeal Residence." She bit off the words. "I am teleporting *right now* to TQ. Be so kind as to thin your shields."

"They are down for Garrett." The Residence creaked disapprovingly.

With the energy of her anger, she remembered everything about the teleportation pad she'd left a few minutes ago, checked that it was unoccupied, and returned to TQ.

"TQ!" she shouted. It felt good.

"It was all my fault." The young House rushed into words. "All. I'm sorry, Tiana. I'm *so* sorry."

Thirty-seven

*W*hat, exactly, did you do?" Tiana demanded.

The whisper she remembered came, along with music that shivered over her skin. "You want to HeartBond."

She should have been able to roll with the revelation, accept, forgive. Instead she said tightly, "You wanted us to HeartBond when we weren't ready."

A creak that sounded more like a cringe than anything else.

"We are allowed to . . . suggest."

"I will want to see a list of whatever rules there are."

"Residence Ethics."

"Yes. You can ask GreatCircle Temple to have a copy made for me and placed on my desk."

"Yes, Priestess."

She bit off more words, stopped the sigh. "It's Tiana, TQ. I love you, but I don't like you much right now."

"That is contradictory."

"No, it isn't. And it's something for you to think about." She paced back and forth, realized her arms were wrapped around herself and she'd hunched over. So she straightened. "I don't want to be here right now."

"Are you going to make me ask BalmHeal Residence to let down its shields so you can teleport into the estate. Again?" The House sounded staunch but with an undertone of pitiful.

"No. I love you, but I am running out of energy." A sigh puffed from her. "I am usually more forgiving and accepting. It's been a . . . trying . . . week. There are always people in GreatCircle Temple, and I have floor pillows that will do well enough for me to sleep on. I will see you tomorrow morning for breakfast. Since Felonerb adventures tonight, he should return to his closet and keep you company. Good night."

"Good night . . . Tiana. I will think on what you said," TQ said humbly.

With a nod she checked a couple of staff teleportation pads at the Temple before she found one free, then returned to the place she'd thought of just days ago as her main sanctuary. Sometime in the last two days, her emotions had switched that security to TQ, and he'd hurt her.

Stupid to be so fragile that every damn little thing hurt her. Antenn, her parents, BalmHeal, TQ. She'd sleep and Heal and be fine tomorrow morning.

*T*Q *brooded. First Antenn, then Tiana left. Because Turquoise* House had been sneaky. And nudged them when he shouldn't have. *Now* he knew all his thinking at the time about whispering to his Family, his couple who weren't quite a couple yet, had been rationalizations.

TQ had contacted GreatCircle Temple to make sure the female part of his Family was safe, and that entity had said she appeared to be staying the night in her office.

The Temple winkled what had happened out of Turquoise House and had been kind and stated that all sentient beings made mistakes. And had called TQ "child." Which TQ *hated*, even though he was centuries younger than the FirstFamily Residences.

He hurt, and from his own stupidity. Was embarrassed . . . and, even worse, fell into his bad habit, and began to glow.

*B*efore *Tiana could settle down into the makeshift bed of floor pillows,* a rapping came at her outer chamber door. She rose and opened it to a smug Lucida Gerania, who had finished officiating a Nameday ritual. Lucida flinched with fake surprise. "I didn't think you were here."

"No? The High Priest and Priestess, the GreatCircle Temple Archives, and the PublicLibrary wanted my thoughts on the ritual I wrote and which was conducted tonight at the Intersection of Hope cathedral." Truth, though Tiana had planned on considering it more deeply before doing such a report because she thought it would be a long document.

That seemed to derail Lucida's thoughts for a moment; she frowned, then she rallied. "You *do* know that odd House you're living in, that Turquoise—"

"—House becoming a Residence? Yes," Tiana smiled. "I know it well."

Lucida's dimples fluttered as she laughed lightly. "Do you? Then you know it is *glowing*, bright enough to light up that whole neighborhood." She raised her brows. "Don't you think you should do something about it?"

Tiana met the woman's eyes, then shook her head. "Maturity comes in fits and starts. No, I don't think I should do something about that right now. I'm sure this isn't the first time it's glowed, nor will it be the last." With that, she closed the door gently in Lucida's face.

And once it was shut Tiana paced back and forth through her chambers, holding her elbows. Feeling all sorts of things and not knowing, really, what she should do.

Eventually, though she wanted to throw herself onto the floor pillows, she knew they'd scatter under her, so she lowered herself to

them and thought of every-damn-thing that had happened that day.
Dissecting it.

The Turquoise House tried to tone down his glowing—there'd be com-
plaints, there always were, but he struggled with his emotions . . .
and then something . . . some*one* passed through the range of one
of his back grassyard cameras. The man had tubes and bottles, rags
in them, and a firestarter. TQ's innermost, smallest timbers quivered. He'd seen something like this when he'd reviewed Tiana's
memorysphere. The prowler prepared firebombs.

TQ had the best spellshields in Celta. But he was afraid.

And wished he weren't alone.

An itching sensation between Tiana's shoulder blades had her tossing
and turning. Perhaps a premonition.

Something *was* wrong! Felonerb? He hunted, paid no attention
to her tug on his link. Antenn? He sparred fiercely with a . . . Holly?
Yes, Tinne Holly, Tiana had seen that man before. Quickly she
checked her parents, Artemisia, Garrett . . . all fine.

Trouble stalked TQ.

She reached for her connection to the House. *TQ?*

There's a prowler on my grounds.

Tiana jolted. *What?*

There is a man walking in my back grassyard, TQ said. *If he
touches me. If he touches my gates that I can control, I can shock
him. But I do not control all of my grounds. My cameras can't even
see all of my grounds.*

Do you want me to call the guards?

Silence hung for a moment, and then TQ said, *I think that would
show me as a weak being. I am not weak.*

That was a male being for you.

But, Tiana, he has firebombs.

What? I'm calling the guards. And coming there.

Do not.

I WILL fight for you, she snapped. She paused only to tersely scry the guards and, now using fear, teleported back to the Master-Suite. She lunged for the wardrobe, where she'd seen a blazer. She bet she could use a blazer.

I have locked the doors, Tiana. You must stay safe.

"Don't you do that to me, TQ. Don't. You've already tried my patience once tonight."

Silence.

"TQ?"

"I have unlocked the front door."

She ran.

*A*ntenn *felt* TQ *scream. In rage, not hurt. "What's going on?" he* demanded, aloud and telepathically with the House.

Everyone around him stopped where they stood or lay, probably experiencing his spike in Flair, his sense of true danger.

An intruder. In my back grassyard! Firebombing ME!

"Firebombing!" he shouted.

"Where?" asked three voices, one of them Vinni T'Vine's.

"Turquoise House."

"Fligger, I don't know that place well anymore, the light and such," Tinne Holly said, expression grim.

"I do," Antenn said, wondering how it was so, but it was, a combination of his spatial architectural Flair and TQ's Flair and presence in his mind. "Link hands." He held out his hands, and Tinne Holly slapped his callused one into one and Draeg did the same into his other. "On three, let me visualize for us."

"Getting gliders," someone shouted. "Pile in."

Depend upon me for your teleportation visual, TQ said, hard-voiced as Antenn had never heard. *My spellshields hold, for my walls, but my north sideyard BURNS!*

"Counting down," Antenn repeated roughly. "One, Antenn Moss, two Draeg Blackthorn, *three*!" He meshed his vision with

TQ's, noted the exact spot where the House wanted him to teleport, and they arrived.

The first thing he saw was Tiana Mugwort running toward a man holding a lit bottle. She wore a light dress that could easily burn.

Antenn lost it. He roared and shot through the air in a leap-teleportation-*something* and took the man down. They both grunted as they hit the ground.

"Got the bomb," Draeg said.

"Contacting the guards," Tinne Holly said, coolly.

Panting, Antenn pummeled the man until Tiana put her hand on his shoulder and said, "Stop."

She knelt near them, and all Antenn's instincts throbbed to protect her.

"You're Arvense Equisetum," she said in a genuinely calm voice. "You look much older than I recall."

He lunged to spit at her but didn't move much under Antenn's hands, and the slobber hit Arvense's own cheek.

"The younger Mugwort girl. Got your complaint served on me today. You ruined me! You're taking my estate away after I worked hard for it for my fliggering cuz. After I slaved to make it profitable." An edge of gleeful madness shone in his eyes and his smile. "And because we like to watch fire burn."

"*We?*" snapped Antenn.

Arvense's chest rose and fell with shaking laughter. "We. We experiment with fire. We watch it. We love it. That puny stupid Cross Folk ritual that supposedly set spellshields in the fliggering church foundation blocks? Can it keep our fire out?" With a sneer he shook his head. "I don't think so."

Jumping to his feet, Antenn grabbed the first two people's hands he could. Tiana. Of course she could be with him. Should be with him. And—Vinni T'Vine? Didn't matter. "I'm teleporting to the cathedral site on three. Keep still and let me handle the action."

"I will. You're the only one who knows that land well," Vinni said.

On the ground, Tinne Holly demanded of Arvense, one villain already caught, "Who else is in this?"

"My cuz Elatum. When you bring down T'Equisetum, the fligger, you bring down the whole Family."

"Every individual in a Family is not bad—" Tiana began, and then her voice cut off as Antenn 'ported them to the cathedral site.

He lit well, as did Tiana and Vinni. They stared at the massive cut stones in the nearest trench. Antenn let out a ragged breath. "They hold. The spellshields hold."

"For the cathedral." Vinni's whisper was raw. He lifted a pale hand and pointed. "Not for the whole of the Varga Plateau. Cave of the Dark Goddess, what has he *done*?"

Thirty-eight

A long line of flickering yellow-orange flames stretched across the plain as far as Antenn could see. A man threw bottles lighting the winter-dried plains grass that caught quickly and rolled hot in the wind, torching brush and bushes.

"The ecosystem!" Tiana gasped.

"Druida *City*," Antenn said tightly. He ran for the firebomber, Vinni keeping pace. As he did, great alarm klaxons pulsed from the far city. A stream of lights shot toward them, flashing. Gliders on emergency mode.

"All the mages who best work with the elements: fire, air, water, earth," Vinni said. "They come."

"We're here!" called Custos. He and the other three Chief Ministers joined in the hunt.

Younger ran with a speed none of the rest of them could match.

The villain must have seen him coming, but Elatum's stance didn't alter. He stood as if mesmerized by the conflagration. Younger tackled the man, took him down. Foreman put him out and broke his jaw with a punch.

Antenn, Vinni, and Tiana found Elatum's tools and neutralized them. Tiana and the Chief Ministers cleaned the foundation stones of accelerant, did other chants and blessings.

In a few minutes, guards showed up to help fight the fire, and one pair took Elatum into custody and away.

Antenn lent strength, physical and Flair, to the mages who arrived, milling around, trying and failing to quash the fire with different methods. Three fell.

Finally Vinni T'Vine threw back his head and shouted, "Nuin Ash!" The begrimed eighteen-year-old trotted over to him.

"Didn't I hint at what you should do, Nuin, not more than a week ago, should this happen?" Vinni said through gritted teeth.

The young man's mouth dropped open and eyes widened. He flung his hand at the firefighters. "I am the youngest, the *least*."

"You are a greatly Flaired Fire Mage. You are an ASH! Go organize them. Time to grow up, boy."

Tiana gasped beside Antenn. She stepped up to the youngster, looked up into his face. "You can do it. Blessings."

With a jerky nod, the young man loped away and, through force of will, made his colleagues listen.

Vinni sagged, and Antenn steadied him with an arm around his shoulders. "It could be worse," the prophet mumbled. "I usually saw worse. And the later in the year this happened, the worse it was." He turned his head to Tiana. "Your actions helped."

Then he patted Antenn's hand on his shoulder and paced away. "And yours. You two belong together. Do not forget that. I'm going now. I can sleep now." With a half smile, he left.

Antenn would never forget the two septhours that followed. The cool bright and beaming stars peeking through roiling smoke, white against the night sky, billowing higher than a man. After the flames passed, stalks of bushes showed black against the night. Smoke clogged his throat, the stench of it saturating everything. Pitiful cries of small animals, fleeing or dying.

Many Lords and Ladies arrived from Druida, what contribution they could make was determined by Nuin Ash as he set them to work.

Tiana, along with the Chief Ministers and other priests and

priestesses, succored the injured. Finally when all had quieted, once again Antenn, Tiana, and the four Hopeful ministers remained.

"The cathedral stands," said Elderstone.

"The cathedral stands," Antenn agreed.

"We were all blessed. In many different ways," Custos said.

He looked at Antenn. "We will need to evaluate the land, the damage to the plateau, in the morning—say MidMorning Bell. It is a sorrow that the landscape around our great structure is burned."

Tiana folded her hands into her opposite sleeves. "I am sure the FirstFamilies will do some rituals and send some Healing energy to the plateau."

"We will do so, also, throughout the building of our cathedral. For now, let us go to our old church and pray." He bowed to her and Antenn, joined hands with his colleagues, and teleported away.

Antenn looked at his HeartMate, the woman who'd hurt him so earlier that day. "We belong together." He rustily repeated Vinni's words. "And we need to work things out. Now. I'll meet you in TQ's back grassyard in half a septhour. Long enough for both of us to clean up." He angled his chin. "I want the air cleared." He grimaced at his own words even as he whiffed lingering smoke. He might need an energy drink, but they had to be easy with each other if they worked together.

But he just wanted his HeartMate.

He waited a good long minute for her to protest, then gave her a half bow and teleported to his waterfall room, telling T'Blackthorn Residence not to let his Family know he was home and that he'd be leaving shortly.

*T*iana headed to the Temple and the largest staff waterfall room, cleansed herself, and pulled on an older, comfortable robe that she'd soon retire. Felonerb supervised.

Then she visualized TQ's back grassyard and found her image boosted and refined by both Felonerb and TQ himself. Oddly enough, the place she recalled best was outside the block of the MasterSuite.

When she'd been in her own rooms, she'd spent most of her time in the sunroom or looking out the north window of her bedroom at the side yard.

Two more deep breaths in and puffs out, and then she held her arms out for Felonerb to jump into them, merged their vision of the space, double-checked with TQ, and teleported hom—into the back grassyard of TQ.

Felonerb jumped from her arms and raced around the yard, and Tiana heard rustles as other animals hid or left.

Her gaze fixed on Antenn, across the yard from her. He stood tall, his hair ruffled by the breeze, his tunic and trous dark. Yet the events seemed to have refined him in her eyes, and maybe to himself and others, too, she didn't quite know. He had the bearing of the adopted Noble son but the shadows of the street boy who'd been abandoned and spent his first years in fear. Tough, a fighter, and it was easy to see that, while she'd just discovered the kernel of fight in herself.

Her heart ached for the man, the boy he'd been, his trials—and ached, in a different way, *for* him, a need that didn't feel as if it would be satisfied.

He nodded to her, crossed his arms. With a little Flair, he made his words easily heard, though he spoke softly. "We had a discussion today." He paused, the side of his mouth lifting ironically. "One that didn't end well. I've had some time to mull it over." Now he smiled and his eyes lit with humor. "While sparring at The Green Knight Fencing and Fighting Salon."

Men. She still just reacted when in a dangerous situation, and here he seemed to consider it something like meditation.

"And it's not only me who is wary of being HeartMates, dragging my feet on this, not ready."

"Oh?" She jutted her chin.

"I trust you more than you trust me."

"Untrue."

"Let's just try a little experiment. We're HeartMates, right?"

Though she had to swallow before she replied, she said, "Yes."

He nodded, raised his voice. "TQ, can you hear me?"

"Yes," issued a voice from a speaker.

"Can you use one of your spotlights or project your Flair to make a light-spell beam to 'draw' a line bisecting the yard?" Antenn asked. "We'll start out twenty paces away from each other and walk to the line."

"What is this, a duel?" she asked.

"Hmm," he said, and she could now see him better. He'd raised his brows. "You might think of it like that. A duel of hearts." He grinned and gave her a flourishing bow, and the lightening of his spirit swept over her, simply charming her. "All talk and discussion aside, we'll see who's brave. I'll meet you at the line of light, halfway. When we meet, we'll join hands and state our intentions to be HeartMates."

She didn't say anything.

"All right?" Pure challenge from him.

She nodded. "All right." Her voice sounded a little high.

"And to prove that I am sincere in changing, that I have accepted that I must change and *will* change to be a good HeartMate to you, I will . . ." He stopped and drew himself up, glancing over at TQ where a camera angled toward them.

"TQ, according to my schedule, the cathedral will be completed in six months. I wish you to issue an invitation, *right now*, to all the FirstFamilies Lords and Ladies, as couples, to attend a celebratory al fresco banquet in the back courtyard of my place of business on the first-quarter twinmoons of the month of Vine, in six months' time, at the rise of the twinmoons in the evening. Please have them RSVP." Antenn crossed his arms and stood hip-shot, his gaze burning with intensity.

"There. I've faced that fear—the fear of being rejected by the FirstFamilies, never being acceptable to them, never being good enough for them." As if he noticed how tightly he held himself, he dropped his arms and stood more casually.

They looked at each other in silence, and his expression softened. "I know *you* are changing, too. You've started fighting for your rights. I will be with you all the way on that."

Tiana found her voice. "Thank you."

HERE you are, said Pinky telepathically, teleporting in from somewhere to the grassyard. He promptly hissed at Felonerb across the width of the grassyard, turned with lifted tail, and hopped onto a cushioned chair at the patio.

"Thank you for joining us, Pinky," Antenn said.

"Greetyou again, Pinky," Tiana said.

TQ said, "I have already received acceptances to your invitation from T'Blackthorn, T'Vine, and T'Hawthorn," he said.

A small breath whooshed from Antenn. "My parents and two good friends." The line of his shoulders shifted. "Well, it's a start."

"Absolutely," Tiana said.

His gaze focused on her again and his lips quirked up. "And now we will see about our relationship, and whether you will be welcoming guests with me that evening."

"Proceed!" TQ said. Just the one word let her know the House was enjoying this. Their Fams, Felonerb and Pinky, sat on the sidelines illuminated in the stripe of light, Pinky at the edge of the patio, Felonerb across the yard, just outside a leafing bush.

With a steady step, his gaze on hers, Antenn started toward the lightbeam in the middle of the yard.

She began, too, aware of the eyes of feral animals watching them from the bushes. Amusement came from them as well as TQ. But at fifteen paces, her nerves began to twang and her steps slowed. At ten paces, she had to force herself to continue, but her steps lagged and became smaller.

At five paces, Antenn was already at his edge of the fifteen-centimeter-wide lightbeam and stood in what appeared to be a relaxed manner, but watched her with hooded gaze. She sidled one step, another to him.

If he held out his hands, it would help her. But he didn't. His expression still wore that half smile he'd had when they'd started this experiment—that was turning out to be much more difficult than she'd expected—but the feeling she got from him now had no hint of amusement.

She thought he didn't even look at her anymore, fixed on something in his mind's eye or tried to distance himself from the situation. No, he wouldn't offer any more than he had, standing there with the white light from TQ crossing the tips of his boots.

He probably couldn't offer any more. She stopped and closed her eyes, wondered if she'd hear him gasp. No.

Centering herself, learning herself, the new self blown open earlier that night, still raw with uncertainty. She'd been angry with her parents, had felt for so long that she couldn't trust them. And not to put her needs first.

No one had put her needs first, not even herself, as she conformed to the expectations of a priestess.

But here was a man who could. She examined their bond. He was painfully sensitized to her movement, spiraling high into hope, crashing into despair. He'd never be an easy man to live with, but that didn't matter, because he was just the man she needed. Her HeartMate. They'd give each other a home.

Opening her lashes, she saw that he appeared just the same as before. One last big breath for courage and she ran, sped to him, across the light separating them, and leapt.

His arms opened and embraced her. And his breath shuddered out against her, and she realized his whole body trembled. With fulfilled hope.

Leaning her torso away from him so she could look into his eyes, she said, "We are HeartMates. I accept you as my HeartMate, Antenn Blackthorn-Moss."

"We are HeartMates," he replied, his voice rough. "I am honored to be accepted by you as your HeartMate, and I accept you as mine, Tiana Mugwort."

All those words sank into her, but she felt his need and her own for more. "I love you, Antenn Blackthorn-Moss."

"I love you, Tiana Mugwort. Stay with me, here, with the Turquoise House for the rest of our lives."

"Yes."

"Hold on," he said, keeping her tight against him, then sent a message mentally. *TQ and Fams, we are teleporting to the bottom of the secret stairs of the entryway to the HouseHeart.*

TQ replied, *My FAMILY!*

"Yes," Antenn said aloud.

"Yes," Tiana said.

Felonerb and Pinky purred in agreement.

I have redecorated my HouseHeart entryway. Especially for my Family! TQ said.

"Oh, good," Antenn murmured, lifting and dropping his brows.

You will enjoy it! TQ assured them.

"All right. Can we still teleport to the bottom of the stairs?" Tiana asked.

Yes! That area is clear. More clear than before.

"Thank you," Antenn said politely, and then they were gone as he 'ported them—both Tiana and TQ giving him exact coordinates.

The light was brighter and before them stood a series of four different doors set into a white clapboard wall: a bright red one with brass latch and knocker, a turquoise one with an intricately engraved silver knob, a black door with a pattern of gleaming copper diamonds, and a green door with painted yellow button flowers.

"It's a maze!" TQ caroled. "You will love it!"

"Uh-huh." Antenn let her slide down his body. He was ready for sex, and that stirred her, too. He took her hand and they faced the doors—each wide enough for a couple—for *them* to walk through together.

Thirty-nine

And it will be easy for you, because I know you and you know me!"
TQ said.

"Do we say the rhyme?" Tiana asked.

TQ paused. "No. I have disabled the rhyme until we can craft one together." One of the door latches rattled, though Tiana couldn't tell which one. "The cats are delayed because they are fighting." TQ sighed. *WE WILL ALL MAKE A RHYME FOR THE HOUSE-HEART TOGETHER, EVEN CATS!* TQ projected.

The cats grunted, almost in unison, then continued with their fight.

"They'll be down later," Antenn said absently. He'd been studying the doors. He squeezed her hand and grinned. "You take the first door."

Naturally she walked to the green door with the Mugwort flowers. She didn't even have to touch the handle.

Once they were inside, the wall behind them became solid and another wall with four different doors appeared on their left.

With a little laugh, Antenn led her to the very feminine white door with a heart-shaped window and tiny turquoise hearts running along the edge near the hinges. Again, when they approached, the door opened. Once more the wall solidified behind them, and they turned to the right and saw another set of interesting doors.

The Turquoise House was right. The trip through the maze was easy and fun for them . . . the light changed overhead, as did the flooring: fuzzy spellglobes beaming the yellow light of the Earthan sun, a moonless night with only colored galaxies illuminating the sky, deep forest branches above and leaves below, a touch of rocky cavern.

They reached another small room with a door in each wall, but the one to their left Tiana recognized as the HouseHeart door. Antenn squeezed her hand and she turned with him to face it.

They sighed together, and Antenn let go of her fingers and studied the other walls. The last door they'd come through had remained open for once and beyond that, Tiana could see the maze of all the variety of doors. "That is fabulous, TQ," Antenn said, taking her hand again. He must figure that they were so in tune they'd move together . . . and since they'd done so instinctively through the maze, he was right.

"I liked it a lot," Tiana said.

The nearest door, a red one with a circular window above a shiny brass knocker in the shape of a hand, glowed. *Thank you*, TQ sent to her mind.

"You're very creative."

The door to their right hummed and they swiveled to see it—also shining turquoise and with a crackling of electricity like lightning.

Tiana chuckled. "Show-off."

"Cut the electricity, TQ. You know us."

"Yes. My Family."

"Almost," Antenn said. He tilted his head, and then Tiana heard it, too. Yowling threats as two cats threaded through the maze.

Stupid doors! Pinky said, with a hint of panting even in his mental voice.

You are just little and fat. See ME jump through this window! See ME open this handle with my NOSE!

"Talk about show-offs," Tiana muttered, but sensed both Cat-Fams were easily negotiating the maze. And before she could say anything else, Felonerb sat by her feet, beaming up at her. He'd never be a beautiful cat, not like Pinky, but his fur looked healthy and smooth over his lean but not skinny body. He had no new scratches.

And he smelled good.

At the same moment, she and Antenn placed their hands on the door and chanted a jingle. Soon, soon, her muse would demand that she write a tiny ritual for her home and her Family, the Family that would come from her and Antenn, to enter the HouseHeart.

The door swung open and they walked in, the floor under her feet soft and springy, giving up a rich scent—moss. "Very nice, TQ," she said, and paused a pace inside the door as her eyes adjusted to the lower light.

Felonerb and Pinky hurried by her, along the wall.

See, she is here. She still has not moved, said Felonerb of the cat on the wall. He sat in front of her.

Pinky sat beside him. *We must send her energy and love. I know this.*

I would rather go hunt rats, Felonerb grumbled.

Our humans will soon get boring and we will go hunt, meanwhile a little love for the Cat will be just right. Pinky purred and kneaded the moss.

Tiana laughed, heard Antenn's chuckle, too.

Then her vision sharpened and she saw the mural on the opposite wall, no longer Maroon Beach. Her avatar and Antenn's, prominent in the foreground, golden auras about them showing they were HeartBound.

Not yet. But soon. As soon as they bored the CatFams. Her body began to ready, her sex to crave release. From the corner of her eye, she saw Antenn's body harden.

"Huh." He frowned at the mural. Tiana followed his gaze and blinked. In the far background, over the treetops, rose a hill with a winding path. Atop the hill stood a castle of domes and spires and round towers, one too fanciful for even an Earthan Colonist to build in NobleCountry when they'd landed on Celta. An imaginary castle. Especially since the stone glowed turquoise. "What's that?"

Antenn followed her gaze, then flushed and muttered something she didn't catch.

"What?"

He stood straight, took a pace away from her, opened his hands, palms up, and then closed his eyes. His mouth formed silent words. A moment later, a model of the intricate castle appeared resting on his spread hands.

Tiana gasped, stepped close, and touched her index finger to a glass dome that she could see through to a tiny grand staircase.

Antenn's breath whistled in and he stiffened more, pushed the model toward her. "Dearest Tiana." His voice strained, he coughed, and continued, "Dearest Tiana, do you accept my HeartGift?"

The sexual energy that emanated from HeartGifts was banked, so the gift itself had a spell to minimize lust on it.

She discovered her mouth had instantly dried, and she stepped back, more to see the entire model instead of fantastic details, but it was the wrong thing to do. Antenn's mouth twisted.

So she shot out her hands and grasped him around his elbows, taking the weight of the model on her arms, too, and met his hazel gaze.

"Yes, I do." She coughed slightly.

TQ said, "There is a table in the northeast corner here for the castle."

They turned and looked at the table, dark wood with diamond-shaped studs of silver. Antenn made to take the model, and Tiana held on to it fiercely, scowled at him. "This is *mine.*"

You are giving the fun-thing-to-look-at AWAY? wailed Pinky.

Antenn grinned, said an anti-grav couplet, and let her have it.

Pinky continued to whine. *It has little peoples in it I want to bat around!*

Slanting a look at his cat, then Tiana, Antenn said, "He was such a sweet cat when we were younger."

Peoples I can bat around? Felonerb hopped up to Tiana's shoulder and looked down. *I do not see.*

Pinky sat and licked his paw. *Have to take roof off.* He lifted his nose and stared in another direction. *I know how to do that.*

"I don't want either of you Fams to do that," Tiana said as she carried the castle over to the table, a difficult process because she kept seeing tiny details that delighted her. "Who are the people, Antenn?"

"Uh, the last Captain of the starship *Nuada's Sword* and his wife, Fern. I saw a viz about them once. They were my heroes as a teen."

Everything in Tiana softened. "Lovely."

"Yeah, yeah. You need help?"

"No, it's light and there's a groove in the table. It's a fabulous table, and just exactly right for the model!"

"I had it made," TQ said. The room rustled around them. "I have been linked with Antenn for a long time."

"Oh."

"I didn't know that," Antenn said roughly.

"Yes, in the back of your mind, or the depths of your heart," TQ said.

Antenn hunched a shoulder.

"I like the model very much, but I think Pinky is right," Tiana murmured.

I am always right. The small beige cat preened. *About what?*

"It's a wonderful thing to look at. I think I'd like it in the MistrysSuite rather than down here in the HouseHeart."

Antenn joined her. "We can translocate it later. And I'll show you how to open each wall and the roof, later, too." He cleared his throat loudly. "I gave you my HeartGift and you accepted."

She looked up and found his intense gaze fixed on her. "I accepted your HeartGift. I accepted, earlier, that we are HeartMates, and so stated." Heat washed through her. "I accept that when we next make love, we will HeartBond."

"I gave you my HeartGift," he repeated.

Felonerb thwapped her on her head with a paw. *You must give him a gift.*

Antenn stepped back abruptly. "I know I wasn't closely connected with you."

She nodded slowly, suddenly breathless; time to take another level of commitment to this man, their relationship, the Family and home they would share. She'd wanted to put this moment off a little, because she was still overwhelmed, but she would not hurt him further.

Her eyes looking deep into his, she held out a hand, *felt* where her HeartGift was, and translocated the scroll to her palm. It felt as it had before, a heavier, weightier papyrus especially created for very important documents out of top-quality linen.

She'd made the papyrus herself during Passage, a dreamquest that freed her Flair and had her reaching for her HeartMate.

With a big breath, she held the rolled papyrus tied with a white velvet ribbon between them. It, too, had an anti-lust spell on it, for the moment. Concentrating on not rushing her words, she said, "Antenn Blackthorn-Moss, do you accept my HeartGift?"

He nearly snatched it from her grasp. "Yes." But they yet stared into each other's eyes. "What is it?" he asked, and she felt flushed warmth staining her cheeks again. "It's a wedding ceremony, with my vows . . . and yours."

His eyes widened and he broke their gaze, but his fingers trembled as he opened the papyrus. He blinked and his eyes focused on a phrase, and he read: *In all the world, at the setting sun, under twin-moons and bright skies, I have found you and found love and love you, my HeartMate, the one who completes me.* He swallowed, let the papyrus curl up, opened his mouth, shut it, and shook his head, though he didn't hide the sheen in his eyes, the huge welling of love flooding their bond, the acceptance of her, his *need* for her.

As she needed and accepted him. So she cleared her throat and said, "Will you marry me, Antenn Blackthorn-Moss, as day turns to dusk in the outside grove at GreatCircle Temple, next full twin-moons, my HeartMate?"

"Nearly two weeks," he croaked. "So long."

"And will you, Turquoise House, accept us as your Family?" Tiana asked. "Where we can live and raise our children, who will be yours also?"

"Will you do that, Turquoise House?" Antenn asked.

"YES, TIANA. YES, ANTENN! You have always been my Family."

Forty

Six Months Later
Summer, First-Quarter Twinmoons
Evening

Antenn and Tiana kissed the last of their guests, his parents, Straif and Mitchella Blackthorn, good-bye. When the couple vanished, they glanced around the courtyard behind Antenn's business. The caterers, a male couple, and their staff efficiently boxed the food and dismantled the tables and chairs, translocating them to their storage.

The food served to the FirstFamily couples had been the best and the most expensive that Antenn could afford. It had looked great, and despite his deep nerves, which he hoped hadn't shown except for an instinctive twitch or two, conversation had flowed easily among the group—those who'd shown up. Mostly the younger set and the more liberal of all ages had come.

The Birches, who'd suffered burns from one of the firebomb-spells his brother had used to murder people in the FirstFamilies council, had not even acknowledged the invitation.

But others who'd been burned, like T'Reed, had accepted his hospitality. Even others who'd inherited after they'd lost their relatives to Shade's murders, like the Rowan and Elder Families, had greeted him and eaten his food, and talked to him about the cathedral. The most conservative Family, now, the WhitePoplars, hadn't attended, and a few more.

Neither had the Yews, though no one in any of the Councils seemed to know what was going on with that Family or Residence, since the Heir was only a girl of fourteen and had never been seen.

"That went well," Tiana said, and Antenn luxuriated in the sweet peace of her. He'd realized a while back that when he'd met her, her natural personality hadn't shown through . . . and now that she'd—they'd—grown together, she really shone. He loved being with her.

She nudged him with her elbow. "I said that went well."

He chuckled. "Yes, I accept that there are people who will never tolerate me because of what my brother did." Antenn paused. "And what he did was terrible. But I also don't care too much about what those people think." He smiled himself. "I had many more people accept my invitation than I'd anticipated."

"You aren't as disliked as you thought."

"You're right." Now they were alone, he stretched long, working leftover tension from his muscles, and let his gaze focus on the treetops, then wander in the direction of NobleCountry, where most of his guests lived. "Many of my childhood fears have been laid to rest. But this was the right time for this gathering. The FirstFamilies are intrigued by the cathedral and know the building will last for centuries. It's also good to understand that no one will ruin my career because of what my brother did." He put an arm around her shoulders and led her to a bench to sit in the shade as the heat of the summer's day faded into evening.

"We promised my mother that we'd meet her at the cathedral tonight," Tiana said.

"And we will, but let's take a few minutes for ourselves." He drew her down to sit beside him. "By the way, the clerk sent the papyrus closing your complaint against T'Equisetum and your petition to the NobleCouncil here. Got them today."

"Ah." She sat and smiled—and not one of those compassionate priestessly smiles.

"He got the justice he deserved," Antenn said. His arm dropped to her waist and he squeezed her tightly, until she squeaked. "Satisfied?" he asked,

She'd told him before, but he always pressed. "Yes. We all are." She leaned against him, and he closed his eyes better to see deep into her emotional aura, and was pleased with the clear and golden result. No seed of discontent at T'Equisetum, or the actions of her Family as a child, lived within her. She'd seen justice done and that had settled her.

Antenn stretched out his legs and a sigh rattled from him. "I liked it best when he had to admit he did wrong before the whole AllCouncils membership and the newssheets and ask pardons from each member of your Family."

She nodded. "He had to admit to hubris, arrogant ways. A good lesson for all."

Equisetum hadn't wanted to do that; what man would?

"I don't think he even understood he was flawed or believed he was wrong until we forced him into treatment with a mind Healer."

"Nobles keep having to learn that lesson," Antenn said. "That wealth and power and birth and status don't automatically give you a right to harm others by word or deed for your own ends. That just because you have wealth and power and birth and status, whatever you believe is *right*."

She sighed. "I don't think he would have learned that without having to experience all the memories each of us had of that night. The man had no empathy until it was forced upon him."

"Justice," Antenn said; his jaw tensed and he relaxed it. Justice had been done; he didn't get to call harm or duel on the man. "Neither he nor his son is allowed to participate in any council, anywhere. They had to let his daughter take the title of GraceLady D'Equisetum." Antenn couldn't prevent his lip from curling. "They were lucky they retained their estate, wealth, and title."

"I heard the former GraceLord T'Equisetum is moving to Gael City." Tiana laughed lightly. "He will receive only a pittance of NobleGilt for his new work, based on his creative Flair."

Antenn drew back so he could see her. "I don't know what his creative Flair is."

"Stunted," she said. "He denied his creative Flair, never practiced it—two-dimensional painting."

Antenn contemplated what kind of hideous painting—subject matter and technique—the man might produce. "I don't want anything of his *near* my buildings." He paused for a trifle bit of consideration. "I think I'll notify all of my subcontractors of that, and my mother." He grinned. "*And* I think I'll send a brief note to the ex-Lord not to submit any of his work to my business."

"Until he is a master," Tiana said.

"What? No."

She put her arm around him and squeezed back, adding a little Flair to make her point. He didn't mind; any moment she had her hands on him was a good moment. "If . . . when . . . he masters his art, you will consider it. He is now in his apprenticeship. If he puts in the time to move from apprentice to journeyman to master, you will consider it."

"All right." He stood. "Let's go look at *my* masterpiece." He'd brought the cathedral in under budget and under deadline. It had been open a month.

"Let's."

He stood and took her inside to the teleportation pad, and set the spellshields. He could hear the FamCats gorging in the kitchen on leftovers, and he sent telepathically, *We are going to the cathedral now; then we will be at home.*

All right, said Pinky.

All right, said Felonerb.

Neither cat bothered to tell them whether he'd follow to the cathedral or not. Antenn reckoned they'd just lie quietly in the kitchen after their feasting until they got the energy to teleport again.

He took a quick moment to study the aura of his office building. It wasn't a sentient structure; maybe in a decade or two. The place was in CityCenter and at least three centuries old but hadn't had a steady Family, owners, or renters in that time.

Antenn had moved the incipient HeartStones to a secret safe when he'd rented the space, and added more from places that were self-aware, like T'Blackthorn and D'Elecampane Residences. Still, the atmosphere felt . . . as satisfied as Antenn and Tiana were. Pleased. Proud. Good qualities to have in HeartStones, and he sent a little Flair to them.

Then he stepped behind Tiana, wrapped his arms around her, and pulled her against his body to teleport. She leaned back and put her hands on his.

They 'ported to one of the designated areas outside, near the vital adult door and arm of the cathedral. The building rose, impressive, elegant against the hot blue summer sky, bathed in the white light of Celta's sun. They stood for a moment and looked at the wide window and two tiny towers of this entrance.

"Beautiful," Tiana breathed.

"Yes." Pride filled him; he thought it might exude from his every pore. *He'd* designed this, helped build it, and the structure matched the vision he'd seen in his mind. Mighty, graceful, a spiritual sanctuary that reflected the Intersection of Hope religion which would last for centuries.

Without another word, and hand in hand, they entered.

The last sunshine beaming through the tracery of the clerestory windows filled the cathedral with gorgeous light, accenting the art within—the sculptures and, most importantly, the four magnificent holo murals. One or two windows had clear glass replaced with brightly colored stained glass, the current continuing project of the Hopefuls to embellish their cathedral.

Already, a reverence imbued the very stones of the building, dusted the atmosphere with a sensation unique to the Intersection of Hope folk, as individual as their chants and their incense. But all visitors would feel that this was a cherished holy place.

The cathedral had become a small tourist attraction, an outing for people living in Druida, and a Hopeful staffed the structure around the clock, usually a volunteer. This evening, GraceLady Quina D'Mugwort guided people through the building, explaining her religion and the meaning of the art. Each visitor received a free pamphlet on the Intersection of Hope faith and was asked to make a small donation for the tour.

The four awe-inspiring holo murals of the godhead—two male and two female—drew the eye and had been brilliantly executed with great Flair by a new convert, Avellana Hazel.

As they proceeded down the transept, the cathedral cat, a slinky all-black tom, greeted them.

He leapt at Tiana, fully confident that she would catch him, and she did.

"Are you happy here?" she asked, petting him.

"Yesss," he vocalized, then slitted his eyes and settled into her arms with a purr.

Along the inner walls of the arm representing the eldest were small rooms for the ministers and the volunteers to relax, sleep, even eat. The guardian spirit arm held rooms for counseling; the vital adult wing had tiny individual meditation stalls.

Though Antenn could hear Tiana's mother's lifted voice as she pointed out the beauty of a sculpture, they didn't interrupt her, but continued to the center of the cathedral and stopped near the altar.

He tilted his head back, closing his eyes and soaking in the ambience, breathing deeply and steadily. Then, opening his lashes, he looked—for the first time without a critical eye—at the beauty the artisans of Druida had achieved in stone carving and wood carving, statues, painting—holo and two-dimensional. He glanced down at the painted flagstones and simply breathed in wonder. This, too, was the first time he just let himself experience the full structure as a building. Not a project he'd designed and helped construct, but a space he walked into, as one of many.

Breathtaking. Blood began to pound through him and he folded over, hands on his knees, head down, gasping.

"What is it?" Tiana asked. He heard the thump as the cat landed on the floor, saw a black tail and rump sashay away in offense.

"I. Did. This."

"Yes?"

He straightened enough to show her his trembling hands. "I designed this and it's built and . . ."

"Wonderful."

"Yes. Full of wondrous items, saturated with wonder." White spots danced before his eyes, sparking and fading as he dragged in breath after breath. He thought the blood had drained from his head to settle in his belly and upset it. Tiana embraced him, pressed her warmth to his chill body. As designed, the cathedral kept scorching summer air out.

As designed.

He'd conceived of the building.

He'd drawn it.

He'd *done* it. Built a cathedral that would keep his name alive for centuries. Achieved one of the major goals of his life. And as he hung on to his wife, his HeartMate, joy sizzled through him that an even more precious goal had been obtained, he'd found his woman.

Lifting his arms, he put them around her, felt his breath steady with hers, his pulse slow. "I did it," he whispered.

"Of course you did."

With a shake of his head, he straightened fully, scrubbing his scalp that had prickled with sweat. "I guess I've been so focused on getting it done, maybe even doubting it *could* be done, that I just didn't stop to appreciate it. Until now."

"You designed a great cathedral that will stand for ages. Congratulations. Now breathe."

He let one arm fall, kept the other loose around her waist as his gaze gently scanned the cathedral, nodded once. "It's good." Then he let happiness bubble through him and smiled. "Wondrous. Wonderful."

Quina D'Mugwort glided up to them with a satisfied smile on her face that told him she'd gotten a sufficient amount from the tourists for her church.

Reluctantly, he withdrew his arm from Tiana, missing the physical connection though their emotions linked. He bowed to Quina. "Good evening, GraceLady D'Mugwort."

She dipped a curtsey in return. "Good evening, Antenn and Tiana." Her slight frown cleared. "I see the banquet went well."

"As well as could be expected," Antenn said.

"It went very well," Tiana said in her priestess voice that told him he'd been less than gracious.

"Everyone asked and spoke about the cathedral." He made a sweeping gesture. "I think you Hopefuls will have some visitors from the highest Noble class."

Quina rubbed her hands. "All to the good." Her chin lifted. "And our beautiful cathedral can match the loveliness of GreatCircle Temple any time."

"Yes," said Tiana. She curled fingers around his upper arm. "Mother, did you and Father go and look at the estate the Noble-Council awarded us today?"

Quina's eyes shifted and she took on a defensive stance. "We did. We didn't stay very long."

"Didn't you like—"

Tiana's mother shrugged; her gaze met Antenn's. "It's a sad place, since the last of the Rhinanthus Family passed on to the wheel of stars." Her shoulders straightened. "We already have a wonderful home."

The legendary FirstGrove, the secret garden, the secret sanctuary . . . and the grumpy BalmHeal Residence, which had grudgingly accepted Antenn as a member of the Family.

He'd have liked to spend more time exploring the grounds, that stayed closer to the original layout of the Earthan colonists than any other place he'd seen. With blatant flattery based on sincere admiration he could pump the Residence about its past and its structure, maybe even get its original plans.

But Quina Mugwort stared at him, and his neck heated as he knew he'd missed a question. "Of course we can add to the House-Stones of our new estate in the city," Tiana clued.

"Yes," Antenn said. "We can. As a full *Family*." He cast Quina a stern glance. "You and Sinjin and Artemisia will wheedle a couple

of stones from your Residence that we can take to the new Mugwort estates here and in Gael City."

"But Artemisia and Garrett and their children will be living at
our home, and yours and Tiana's at the Turquoise House—"

Antenn smiled and rubbed his hand up and down Tiana's supple
back. "The thing I know about children is that they rebel against
their elders, even though it might take them a while. We, as a Family, the Mugwort-Moss-Primross-Blackthorn Family, will care for
our new Houses, and nurture them, and when one or two of those
children wish to *not* live in our Family homes, they will have their
own places."

"And stay close with us. An excellent idea." Quina nodded.

"We just haven't spent the time to discuss this much," Antenn said.

Quina smiled, spread her arms wide, and turned slowly in a
circle. "I gave the backed-up amount of my NobleGilt to help with
the cathedral expenses."

"Something I'm sure the Intersection of Hope ministers greatly
appreciated."

She sighed. "Of course. And I am pleased to have another place
to come to in the city." Her smile trembled as she glanced at them.
"We, Sinjin and I, are doing better in that regard."

"Yes." Tiana hugged her mother. "It takes some Families . . .
and Residences . . . longer to bond than others, like yours."

D'Mugwort laughed, blinked tears away from her lashes, and
shook her head at them, putting her hands on her heart. "Four days.
I still can't believe that it took you only four days to bond, and with
the Turquoise House, too."

"We were ready," Antenn said, stepping up and circling his wife's
waist again.

Footsteps sounded and the four Chief Ministers converged upon
them. They all bowed and greeted Antenn, then Tiana.

Antenn bowed back, coordinating it with Tiana's curtsey so he
could keep hold of her.

"We are very pleased that you honored GraceLady D'Mugwort's
request to meet us here," Custos said.

Antenn hadn't known that was part of the deal, but said nothing.

"We want to express, once again, our gratitude that you took our commission, treated us fairly and with respect," Younger said.

Antenn smiled, deliberately stared around him. "This was the project of a lifetime for me. I couldn't refuse." He let his smile broaden. "And I thank you, once again, for the bonus."

"A good workman is worthy of his gilt," Foreman said gruffly.

"If you will follow us," Custos said. He gestured to Foreman, who'd turned on his heel and begun to stride down the transept dedicated to his portion of the Journey, followed by Custos, Elderstone, and Younger.

Quina beamed. Tiana held Antenn's hand and chuckled in her throat. Antenn's heart began to pound in anticipation. They paced to the end of the arm and the two great bronze doors that opened to the outside. Foreman planted himself by a large plaque that showed the floor plan of the cathedral and a wall elevation showing the different sections from flagstoned floor to the arch of the stone vault at the top. Below the drawings was his name in raised letters:

ANTENN BLACKTHORN-MOSS, FIRSTLEVEL ARCHITECT.

Pause your Journey to gaze around
and appreciate his Mastery.

Antenn's insides contracted, his eyes stung, and he had to pull a little Flair from Tiana to keep his composure. Then he bowed formally to each of the ministers. "Thank you," he said roughly.

Linking her arm with his, Quina said, "Now that you've finally finished your work on the cathedral"—her tone scolded subtly—"will you stay for a cup of celebratory tea? I commissioned a blend specifically for us Hopefuls from GreatLady Camellia D'Hawthorn."

Foreman grunted and frowned. "Cups and cups and cups of tastings until we found one we agreed upon."

"It's good, though," said Younger. "Please join us."

Antenn let the ministers persuade him. The tea was tolerable and the flatsweets great, comments from the cathedral cat amusing. The small courtesies smoothed out the emotions of the day.

He'd always remember the moment when he saw the plaque. And he had no doubt that in the years ahead he'd learn how light fell on it on all hours and seasons. It would be an anchor for his spirit, when he doubted himself.

Soon enough, he slanted a look at Tiana and they rose and excused themselves to Quina and the ministers and walked to the private teleportation area. Once again he wrapped his arms around her. "Home?" he asked.

"Home," she agreed.

*T*iana settled into the embrace of her HeartMate, and their minds tuned together and meshed the vision of the teleportation area of the courtyard of their home. Heart-fulfilling home.

They arrived as day transitioned into night, a precious time to her, now, and to Antenn. *Their* special time, when they acknowledged the changes of the day and the changes in their lives.

"I love you, wife and HeartMate," he said.

"I love you, husband and HeartMate," she replied.

The last rays of golden-evening sunlight speared onto the glossy turquoise finish of their home.

As they approached, the moss-green door opened and they stepped over the threshold together.

The cats sat in the entryway, tails curled around them, and mewed in unison, sending love at seeing them again.

"Greetyou, beloved Family," came from the walls in a deep, resonant voice.

She glanced at Antenn, words unnecessary.

"Greetyou, beloved Mugwort-Moss Residence," she and Antenn said in unison.

Startled silence, then a wave of love came from the one who had been the Turquoise House. "I have found my Family!" he yelled.

We found YOU, the cats said.